REVELATION

POPPET CYCLE BOOK 1

DONNA J.W. MUNRO

Hydra
Publications

ISBN: 978-1-958414-06-4

Hydra Publications

Goshen, Kentucky 40026

Hydrapublications.com

For my daddy, Ed Wagenblast, who always believed in me and my husband, Matt Munro, who is my favorite.

Wester-Marium Dictionary circa 2000 CE, Antedevolution Period

POPPET noun pop·pet \\'pä-pǝt

1. <u>a</u> doll, usually handmade and cloth
2. beloved child

Examples of <u>POPPET</u> <grandma calls me her poppet>

Wi-fi-pedia Encyclopedia definition circa 2020 CE, Antedevolution Period

Poppet: The word **poppet** is from British English, meaning a small child or doll. In folk traditions, a poppet is a doll that represents a person for casting curses against or to aid that person through magic.

Other uses: A term expressing love or affection from an elder to a younger person.

The History of the Devolution and Development of US NOAM

Textvid by Prof. Venkma of the Academy de Bellum. Published US NOAM Year 80

Poppets: Servant biomachines created using the remains of the recent dead, DesLoge Com's proprietary chemical formula, and biochips programmed with the manual skills required by the consumer. Following the class wars, poppets replaced all manual laborers in the US NOAM economy. Tireless, easy to train and replace, poppet labor revolutionized the modern economy.

A MEMORY OR MAYBE A DREAM

Little Ellie toddled away from her mother. Happened all the time. Her delighted smile was lost on her mother, who was busy trying to fit in with Auntie Cordelia's fancy society friends sitting in their afternoon finery, sipping tea and nibbling the honeyed scones poppets offered. Each woman was attended by her own high-mannered, impeccably dressed poppet servant.

Ellie didn't know that Thom, her auntie's poppet, was nothing more than a chemically reanimated corpse. She was too young to understand. The words "undead" and "zombie" weren't in her three-year-old vocabulary. For her, Thom Poppet listened and cared. She thought he loved her.

"Watch me, Mama! Watch me, Thom!" Ellie squealed her delight as her plump baby legs carried her away from the old ladies and toward the dock. If she jumped in like she had with Mama yesterday, everyone would laugh and pay attention. Yesterday, she'd jumped so well that even Auntie

Cordelia clapped. Mama caught her and showed her how to kick and flap her legs to swim. Ellie knew she'd jump in and swim, and everyone would stop talking and watch her.

She ran to the dock and out onto the wooden planks, white shoes clumping across the graying surface. Driven by the false tides of passing boats, the water lapped at the wooden piers and jetted up between the planks, drawing Ellie's attention as she stomped on the spouting liquid. The water had been warm yesterday and bright silver like the dome sky, but now, as she peered over the side of the dock, it was a dark steel gray. For a minute, Ellie thought about running up and asking Mama to play with her or lift her into the trees, but she knew that she wouldn't get her attention that way. Nope, she needed to jump in, even if the water seemed mean today.

She leaned out over the side, farther, farther, whipping her arms forward and back like her mother showed her. She danced there on the edge, leaning, and laughing.

"Mama, look!"

None of the women looked up from their business. Only Thom turned toward her voice. Only her poppet seemed to hear. Her arms wheeled around as the breeze brushed past her cheeks, warm like a kiss.

"Mama!" She leaned forward more.

She hit the water not with a splash that would have brought sensible mothers running. Instead, she slid in silent like a knife. For a moment, her flapping arms held her up, then she sank to the bottom, her hands clawing for the surface. She cried out, her open mouth letting water rush down her tiny, gaping throat—a sad ending to a quick life.

At least it should have been an ending. But strong hands broke the rippled surface of the lake and grabbed for her. Thom's hands.

Poppet Thom walked into the lake, lifted her, and walked back to the shore. His shining leather shoes squished with puddled mud, and his trousered legs were tangled up with seaweed. But Mama didn't see. Thom carried her to a bench and dropped her down, then he wandered back to service.

Ellie loved him, even if Auntie Cordelia always told her it was like loving a hammer. She loved him and never forgot, though the memory softened until Ellie imagined it was just a dream.

DOCUMENT 1: ADVERTISEMENT FROM YEAR 5 OF US NOAM

Poppet workers for your home ... Maxplosive™ guaranteed

DesLoge Com Labs presents the newest version of Poppets™ with safety built in.

Never again will yesterday's "zombie" be a worry. Inventor and industrialist Harold DesLoge's new Poppets™ feature a combination chemical and bioprocessor-based method of revival and control that halts the decomposition of flesh while training it to do whatever needs be done. The old "zombie" aggression is gone, and what remains is loyal, mindless service—the perfect Poppet™ servant.

For your safety, we inject all modern poppets with our patented Maxplosive™. If triggered, the resulting detonation affects only the head of the nearest poppet, not the goods or environment beyond. Maxplosive™ has been tested on thousands of Poppets™ and is endorsed by the US NOAM government as a solution to the former violence problems in early Poppet™ models.

The button trigger for the Maxplosive™ is encased in our beautiful Joltlace™ collection. Developed by US NOAM renowned jewelers, our necklaces will keep you safe and enhance any ensemble. Custom-made Joltlaces™ make the perfect anniversary, wedding, or coming-of-age gift. With just a simple push of a button, you and your family are safe from the fears of yesterday.

Safe, useful, fashionable, and yours.

Purchase your Poppet™ today from DesLoge Com showrooms near you.

CHAPTER 1

"Oh, no. Forgot it again," Ellie mumbled under her breath as her hands brushed along the bare skin of her naked neck. She had to hurry, or Cordelia would catch her without it.

She raced up the polished oak stairs to look for her missing Joltlace. Aunt Cordelia expected so much from her now that she'd turned sixteen. So many things to remember and to do. Half the things she *should* do she didn't because she couldn't remember them all. Cordelia usually forgave the small things. Things like dirty rooms and bare feet and uncombed hair had all been at one time or another forgiven, forgotten, and laughed about. But forget ting to wear her Joltlace wasn't one of them. Aunt Cordelia had spent many thousands of her billions on one just for Ellie—a precious twinkling sapphire set in platinum and backlit by the soft twinkling glow of a linked kill switch inside the jewel. Just one squeeze, and poppets would fall. Everyone who was anyone had one and wore it with pride. Why did she always forget to wear hers?

She topped the stairs where her ol' Thom Poppet dusted, balancing on a personal lift disc hovering ten feet up, near the top of the collection of family portraits that lined the tall curling staircase. The venerable DesLoge ancestors going back to before the War of Devolution, their mouths set in brave sneers and gazes that pierced the air like needles, stood silent judges, always watching. Thom's spindly-knuckled hands dusted each intricate mahogany frame with the care and patience that only a poppet spends. Ellie knew that her Thom had already spent hours at this job with no break, no rest, or food. A poppet works until the job is done, guaranteed, or your money back. At least that's what the teach-vids and commercials said. That's the thing with poppets—they're just like machines. Though Ellie wasn't so sure when she looked into Thom's eyes, brown and soft like syrup, even if they stared off into space all the time.

"Good morning, Thom," she said as she slid past him, slowing to try to catch his gaze. She always tried, even though they said poppets can't see anything that doesn't relate to their job. Can't. Won't. Ellie was never sure what actually dictated their lack of eye contact. She only knew that all poppets wore the same slack-jawed, wide-eyed emptiness like a uniform.

"Umnnggg." Thom's guttural response was the same, no matter who greeted him. They say poppets all sound the same. Maybe someday she and Aunt Cordelia could whip up some kind of chip upgrade to soften the grunts or even allow for some speech—nothing too disturbing or complex. As

Cordelia often said, "Poppet brains could only handle so much."

Ellie opened her door with a bang and tossed aside the mess of clothes on her bed. She'd tried all of them on that morning while searching for the expensive toy Cordelia had given her. Thom hadn't been through to clean up yet, thank goodness. Something about Thom handing her a kill switch didn't sit right.

"Where is it?" Ellie bit her thumb in concentration as she shifted her personal compad, hoping the Joltlace was underneath, perhaps hidden from last night's studying. Nope. Where could it be? On her pillow? In her jewelry box? She shuffled through the gold rings and precious jewelry befitting her station in the DesLoge family, all presents from Aunt Cordelia. Still nothing. She gazed around the room, eyes skimming her extensive collection of books. Actual print book antiques that were all hers. Only the heir to the DesLoge fortune could afford that many real paper books. There! The chain glimmered, hanging out of the side of her copy of *Golden Treasury of Antedevolutionary American Lit*, one of the last print books made before the vidbooks replaced them.

That's right, Ellie thought, and grabbed the Joltlace from the book pages. She'd been reading the uplifting lyrics written by the twentieth-century band named Journey. Of course, the song's streetlight people really referred to the sexual slavery that existed in the twisted free market system of the bad old days before the Devolution. Imagine live women driven to using their bodies as capital. What a horrible time that must have been. Now, the poppets fulfilled that function for society, though people of breeding didn't openly discuss such things. She imagined someday she'd be let in on the intricacies of the poppet trade, maybe when she took over from Aunt Cordelia as the CEO of DesLoge Com, which wouldn't be anytime soon.

Thank goodness for Aunt Cordelia, she thought as she smoothed the chain of the Joltlace between her finger and thumb. She often wondered if she'd ever be ready for the DesLoge mantle of power that Cordelia carried with such grace.

She pulled the Joltlace over her head and snagged it in her thick brown hair. She jerked it through, but not in time. The soft pop was unmistakable.

"Forgot your necklace again, child?" Aunt Cordelia's voice issued from the wall vid unit.

Caught again. The entirety of her bedroom wall was lit with the larger-than-life face of her loving aunt and benefactor, the formidable Cordelia DesLoge—richest, most powerful woman in the seven zones of US NOAM. The slight crazing of crow's feet did nothing to diminish the beauty of Aunt Cordelia's deep blue eyes, harvested just a few weeks before from a poppet of astounding beauty. Like so many ladies of means, Aunt Cordelia could pick and choose replacement features from the finest poppets. The surgeons at Parker Cosmetics, a DesLoge Com partner company, transplanted them without delay. What do poppets need with such beautiful eyes, anyway? Those eyes seemed locked on Ellie with a sharp interest that made her feel five years old again.

"I can't keep you safe all the time. What if they turn on

us, Ellie? They can be so strong. They'd kill you in a minute, and then what would I do?"

Ellie turned away to roll her eyes so Cordelia couldn't see. She straightened up, put on her I'm-a-good-girl face, and said, "Aunt Cordelia, you and the Corporation have made them so dependable. It's been what...thirty years since the last poppets went rogue?"

"That's right, Ellie, but twenty-two people died. You *will* wear your Joltlace. It's not negotiable." Cordelia's face lost its indulgent softness and stretched into a mask of severity—a visage usually reserved for the most serious company offenders.

Ellie nodded because she knew a lost cause when she saw one and settled the twinkling remote pendant around her neck. The triangular stone settled into the hollow at the base of her throat, a weight that felt much heavier than it really was. So heavy, because the glittering device sparkling there against her skin could blow Thom's head off with a simple squeeze.

"Sorry, Aunt Cordelia," she said, and she meant it. Aunt Cordelia loved her in her way. Cared for her as her own mother couldn't. Why was it so hard to remember this one little kindness? What did it cost to wear the necklace if it meant so much to Aunt Cordelia? She'd just have to be careful with it around Thom and the others. More than one loyal poppet had lost its head to the careless squeeze of a Joltlace.

It bumped with each step as she hurried out of her room. She was expected downstairs to sit with Cordelia as the decisions of the day were ticked off. "Training," Cordelia called it. Ellie called it torture. She stepped back out onto the landing where Thom Poppet had been. Done with the frames, he'd moved on to the next task of precision and monotony. As Ellie's feet found the top of the stairs, she noticed his lift disc floating off to the side of the landing in safety mode. Thom squatted mid-staircase, working on the spindles of the banister with lemony oil and slow, studious wipes of his cloth.

A quick test wouldn't hurt, would it?

Ellie pulled the hover disc out and stepped on board, activating it. She took a deep breath and lunged over the staircase edge. The disc carried her swiftly down, each step catching, dropping her weight, then lifting her back up in a jerky tumble down the edges of the risers.

"Thom!" She screamed as she flew past his crouched, black-suited form. "Thom, save me!"

She threw her arms out, as if she would fall. Her body bobbled left and right, making it seem as if she might tumble off and down the steps to her death. She shrieked and moaned, trying to get a reaction—any reaction.

Thom didn't respond. He kept his pace on the spindles without a twitch.

She thumped and bumped and screeched as the lift carried her down the last of the steps to the marble foyer and settled her safely on the floor.

Ellie stepped off and turned back to gauge Thom's reaction to her near deadly antics.

None. No reaction. Just the poppet effect. Slack-jawed, unfocused eye, and the occasional drops of drool down a less-programmed poppet's chin. Exactly what society had told her he was capable of.

Was she wrong about Thom?

She turned and moved across the vast marble entry vestibule, where the stairs had spilled her out on the floor. It hadn't worked this time, but she'd keep trying to get a reaction from him. He'd helped her once. Sometimes, she'd snatch little images of water closing over her head. Thom's blue, withered hands reaching and lifting her. Could be a dream, but somehow dismissing it like that hurt worse than any rejection from her mother, Juni, or failure with Aunt Cordelia. She glanced back at him, her sweet old

Thom, and turned into the wider hall.

Ellie shook her head and smiled as she evaluated her latest attempt to get Thom riled up. The whole "pretending to be in danger" test was something she tried on Thom once in a while. Once she'd lain in the bathtub face down for an hour with a straw as her only source of air. Another time, she'd thrown herself in front of a speeding hover truck, only to have it zip off the track and into a tree. All that work, and Thom had never reacted. He stood by, watching as she thrashed in the water or rolled downstairs. His gaunt face framed in the shadow of a smile that death had frozen on his lips. Blank and full of nothing, just like the textbooks and DesLoge sales vids promised. Only, if he was smarter than what everyone believed, then he had to know that she wasn't really in danger when she skidded down the stairs on the hover disc. Still, if she did something more dangerous, something really risky, and he didn't save her, well...better not to think about that. And honestly, if anyone ever figured out that she was baiting a poppet to try to get a reaction outside of what the poppet programming allowed, she'd be a laughingstock. Imagine the DesLoge heir believing her poppet was human? She'd be called crazy or, worse, a Resurrectionist.

Her cheeks flushed as she imagined the shame she could bring to Cordelia and the DesLoge name. She bit her lip, suddenly ashamed of her own childishness.

She walked into the formal dining room, where Cordelia perched at the end of the long mahogany table. Her aunt hunched over a glowing compad, punching up a projection that Ellie knew well. A holovid Hobbit with huge blue eyes and a gentle face glowed above the compad in front of Cordelia. The image was a vid page from Antedevolution classic novel, *The Hobbit*, which was Ellie's current literature project from the Academy. Cordelia swiped the face of the compad's screen, turning vid images with dismissive shifts of her elegant white fingers.

"They have you reading about Hobbits? Hairy-toed little bastards and their smug little green buildings...hovels, really. Why would they have you read a book that is clearly designed to inspire class warfare?" Cordelia waved her vaporarette around for emphasis, leaving foggy tracers in the troposphere. "Haven't we all had enough of that sort of thing? You know—the horror and the fantasizing?"

Ellie steeled herself for the morning rant. It was always something. She just needed to listen, let Cordelia make her point, then the lessons would begin. These breakfast meetings were the only time Ellie could count on spending time with her aunt, who would spend the rest of the day on company business either at the factory or with politicians.

This was the hardest part of Ellie's day, but she always looked forward to their time, because it was just for her and no one else.

Even Ellie's mother, Juni, didn't get such loving attention from the DesLoge matriarch. That was okay, though, because Juni had a plan. She worked hard to make Ellie aware and forgiving of Cordelia's shortcomings, her oddities, and her bitter, controlling methods of rearing her, the next heir. Juni wanted Ellie to manufacture the one thing that would win Cordelia over completely—love. Juni wanted her to pretend the shadow of love for the aunt, who could keep them safe and rich in the enclosed dome of Santelouisa with poppets and parties aplenty. Strangely enough, and in spite of Juni's clumsy efforts, love perched in Ellie's heart like a starved baby vulture. She did love Cordelia—oddities and all.

"Ellie? Where did your mind go just then? I declare, you are worse than the poppets, and they're brain dead. I was saying, before you disappeared into that pit of a brain, why would that school of yours teach such unnecessary things? This world needs no more fantasies written or read. Death to fantasy and horror. Their time is done. Have you not looked around you, silly girl? My money keeps you and Juni safe, but outside the dome, there's horror aplenty. People starve. People fight and die and suffer. People are poor out in the wilds. Thank the Lord that my Harold took his money out of that damned market before the crash, and thank goodness he created the poppets."

It was a prayer Ellie had heard once or twice before.

She nodded and gave her aunt a bright smile as she pulled out a chair next to her. She reached for the compad to scan the DesLoge Com production reports with its endless numbers describing the trade in poppets and all the effects of the DesLoge Com empire's proprietary treasure. As she scanned, Cordelia waxed poetic about dear Harold DesLoge. Ellie knew the story by heart. Brave, prophetic Uncle Harold saw the writing on the wall. He rid himself of all stock in blue chip Dow-traded corporations. He invested in the new medicines—tonics that restored dying organs, revitalized decaying limbs, and eventually raised the dead from their graves. Just the freshly dead, mind you. Fresh because spoiled things, things with more bone than flesh, hadn't the muscle or will to get up out of their lead-lined beds.

Harold, according to the history books and Aunt Cordelia, ushered in a new age. After several years of testing, positioning, quietly building legislation to protect himself, his product, and the profitable living to be made from raising the dead, he introduced the drugs first to the military, because he was a patriot. Of course, Ellie suspected the truckloads of gold the military paid him hadn't hurt. After a year of the military being purged and replaced by poppets, Harold began marketing his formula, in a weakened version, to regular people.

Ellie pulled closer to the table and glanced at the compad report her aunt sent her. She pretended that the scrolling figures of world domination through rising sales impressed her, as Aunt Cordelia wanted them to. She nodded in the appropriate pauses during her aunt's morning lecture about poppet supply and demand. But Ellie's mind couldn't stay focused on the business of DesLoge Com; instead her thoughts wandered back into the history of the family's great gift to humanity—the creation of poppets.

Because Ellie had Aunt Cordelia to tell her about it, she knew the whole history. At first, it had been a slaughter. Families, shocked at the loss of their loved ones' souls or any semblance of a personality, turned in their poppets to the authorities for removal, destruction, anything that would keep dear old dad from trying to strip skin off of junior or chew on Grandma's face. The government had rounded them up by the thousands into pens for destruction—a bolt shot through the brain just like they did with cattle at slaughterhouses. Good old Harold had been on hand for the first round of executions. Brutal, he'd called them. He'd shed tears over the waste of his creations. So he went back to the drawing board. After adjusting the chemical recipe, the first mass-consumption poppets were born.

Tick, tick, tick—Aunt Cordelia's lacquered nails rapped a smart rhythm on the glossy tabletop, jerking Ellie back to the figures at hand. She quickly rescanned them for the upcoming quiz that happened every day over breakfast in the DesLoge mansion. A quiz she never seemed to pass.

"What is DesLoge Com's standing today?" Cordelia leaned back in her chair, bright blue eyes gazing right through her.

Ellie slid her fingers across the screen's surface, flipping through files and digital sales reports, scanning for the information she'd been trained to find.

"Hmmm... sales are up in the blue sector by forty percent. We are not meeting demand for mine poppets. House poppet sales down by twelve percent."

"Why is that?"

Ellie shook her head and flipped through the stack of reports from the seven regions' managers, people who expected her to understand this complex business with only a pass of her eyes and a few seconds' thought the way Cordelia could.

"So...maybe people have enough house poppets right now?" Probably a wrong answer, but she had to say something. Silence is weakness.

Cordelia pressed her lips together in a thin pink line.

Ellie had guessed wrong. She always guessed wrong. "Sorry, Aunt Cordelia." Ellie closed the reports and pushed them aside. She lifted the delicate china cup, filled with Citrocon tea, a poppet-grown product from the Geolina Region, and sipped.

Understanding the tea, produced on poppet-laboring plantations, was piffle knowledge. "Piffle and puff," Cordelia would say. Knowing where a product was from or which region produced it was a start but knowing how to predict the need for the product or how much poppets could produce or knowing the ins and outs of managing that district and the six others that made up the DesLoge commercial empire—that wasn't any piffle.

"Maybe I just don't have a head for business like you."

"Nonsense, dear. You are a sixteen-year-old with a head full of fluff and flowers. You will grow into it." Cordelia lifted her own cup to her lips and took a sip. She lowered it and folded her hands into a graceful nest.

Most women, Juni had often told her, show their age in their hands. But Cordelia's looked ageless and vibrant, even though she was over one hundred years old. Her silky skin lay plump on her bones in a way that only the Plastiques and injections of the best Parker Com preservationists could achieve. She was like the *Mona Lisa* or the *Monroe on a Subway Grate*—timeless.

"Someday, you will make a fine CEO. For now, you make a fine schoolgirl and a lovely niece. Come and kiss me before you fly away, little Ellie Bird."

Ellie smiled, set aside her tea, and gave her aunt a kiss on the cheek. "I'll try harder next time."

"I know you will, sweet." Her aunt waved her away with a smile that warmed her icy eyes and turned back to the scrolling reports. Moments of love were fleeting in the DesLoge house. Best to grab them and tuck them away in her heart, since someday she'd need to be the heartless bitch that Cordelia had become after Harold's sad and untimely death. That was the plan, anyway.

"Auntie, I'm going into the kitchen. Do you need anything?"

"Now, my silly bird," Cordelia said, her bright blue eyes never leaving the sums and figures she studied, "if I needed anything, Thom would get it. Yes?"

Ellie nodded and smiled but still rose to get her own food from the kitchen. She'd lived in the DesLoge mansion for most of her life but knew she didn't really belong. Her mother, Juni, had told her she'd be out on her butt if she made even the smallest mistake. Ellie didn't know what it was, but she knew that Juni had made some mistake since she was and disinherited. Ellie was Juni's best hope, and she never let her forget it.

Ellie walked from the wide archway of the dining room past Thom, who'd finished his spindle wiping and halted, stiff-bodied and waiting for orders next to the kitchen door. She patted his cold hand as she walked past. Even though he didn't respond, he was always her Thom. The kitchen door swung open, revealing the bright white everything within— wide counters, brightly lit cabinets stacked with bone phosphorescent china, shining appliances, and a staff of cooking poppets that any family of means would be proud of.

She walked to the cooler to dig out a crumpet and juice, staying out of the way of the busy kitchen staff. Baking, rolling, chopping, cleaning—all jobs once worked by illegals from other nations or the desperately poor—now taken by poppets. Families did well selling their skilled dead. Maybe Uncle was a machine mechanic, and on the corpse market he'd fetch a small fortune. He could do the work even without his higher thought centers, because after a lifetime of working on machines, the abilities had become rote.

After Uncle Harold was killed by a poppet whose control formula had failed, the company scrambled for solutions. First, poppets were treated with formulas that woke them to their poppet life. Processors injected into their frontal lobes directed non-muscle memory and contained programmed actions not part of a poppet's former life skills. Thom, Ellie's poppet, was an old white-skinned banker who had pissed off Uncle Harold by not investing in DesLoge Com. He'd announced publicly that he thought poppets were unseemly, against the intentions of the creator and other such nonsense.

When Thom died, his family had sold him for a huge

amount to pay off the debt he left after the market's crash. Harold's treatment of Thom had been gleefully cruel—beatings and taunting mostly. After Harold died, Cordelia repurposed him as the butler because of his refined walk and agreeable features. His years as a banker to the rich had set his face in such a way that it seemed like he smiled gently. Ellie never hit Thom like Aunt Cordelia did. His quirky face made her feel welcome in the fortress mansion that Harold's peculiar institution had created.

Back in the beginning, they'd called poppets like Thom zombies, but no more. The Z word was the newest never-say, soap-in-the-mouth, dirty word. Don't call a poppet a zombie because zombies ate people. Zombies were shambling, bumbling, cartoon monsters and, really, sympathetic. No one wanted to sympathize with the poppets, because then...well, everything everyone knew would be upside down. The duty of every citizen of US NOAM was to understand their place, preserve their way of life, and protect the dome cities. That included treating poppets as what they were—reanimated, empty-headed dead servants. The name "poppet" had been Aunt Cordelia's genius. A harmless sweet name. A name that denoted the place of the servant dead in the new republic. Poppets—small and useful items, like the dollies of old they were named for. The name represented the new creature's lack of status and rights.

Thom shuffled in with a tray full of freshly cut fruit.

Beautifully cut little roses and tiny ships with floating hummingbirds suspended on tiny, edible hover discs painted their color of the ruby bellies. One of the kitchen poppets had in life been a famous chef. She wondered how Cordelia had acquired him. If his family had sold him, they certainly hadn't needed to. His fortune massed for years after his death due to sales of books, spices, and the pots and pans that bore his name. Ellie suspected instead that Cordelia had paid the Grave Hawkers to rob his grave. What family, even one with such wealth, would ever begrudge Cordelia DesLoge a world-class chef?

Em, as Cordelia called him, was a genius in the kitchen. Em's particular talent—cooking, slicing, prepping—kept him in constant reach of things that, if the chemical cocktail that kept him from wanting to crack open your skull failed, he'd be a knife wielding maniac. Hence, Joltlaces.

Her family legacy. Harold watched his wealth, his empire of poppets grow from a fad—*Own your own personal poppet! Be the envy of the neighborhood!*—to a full-blown economic sector responsible for most of the economy, either through production, sales, or what the poppets themselves produced.

Ellie walked back into the dining room to eat her crumpet. She bowed her head for a moment.

"Bless Uncle Harold." Ellie prayed this because she believed it. It had been taught to her and every other dome-safe child in the world, and it was true. She owed everything, her life and her safety, to him. To him and Aunt Cordelia. "He saves me every day, and so do you, Auntie."

Cordelia nodded, a satisfied jerk, then lightly punched the buttons on her compad. A smile flitted across her aunt's features, and Ellie knew she'd gotten through to her, just for a moment. She smiled back and chewed her crumpet. Thom wandered in with light steps, carrying her book bag in his hands as Cordelia had ordered.

Ellie took the bag, gulped the last of her juice, slung the bag across her shoulders, and leaned in to peck Thom on the cheek. "Thank you, Thom." Damn it, she thought.

If she could smack herself for being stupid in front of her aunt, she would. And then go back and take away that kiss. Cordelia had tolerated her loving actions toward Thom when she was a kid, but now? Her aunt's face hardened and erupted into a sharp poisonous scowl of bright, squared teeth and perfectly plumped lips.

"Ridiculous. Why would you do such a thing?" Cordelia pushed herself up out of her chair, her tiny body seeming so much bigger when she raged. She ticked her well-shod feet across the floor. "Thom is just a creature. A machine, at best. He is not aware of your esteem. He does what his chip tells him to do. What I programmed him to do."

"He's just meat driven by wires and chemicals. He's not even as important as a lump of meat."

Aunt Cordelia whipped her hand back and made to slap Thom once again, but Ellie moved between them, took Cordelia's hand in hers, and squeezed it. In the corner of her eye, she thought for a second that she saw Thom take a step back, but that was ridiculous. Poppet or not, Ellie couldn't believe it was okay to hurt him. He was her family.

She shook her head. Good thing she hadn't said that out loud. No matter how she felt about him, she couldn't let Cordelia see because she'd be ashamed. Ellie didn't ever want to be a source of shame for her family. Family meant everything, and Cordelia was the most consistent, involved family she had. Her approval, her love, meant more than any inheritance. That's why she had to get this right. Thom was just a poppet. Just a revived machine.

"Yes, Auntie. Meat. I just forget sometimes. I won't do it again." Ellie switched her book bag onto the shoulder closer to Cordelia, as if it could shield them from her wrath. "I need to get to school."

"I'm serious, Ellie. You have to grow up. They are products. We *sell* poppets."

"Yes, of course, Aunt Cordelia," she nodded. She hoped her eyes would open wide enough, be earnest enough to convince her aunt that she took her seriously. "I'll try to remember better."

Thom glided away as Cordelia allowed Ellie to hug her lightly. The clouds of anger lifted from her face, and Ellie felt she could go. Thom walked her to the door, held the door open, handed her a jacket, and waited for her to walk out, down the steps, and into the waiting autocar.

Ellie stepped into the autocar, shut the door, and ordered it to drive to the Academy de Bellum. As she pulled away, she stared back at Thom, who stood stone solid in the doorway, still, and waiting for instruction. He would be waiting there when she got back. Ellie laced her fingers together to control her urge to wave goodbye to Thom.

DOCUMENT 2: FROM THE SANTELOUISA VID GAZETTE

HB 8652B US NOAM PASSES. PRO-EARTHERS REJOICE

The debate between burial and cremation is finally over as the Senate passed the "Body and Soul" law. Pro-earthers have long held that bodily cremation is tantamount to treason. They reason is that once a soul has left the body, after medical and brain deaths have been declared, a citizen's body becomes the property of US NOAM to use for poppet labor or as soldiers. This view was considered radical a few years ago, but as the border wars continue, the need for labor is undiminished.

Polls show most US NOAM citizens support the sale of deceased family member's remains to supplement their incomes or support the state. The latest trend is to will yourself specifically to whatever portion of the economy you imagine your body best suited for. Counselors and post-life planners are available to help for a small fee from DesLoge Com.

Pro-ashers fought the bill, believing that the dying

should have the choice to give their bodies to DesLoge Com for repurposing or to cremate their remains. Some have argued for religious reasons, for their preferences, and as citizens and taxpayers, they should be able to choose whether to give their bodies over to being poppets.

The recently passed "Body and Soul" law now prohibits the destruction of remains. Families may still choose to bury relatives with the understanding that for the good of the state, DesLoge Com may claim remains at any time, even during funerals, ceremonies, wakes, or lay-ins. This precedent was crafted in response to one family's attempt to block collection of their deceased by holding a prolonged lay-in with the intent to keep the collection agents out until the remains spoiled. US NOAM marshals, along with Grave Hawkers according to some witness reports, did intervene, though the resulting firefight offered the state the opportunity to collect more deceased for border skirmish repurposing.

CHAPTER 2

Ellie climbed the white marble steps leading to the Academy de Bellum's main hall—a rough-hewn stone castle with turrets and climbing ivy. Antedevolution and made to last. Dusty, but it was a dust with generations of breeding. The moneyed and the name-bearing kids of Santelouisa learned from the greatest minds and rubbed elbows with the right people. Ellie never felt like she really belonged, though her name, DesLoge, seemed to be emblazoned in every other hall's marble marker or bronze plaque.

Take, for example, her first class. Literature of the Antedevolution, the literary history of the time before poppets, most interested her. But beautiful Joceylin Parker and her tribe of silky-skinned socialite harpies talked over the vid lectures. Yes, they talked *to her*, but they only did that because of *who* she was—DesLoge. Being the future queen of the poppet empire made making friends, real friends, nearly impossible. When Joceylin talked to her, she was trying to win her over. She felt like some prize pony for Joceylin's stable. Ellie tried to be nice, but the harder Joceylin pushed, the less she wanted to have anything to do with her. Why did she need her so badly? Joceylin was literally the most popular girl in the school. Couldn't she just be happy with that?

Cordelia's eyes had flashed when Ellie told her of Joceylin's constant pursuit. She'd said, "You will have to deal with her and her horrible father soon enough. Keep it courteous and distant. Arm's length at all times, or else you'll wind up bleeding, my girl."

Cordelia didn't say such things lightly. So since then, Ellie did as she'd been told. Avoided, obscured, smiled, and walked away. But Joceylin wasn't one to give up. Even as she walked toward her next class, Ellie felt an approaching wake as if the wave of blonde ambition were a palpable thing. She turned down the hall of cubby lockers to escape, weaving through the crowds of uniformed scholars punctuated by the occasional poppet mopping, shining, carrying—all wearing the bibbed uniform of the Academy de Bellum poppet staff. Since some of the students were, like Ellie, prone to forget their Joltlaces, the walls of the Academy sported a blue glowing glassed-in switch every ten feet. Ellie shook her head as she walked past one of the small poppets, perhaps in life a nine-year-old who'd died of some fever or wasting disease in the wilds. The bowl-cut, freckled poppet scrubbed the marble floor on his knobby knees. The school had at least 40 of these small poppets. Maybe they preferred the smalls because they were less threatening? Ellie found them distasteful. Who wanted to be reminded that children die in this age of wonders? Not her.

"Hey, Ellie!" Sasha gave her a quick wave from across the marble-floored hall. Sasha, as Ellie's formal "bestie," should have offered the formal arm clasp and greeting that acknowledged their status and duties to each other, but they'd long ago become real best friends and stopped with the pantomime. "How'd history go?"

"Same as usual. I'm going to fail my tribunals because of Joceylin's silly mouth."

"Whose silly mouth?" A deep, confident voice whispered just behind Ellie's ear. Natan, Sasha's brother and Ellie's beau, stepped around and bowed to them both. He was a perfect reflection of Devolution courtesy. Always following the traditions. Always so gallant to Ellie, though she often caught his eye on other girls when he thought she wasn't looking. She worked hard not to let the jealousy get to her. It's not like they had signed a marriage pre-contract. She should be grateful that he was interested in her at all. With his athletic body—muscled from years of cricket, baseball, rugby, and poppet-polo—his blue eyes so deep like wet velvet, and his dark brown hair, soft, and naturally sideswept. It was shocking that the most gorgeous of the society boys at Academy de Bellum was interested in her, but he was. Aunt Cordelia thought it a good match, though she often grumbled about his motives—that his family sought connection to DesLoge wealth and DesLoge power. Behind closed doors, Cordelia talked often about how Ellie would always have to guard herself against her potential mates, no matter who they were.

Natan leaned in, grabbed Ellie's hand, and pressed it to his soft lips, a moist warmth crept up her arm and into her cheeks. "Ellie, you look beautiful today. Now, what's this Joceylin problem you have?"

"Nothing." Ellie shifted from foot to foot. Squirminess, her comportment teacher would call it. And unladylike. She straightened up her shoulders to equal Natan's perpetually perfect posture. "Well, she's just always talking. She's so full of herself and bossy. I can't even hear the vid when she gets going in class."

Natan looked to his sister for a moment, then shrugged. "Say something to the Proctor Principal. She'll listen to you. I mean, you are Ellie DesLoge," Sasha said, her coppery red hair wound partially in braids around her head, while the rest snaked down her long back into a loose stream. Sasha opened her cubby locker and stepped in, switching books and freshening up her face with a quick Plastique spray. Ellie stepped in and sat on the cushioned bench near the bay window. She had a cubby locker of her own, the most spacious one at Academy de Bellum, but she didn't go often. Seemed silly to use all that space for a few lab supplies and a printer, so she just stashed her things here with Sasha's stuff. Jule stood near the bay window holding Sasha's cloak and bag from the morning. Ellie couldn't stand that Sasha left Jule waiting in her cubby all day. It seemed cruel to make her stand there, holding her things like a fleshy coat rack. But Sasha had no problem letting her poppet wait. Ellie couldn't imagine doing the same to Thom, dragging him all the way down here just to stand like some bit of furniture.

Jule was Sasha's personal poppet, a young blond with

thin arms and legs but beautiful long hair. Quite an expensive poppet to own. Sasha had once told her, not in a braggy way, that Jule had been a supermodel in the Antedevolution days. She'd died of cancer. The silly things people died of in the old times never ceased to amaze. So, when Jule died, they cryo-froze her and kept her in case of a cure. Well, the cure for cancer came, but there's not a cure for dead. Sasha had revived Jule as a personal maid. Quite a step down, but Jule didn't know it. Ellie always thought that their loss of higher thought was a blessing, especially when she watched how Sasha treated Jule sometimes.

She turned away from Sasha and Jule, back toward the door and her handsome beau. He'd waited so patiently for her to attend him, she tried to involve him in the discussion. "What do you think I should do about Joceylin, Natan?"

Natan nodded agreeably like he was really considering all she'd said, but his eyes shifted toward the guys clustered down the hall—his baseball team. He leaned toward them like wheat in the wind. "She can be a pain. Maybe old Proctor can get her to shut up. Or maybe we can put some Plastique in her food and freeze her tongue, eh sis?"

Sasha smiled and waved the bottle of Plastique menacingly in the air.

"Oh Natan, cut it out." Ellie gave him a playful shove toward the guys he clearly wanted to go talk to. "You should go to your team. They're waiting for you."

With a smile, he bowed deeply from the waist and turned in such a fluid movement that he might have been dancing.

Ellie watched him walk away, her heart still racing. It still felt so unreal that he was her beau. If all went well, he'd be hers forever, joining the DesLoge and the Parker fortunes and families. It made her nervous to think about that part of her life, so mapped out and appropriate. Sometimes, it frightened her how pat her future seemed. Any girl would feel honored, even blessed, to have such wonders in her future. To be the head of the greatest industry, bringing the comforts and benefits of poppet labor to the world. Then to marry one of the heirs of the next greatest industry, Parker Plastiques, which had the potential to extend lives and youth for near ever. Their future was so bright. Why did it make her stomach turn inside out when she thought about it? They were at least a few years from any formal engagement. No sense letting her nervous- ness overwhelm her. Ellie rolled her shoulders, willing the weight she felt there to tumble away. She glanced at her bestie. Sasha never struggled with her place in the world the way Ellie did. She seemed ready to eat up any banquet thrown her way and then ask for seconds.

If only she could be more like Sasha.

Sasha leaned in toward a mirror, patting the sides of her face. Though she was one of the better-looking girls at the Academy, Sasha's natural cheeks bothered her.

"Blubber," she said, pinching and twisting them.

They weren't that bad, but Ellie couldn't convince Sasha of that, no matter what she said. Her slightly floppy cheeks were weak spots on an otherwise lovely facade, as she liked to say, fashioned by daddy—the leading esthetician doc in all of US NOAM. Dr. Parker's Plastiques line revolutionized aging. Stopped it. It really wasn't designed to be used on young skin, but since Sasha's daddy didn't have time for her cheeks right now, Sasha used a few drops of bottled Parker magic here and there. Sasha dabbed the Tighten Plastique on her face, then started grabbing the things she needed.

"Well, are you going to say something about Joceylin?" As she moved about the cubby, Sasha's cheeks perked up tighter than the beauty sales girls on the vids. Glamour in a bottle, and Sasha had all she wanted.

"I don't think so. Proctor will listen to the poor little rich girl with a wing and a street and everything you can imagine named after her. I don't want to use my family name, I mean...I hate that," Ellie said, leaning on the door frame and watching Joceylin hold court in the hallway. The tiny terror, Sasha called her. Blonde, beautiful, and bossy in a way that every boy loved and every girl hated. Every move that girl made was calculated and weighed for maximum impact.

Sasha stepped out of the cubby into the hall. She turned back and said, "Want to go shopping today? I'll have Jule get an autocar for us."

Ellie nodded, walking out into the hall behind her. Why not? Cordelia would approve. Sasha was both an appropriate acquaintance and a good friend. The only one she had when she really thought of it. Everyone else at the Academy liked her only for her name and her power. What a pain. Constant butt kissing, her mother called it on her infrequent visits and in between her social soirées. Mother told her to enjoy it. Power opened doors and created opportunities for her. But Ellie always felt uncomfortable when people fawned over her. Sasha was different. Sure, she wasn't the future CEO of DesLoge Com Poppets, but she was financially independent, future CEO of Parker Plastiques, if her father had any say.

She lived in her own mansion on her own hill, and much to Ellie's relief, she was real. Sasha laughed with her mouth open. Sometimes she dropped food on her shirt. She openly gawked at the cute boys and blushed when they gawked back. She made Ellie feel like a real person, not just an idea of her mother's or the heir of the empire. It was good to have a friend.

"Shopping, huh? Sounds like fun," Ellie said. As she looked up, she wished she could suck those words right back into her mouth. Joceylin stood there, a few cubbies down, clearly listening in. Their eyes caught each other for a long few seconds, then Joceylin flicked her hair over her shoulders.

"Are you going to Lord's Mall?" She and her hangers-on were arrayed in near-perfect wedge formation behind her. "We could meet you there. You know, make it a girls' day."

Her eyes were eager and wide, her gaze shifting between Sasha's and Ellie's.

Sasha shook her head, upper lip curling slightly. Just enough to let Joceylin know what she thought. "Sorry, Joceylin. We've got a private fitting. Not enough room for you all. Maybe next time."

Joceylin's shoulders tightened but quickly relaxed. A hardness settled between her eyes, even as she smiled sweetly and stepped back. "Oh sure, Sasha. We'll try some other time."

Joceylin stepped away, and her ladies-in-waiting folded her into their embrace. Whispers of "bitch" and "snotty" and "stuck-up" reached Ellie's ears, even as Sasha pulled her in the opposite direction.

"Don't let it get to you, Ellie. Seriously, she's a shit. All she'd do is brag to us all day about her father's connections to Cordelia and his money, then brag to the school about being better than us tomorrow. Let's just remove the middle-man, shall we. Let's go straight to bitch and let it go." She linked her arm in Ellie's and laughed at her own joke.

They made their way to class. Devolution History. Not her favorite. Might as well be called DesLoge Com history. They walked into the high-ceilinged white classroom, where students sat in bunches, gossiping and rolling their eyes as she passed. Joceylin and one of her cronies, Alys maybe or Betrix—so hard to keep track of Joceylin's court of cattiness —muttered and flipped her hair in a pretty dismissal as she approached. Such disdain, just like the sudden intense worship that happened on occasion, came with having the name DesLoge. Though it bothered her to have these people saying things, thinking things about her, she straightened up her shoulders and walked with the measured grace that Mrs. Ambrose's careful comportment training had lent her. She settled into her seat between Sasha and Natan, who was fully engrossed in a description of a recent dome defense from Josep, a dome defense colonel's young nephew. Ellie nodded greetings to both, then turned back to Sasha.

"Mmmm, Doc Vinkma is actually here today." Sasha sneered and slid into a padded desk and clipped her compad into the holoscreen.

"Yeah, that's different," Ellie said. She cued up the note file on her compad.

Vinkma flicked on the holovid and turned toward the

class. "Today, we will review the institution and it's creation. Please clip in your vids for note transmission."

Ellie groaned. The "institution" was how polite people referred to the economy, lifestyle, and culture that grew up around poppets. The history of the DesLoge family wrapped around everything they were learning. Honestly, it embarrassed her every time her teachers brought it up.

Dr. Vinkma began her lecture with a wave of her arm, as if she could draw them back with her into the Antedevolutionary past. "It was only 150 years ago that the Worker War erupted. The stock market crashed and never recovered. Debt, poor governance, democracy, regulations on the companies, and the general laziness of the working class all contributed. Workers rioted, attacked rich neighborhoods, and kidnapped the wealthy in their rage at being laid off from those failing companies."

Ellie imagined the brutish working class, smeared in filth, toppling the profit margins and destroying the delicate Antedevolution economic system. The attacking workers and soldiers were vital to the economy, but they demanded terrible concessions. Limited workdays, days off, vacations, high wages, something called insurance. How stupid were they? They destroyed their own livelihoods with their demands. Did they think that the producers would just allow their attacks? Roll over like some dairy cow waiting to be milked?

Dr. Vinkma continued, peering out under her fashionably bushy eyebrows, "The workers and the soldiers of the United States of America joined together against the producers, the companies and the wealthy—against the very backbone of the economic system. Their attacks were brutal. They used chemicals that killed children in their beds and bombs to scorch the skies. In nearly every gated community of the old America, there were battles and attacks on good, hard-working company owners, doctors, and the like. No one was safe from their terrorism."

Ellie felt color rise in her cheeks. She used to be proud of this history, but the more she heard it, the more it sounded hollow in her ears. Especially since when she asked Aunt Cordelia questions, and Cordelia answered with laughter. With a curt dismissal, Cordelia had told her to learn the difference between the true history of Uncle Harold and the US NOAM patriotic tripe that teachers and holovids served up on silver spoons. She'd been shocked by her aunt's flip attitude, but quickly learned that this attitude really reflected Ellie's position; that she'd need to look beyond what the common story was. This was a lesson in subtext and diversions. Harold did all the things that the vids preached. It's just that his reasons might have been more profit-driven than the vids let on. Ellie fanned herself, trying to get the flush out of her cheeks.

"At first the producers rolled up their own sleeves, building walls, and eventually the domes, to protect citizens from the vicious attacks of the workers. The domes were the first invention of our own greatest citizen—Harold DesLoge."

The holovid lit the middle of the room, showing a larger-than-life image of Uncle Harold, cigar clenched in his teeth, arms crossed and silver hair waving in a virtual breeze. His wrinkles were heroic, his bushy eyebrows venerable. His eyes were like the twin souls of God, burning with naked purpose.

Students around her straightened up in their seats. Harold, like Noah of the *First Book of Mysteries*, led civilization out of a flood. He was to be idolized. Respected. This lesson they all knew. Ellie shook her head and stopped taking notes.

Sasha turned toward her and waggled her eyebrows. Yep, this old lecture again. Only Sasha knew how much it made Ellie want to vomit.

"To combat the workers and the traitor soldiers, Harold DesLoge next invented our poppet soldiers. Fast, vicious, not tamed like our house and servant poppets today. The soldier poppets tore through the ranks of workers and soldiers with no mercy—just as they had destroyed our homes and cities with no mercy."

The vid crackled to life across the center of the room, immersing all of them in the colors, the reenacted violence of the Battle for the United States. Poppets with gnashing teeth tore through the camo and skin to the bone of the rebels. The massacre reached a scale that even the holoscreen couldn't contain. The images swam and spun and vibrated before her eyes. And above it all, Harold's head floated in majestic glory—the hero of the future US NOAM. Most kids around her in class began to hoot, clap, and tap their fingers against the tabletops in appreciation. It all made Ellie's head spin.

She looked at the students around her; all had rapt gazes cast upon this most famous, most brutal scene from their history. So embarrassing. As the fury of the battle died away and the vid flickered back to line upon line of notes, she shifted her gaze to the right and grinned. At least Sasha wasn't in on the hero worship. Sasha picked her nails and watched blond, beautiful Cole Newlin, the Rugby stud whose dad worked for DesLoge Com. She shifted her gaze left where Buell, son of a scientist in the DesLoge Com black hole building, yawned, and took notes on his compad. All of them owed their lifestyles and livings to good old Uncle Harold.

"At the end of the war, the few lower-class rebels left were disenfranchised and their properties seized. They were driven from the cities into the wilds where, if they wanted, they could live or die by producing goods we in the dome cities needed. We left them, outside the domes, in the mess of pollution and chemical destruction they'd created. Some choose to live in edge towns where they direct poppet laborers creating the products we need inside the domes. They are dependent on cities to provide them with a livelihood. That's how they live, even today. They aren't citizens of US NOAM." Venkma's voice swelled, filling the air around them. "They were traitors. They forfeited those rights when they rose up against their country and government."

A brittle sigh rattled behind Ellie. If a sigh could say things, this one said anger, not boredom. Anger? She turned and found herself nearly face-to-face with a boy she didn't know. Someone new at Academy de Bellum? No one new ever came here. If you were from the enclosed city of Santelouisa, then you went to one of three schools. De Bellum is the school for the tippy top, richest, and best kids. The other schools are for bad kids and kids who don't learn well. If you didn't fit in one of those categories, you didn't go to school, and eventually you didn't stay in Santelouisa. Better to work for the company or to seek your fortune in the wilds if you couldn't afford the education of Academy de Bellum. This guy should be someone Ellie knew, but she didn't. She'd have remembered him for sure. Brown eyes with gold, even some green. A thick, masculine nose. Soft hair, hard chin. A boy on the verge of being manly. Lips set in a hard line. He wasn't looking at her but at the vid. Disgust turned his lips ugly. Did he disapprove of the retelling?

"Once their uprising was broken and the threat of invasion quelled, Harold DesLoge..." a slight nod of deference in her direction. The whole class turned to look at her. His eyes were on her too, only they were not the normal awe or naked jealousy that burned her so badly. His eyes were appraising her. Weighing her. "DesLoge invented the next serum, which took the rage out of the poppets. From that point on, through all the various improvements, the DesLoge poppets became essential to the newly formed United States of NOAM. The company provided all of the labor to help us strengthen our walls and domes around the unified cities: Geolina, Atlton, New DC, Minipaul, Ausodotex, Vega, New Jersey-Yorktown, and, of course, Santelouisa. The poppets were the workers that plantations needed to provide our food. Eventually, poppets became whatever we needed them to be."

Ellie knew more than them. More than even Dr. Vinkma. Aunt Cordelia had told her how many workers and soldiers had died. The numbers stunned her every time she thought of them.

"Truth is a luxury that people can't afford. Better to leave them their sweet histories," Aunt Cordelia had said.

Her stomach churned when she thought about the dead soldiers being turned by overhead serum sprays. The shambling dead ate their way through millions. Finally, after the walls and the parades, Harold had fixed the formula and created the tame poppets. Ellie felt her face getting hotter and hotter as Dr. Vinkma's voice rose and rose until she seemed to be screeching. She'd never liked this history. Never. Harold's head floated above it all like some thundercloud filling the horizon with sound and fury. She needed to get out, or she might puke.

The new boy looked at her again; this time his eyes weren't hard or angry. They seemed softer, wide, and sad.

"Dr. Vinkma, I feel sick," Ellie said. She couldn't take it anymore. Any of it. But especially his pity. Her stomach tightened against her throat, and her tongue felt dry like dirt. If she didn't get out of here...She stood and waited to be released.

Vinkma fluttered her fingers, gesturing her toward the door. Ellie rushed out into the hallway with an untoward, shambling gait. Her comportment teacher would be horrified.

Sometimes she loved being a DesLoge with all of the perks and privileges. Who wouldn't? But at other times, her name wore heavy on her like a stifling coat that smothered her breath from her. She walked away, putting distance between her and Harold's floating head. She opened the door of the Academy and stepped out into the muted light of the dome-noon. She looked up at the opaque surface of the field that surrounded them—the dome that kept out the wilds, the Resurrectionists, and all the forces of history. Ellie took a few breaths deep into her lungs as she collapsed on the marble steps that led out onto Vanderventer Avenue. With each breath, the vid of battle and death receded from her mind and became less oppressive. Queasy gurgles in her stomach settled a bit as each breath passed her lips. She lowered her head to her knees, fighting back tears fueled by anger as much as anything. Why did she act like this? She should be proud of Uncle Harold.

The door squeaked behind her. Ellie wiped her traitor tears with a quick pass of the back of her hands. Of course, Dr. Vinkma would come after her. Students didn't just walk out without repercussions. Ellie whipped around to explain.

"Sorry, Dr. Vinkma. I—"

She turned to see him standing there. His dark blond hair, cut shaggy but close, fluttered in the dome breeze, a fake air current created by the careful ministrations of some dome scientist somewhere. He walked over and sat next to her on the step.

"Are you okay?" He reached out toward her but pulled back quickly like he'd been burned. Of course, since they weren't properly introduced, his touch would be too forward.

He folded his hands together instead in a much less threatening gesture. Clearly, he hadn't had comportment classes since primary school, like she'd had. Her hands never wandered. They were trained sentinels, keeping clear of anything that might shame her. His gaze met hers and then dropped to his hands.

"I'm okay, yes." She drew her knees to the right, aware suddenly of how close his body was and how it might look if someone drove by and saw them.

"I'm Moze," he said.

The name soothed her a bit. Smooth like a piece of chocolate. Moze.

He looked up at the dome-noon's distilled light—milky and swirling whites, soft grays, and blues.

"Ellie DesLoge, right?"

She nodded. There was no use in pretending she wasn't a DesLoge. Everyone knew. That was just reality. "Are you new here?"

He nodded. "I didn't mean to be rude or forward. I know that debutants have rules and traditions and such. I just wanted to make sure you were okay."

Her arms folded around her, hugging in the discomfort she felt. She let her gaze trail across the marble-fronted buildings of the art district across from the Academy, the glittering street lines of the autocar tracks, and the scrubber plants lining the clean alley walkways. The only un-beautiful things in this part of town were the dome's dull light and maybe herself. She drew in a bit more, hoping this moment would pass.

He could have said anything. Anything.

What he said was, "Have you ever seen the sky?"

Ellie caught her breath. Few people ever get outside of their home city's dome. Few because life outside of the islands of civilization in US NOAM was said to be ugly, brutish, and poisonous. She shook her head and drew her knees tighter into her chest.

"Have you?" she asked.

He nodded and pointed straight up and to the right of the center prism that marked the top of the dome.

"There, if you could see it, there is the star of the north. It sits up there bright like the crystal earbob or tooth lights from a Santelouisa deb cotillion."

She followed the tip of his finger, as if she would see it.

His finger was long, like his arm. Strong. She forced herself to think about what he was saying.

"It's beautiful. Twinkles and shines, and you'd never even know it was there because of what your uncle did."

"What my uncle did?" She felt herself draw back from him, scooting away on the dusty step. In the stunned silence, she saw a poppet skimming the sidewalk with a blastbroom that crackled and seared the dirt and litter from the street. In a dome, such cleaning saved lives and kept them all breathing. She watched the brown-skinned poppet shuffle by, his broom an extension of himself. She bit her lip against the rising anger.

She turned toward him, face flushed and body rigid. "What? That he saved us all? That he preserved us and our way of life? He's a hero. What have you done? And who cares about what is outside of the dome? Here we are safe and prosperous and happy. Why would I care what is out there?"

Moze drew back, his eyebrows pulling together and palms up in an "I surrender" kind of gesture. He stood quickly and moved away. She thought she saw his lips pull up in a near smile. A smirk. A nasty, smarmy smirk that made her even madder. He bowed to her, deeply. Though it seemed the height of politeness, to Ellie, it felt more like a slap in the face.

"I'm sorry if I offended you, Miss DesLoge. I meant no disrespect to you or your illustrious uncle." He turned toward the street, stepping down the marble steps and onto the sidewalk. He gestured to the buildings surrounding them, the brownstones, the businesses with colorful swags, the poppets carrying things here and there, the beautiful residents wandering between the facades of each. "When I look around here, I don't see what you do. I'm not from here, and I guess I just take it for granted that everyone feels as I do about the past. I apologize."

He leaned in too close, near her ear, one leg on a higher stair, his breath warm and sweet-smelling. Here his eyes looked like liquid bronze.

"I mean no harm. I just... I thought that you... I thought you found it as ugly as I do."

"Ugly?" Ellie repeated his word because she still didn't know what to say to him. Her insides twisted around her middle, and her tongue felt thick.

Moze nodded. His voice was so soft it took her a moment to even hear it. "Ugly because you can't see the sky. Because you live inside a wall."

"It's safe. You know...clean," she said back, tasting the words like they were from someone else's mouth.

An autocar floated by, drawing his eye away from her. He stared after it, not moving closer, but his voice dropped lower and felt closer than before. A whisper just for her. "It's all very calm. Safe. But Ellie, it isn't right."

The door to the Academy swung open with a slam. They both jumped and turned, pulling back from each other to a polite distance. Dr. Vinkma stared down at them, her gray eyes fairly blazing with an anger that only self-important teachers can conjure.

"Mr. Grayson, Ms. DesLoge, will you be returning to class

anytime soon?" Dr. Vinkma asked, her arms crossed on her narrow chest.

Ellie stood quickly, brushed the dust from her skirt, and hurried up the stairs, aware that Moze was right behind her. Why did she care what he thought about her uncle or Santelouisa or how they lived? Who was he, anyway? She straightened her shoulders, headed back into class and held her head high, not giving him even another glance. She sat back in her seat, took up her compad, and felt everyone's gazes burning on her back—even poor Uncle Harold's frozen vid head, paused mid-speech, whose gaze seemed to pin her right through the soul.

DOCUMENT 3: US NOAM HIGH COURT RULING ON POPPET RIGHTS.

HIGH COURT RULING

Liza Jon, who owned a poppet named Dia, hired her out for a month to Mann Vin in order to pay debts. Her contract with Mann gave him temporary ownership of Dia. Mann shot Dia, destroying the poppet utterly. Though the reason for his action was unclear, he suggested that he was within his ownership rights. Jon, the original owner, brought suit for damages against her property in lower court. Mann was found guilty of destruction of personal property by the jury and charged a five-hundred dollar fine.

Mann appealed the decision based on his rights as temporary owner of Dia. The NoCal High Court overruled the fine on the grounds that poppets were the absolute property of their owner or temporary owner through rental or other such means. Owners of poppets cannot be held liable for damages to their own property. During testimony, Liza Jon suggested that Dia's difficulties with

Mann might have been due to loyalties to Jon. That Dia should have been brought back to Jon, not destroyed. Mann argued that poppets have no rights, no feelings, and no loyalties and that Dia was a bad poppet. Liza Jon lost her case upon appeal in Judge Ruff's court, whereupon she left weeping, having lost a poppet she valued highly with no recourse or compensation.

Judge Ruff stated that "the power of the owner must be absolute, to render the submission of the poppet perfect." Ruff, however, made it clear that his opinion was a legal one, and his sympathy lay with Liza Jon and Dia, the destroyed poppet. He wrote that "the struggle, too, in the Judge's own breast between the feelings of the man, and the duty of the magistrate is a severe one, presenting strong temptation to put aside such questions of loyalty and feelings, if it be possible. It is useless, however, to complain of things inherent in our political state."

Judge Ruff was disbarred a month later with no state support for having made such traitorous Resurrectionist statements. He disappeared from NoCal and is thought to be in the wilds.

CHAPTER 3

When classes released and Sasha and Ellie stepped into the waiting autocar, Sasha's poppet Jule shut the door behind them and sat on the jump seat on the outside. Jule's beautiful golden hair flowed behind her as her slight form, dressed in the silks that usually were reserved for the wealthiest people, was buffeted by the rush of the autocar's acceleration. The poppet's hands crept up to shield her eyes from her hair whipping in the wind as the car raced across town. Ellie shivered in the low-G interior of the autocar in sympathy for the poppet as they dropped from the high fast lane in near free fall some thirty-five feet. All the while, Jule's body leaned, seemed to collapse back, then recover from the extremes of their travel. She would have liked to have Jule sit in the autocar interior with them, but Sasha had been raised to separate from poppets. Aunt Cordelia had tried to drill that into Ellie, but she'd never been able to swallow down the rigid separation. Sure, it was around her every day, but her stomach turned at every cruelty, though she could never say that out loud.

"Here. Stop here." Sasha's always-so-sure-of-herself voice demanded. The car swerved off to the curb, and the door retracted. By the time both of them tumbled out of the auto-car, Jule stood waiting for them to direct her. Sasha stopped in front of the poppet, appraising her in a swift, severe glance. "Fix yourself, Jule. You look a mess."

The poppet's hands smoothed her hair methodically, flipping out the ends like she'd done so often in her life from before. Jule's rumpled clothes still looked good on her thin frame, but Sasha still fussed over them, clucking angrily. "Just keep up, Jule. You are such a pill."

Sasha locked arms with Ellie, towering a whole head over Ellie's compact, shorter form. They were an odd pair. Ellie, short and pale with long dark hair and what her aunt called a "guileless face," which meant she looked naïve and baby-ish. Sasha looked gorgeous, of course, with her coppery hair, tall and thin body, including the willowy legs and arms that the boys always admired. Even with the big differences between them, it still felt to her like sisterhood. Ellie smiled. It was good to have a true friend.

Jule followed four feet behind as they walked. Sasha prattled on about class and about Joceylin's obviously repurposed green, crystalline eyes and about her own unhappily shaped cheeks. Ellie thought they were actually darling but couldn't get Sasha to believe it. The bright signs of the shopping district of Santelouisa unfolded before them in their millions of colors, breezy scents, and clicky heels of salesperson entrepreneurs.

They could shop anywhere. Both of them carried the highest credit markers. Their names alone would open any shop door, even after hours. Joceylin and her tribe of petty, pretty girls probably would expect them to shop in the private galleries of CoVoLaRouche and Jason Jones, designers to the highest circles of society.

Instead, Sasha and Ellie liked to go to the vintage shops where Antedevolution fashions, books, jewelry, and vids lined the walls. Posters of olden stars of film like Charlie Chaplin, Elizabeth Taylor, Brad Pitt, and Kim Kardashian lined the white ceiling vaults. Strains of the incomparable hair bands of the 20th century played softly out of the ceiling and floors, soothing the shoppers as they spent.

Sasha's head bopped to the music as she sorted through acid-washed jeans and track shorts. All were new, of course. They were just styled to be like the fashions of the world gone by. Ellie wandered away from Sasha as she piled up Jule's arms with things to try on. "Come on, Ellie. Won't you try anything on?"

"Not today." She wandered over to the artifact collection, her favorite section of the store. "Be right back, Sash. Promise."

"Okay, you freak." Sasha laughed. Ellie knew that Sasha understood, or at least tolerated her fascination with what came before. As she wandered past shelves of bygone technologies like books, DVDs, iPods, and cell phones, she trailed her fingers across their surfaces. At home, her walk-in closet was a museum filled with things she'd found here. Beautiful things, things that caught her fancy, things that made her laugh. Finding something to save always made her heart flutter. It made her feel important in her own right.

She stopped in front of a book called *A Brief History of Time* by a man named Stephen Hawking. She thumbed through the pages that described the physics of the universe in the lofty terms that only the old ones used. He talked about things no one had ever seen or touched—things as fantastic as hobbits and elves. The DVDs interested her, but the players had been outlawed long ago. So, if you bought a DVD, it had to be turned in and decoded, approved, and uploaded to the vid system. She always bought every DVD, because if she didn't, who would save them? She'd turned in dozens, and so far, fifteen of them had been released to Santelouisa citizens. Each time, they'd been released with her name as the benefactor. She didn't spend the thousands of credits for fame, though it was nice to have done something kind of on her own.

"No DVDs today, Miss Ellie," Gertrude said. The silver-haired and wrinkled owner of the store took much pride in having caught Ellie's attention with her antiques. She did everything to help feed Ellie's growing obsession with the past and its leftovers. "There's a new box behind the counter I haven't had a chance to go through. Grab yourself a sweet tea from the coolie and have a look-see."

Dear Gertrude. She'd been a nursemaid for Ellie when she was a young thing, teaching her songs and rhymes while mother shopped in other stores. She'd always had the time for a silly little rich girl who felt so out of place at her mother's side. But Gert made her feel like she belonged somewhere.

"Jule!"

Ellie looked over her shoulder at Sasha, who had nearly buried Jule in a pile of clothes. Sasha barked orders at her poppet as she continued to search for the elusive pieces that would make her wardrobe sing every morning when she opened the door and stepped into the entry of Academy de Bellum."

"Go ahead, Miss Ellie. If she looks for you, I'll keep her busy." Gertrude smiled with a quirk of conspiracy on her curled lips.

"Don't call me miss, Gert. Really. You practically raised me."

Gert put her hands up and her fading blond head nodded, her teased bun seeming to shift atop her head and nod along. Mock surrender. Ellie knew they'd have this conversation again the very next time she came, but it was what they did, and she enjoyed it.

Ellie slipped behind the counter, back into a dusty area less organized than the cluttered but clean shelves that surrounded the round and tiered clothing racks of the main store. She grabbed a sweet tea, popped the air seal, and took a swallow. The sun-steeped tea came all the way from the fields around the dome city of CharLanta—a real luxury that made her tongue feel candied. To her, it was the taste of summer, produced on a plantation and made from poppet-grown leaves. Thank you, Uncle Harold.

She pulled the hoverbox closer and settled onto a stool. It bobbed and wiggled until she had it in place next to her. She thumbed the lock button, and it settled to the floor with a hiss. Her eager hands rooted around. So many interesting items to look at. Rubber ducks, hardened and cracked with the years. A clock with hands instead of digits. A handkerchief stitched with letters and flowers. A pencil made of wood, rubber, and graphite. Her hand settled on a thick cardboard wheel with two circle layers attached in the middle with a pin. She pulled it out and wiped the face of it, smearing away the dust. It said "star wheel." As the top wheel spun in her hand, a window showed starred patterns connected by lines. It reminded her of what Moze had said about the sky. She had to have it.

She set it aside and rooted around again. Her hands passed over many items but finally stopped on top of a globe. She took it out and looked inside the scratched-up foggy plastic. It needed a good cleaning, but if she squinted and stared hard at it, she could see that on the inside, in a layer of white flakes and encased in water, there was a little city. A skyline. In the center of the dome were the words "Gateway to the West," etched into a silver arch. She shook it and watched the white flakes fall atop all of the little buildings. Her thumb ran along the lip of the bottom and found letters there. They said Saint Louis. The old city. She laughed with delight.

She wondered if Aunt Cordelia would like this as a present. Cordelia often talked about her childhood, visiting the massive silver arch before it fell into the Missip some thirty years after the Worker War. Such a shame, but it was outside the dome. Why would they waste resources on such a thing?

As she stood to leave with her treasures, she noticed one more item near the bottom. A photo. It showed a family, a

mother with brown, straight hair parted down the middle in
an orange sweater that folded at the neck and practically
swallowed her head. A daughter with high ponytails on
either side of her head, thickly rimmed glasses that seemed
to magnify the child's large dark eyes, and a smile punctuated with metal. Cordelia had once called these things
braces, mocking Antedevolutionary people for their
attempts to perfect such weaknesses in their bodies with
temporary corrections instead of replacement parts. Finally,
there was a father. He was kind-eyed, with a ring of black
hair around a bald head covered by a row of long hair pulled
comically across as a false cover. The man wore a shirt too
small for his roundish middle. But he seemed so happy,
arms around his two girls. A family, whole and awkward and
so beautiful. Ellie felt tears come up in her eyes, blurring
her view. She sniffled them back, took some breaths and
stood. She always took pictures of fathers. She couldn't
help it.

"Gert, I'm done. What will I owe you for these?" Ellie
asked.

Gertrude met her at the counter, took the items, and
appraised them quickly. "Good eye. If you weren't the
DesLoge heir, I'd suggest that you become a history doc or
museum curator."

Ellie smiled, pleased to have done well.

"This photo is yours, free. Without a name, I can't sell it
to a museum. It's worthless to anyone who isn't interested in
the story inside their mind from looking at it. I mean, who
would wear ugly clothes?" Gertrude giggled at her own good
humor. Ellie smiled along with her. "The star map is a trea-

sure. I'll need 2000 credits for that. Its paper, and paper articles are rare now, yes?"

Ellie nodded. Two thousand was nothing much to her. The possibility of understanding Moze's words seemed more important than money.

"The globe is quite historical, isn't it? Saint Louis, it's our old city. You can even see some of these ruins in the open museum of Westown Santelouisa. So, this, I think, is the most expensive. Five thousand more?"

Ellie sensed an opening. Gertrude had taught her to haggle, a skill, an art she said the Santelouisans were losing.

"5000 credits for the lot," Ellie said.

Gertrude smiled, then pursed her lips and shifted them to the side in a gesture of deep thought. "Let's say 6500."

"6000."

"Deal, 6000." They shook, and Ellie typed her code into the compad that Gertrude offered, signing off on the transfer of funds. "I'd have given the whole caboodle to you for 5500 credits."

"Gertrude, you shrewd shark," Ellie said. She didn't mind spending extra money. She took the bag of treasures, leaned in, and pecked Gertrude's rose powdered cheek. "Thank you."

"Get out of here, you bandit. Go help your friend decide on some clothes before she wrinkles everything in the store." With a final pat and a chocolate from a secret stash pressed into Ellie's hand, Gertrude turned back to her work.

Ellie smiled and shifted the bag over her shoulder. She hurried toward Sasha's dressing room—the one with the scattered piles of clothing, helter-skelter shoes, and belts draped here and there. Jule stood stoic and beautiful by the door, holding brilliantly colored blouses and silken pants, face frozen with her trademark smirk—a smirk Ellie had just seen in the pile of Antedevolution fashion magazines on Gertrude's shelves.

How could poppets with limited cerebral use continue to get things like that right? Thom at home was the same, with his perpetual soft smile.

"Jule, what the hell?" Sasha, wearing a floating electric blue dress with gold details that shifted as she moved, grabbed Jule hard, shoving her. "You are wadding them!"

Ellie hated that Sasha was so rough with Jule all the time. She almost felt bad, but then again, Jule was just a poppet. The shove didn't matter to her, really.

Sasha said, "She's so useless."

Laughing nervously, Ellie stepped in between Jule and Sasha to sort Sasha's finds, laying them nicely in Jule's arms. Luckily, Sasha was too preoccupied with her latest outfit to notice the intervention. As she worked on the clothing, smoothing it and hanging it straight, she noticed an older woman with hair silver-gray and long. Gray by choice. Such a statement in an age when your hair need never fall out, gray, or thin. Widow Douglas, Cordelia called her. Marie Douglas, wife of the late Marl Douglas, Mayor of Santelouisa, and a senator in her own right, cut quite a figure in society. Between her dedication to the crafts and arts, as well as her continual donations to the beautification funds of the great walking alleys of the city, everyone knew and loved Widow Douglas.

"Mrs. Douglas." Both girls greeted her and curtsied in unison.

"Why, Sasha and Ellie. Aren't you both a sight?" She nodded a polite greeting back, acknowledging their clever bows.

The girls smiled and lined up for inspection. Widow Douglas reached out and squeezed a shoulder from each, smiling warmly and making them feel like they mattered. Ellie thought she was one of the most genuine people she knew.

"Girls, I have a favor to ask." The widow's eyes shifted from side to side, and she lowered her voice as if conspiring. "My nephew is in town. He's started at the Academy today, and I'm worried for him. You know all the old blood and snobbery there. I'm worried they won't treat a newcomer well."

They nodded eagerly, and Sasha gave Ellie a sidelong glance that seemed to say, "Are you thinking what I am thinking?"

Moze. The only new kid since, well, ever.

"I think we met him today, Mrs. Douglas. Moze, is it?" Sasha asked. The sheen on her kind words had dulled a bit. Clearly, Sasha didn't care for Moze.

The widow withdrew her hands and clasped them together, as if in prayer. "You did. Oh, good. I worry about his fitting in. He really is a fine boy; he's just...he's from the wilds, you know."

Ellie gasped. It was rude, but she couldn't help it. The wilds? She'd assumed he was from another city or a plantation on the edges. But the wilds? That was something new.

Resurrectionists and lawlessness—how had he survived? And his manners. Weird, but not rude like she'd expect from someone from the wilds. Suddenly, much of the brown-eyed oddity she'd met in class made sense.

"Oh. Well, that's...interesting," Sasha said. A smirk bloomed on her lips, as if this explained all she needed to know.

Ellie hated it when Sasha did that, but she didn't argue. It did say something about him that he'd lived among the savages. "Why is he here?"

Widow Douglas' lovely blue eyes filled with tears, and she looked away for a moment. She sniffed and dabbed her face with a silk hankie, then smiled with tight lips. "His mother left here when she was just a whip of a thing. Fell in love with a..." Her voice dropped to a breathy whisper. "Free Resurrectionist."

Sasha's eyes widened, and her hand reached out and grabbed Ellie's elbow. "No!" Few things scandalized dome city folks more.

The widow nodded. "Moze wanted to come here. I offered him the benefit of my name and fortune. I couldn't let him stay out in the wilds, especially after his parents, rest them, were killed in a raid. Gone, just like that."

Ellie's hand found Sasha's and pried it from her elbow. It hurt. It was not something to talk about in polite company, but of course they'd died. The Grave Hawkers didn't protect Resurrectionists. The plantation owners and the manufacturing men outside the dome took to night riding when the Resurrectionists stole poppets from them—what the Resurrectionists called liberating them. Hogwash. Still, the night rides smacked of murder to Ellie. The law of US NOAM guaranteed you could believe in resurrection and worship in your own way, and if it led you to steal your neighbor's property, then you'd go to jail or pay fines. It's just that polite society, the leaders, and those who were in charge quietly wanted to deter such acts more stringently than the law allowed. Hence, the night rides. Few talked about them, but most folks thought it served the Resurrectionists right. Ellie wasn't so sure. Especially with Mrs. Douglas crying over her lost daughter, Resurrectionist or no. And poor Moze.

"Perhaps we could see about a dinner with Aunt Cordelia to introduce him around, Mrs. Douglas?" Ellie offered. Sasha elbowed her in the ribs, a nasty little jab that struck bone. She didn't approve.

"Why, Ellie, that would be lovely. You'd be a dear to see to it. Tell your aunt I would be so in your debt. My place is a fine house, but it isn't set up for such a crowd. I'm sure Moze will be glad, too. He seems a bit lost here, I'm afraid."

Ellie nodded. "Yes. We'll get the details worked out."

Widow Douglas smiled and patted her cheek like she was a dear pet, then left in a swish of skirts.

As soon as she was out the door, Sasha turned, her lovely face twisted in frustration. "Why would you do that? That boy is creepy."

Ellie shook her head. "He's all right. You just haven't gotten to talk to him yet."

"I don't want to. He's not one of us." Sasha turned back to her clothing finds and waved Gertrude over to ring her up. "He won't ever be, even with the widow's name. Why... he's a Resurrectionist's child. Nothing worse than them."

"How would you know? You've never even met any. Besides, since when do we blame a child for his father's sins?" The grit edge of frustration tightened her words in a warning. Why did Sasha care about this so much? Just because she didn't agree with them for their stance on poppets. "They have a right to believe what they want, even if it is stupid. That's the law."

"Yes, but imagine." Sasha picked up her bag and began to walk out. She lowered her voice so that none of the other shoppers would hear. "Freeing the free poppets?"

Sasha grabbed Jule's face and turned her to face Ellie, nose to nose. "Like this empty-headed, unfeeling thing should ever be released into the wild." Sasha pushed her back, disgusted. "Resurrectionists are idiots. I'm not coming to your little dinner, El. I won't sit at the same table with him. Besides, don't you think that he'll get the wrong idea? What about Natan?"

"It's just a party to welcome him! Natan will be invited, too." Ellie followed her out and down the street. "Come on, Sasha. It won't be a party without you there! Come on, please?"

"No, I just won't do it."

"I'll invite Cole." Ellie smiled slyly, knowing Sasha's Achilles heel.

"Ellie!"

She got into the autocar, knowing it was just a matter of time. She'd wear Sasha down, send out the invites, and they'd have a party for Moze. She peeked into her bag at the sky wheel she'd bought. Maybe then she could show him that she'd found his beautiful night sky. Maybe that would pay back his odd kindness to her on the steps of the Academy. Maybe if she did the party for him and got to know him, she'd untangle the odd anger she'd felt mixed with such a dose of hope. What was that? Getting to know him and having him in her debt might make understanding things easier. She smiled and leaned back into the seats as the car carried her home.

DOCUMENT 4: MISS ELLIE DESLOGE'S SCHOOL TRANSCRIPT

Miss DesLoge, heir apparent at DesLoge Com, was well regarded by her teachers and fellow students in her second year at de Bellum.

Academy De Bellum

The finest education money can buy

Transcript Report: Miss Ellie DesLoge

Legacy 3rd generation, active alum-Juni DesLoge, Cordelia DesLoge

Primary School:

Passed Intermediate School: Passed Secondary School:

1st Year—

Comportment: A /Mrs. Aubush

Comments: Shy, sometimes a bit awkward in her conversation, generally excellent manners.

Devolution History: B+/Dr. Vinkma

Comments: Shows little of the DesLoge fire in studying, discussing this subject. A very nice girl.

Music Theory: B/Maestro Choi

Comment: Little natural talent, but an excellent ear.

Maths: C/Mr. Maro

Comment: Trigonometry is not a natural talent. Suggest private tutoring to develop skills.

Dance: B/Madame Lasalle

Comment: Passable. Not creative enough for advancement in dance as art, but proficient in social dances.

Physics: A/Dr. Penneu

Comment: Bright.

Literature of the Devolutionary Period: A/Mrs. Loar

Comment: Bright, critical thinking top notch, a good little writer herself.

2nd Year—

Comportment: B+/Mrs. Aubush

Comments: Doesn't always participate. Generally good manners.

Devolution History: B/Dr. Vinkma

Comments: Adequate progress. Lacks sufficient interest in the subject.

Art of the Antedevolutionary Period: A/Dr. Boesch

Comments: Excellent work. Very bright.

Maths: B+/Mr. Maro

Comments: Recommend continue private tutoring to progress beyond calculus.

Rhetoric of the Institution: A/Mrs. Loar

Comment: Writes excellent themes and papers, but the

strength of her convictions in defense of the Poppet Institution, DesLoge Com, and the US NOAM need sharpening.

Chemistry: A/Dr. DeMayo

Comment: Demonstrates exceptional interest in the chemical processes behind the reanimation of tissues.

Literature of the Antedevolution: A/Mrs. Loar
Comment: Always a pleasure. Her interest in ancient literature is commendable.

3rd Year—Not achieved

4th Year—Not achieved

Post Graduate Plans—

Ellie DesLoge is the heir apparent to Cordelia DesLoge in the Des Loge Com holdings. We recommend that she attend intensive postgrad with business, politics, and rhetoric as her majors.

CHAPTER 4

Juni DesLoge blew through the massive front door of the DesLoge mansion, her perfume a flowery fog and her silver-plated spike heels clacking with self-importance. Her personal poppet, Dovey, brown-skinned with black shimmery hair down to her waist, trailed behind at a respectable distance. Juni had her own house over on the heights, a trendier section of town where the houses were made of glass, steel, and Plastiques with splashy bright exteriors shaped like stacked boxes and geometry word problems. Aunt Cordelia hated that part of town but preferred that Juni live there among the party socialites who planned the constant balls and cotillions that made up the daily grinding social schedule that Santelouisans enjoyed. Aunt Cordelia hated it but believed someone from the DesLoge family should attend all the teas and fashion shows. Juni lived for the social swirl, while Aunt Cordelia and Ellie both only attended what they had to.

Juni's social calendar left her with no time to be a mother. Ellie didn't mind it, though, because Juni was vapid and anxious and didn't like being touched. As grumpy as Aunt Cordelia could be, at least she had an honest interest in how Ellie was doing and even showed affection when she thought of it. The only reason Juni had bothered to show up was because she wanted her name attached to the DesLoge party that Ellie was planning.

"Oh dear, these plans will never do. A sit-down dinner for twenty? Why, that would be an insult to most of Santelouisa. No floating message boards? How ever will our guests be able to flirt? And what's with the lack of costuming plans?

Why, this party you've planned is so... backward." As Juni fanned herself, wisps of her black silken hair flew about her head in a near-miraculous halo. She popped open her purse and extracted a mirror to admire the effects of her many Plastique upgrades.

"Notice anything different?" Juni asked. She turned her face this way and that for Ellie and Aunt Cordelia to admire, watching herself the whole time in her 360-degree projection mirror. A minicam spun around her head, taking in the entirety of her face and head and projecting it back to the handheld receptor. "Well?"

Cordelia didn't give her a second glance. Instead, she snapped her fingers to call Sabine, her own poppet maid, to get the compad she'd been looking at. Sabine brought the factory compad for the daily round of signatures required to run the most important organization in the world.

Ellie watched her mother stare at herself in the mirror.

Dovey and Thom both stood behind her, waiting for any order that might come through their chips or from Juni's lips.

"Mother..." she started, knowing how it annoyed Juni.

"Call me Juni, dear."

"Juni, we have things to do. Why don't you just tell me what's different?"

"Just guess." Juni put the mirror away and smiled brilliantly at Ellie, as if this mystery were the most fascinating thing in the world.

Nothing would get done if Ellie didn't figure it out.

"You've had your eyes done. Poppet eyes?" Juni shook her head. "Teeth then? Maybe a jaw replacement?" Shake. "Ummmm," Ellie stalled, running her gaze quickly over her mother's lovely face. Perfectly formed forehead, hair just high enough to suggest good breeding. Chin, slightly pointy but not aggressively so. High cheekbones. Perfectly shaped eyes, brown as sable. Skin taut and stretched and impressive for an eighty-year-old. But what was new? Ellie bit her cheek and ran her eyes across her mother's beautiful, stiff face once again.

"She's had her shoulders replaced." Cordelia didn't even look up from her compad and figures. "They're much wider. About three inches. Right?"

"Auntie!" Juni banged a fist on the table like a petulant child. "Ellie was guessing. Why did you ruin it for her?"

Ellie and Cordelia's lips drew up in near-matching curls of disgust, though Juni seemed not to notice anything beyond her whirling reflector.

Aunt Cordelia set aside her compad and turned her full

attention to her nieces. "Let's get this planned. I have too much to do to play your empty-headed games, Juni."

"Fine." Juni pouted her lips in a wrinkled pucker.

Ellie sighed and opened a sample vid she'd created. "I thought we could just invite the Parker family, the widow, and her charge Moze, perhaps some of the other senators and their spouses. You know, keep it small. That way we can—"

"No, no, no...the boy will never make friends that way. We need to invite everyone. Really do it big. You know, decorate and everything. This will be the event of the sea-son!" Juni's voice rose, and her breath seemed to weave in and out of her words too quickly for the sounds.

Cordelia nodded. "We don't do things halfway, Ellie. If you are introducing Widow Douglas's ward to Santelouisa, you must do it right. We need to host a big party, not a dinner party."

"Oh, Aunt Cordelia, you just want a chance to lean on the widow for more support in the legislature. She seems to be backing the company less these days." Juni picked at her nails, pulling a bit of skin from the side of her thumb.

Cordelia leaned on the massive oaken table of the dining room. "She has another five years in her term. That's five years I need to make her a bit more receptive. That's why Ellie is my heir, Juni darling. This party of hers is the perfect opportunity to seal an alliance. If we get in good with her boy, then maybe..."

"Why should Ellie be the heir? She's just a child, and I want to help you too!" Juni pouted unprettily.

Cordelia shook her head. "We've discussed this before. Just help us put on this party, will you?"

Ellie walked toward the window, leaving them to discuss decorations and the like. Her mother always acted distressed when Aunt Cordelia called Ellie her heir, as if she really wanted the part. Why did she pretend to want the job? All three of them knew Juni found the actual making of the money, the running of the business, and anything related to decisions distasteful. Cordelia and Ellie both accepted the fiction of her complaints since Juni would flit back out of their lives soon. The window stood open to the cool, filtered breeze, and Ellie leaned into it. As she did, Thom moved toward her in the slowsteps that his feet naturally performed.

"Fine." Juni waved to Thom to bring her the treats on his silver tray. Canapés. Thom shuffled over to the table and leaned in to let Juni pick her favorites from the tray. Then he stepped back to stand near the wall, close to Ellie. Cordelia ran her finger down the compad, summoning images and lists. Juni moved closer to watch the holovid, reeling off the names.

"Ellie." Aunt Cordelia never even looked up from her work. "While we work on the invitation list, could you look for the invitation paper? It will be much nicer if we write some of these by hand on real paper."

Ellie walked toward the credenza to carry out the errand. She'd been the one to come up with the idea of the party, but she wasn't fool enough to think that she'd actually be the one to plan it. Nope, the intensity of politics and alliances made in each spoonful of caviar or polite waltz card order must be handled by professionals, by people who understood the intricacies of polite US NOAM society.

She pulled out the top drawer, hunting for the linen paper shot with threads and flecks of gold that they used for invitations. Her hands shuffled through the mess of sheets and miscellaneous trifles. Nothing. With a push, she closed the drawer, then yanked open the next one.

"Widow Douglas would want the legislative families invited," Juni said. "They are like her family now that her husband is gone. What kin were the boy's parents to her?"

Ellie's hands skittered across the velvet-wrapped silver in the second drawer. Her hands kept feeling, but her mind focused. Moze. They were talking about Moze. Her heart beat a bit faster, louder. She took a quick breath deep into her lungs to calm it. She shook her head a little at the reaction her heart had to his name, even when she whispered it in her own head.

"Her daughter," Aunt Cordelia said, a grimace marring her lips.

"You mean Josine? He's Josine's boy?" Juni asked. Her frivolity dried up, and age seemed to bloom around her eyes. "Josine, my bestie? Why, I thought she married? Didn't she move to New Chi Town?"

"Seems like you two besties are more alike than not," Cordelia said, her icy gaze fixing on Juni. "Girls with very little sense about their responsibilities to family."

Juni's brow furrowed for a moment like she'd been stung. "Will you not forgive me even now, Aunt Cordelia? I came back. I stay out of trouble...for you."

Cordelia stared at her, chin tilted, and lips set in a soft, cruel curl. Ellie had stopped shuffling through the credenza during this exchange, wondering what it could mean. The two women she loved most seemed to be engaged in some silent, painful conversation that Ellie only wished she could understand. Cordelia glanced at Ellie and seemed to signal to Juni that Ellie was watching with a quick twitch of her head.

"When she married that Grayson boy in New Chi Town, they decided to leave the dome." Cordelia's voice had dropped to a low, rumbling whisper as if the information was too much for her mouth to bear. "To Kansas."

Juni's ragged shudder betrayed her shock. Ellie's hand covered her mouth even though she'd known Moze was from the wilds. Kansas? The widow had said the wilds, but Kansas was so much more than that. Kansas territory meant the complete exit from US NOAM-held land—Resurrectionists were the least of the villainy there. Wild bands of pre-serum zombies and people with no allegiances but lawlessness and death ruled in Kansas.

"Paper, Ellie?" Cordelia demanded. "Check the hall sideboard."

Ellie nodded and moved out to the hallway. She didn't want to miss the conversation in the other room, but clearly, she was being dismissed so the adults could talk. She pulled open the doors on the sideboard, shuffling through them. Nothing. Ragged linens, boxes, old books. Meaningless stuff. She tried to be as quiet and quick as she could be, hoping to hear some of what Cordelia and Juni were saying. Even so, she only caught snatches of the conversation.

"Attacked."

"Found decapitated."

"Resurrectionists."

She turned to search another door and spun right into Thom. In his hands, he held the invitation paper. A drawer much farther down the sideboard stood open.

"Thank you, Thom."

A nod from him, then he ambled away toward the dining room ahead of her.

She tapped the papers into a clean stack, shut the sideboard and went to shut the drawer Thom had opened, wanting to hurry back into the room, but her gaze stopped on a fine wooden box inside the sideboard. A branded inscription in the lid said, "Ridley Brown" in gilded, stylized script. Her fingers traced the name and the edges of the box, which was maybe a foot across and half a foot deep. A tiny lock glittered at the opening hasp. Ellie pulled her hand back. It wasn't hers. But for some reason, she felt that wasn't right. Somehow, she knew it *was* hers. Hers to open. She shook her head and pushed the drawer back into place.

Back in the dining room, Ellie handed the papers to her aunt and sat back at the table with them.

"Poor Josine," Juni said. Genuine sadness, so foreign in her mother's usually overly bright voice. "I wish I had known."

"What could we have done, my dear?" Aunt Cordelia asked, a tender voice so different from her usual sternness.

Ellie's gaze bounced back and forth between them. Stupid paper. She'd missed something.

Juni wrung her hands. "Who attacked?"

Cordelia shook her head and stood. "No one knows. The town is full to the brim with Resurrectionists. Could be them. Could be rogue poppets. Let's not think about it. Let's do our best to raise the boy's prospects here, shall we? Ellie, you will be his bonny friend. Introduce him around. Be kind to him."

Nodding, Ellie understood that this kindness meant a gain—closeness to the powerful widow, but Auntie's voice contained true care in it. Of course, it would. If his mother and Juni had been besties, that was a powerful bond, indeed. It joined their families only a bit less strongly than a marriage would.

Juni had a decor scheme projected on the table in front of her. Ellie studied the holovid showing the banners, lights, projections, and floating confetti launches strategically settled in the most festive configurations. No corner, no hall, and no space would be left unbeautified by Juni's adept hand. The color and theme reflected Antedevolution. She couldn't wait to see guests in their costumes from before the war—old movie stars, famous presidents, infamous villains from her texts.

"Oh Juni, you've outdone yourself," Ellie said.

Her mother nodded, the grave set of her features melting away in the warmth of Ellie's compliments.

"Give me a peck, darling. I'll finish this at home and in one week's time, like magic. I'll take the paper with me too. I have the nicest handwriting." Juni stood, took Ellie's peck, and clacked back out of the DesLoge mansion and her life. At least until the party.

"Ellie, dear, I am expected at the factory tonight. You can

get yourself dinner, right?" Aunt Cordelia walked away, not waiting for an answer.

Ellie sighed and grabbed her compad. She keyed in her dinner request, a simple sandwich and salad to be served in just fifteen minutes. Access to one of the greatest chefs in the world, and she requested peanut butter and jelly. At least as a poppet, he wouldn't be insulted by her immature taste.

She wandered around the dining room, looking at the portraits on the walls. Here was one of Harold, standing against a background of a white columned building with huge dark doors. On the steps of the building, several poppets stood at attention waiting for orders. The silver plate at the bottom of the thick scrolling frame said, "Harold DesLoge: Liberator and Savior. Year One." In this picture, Uncle Harold looked stern, but loving. His eyes set on something in the distance, filled with a bright warmth. Crinkled skin and deep smile lines made him human in a way that the holovids never did. Here was the man she was proud of. Not some monstrous inventor hanging above it all. Just a great man trying to make the world better.

She walked farther down the richly papered walls to the matched picture of Cordelia standing in front of the same building. Sweet old Cordelia looked as young then as now, even though the portrait had been completed when Harold first came to power. Cordelia's real eyes had been a regular grayish blue then, but no less beautiful in their way. Her long, ash blond hair spilled across thin shoulders. The evening gown she wore with an air of command, even before she'd assumed the mantle of DesLoge power.

Ellie wondered if Cordelia had walked out of her mother's womb a powerful and organized woman. She could never have been helpless or dependent, so she couldn't imagine her as a baby.

Ellie walked past the far end of the room toward the entrance, the place where Cordelia had given a wall over to family snapshots that rotated in flickering frames on the wall. Images of her at various ages dominated the snaps. Ellie's eyes, almond-shaped with deep brown irises so rich that the pupil seemed to fade into them. Her long brown hair, thick and shiny, framed her face in a flippy bob. Little Ellie at school. Little Ellie swimming. Ellie with Juni on a swing set. Ellie on Cordelia's lap. Whenever Ellie looked at this wall, it gave her a boost just knowing how important she was to her aunt.

Most of the pictures with Ellie also featured Thom. Her silent friend. Thom in the background, carrying her books, holding her umbrella, always doing for her. She smiled and looked at Thom, who was setting her dinner on the table at that moment.

"Thank you, Thom. I appreciate it."

Thom bowed and walked out. Though she tried to do things for herself as much as she could, Thom's help felt more like love than servitude. Taking his help and letting him care for her didn't inspire guilt. She knew it didn't really make sense, but she couldn't give up Thom's constant help.

She focused back on the photos, watching them cycle through. A picture flickered through the family photo feed that she didn't recognize. How could she never have seen this one? The image showed two young couples, laughing, heads tilted together in a secret sort of alliance, the kind of comfortable relationship Ellie often wished for. Ellie reached out and froze the picture with her forefinger before it could escape into the house's memory.

"Copy to my compad," she said.

The image flashed twice in confirmation.

She stared at the picture. The couples, two men and two women, stood close and smiled with a natural brightness. She didn't recognize the men standing behind the women with their arms draped across their women's shoulders, clearly great friends or brothers with much love between them. But the women were familiar to her. Both seemed to have eyes she recognized. Suddenly, the features of one of the women came together in her understanding. Juni! It was a picture of her mother when she was younger and less Plastiqued. Who were the others? Who was the man in the photo?

Could it be her father?

Ellie's stomach dropped to her feet. The man's face seemed to swim before her eyes. His kind eyes, his huge, toothy smile. She'd never seen him before. Juni and Cordelia acted as if he didn't exist. He was a topic that neither would broach. Only every once in a while, would Cordelia promise to tell her about her father someday.

The father she imagined haunted her dreams, even if she never brought him up to Juni and Cordelia anymore. Could this be him?

Thom appeared next to her, the sandwich on his tray.

She looked at him for a moment.

"Thom, this could be my father. How am I supposed to know who I am if I don't know who he is?"

She reached absently for the sandwich and took a bite. Thom wandered away, allowing her to eat and stare and wonder.

When Ellie sat down to do her calculus, she struggled to keep her mind on the subject. Every time she considered the derivative before her, her mind returned to the photo. How could she figure this out without her aunt or mother's help? It seemed so hopeless.

Thom came back, placed her hot chocolate on the desk, and began to brush her hair—their nightly routine.

"I can't focus, Thom. Why won't they tell me about my father?"

He grunted his inhuman answer, a noise that happened as the air required for perambulation escaped from his lungs and vibrated his mostly frozen vocal cords. At least that's what Aunt Cordelia said.

"I know. I'm being ridiculous," Ellie said. She'd always imagined the other end of their conversations, answering things she wished Thom would ask or say to her. Maybe that's why Thom had always seemed so human to her.

Her compad beeped, announcing an incoming call. It was Sasha.

"Answer. Hey, Sash."

Sasha's face materialized, floating above her desk.

"Ellie, I hear the party planning is going well."

Ellie put her hand up to stop Thom's brushing. The poppet moved out of the way, back toward the door. "Oh, I guess my mom called your mom about some kind of touch-up for the party?"

Sasha nodded. "Her neck. But I also just got this."

Ellie could see her hand clutching a gold trimmed envelope with an invitation peeking out.

"Already?" Ellie asked. Cordelia's assistant must have taken care of the invites while Cordelia toured the factory. "I guess she didn't want to wait for Juni to get them done by hand."

Sasha nodded. "She must have hired an army of poppets."

Thom pulled the blanket down for her, smoothing the pile of comforters and quilts into an inviting nest as she got up and moved toward her closet. The vid feed floated, following her in.

"I guess I'll need to find something to wear, right?" Ellie asked, knowing that Sasha, fashion maven that she was, would want to discuss such things. "I don't have too many Antedevolution pieces in my wardrobe."

She used her finger on the closet screen to scan through outfits prescreened and selected for their fashionability. Her eyes measured her purple evening dress's potential as a costume if she paired it with something from her collection of Antedevolution artifacts in the next room.

"No, no, my friend. That won't do." Sasha accessed the closet through a compad link they'd set up last year. "Let's try this."

The clothes streaked by, settling finally on a white halter dress.

"Add a little bit of this." Sasha tweaked something, and pleats appeared in the dress. "A tuck here and some extra decolletage—that's cleavage, if you didn't know."

Ellie snorted with laughter, looking down at her less

than-stellar chest. Sasha added a temporary blond hair piece, a short strand of pearls, and heels to the screen, and Ellie realized just who Sasha was dressing her as.

"Oh no, you don't, Sasha. You could be Marilyn Monroe, but me? I'm two feet too short and too thick-hipped to be her. Are you kidding me?"

"It's not you silly," Sasha said. "That's for me. Do you mind? Your poppets are so much better at sewing than mine. Cordelia always seems to dig up the best of the designers and seamstresses."

Ellie shook her head in dismay.

"Come on." Sasha threaded her hands in a mock prayer and started to beg and whimper.

"Okay, sure. Just find something that good for me, too."

Ellie paced back and forth as Sasha flipped through her closet. She mumbled as she worked, but Ellie didn't make fun of her. This was part of her friend's personal genius. She knew Sasha would create something incredible for her that perfectly suited her own body type. So, while she worked, Ellie picked up the bag of goodies she'd bought earlier from Gertrude. She walked to the back corner of her closet and pushed on the shelf stand that held her collection. Thom, right behind her as always, held his arms out. Ellie put the items gently into his hands, letting him carry them into the closet and put them away. No one else touched her collection. Only her and Thom. She watched him set them on a shelf, grouped, and facing outward so she could admire them.

"Okay, try this..."

Ellie's hand trailed across the image Sasha had created.

The DesLoge sewing poppets were going to be busy. The design Sasha had worked out included a full, floor length skirt of green velvet with a lighter lime underskirt tied smartly in the middle with heavy yellow gold tassels. A hoop popped the skirt out to almost obscene proportions. Then, there was a hat that would sit sideways and pointed atop her head.

"Do you get it?" Sasha asked. Delight swelled her voice and raised it a few notes to a trill. "Scarlett O'Hara. You know?"

"Yes, *Gone with the Wind*. We're watching that movie next week in class, aren't we?"

"Exactly! Perfect timing since the party will be the day after we watch it!" Sasha's words came quickly, and Ellie couldn't help but be swept away with them.

"It looks beautiful. I'll put in the alteration request now."

"Good. It'll look so live on you. Gorgeous!" Sasha's holovid face beamed with excitement.

With a loud beep, a second holovid announced itself.

Ellie slid over and checked who it was from. "Natan."

Sasha smiled and started chanting. "Ellie and Natan sitting in a tree..."

"Oh, shut up. Speak to you later, okay?"

"Ta, dear." Sasha's holovid popped and disappeared.

Ellie turned to Thom and signaled to him to bring the brush. He came quickly, slack-jawed, but moving with punctuated steps. She took the brush from him, mumbled her thanks, and ripped the brush through her thick hair, straightening it with the strokes. She shoved it back into Thom's hands and said, "Answer."

Natan's handsome face, blue eyes twinkling, and strong jaw clenching in a restrained smile that even as a holovid lit up the center of her room. She was glad that Cordelia had insisted on giving her such a large, dignified room. No little girl frills or posters. It was the room of an heir, a future captain of industry. Ellie always wanted Natan to remember that. His eyes slid hungrily across the room, taking in the wealth, the sumptuousness of the bed covers, the huge wall vid, the chameleon wallpaper now set to reflect the *Gone with the Wind* theme Sasha had requested, and the hand-blown carnival chandelier. She knew she looked a little...insignificant surrounded by the finery, but at least he saw her as part of that world.

That's why he wants me, she thought, but not with bitterness. She'd been told that her money and position would dictate her place in society. She knew a good marriage didn't mean love. Instead, it was a link to be forged between two powerhouse families. She wouldn't be like Juni—that much she'd promised Aunt Cordelia.

Juni hadn't done what had been expected of her. She'd fallen in love and married Ellie's father, a father no one spoke of. She'd been disinherited for that. Sure, she had money. Just enough to keep her happy and out of trouble. Just enough because she had given Ellie to Cordelia. Until she'd surrendered Ellie when she was just four years old, Juni suffered in an average brownstone, without access to parties and shopping. Ellie was payment for what Juni owed, and Juni was forgiven.

"Good evening, Ellie." Natan bowed. So gallant. "Natan, good evening to you." She curtsied back, smiled, and tried to look as charming as he did, but she knew that goal was as out of reach as Moze's stars. Ellie blinked. Why would Moze come to mind just now? She pushed the image of his earnest face right out of her head, focusing instead on her beau.

"I'd like to ask you to save a spot or two on your dance card for me at the party."

Ellie nodded. Of course, she would, but it was nice of him to ask.

He cleared his throat. "I think we should go on a date soon, don't you?"

Her stomach skidded around inside her ribs, but she managed to stay calm, look serene, and say, "Sounds lovely."

He bowed, smiled at her—all teeth and daring, though it was the same smile she saw him flash at school all the time for other girls. Still, this time, it was just for her.

"Good night then, dear Ellie." His image faded with a pop.

Ellie's stomach churned from the excitement. He'd asked her out. Not formally, of course. That would have to be done through Aunt Cordelia and probably Mrs. Parker, Natan and Sasha's venerable mother. They'd negotiate the place, the time, and the chaperones for such a momentous occasion. Formal courting. It was a big step. Ellie searched her feelings. This squelchy stomach of hers wasn't what she'd imagine she'd feel on such a wonderful occasion.

She should be jumping up and down. She should throw open her door and scream for the whole house to hear. But somehow, the request had only excited her a bit. Maybe it was all this talk about her mother and Josine or the image of them with their beaus. That was what love looked like. With all the pre-planned courting and their futures written by family politics, would she and Natan ever feel that rush of love or excitement? She wasn't sure, but she knew she couldn't let herself be swept away. Not like Juni and Josine. Swept away into danger and disinheritance. The thought alone made her shiver.

Ellie went into her closet to change into the pajamas that Thom had laid out on the bench that sat in the waiting area there. As she picked up the silky shorts, she saw something there she didn't expect. The box. It was the wooden box from earlier. Its burned, gilded lettering and tiny little lock glittered in the light.

"How'd this get here?" Ellie flipped the heavy box over in her hands. Things rattled and clunked inside.

She wandered back into her room, where Thom was setting the vid wall to her favorite night scene, a beautiful painting from the period in history called the Renaissance. The scene was a whirling view of what those ancient people thought heaven looked like, with saints and angels, God, and the Mother Mary. At the center stood the figure of Jesus, angry, vengeful arms thrown up, and muscles bunched. So vivid and alive.

Ellie sat at her desk, turning over the box. "Who brought me this, Thom?"

Thom slowly walked over to her side, but, of course, didn't answer. She pulled open her desk drawer. Rustling around, her hand clasped the metal file with a thin hooked end she used on her nails when the poppets missed some rough spot. She lifted the tiny lock and jammed the end of the file into it. For a moment, she thought about the fact that this box wasn't hers. Would Aunt Cordelia be angry when she found out? Why did she feel like opening this box had to be done?

Ridley Brown, the lid said. The name was meaningless to her.

Why did she feel the need to do this?

Ellie went to her bathroom suite. She picked up the mouth laser and set it against her teeth to allow it to bake away the day's decay. She didn't know who'd brought her the box, but she knew she shouldn't mess around with things that weren't hers. She'd just have to take it back downstairs to its drawer before Cordelia missed it. The laser clicked and shut off, so Ellie set it to the side, took a mouthful of tooth vitamins, swished them, and then spit into her sink. She looked into the mirror at her face. Her mother was there in her dark hair and cheekbones, but was her father there, too? Did she look like the man hugging her mother in the picture? Maybe his chin. His smile. She went back to her compad, flicking across the surface until the picture returned to view.

"Project." The picture popped up as a holovid floating in the air above her desk. She used her hands to manipulate the photo until it was just the man behind her mother. Was it her father? She'd never know if Juni and Cordelia kept mum about it. But here in this picture, maybe it was in the way his eyes crinkled a bit with his bright smile or the tone of his skin. Maybe it was the swoop of his thick hair. Maybe this was her father. She stared just for a few moments, trying to see connections between her and him, but it was too much like a puzzle missing all the edges. How can you know what goes where?

She sighed and stretched. No sense going on about something she couldn't do anything about. Shaking her head, she forced her thoughts to turn away from the pic. She flicked her hand across the screen, dismissing Juni and Josine and their beaus. Best to think of the things she did have to deal with. Just five days until the party. School and Cordelia's lessons and Natan's gentle attentions. Those were pressing and real, so those would be her focus. She yawned.

"Thom, instead of *Gone with the Wind*, can you switch the walls to the night sky outside the dome?"

He turned toward the screen with his usual mechanical gait and flicked through images of sky from before the dome: bright blue mornings, sunsets in pinks and oranges. The images flicked past in a circle. Thom couldn't find what she wanted.

"That's all right, Thom. It was worth a try. You can go now."

He grunted, bowed, and walked toward the door. As she turned for bed, she heard a soft metallic clatter. There on her desk. The metal file had moved from where she'd left it, and the tiny lock hung off the metal hinge, open wide. Ellie watched Thom's back as he walked out the door.

Thom.

That was just not possible.

Her hands found her Joltlace and absently touched it. Thom had opened the box. Someone must have programmed him to do it, but who? Only she and Cordelia had access to Thom's chip. Was Cordelia trying to tell her something? That had to be it.

If Cordelia wanted her to see this box, if she had programmed Thom to bring it to her, why didn't she just give it to her herself? It didn't make sense.

Ellie opened the lid slowly. She breathed in the smell of old paper, leather, and some other thing she couldn't identify. Her hand floated above the papers in the box. The name Ridley Brown sat heavy in her mind, like a weight she couldn't quite lift.

The papers were yellowed, but definitely of the Devolution period, since the paper had the tiny teeth of mini processors that would project holovids, though many of the teeth were broken off. Ellie wondered what the papers would have told her. Without those teeth, there was no way she'd be able to get the papers to play on the compad. But maybe she could find someone to help her.

Besides the file thick with papers, she found a bulging palm-sized leather bag tied off at the top with a cord. The leather bag's cord resisted but then gave up its knot, opening under her insistent fingers. She tipped it, spilling the contents into her hand. Out fell a two-inch-tall female carving, like a chess piece. A woman not in a formal dress, but a working dress, hair tied up in a wrap. Her face was sour, set in a savagely serious pose. On her forehead, a massive dent rose above her brow and into her hairline. Ellie's finger skimmed the dent with her finger. It didn't feel jagged like a gouge or crack. This woman's face had been broken somehow and not fixed—absolutely unheard of in the Devolution world. The ugly scar didn't seem out of place, though.

On the face of this tiny figure, it projected a powerful, almost regal air. Ellie imagined the world and its trivial concerns were beneath the figure.

She shoved the tiny statue back into the bag and flipped through the file. The writing scrawled across the page at staggering angles. What was this language? She flipped it over and on its side. No matter how she turned it, it didn't look like any language she'd ever seen before. Page after page, she flipped the sheets over, smelling their age. Beautifully drawn sketches of trees, hills, and people hid among the documents every few pages. Was Ridley Brown an artist?

Underneath everything in the box, under the file and papers and pressed leaves, lay a picture, small and grayed-out, dog-eared and wrinkled, as if the picture had a life of its own. It was him. Him! The man in the picture she'd seen in the dining room. The same man was in the picture with a baby. Behind him, she could see the old oak that still stood behind the DesLoge mansion, where she'd made the poppets build her a tree house. She could see the edge of the Mizzourah River snaking through the top of the picture, just like it snaked through the grounds behind the mansion. Was this Ridley Brown? Was he her father? Part of her wanted that baby he held to be her. Part of her longed to have her past finally solved. She wanted to be that baby in his hands.

Ellie's temperature went from cold, hands clammy with a full body chill, too hot, reddening her face, back, and cheeks with a fire from within.

She picked up the toothed papers and examined them closely in the light. All of them had damage, missing teeth in the same place. That had to mean they were destroyed on purpose. Someone didn't want the vid attached to the documents to work. She tapped the papers against her desktop and shoved them back into their folder. Who could read these for her? Ellie bit her lip. Thom brought this to her, and she had assumed that Cordelia had given it to him. But now that she thought about it, that didn't seem right. Cordelia wouldn't have sent this to her without explanation. This box and all its contents had been locked away. Maybe Thom's bringing it to her was a mistake in his programming or something. That meant she really wasn't supposed to see this.

Her stomach knotted at the thought of her own disloyalty. She had opened this box without permission, but it was her past, wasn't it? She had a right to know about herself. But if Cordelia didn't want her to see this or to know about Ridley Brown, then she really had to be careful. Again, the disloyal thoughts made her gorge rise. Maybe it would be better to just lock the box and everything in it back up and put it right back in the sideboard. She piled the folders into a hasty pile and shuffled them and the leather bag back into the box.

She heard the wall vid pop on with a self-important click. Cordelia.

With a shove, Ellie hid the box behind her body and leaned against the desk as guilty goosebumps pricked up her arms. Her aunt appeared, smiling with a distracted air. Behind her stood a line of poppets dressed in factory smocks, lined up against the neon lit machinery embedded in the factory floor and hanging from the ceiling. Ellie had been there a few times, but Cordelia tended to keep her away, saying she wasn't ready to learn that part of the business yet.

The factory poppets' constant moaning, their grunts, and rocking made Ellie's skin crawl with ice every time she saw them, so maybe Cordelia was right. Ellie hated her weak stomach.

"Aunt Cordelia," Ellie said. She dipped in a curtsy.

"Ellie Bird, I will not be home this evening. There are big things happening in the wilds. Some of our plantations along the Mizzourah are under attack."

Though Cordelia took up most of the vid screen, Ellie could see boots in the right corner of the background behind her. Fancy red rancher boots crossed and set atop a factory table that Cordelia sometimes used as a desk. Imagine some fool rude enough to have his feet up in the presence of Cordelia DesLoge, like he was in his own house watching holoshows. Such a gesture of disrespect in the presence of the greatest woman in US NOAM! But clearly, Cordelia tolerated the boots and the owner. Who would do such a thing?

"That's terrible. Is there anything I can do? "Ellie's moved her hand back slightly, touching the soft glossy side of the wooden box that she hid with her body. How hypocritical she was, fuming about the insults of the man with the boots on Cordelia's desk as she herself hid this box, her own disloyal act, behind her. Her cheeks lit with the shame she felt.

"No, my dear. Just get your rest. You look a bit flushed." With a wave of her hand, Cordelia dismissed her worry. "I just wanted to say goodnight and give you my love."

"All my love and be safe," she said.

Aunt Cordelia smiled at her, a warm smile she only saw once in a while. Cordelia wanted her to see, wanted her to have that. It was a sweet gesture in a usually dour existence. Cordelia nodded and turned. Ellie could see her hand rising to wave away the compad filming her. In the second between Cordelia's dismissal and the flickering black filling her vidscreen, she heard a voice. It had to be the voice of the man with the boots.

His words stunned the breath right out of her. He said, "Was it Ridley?"

Ellie gasped at the name. Ridley from the box? She grabbed the box, surprised by its weight. With quick steps, she carried it back into her closet and her hidden museum. The tapestry with dogs playing poker hanging from the ceiling concealed a small bookshelf with her greatest treasures. Things that meant a lot to her. Her own art, gifts of great value from Aunt Cordelia, a second-grade love letter. The pieces of her life that she owed to no one. She placed Ridley's box on that shelf, covered it, and headed quickly to bed.

As Thom returned to pull up the sheets and took his post next to her bed, Ellie's mind spun with the possibilities.

"Turn on containment," Ellie said. The shock field around her bed raised to protect her sleep from any potential poppet attack. The shimmering shield hummed with energy. She turned to her poppet, stationed just outside the field's crackle. "Thom, I have to find out who Ridley is."

The poppet grunted, dimmed the lights, and lowered to his floor mat to rest.

"Good night, Thom," she said. Though sleep didn't come easy.

DOCUMENT 5: VID-AD IN ALL MAJOR DOME CITY NEWS STREAMS

Additionally, this is the transcript for many of the vid-show sponsor commercials that ran throughout the Devolution period of US NOAM.

"I owe DesLoge Com my life!"

Cancer. Diabetes. Paralysis. Aging. Impotence. Failed organs.

Disfigurements.

Ugly eyes.

All of these have been cured! Eradicated. They are ghosts of a past we no longer need fear.

Contact your local DesLoge Com Doctor to schedule your retrofit. No matter if you are gleaning poppet organs or features, or if you need a poppet formula treatment, we can save and improve your life.

Remember, before the miracle of poppet treatments, people only lived to be 100 years old.

Who owes DesLoge Com their lives?

Accomplished   Pianist   Choi/Complete   hand replacement

President Jeffa Elison/Age 212

Hortense Vidal/Mother of 5 after uterine cancer treatment

Cordelia DesLoge/Eye replacement, Lung replacement, Age 185

Who owes DesLoge Com their lives?

Employment in US NOAM cities 100%

Life expectancy up by 400%

Literacy in US NOAM cities 100%

Industries and employments related to poppet production or using poppet labor? All of them.

Who owes DesLoge Com their lives? We all do.

Happy birthday, DesLoge Com And thank you for everything.

CHAPTER 5

The week flickered past in stuttering flashes—school, shopping, decorating, preparing. Cordelia, Juni, and Ellie had tasted delicacy after delicacy until Ellie worried that she would have to visit Sasha's father at the Plastique clinic to fit into her Scarlet O'Hara party costume. Juni trotted DJs and bands past Ellie until she wasn't sure what she liked or didn't like anymore. Their sounds melded into a thumping nightmare inside her head. Finally, she'd said, "I don't care. Just pick something good."

Juni had nodded. Ellie assumed with satisfaction that her good taste would win out.

Still, the planning continued. So much to do.

It seemed everyone at the Academy, all of the shop owners, maybe all of Santelouisa, would be at the DesLoge mansion that night for Moze's ball. They all spoke of nothing else. All week, lectures at the Academy were peppered with discussion of the party, what people were wearing, and who would dance with whom. Girls giggled more. Honestly, everyone giggled more. Everyone except for Moze.

On Monday, Ellie had handed him an invitation. She wanted it to come from her, not some poppet or the Widow Douglas. Students walking by whispered as she handed it to him, smiling.

"We are holding a ball in your honor," Ellie said.

Moze looked down at the envelope in her hand like it was a snake about to bite him, but he took it politely.

"Gran said you'd be having a dinner. She didn't say anything about a ball." His whispered voice lilted in a way that marked him from the wilds of Kansas—long a's and a soft o that rolled his words like rocks in a stream whose edges had been worn away. Sort of beautiful if you could get past the fact that the folks in the wild tended to be savages.

Ellie realized she was staring at his mouth. She blinked and quickly turned her head, cheek color rising. "Ummm, my Aunt Cordelia decided that it would be more fitting to honor you and introduce you this way. Your mother grew up my mother's bestie. That made her some family to us."

Ellie rubbed one hand over the other and clasped them in twisted finger knots in front of her. They hadn't considered if this would be too much for him. They hadn't even really considered *him* at all in their planning. She wondered if she should have put up more of a fight on his behalf. Ellie bit her lower lip to fight the nerves. She was never this nervous around anyone. What was wrong with her?

He sucked in a deep breath, looked at her, and smiled. "I would be happy to attend. Will you be my escort?"

"Escort? I..." Ellie was shocked. Did he not know how things worked? For a moment, her mouth hung slack in a rude, shocked O. "I'm sorry. That's not how we do things here. I am too young to escort anyone. I will be happy to dance with you there if you'd like."

Moze's cheeks reddened. "Sorry, I don't know how things are in Santelouisa society. Back in Kansas territory, we are adults at fourteen and can choose our escorts and our own way."

"Oh. Well, that's... Not here. We don't officially become adults until after school—depending on the person, usually twenty or twenty-one."

"Well, I am the guest of honor, right?" Moze asked. His foot circled on the marble floor, and his hands clutched each other.

She nodded.

"Then, will you save most of your dance card for me? I promise to be honorable."

His eyes, a less deep brown than hers, seemed to sparkle as he spoke. So distracting. "I have a beau," she said

"Yes, Natan has told me he is your beau. Several times." He looked at her directly, his eyes earnest and so shot with gold in their brown depths. "I don't need a wife or a lady, Ellie. What I need is a friend. You know, someone kind enough to explain things to me. Someone who isn't a complete snob. I've watched everyone pretty closely this week, and I think you might be my best opportunity for an honest friend."

Moze looked down the hall toward the other students clumped outside classrooms, watching them as they talked.

Of course, the others were hanging on this conversation. Though they stacked books in locker cubbies and leaned into mirrors, checking their Plastiqued makeup and seemed to be having deep conversations about anything else, it was clear that they watched Moze and her like hawks. Ellie DesLoge, future queen of the poppets, had sought out the new kid. She was throwing the event of the year for him. Of course, they would watch them closely to see if there was something worth talking about. Her nerves went away then. Hard to be nervous when you're angry. They were a bunch of uninteresting, clinging social climbers is what they were. She'd show them. She reached out and touched his hand lightly, catching it in a gentle squeeze.

"I already have a bestie, but I promise I will be your friend. I'll dance with you and my beau, and we'll have a great time."

He smiled a smile so deep that his soulful, sad eyes crinkled and lit up. She couldn't help but smile back. The way his eyes lit up his face, the nearness of his joy made her feel right about the political posturing of their families.

When she looked up, she saw Natan standing in a ring of his friends, laughing with an open mouth. For just a second, she thought she saw a hardening of his lips and a drawing of his eyebrow so foreign on his bright, beautiful features. Natan angry? She'd explain it to him later if he asked.

The whole week had been full of small gallantries from Moze and from Natan. It had been almost comical.

"What color will you be wearing? I'll match you." Moze said this one day, Natan the next.

"Shall I bring something?" Sasha laughed in Moze's face when he asked the question during lunch two days before the ball.

Moze carried her and Sasha's books from class to class each afternoon, listening to them prattle on about their finds at Gertrude's shop or about their homework.

Natan spent more time with her at lunch, sitting at her chosen table, even when his besties called for him to sit at theirs.

Moze smiled and bowed every time she passed him. Natan kissed her hand every time she passed him.

She started to feel a bit like an Antedevolution era football being tossed back and forth.

But all that would be over soon.

The ceilings of the mansion were decked in glittering fabric set with embedded diamond bulbs that, when activated, would fill the room with a twinkling light. The walls were programmed to flash scenes from Saturday Night Fever and other Antedevolution footage of the "disco" era.

The parlor, lined with small tables that held various delicacies, dripped with lace and satin and sumptuous velvet. Gold brocade on divans and lace fans in the hands of poppets wearing tall wigs, breeches, or hooped dresses set off the lovely yellow and cream-colored walls.

Ellie's stomach clenched, but she grinned. The guests would be here soon.

"Get dressed, Ellie," Juni sang at her from the entry, where last-minute bags of sand were being dumped in piles near golden pyramids beside a large sphinx, whose head sat atop the winding steps. A gap under its chin opened up as an entrance to the second floor. Ellie ran between its feet and under its chin to her room. "I'm going!"

As she raced into her dressing room, the bells announced the autocar arrivals of the first guests. She opened her closet, where a perfect Scarlett O'Hara dress awaited her.

"It's gorgeous, right?" Sasha blew into the room, Jule following closely behind. "You can thank me now. You know...for my genius."

They both laughed and allowed Jule to help them into their costumes. Once they were both sewn in, they sat and allowed Jule to sweep their hair into the styles they displayed for her on their compads. Ellie's hair was long, curled at the ends, and caught up in a net. Sasha's was tucked under a blond bombshell wig.

As Jule applied their makeup, Sasha turned toward Ellie. "What do you think of Moze?"

Ellie sucked in a breath quickly. "Huh? What do you mean?"

Sasha pushed at the curled ends of her short platinum wig. Jule leaned in to straighten an errant curl, but Sasha's hands flashed out and shoved her away, knocking Jule awkwardly back.

"Moze?" Ellie turned toward the mirror and fussed with her makeup. It felt so heavy on her face since she didn't normally wear much. Girls her age shouldn't, though Sasha and the others often did. "He's new and interesting. A little mysterious. I mean, he's no Natan, but he's kinda cute. Do you like him?"

They were besties, yes, but Ellie didn't share what she really thought about Moze. Sasha was her beau's sister.

"He's okay."

Sasha looked at her from the corner of her eyes as Jule applied lashes tipped with diamonds to her lids. "You've been spending a lot of time with him."

Ellie sighed. "It's just that he doesn't have much family, and his mother was besties with my mother. No big. Will you dance with him?"

"Ow! Jule, stop." She slapped her poppet's hands away from her eyebrows. "If he doesn't ask me, I'll probably ask him to."

"What about Cole Newlin? What if he asks you to dance?"

"Oh, I'd dance with him, too."

They laughed as they gathered their props and drew their silken wraps around their shoulders.

Ellie picked up her compad. "Aunt Cordelia? We're going downstairs. Have you already gone down?"

Cordelia, half made up as Elizabeth I, her flame red wig in pin curls dotted with pearls, appeared on her vid wall. The poppet attending her held a makeup duster filled with white powder to lighten her face. Cordelia leaned into the poppet's reach and said, "No, ladies. You may make your entrance. I'll have you announced."

"Thank you, Aunt Cordelia."

"Yes, just wait a moment, though. I'll have young Moze brought to you. He will be brought in with you both."

"What? He's here already?"

The vid screen flickered and became dark. Cordelia

didn't stay in a conversation she thought was over just because it was the polite thing to do. Ellie shrugged at Sasha, and the two stepped into the hall. From the east wing, two poppets walked beside Moze, who had chosen to dress in a long black suit with a tall stovepipe hat along with a chin-hugging beard and a huge mole.

"Why, Mr. Lincoln, you look wonderful for a dead president," Ellie said, laughing. She reached out her hand to him, which he took gladly and bowed to her.

"Miss Ellie, or should I call you Miss Scarlet?"

He pressed his lips to her palm, showing his ease with Santelouisan customs. Widow Douglas must have worked with him. Ellie hid her grin in her ivory fan, which sparkled with flashing neon light pops.

He then bowed to her bestie and kissed her palm, though not, Ellie thought, with the same tenderness. "Miss Sasha," he said.

Sasha batted her eyelashes at him and sighed out a very breathy sounding, "Mr. President."

They all giggled at her Marilyn act.

"Shall we make our entrance?" Moze asked. He held the crooks of his arms out to each. The girls looped their hands around his elbows. Ellie noticed that he was shaking some.

"Nervous?"

He smiled and nodded. "Gran wants me to do well tonight. I worry that I will fall down the steps and drag you lovely ladies to your deaths."

Ellie and Sasha laughed, though they both used their other hands to steady themselves as they descended the steps. Following close behind them, Thom, Jule, and two other server poppets were dressed as 18th-century servants with powdered wigs and white faces. The lights were on, and people were gathered at the base of the stairs. There were princesses and Charlie Chaplins, monks and pimps, Roman emperors, and Indian goddesses. All were beautifully outfitted and glittering in the glow of the diamond lights and mirror balls. Ellie's heart hammered inside, but she kept the carefully trained smile of welcome plastered to her reddened lips. Only her white knuckles revealed her nerves. Moze's were just as white, so she spared him a little squeeze of comfort on his strong forearm. The walls vibrated with the colors of the refracted lights as they paused at the final landing for their announcement. Two bright spotlights swept across the upturned faces watching them with wide eyes and held breaths.

Emcee Jay, located in the other room with the dance floor and the lion's share of the guests, floated a compad on a little drone jet so he could project himself at the top of the stairs and watch for his cues from the DesLoges. His funny little holovid, a floating head, noted their readiness and, with a nod to them, faded the music. He announced over a speaker system that included every room, in a voice that seemed silky like warmed chocolate, "Ladies and gentlemen, I am happy to announce Sasha Parker, heir to the Plastique fortune, third generation Santelouisan family, and official bestie to the hostess."

Sasha dropped Moze's elbow and raised a hand to the cheer that broke out among the guests. She descended the stairs alone with a natural grace, striding lightly in her tall white heels. Her smile wide, bright, fake—but beautiful—lit her costume like a bulb. She stepped out from under the head of the golden sphinx into an aisle the crowd had formed for her. She walked through it, touching hands, nodding, smiling, and saying a word here and there. When she made it to the head table in the parlor, she sat, still beaming at all the guests, though the smile wasn't so much in her eyes.

Ellie found her ability to do this fascinating. She herself wasn't so good at the fake, magnanimous smile perched on the face of power that Sasha, Juni, and Cordelia had perfected. They were all so good at appearing happy in a well-mannered, sort of distracted way. Ellie practiced that smile in her mirror but only managed to look idiotic.

Moze leaned down and whispered, "Ellie, are you nervous?"

She nodded. "I'm just not wired like her. She knows how to move and how to talk. I'm just not sure I'll ever be good at it." Ellie smiled. "But it sure is fun to watch."

A tap on her shoulder interrupted her.

"Well, if you children think that is something. Why not watch us. We're old pros, Mrs. Douglas and I," Cordelia said. The two women had moved in behind them and now pushed past onto the first step, signaling to the announcer. "We'll go first if you don't mind."

The widow Douglas, dressed as a suffragette with her wide-brimmed hat, long wasp-waisted dress, and "votes for women" sash, smiled at Moze and whispered, "You look so handsome, boy. Just like your father." She said to Cordelia, "Your Ellie is such a sweet thing, and dressed up so, I can see you in her lovely face."

Cordelia smiled at the compliment for them both. Widow Douglas wasn't known for flattery, so it was meant in the best way. Cordelia took the widow's arm in a gesture of familiarity, the bestie arm link—something Ellie had never seen her offer anyone. Then Cordelia nodded to Emcee Jay's holovid.

"Ladies and gentlemen, I would like to announce Mrs. Marie Douglas, heir to the Douglas seat in Congress and current Speaker of the House, first-generation Santelouisa family, and matron of the arts."

The widow Douglas glanced back at Moze, flashed him a discrete thumbs up, then headed down the steps, smiling and waving as the crowd gave her a cheer.

"The hostess of the party and the queen of Santelouisan society, Dame Cordelia DesLoge, owner and CEO of DesLoge Industries, first-generation Santelouisa family and co-founder of the cities, paragon and patron of US NOAM, and mother to us all."

The cheers that greeted her aunt's measured, cultured steps roared and boomed. So loud and long the cheers continued, Ellie wondered if they all thought that Cordelia might be keeping track of them and that later favors might depend on their cheers and adoration. She giggled and squeezed Moze's arm.

She leaned closer and whispered, "Isn't this ridiculous?"

"Absolutely." He nodded with a sweet, honest grin. "Let's get this over with."

They both stepped down onto the landing together, letting the white spotlights blind them. They stood taller as the announcer introduced them, trying to live up to the official introductions coming.

"Miss Ellie DesLoge, first generation Santelouisa family, grandniece to Harold and Cordelia DesLoge, official heir to the DesLoge name and fortune. And introducing her special guest, Master Moze Grayson, second generation Santelouisa family, heir to the Douglas seat in Congress, and guest of honor this evening."

They took mirrored breaths, gulping in courage. As they walked down the steps, Ellie tried not to be aware of anything but her feet hitting the stairs and his arm, so warm and comforting. Before they reached the sphinx head, Moze turned to her and said, "I'm glad I met you, Ellie."

Warmth crept into her cheeks as she smiled her answer. They crossed the dance floor, where all of Santelouisa had turned out to greet them, cheering, reaching out to shake hands, bowing, and saying words of encouragement. It was like being on a sea of warm, soft waves tossing back and forth. She'd done this sort of thing before but had never felt so...comfortable. Moze didn't seem to know what to say, so he kept tipping his stovetop hat, saying, "Thank you. You, too." It seemed to work no matter what they said to him. Mostly. When it didn't, Ellie found herself giggling at his refusal to acknowledge the slight social awkwardness his answers caused.

Natan, dressed as Rhett Butler, spoke around her palm after he'd kissed it with genteel grace. "Don't get too comfortable with Moze, Ellie. I get the first dance. Hear that, Mr. President? I'll be dancing with Miss Scarlet first."

"Thank you. You, too."

"Yes, I promise, Natan." Ellie pushed past him. "Just let us get settled first." She dragged Moze to the head table, where their seats, framed by Cordelia and Widow Douglas, waited. Poppets positioned themselves behind each of them.

"Come dance with me, Mr. President," Sasha said. Her thin fingers laced with Moze's knobby, thick ones. She pulled him away into a quick-footed reel, which he performed admirably though with some old-fashioned flourishes.

As he danced with Sasha, Ellie felt a heaviness settle into her middle—a thickness in her throat so like distaste that she took a sip from the water goblet that Thom held at her side. Watching them spin in each other's arms bothered her. His hands on her hip and laced around her thin, beautiful fingers. Jealousy. Ellie recognized the twists in her stomach and her own knotty anger. Why should she be jealous of her bestie and her new bosom friend? Why would their sweet dance bother her so badly? She tried to smile to cover the clenching stiffness settling in her features. She had Natan, clearly the most beautiful, most eligible beau to be had in all of Santelouisa. She tamped down her jealous distaste and clapped along to the rhythm of the reel and the cleverness of their footwork.

All of Santelouisa swirled around the dance floor like a living tapestry, their costumes creating pools of vivid colors. Cordelia and the widow shared a quiet conversation as Thom Poppet handed them warm toddies and chocolates.

"My lady?" Natan held his hand out to Ellie, his smile turned up and cocky. Glad for the appropriate distraction, she followed him out into the center of the dance floor. Emcee Jay popped on a slow song from the Antedevolution period, one she'd never heard before. Natan's hands went around her body, lightly touching her back and arm. His breath was on her cheek.

Okay, so Natan was still pretty exciting. Very good looking in a leading man sort of way. And he smelled clean, like a minty soap. His arms, thick with muscle, felt so strong around her. Ellie's heart leaped a bit when he pulled her closer. She averted her eyes shyly as he stared into them with a bold, direct gaze.

Still, as she looked around, Sasha in Moze's arms made her feel a twinge of sadness. Moze's eyes found her just then. For a second, they held each other's gazes until the music turned them away from each other. She looked back at Natan's face. He'd caught her staring. He'd seen their look. His brow rippled, and his lips stiffened in anger.

Ellie reached up and touched his cheek with her open palm—a very public declaration of her favor that no one would miss. His features softened. His gaze met hers, and suddenly she felt almost naked dancing this close to him in front of everyone who was anyone in Santelouisa. It felt like the entire floor dipped and tilted toward them as he spun her to the song's heartbeat rhythms. Still, his gaze held her, pinned her. She glanced away, seeing Cordelia watching, her chin raised and pointer finger laid alongside her temple. Ellie laid her head on Natan's shoulder, trying to escape from the pinioning gazes and back into the moment.

"Ellie," Natan said softly, "I was afraid that Moze had captured your heart in all of this pageantry. I know he's from an important family too."

Ellie shook her head. She needed to be very careful with Natan for her own future's sake. But he was right. Moze had made more inroads into her tenderest feelings with just a few exchanges than handsome Natan had in his years of knowing her. Still, maybe it was just how new Moze was to her. Juni often told her that the newest "toys" were the best, as she stepped out with a new man each and every week. Maybe her own heart beat with the same shallow neediness as her mother. She stiffened her back and shook Moze out of her inconstant thoughts. Natan deserved better from her. "No, Natan. He's not my beau. You are. He's just a friend."

The song finished and all the dancers bowed, released their partners, and moved to the next person on their dance cards.

Natan, however, clung to her, holding her a bit too close. "Let's dance again," he said.

Moze walked by escorting Sasha back to her seat. Natan seemed not to see them, or politely ignored them.

"I'm tired out, Natan. Can you dance with some of the other girls? They would all enjoy it." Ellie cast her eyes downward, hoping to appear coy and flirty. "I'll try not to be jealous."

Natan looked toward the crowd, where girls waiting to dance stood. He nodded. "Fine, then. Perhaps we'll dance again later."

He let her go, forgetting to bow, turning, and stalking away toward the giggling girls waiting on the edge of the flashing, strobing neon dance floor.

Ellie retreated to the table, sitting in the high-backed chair between Aunt Cordelia and Moze. Sasha chatted with him about things Ellie caught in snatches—

"...Academy..."

"...Poppets..."

"...Legislature..."

Moze looked bored, nodding politely but casting his gaze about the room, clearly uncomfortable. Sasha didn't seem to notice and had draped her arm across his shoulder. Ellie smiled at them both.

"My brother seems to have found a light-footed partner." Sasha pointed at Natan and his partner, spinning across the floor. When he turned, she saw Joceylin happily spinning in his arms. Ellie forced a smile.

"I said I wouldn't be jealous, and I won't. He's free to dance with who he will."

Sasha laughed. Why wouldn't she laugh? Joceylin was no threat to Natan and Ellie's match and no threat to the Parkers' claims on a partnership with the DesLoges.

It would be only a year or two until Natan would be pressured by his father to start courting Ellie in earnest and then it would only be another year or two until they were wed. Natan and Ellie would both assume their position in their family companies, but until then he was free to pursue his youth as was she. Only he did it with such panache. All the girls chased him. All of them flirted and fawned over him. She couldn't seem to put together two words with another boy without the boy fleeing. Every boy she knew was either Natan's good friend or scared of him.

Ellie sipped the dinner wine her aunt had poured her, enjoying the warm, scorching feeling of the vintage. She wouldn't drink much since it made her head hurt every time. But a little might help take the bitterness out of watching Sasha flirt with Moze. Looking at her friend's happy face,

Ellie knew that it was better this way. If Ellie ever hurt Sasha's brother, they would lose their precious friendship. Kin meant everything to the families of Santelouisa. Soon, they would be one big family in charge of an empire. She swallowed the last of her wine and moved it away from Aunt Cordelia so she couldn't fill it again.

Thom took her empty wine cup and filled it with water. Ellie smiled back at him. "Thanks, Thom." Just like when he'd brought her the box, he always seemed to know what she wanted even before she did.

Sasha prattled on between bites, but Ellie caught Moze looking at her in that moment as Thom grunted and returned to rest behind her.

"Dance again with me, Moze," Sasha said, catching up his hands and dragging him out onto the dance floor. He smiled and allowed himself to be hauled out as a waltz began. The thrumming beat made Ellie's head nod and her feet tap. Natan and Sasha laughed at each other across the floor. Everyone seemed to be dazzled by Juni's decorations—Juni included. She danced with every bachelor of her age at the ball in turn. She threw her head back, her curtain of black hair fanning out as she turned.

"You are such a serious girl, Ellie Bird." Cordelia tapped a vaporarette on the table before lighting it in the silver candelabra that flared in purple and blue jets before her. "Marie and I were just saying that you and Moze are like little old people. This dancing will do you good. Why not get out there with your beau?"

"I will, Aunt Cordelia. I just...I like to watch people dance, but I have two left feet, you know?"

Widow Douglas laughed. "That can't be true. I know your Aunt Cordelia would never let any niece of hers grow to womanhood without knowing how to cut a rug."

"That's right. Ten years of dance lessons. She can do it," Cordelia said. "She just prefers the company of old ladies." She pointed out at the crowd and asked the Widow Douglas, "Maria, how many of them do you think are Resurrectionists?"

The widow didn't seem to mind, though the conversation topic wasn't really a polite one. At school, they called Resurrectionists zealots on a good day and traitors on a bad one. They were the outliers of US NOAM society, believing that the dead should remain dead, that bodies were sacred, and that poppets had souls. Souls! If that were true, then everything they believed, everything that Santelouisa and US NOAM did—the economy, the law—all of it was immoral. Crazies. No one took them seriously. The Constitution gave them the right to hold their services and say what they wanted to say, but that didn't make their beliefs any less ridiculous. And just because it was legal didn't mean that the dome citizens had to like it. More often than not, people who identified themselves as Resurrectionists were met with harassment from the night riders who would take their goods and destroy their property if they were open about their beliefs, usually in response to the disappearance of a poppet.

Ellie was shocked to hear her aunt talk about them. She usually liked to pretend they didn't exist.

"My friends tell me that there are many Resurrectionists here in Santelouisa," Cordelia said. "That they are moving in from the wilds. Infiltrating us. Stealing poppets. Is there nothing that can be done, legally?"

Natan still danced with Joceylin, and Ellie knew she should go, but the taboo was way more interesting. Moze found his way back to sit beside his Gran. On the dance floor, Sasha twined her arms around Cole as a Latin dance began.

"Perhaps there are." Widow Douglas grabbed a bacon-wrapped shrimp offered by Jule. "There's no law against the idea, just against the theft of property. To make their religion against the law—I don't think any of us are ready for that kind of curtailing of rights."

Moze watched his Gran carefully, nodding ever so slightly at her words.

"Attacks on our plantations happen almost every night. Something must be done." Cordelia's voice wasn't one of polite asking. It was a voice that demanded. Commanded. The music swirled, plaited with the mists the DJ released in clouds on the dance floor. The smell was not unpleasant but, mixed with scents of the food, bodies dancing and the crackling ozone of the lights' holoprojections, it made Ellie's eyes water. She struggled to stay pleasant, smiling for her guests. Moze, however, untrained as he was, wore a thinning smile though it had nothing to do with smells.

"My father was killed in Lawrence, you know. And my mother taken. Not by Resurrectionists."

"Hush, Moze. Don't you burden Mrs. DesLoge with our sorrows. Why don't you go take some air?" Widow Douglas's eyes were kindly and soft, though her words seemed edged with iron. For Cordelia's benefit, perhaps? Ellie's aunt nodded in a satisfied manner at the reproach.

"Moze, why don't we walk the grounds? I could use the change of scenery myself," Ellie said. She turned her eyes to Natan, whose hands seemed to be making the rounds of the entire female half of the Academy's junior class and their backsides. Her jealousy aside, he was just being crass now. Maybe trying to evoke a response? She wouldn't lower herself. If he really wanted her, he'd have to rise to her level. She wouldn't shrink to his.

Ellie stood and offered Moze her hand, which he took with a genuine smile. Like her, he seemed to be done watching Sasha and his classmates dance in the style of the early 21st century—sexually close, nearly climbing into each other's skin. The young and old had studied the historic styles of Antedevolution dance, and this one, paired with the thick rhythms of the time, led to near frenzied crowds piling in the center of the floor.

"I've never seen such a thing," Moze said, shaking his head and allowing her to lead him away.

Ellie took him through the wide hall, behind the grand staircase, and out of the delivery entrance. They walked to the grand oak in the backyard, whose roots breeched the soil and stretched back toward the woods and the river. In the dome-moon, the river's surface lay flat and calm, so only occasional ripples gave away the flowing of the current.

"Is that the Mizzourah?"

Ellie nodded. The ribbon of river flowed through the city, past their estate and the other mansions that clung to the cliffs, under the dome, and through the caverns carved by Harold and the US NOAM engineers, out into the wild. Here at the DesLoge estate, the river widened into a mirror that reflected the colors of the woods that hugged its curves.

"If I could, I'd jump on a hover-raft and ride that river back home," Moze said, plopping down beneath the tree. "It's so different here. People are snobs. Not you, of course. I...I don't really belong."

Perched on a knobby root, Ellie plucked some grass from the yard. "I hope you don't go."

Moze laughed and leaned his elbows on his knees. "I don't think your Natan feels the same as you."

"You're probably right."

He looked up at the opaque dome, frowning. "I just can't get used to your sky. It's so dull and closed. Once you've slept under the real stars, it's hard to be here. I wish I could show you how beautiful they are." His eyes held hers for just a moment, but in that moment, Ellie felt like he'd called her beautiful. She turned away from his intense gaze, suddenly feeling shy.

After a moment, she turned back with a huge grin. "I have something to show you. Will you come with me to see it?"

He nodded. She led him back inside, through the poppet entrance and up the back stairs, into the long hall leading to the private wing. They walked into Ellie's room, something she wouldn't do with a boy normally, but Moze's friendship promised that he would be a gentleman.

Besides, in his honest face, she saw no malice. Sometimes, his eyes held a seriousness beyond his age and sometimes distaste, but never meanness. She led him to her closet door.

She hesitated, hand hovering over the doorknob. Having him in her room was bad enough, but to show him her collection seemed so private, so personal. For a moment, she wondered if she'd made a mistake bringing him. "You can keep your mouth shut, right? A secret...just between us?"

Moze nodded and leaned forward. She wondered if he thought her childish for extracting this promise like a petulant little girl. Still, his promise made her feel better. This room wasn't something even her bestie knew about. Sure, she saw her purchase some of the things inside, but they'd never discussed that she collected the old things or what they meant. She'd never shared this with anyone. She took a deep breath, turned the knob, and pushed the hidden door open that led to her treasure trove.

"Lights on." The ceiling's internal lights flared, illuminating the rows of shelves that sprouted from the cream-colored walls. Moze's eyes lit up as they passed over the artifacts.

"Oh wow. Wow!" Moze picked up a photo book with images of places around the world that they would never see. The Colosseum before the earthquake destroyed it. The Parthenon still stood, encased in plastic, but with wars and pestilence still raging there, no one traveled across the sea for pleasure anymore. He put the book back and walked the length of the room, picking up plastic kittens with big eyes, glass birds that dipped to sip from a cup, postcards, and stereocards.

"We had some of these cards. Do you have a viewer?"

Ellie shook her head and grabbed the star wheel she'd bought for him. It seemed a bit silly now, a cardboard antique to take the place of the real vault of sky he was missing. Still, he seemed the type to appreciate a kindness.

He was distracted, looking at a book of speeches from the early times of the old United States—speeches she'd read once and tried to understand.

"I learned these in Liberty Lawrence. My mother loved these words more than any others written." He flipped the book over so the cover showed and ran his finger along the embossed gold lettering that said *Collected Works of Freedom*. "I loved listening to her read these. She'd make all the voices and stop to talk about the big words. Abolition, rights, equality—I'm sorry. I'm prattling on. What did you want to show me?"

"I got something for you. It's nothing really, but..." She didn't know why she'd gotten it for someone she barely knew, and she didn't know how to explain it to him now. She decided not to. She clutched it lightly as she handed it to him. "It's a starwheel."

"This is great!" He held it up and smiled. "I had one of these when I was young. Do you know how it works?"

Ellie shook her head with short jerks. "I mean, I think I understand it. It's like a map, right? You can find things in the sky by spinning it."

Moze held it in his fingers, spinning it slightly back and forth. She hoped for a reaction, a thank you, an "I hate it," or something, but he stayed fixed there staring at it for a solid couple of awkward minutes. Ellie searched for a witty way to excuse her stupid gift, swallowing down the stinging disappointment she felt at his reaction. She had to clear her throat to go on without a tear rising to her eye. He looked up at her, not with a smile or a joke as she feared—what Natan would have said after such a trivial gift, and his mocking laughter would have shamed her. But this was Moze, not Natan. His unblinking gaze held hers for a few seconds. He pressed his lips together and clutched the star wheel in his hands with a delicate immediacy, like he was afraid someone would take it. Then she knew his hesitation to say anything for what it was. He was just nervous. Ellie's bubble of fear popped and, with an exhale, she allowed herself to smile at him, hoping her relief didn't broadcast itself openly on her features.

"This is the nicest thing someone has done for me... since...." He trailed off and went back to spinning the star map. His voice promised more than he seemed able to give. Something about the tone told her this place—this subject— was dangerous for him. She put her hand on his shoulder, her palm resting on his back with a light touch.

He continued with a broken voice, words coming in jerking, halting bursts. "Since my parents. They gave me everything they could. They were...they were the best."

Writhing in his voice, in the silence between words, she could feel his pain and loss. "This is just like the one they gave me when I was a kid. See?" He spun the wheel and turned it toward her. "You could find things in the sky, but you could also find your way with this."

He walked toward the window and pointed the wheel at the sky. The wheels showed a shape that arched up and formed a rectangle. He pointed at one of the stars on the shape. "That's the fixed star. The olds called it the North Star. If you follow the flow of the river with that star over your right shoulder, you'll get to Liberty Lawrence. My town."

"Where your parents were killed?" Ellie knew it sounded awful when it came out of her mouth, but it was like one of those things where your thoughts became words before you even knew they were there. "Sorry...I didn't mean—"

He drew her toward the window, pointing to the river that glowed under the reddening tinge of the dome's twilight.

"No, it's all right. I just miss them so much, you know? They loved the river. It made up the eastern border of our farm. Me and Da and Ma would fish it. Big catfish with whiskers and spines sure tasted good over open flames and under the black sky."

Thom appeared at the door, carrying a silver tray loaded with sandwiches and lemonade, clearly not party fare, but the perfect kind of snack for their conversation. "Thom must have read my mind," Ellie said with a smile.

Moze followed her out the door and sat with her at the table in her sitting room. They lifted the glasses from Thom's tray and at the same time said, "Thank you, Thom."

As Thom grunted and stepped back to the wall, Ellie giggled that she and Moze had said the same thing at the same time. Moze didn't giggle.

He became thoughtful for a moment, took a bite from the sandwich, and said, "That's incredible. Peanut butter and jelly."

She nodded and took a bite. "It's good."

"No, you don't get it. I said in front of him earlier that I'd like a peanut butter and jelly instead of the rich food at the party. I said it to Sasha, but here you see...he brought it to me."

Ellie shook her head and swallowed the bite in her

mouth. The company line spilled from her. "That is impossible. The chemical neutering process allows for no higher brain function. He brought a snack, just what was available because that is what his chip told him to do. That's all."

Cordelia's words felt bitter in her mouth. Ellie took a drink of lemonade to wash them away, glancing at Thom as she did.

Moze touched her hand, a very forward gesture, but somehow, Ellie didn't mind. "You don't really believe that, Ellie."

"What?"

"You don't think he's just some machine. I know you don't. I've seen it in your eyes. The way you care for him, especially. Plus, you're kind to every poppet you meet. You thanked him, Ellie."

She sputtered but didn't say anything. What must he think of her? She couldn't deny the truth.

He took her hand in his, petted it softly, and smiled. "It's okay. I feel the same way."

Thom stood stock still, not blinking and not reacting. A perfect poppet waiting to serve.

"Your uncle's miracle brings them back. Supposedly, they have no soul, no intellect beyond the chip's directions. But Ellie, how did Thom know we'd be here together? How did he know to bring this snack here and now? Why does he choose to follow you, loyally and constantly, when other poppets wait to be called?"

Ellie shook her head. She couldn't deny her own feelings of closeness, love for this poppet who'd been in her life all along. "I've always felt close to Thom. He means more to me than...than my mother, even. But Thom has no soul. He's just a reanimated thing doing what he's told. He's been programmed. Don't you see? If I start thinking of him as more than he is, my heart will only break more when he's taken from me or when his chems fail. Poppets are only as good as the chems, the chips, and the nutrients they are given."

Ellie realized for the first time just how rigid she sat in her chair and how her blood pounded in her chest. How could he make her feel this way with just a few words? Like everything her family did, and was invested in, was somehow immoral? Who was he to tell her what she felt or should believe, anyway? She showed him what Cordelia had called her "bitch face." Eyes distant, hooded. Chin tilted and head cocked. Everything soft and pleasant about her features made into rocky edges and stiff cliffs.

He looked at her hardened features and seemed to deflate as he sank into the chair. He took another thoughtful bite of the sandwich, staring up at the ceiling. After a few moments, he spoke again.

"My Da and Ma were killed by Grave Hawkers in Liberty Lawrence."

"That can't be right." Ellie's resolve melted immediately. "Are you sure? Grave Hawkers are on our side."

Moze's features hardened, his cheeks reddening. "*Our* side? Not *my* side! They broke into our farm, gathering up the free poppets and the live laborers alike."

Free poppets? Live laborers? The words collided in Ellie's head, striking against what she thought she knew. Why would his farm have live laborers? Such a thing didn't exist anymore, did it? And what was a free poppet? None of it made any sense. She studied his face, looking for some kind of hidden meaning or veiled joke. She only saw truth perched naked in the brown depths that gazed back at her.

"They took them all, don't you see? Loaded all of them into tram hover trucks. Didn't matter if they were poppets or live laborers." Moze scowled, clouds and thunder building on his brow as he explained. His words splattered, fat with anger. "When my parents resisted the Hawkers, they demanded that they give back the people of the farm and showed proper papers that should have protected them from the attack. The Grave Hawkers laughed at them. Laughed in Da's face!"

"Where were you, Moze?" Ellie asked. "Did you see all of this happen?"

He nodded. "When the tram hover trucks first pulled up to our farm, Da recognized the markings. Told me to hide up the tree, high in the branches. He didn't want me inside or with him. He said, "Don't be taken by them, son." I wanted him and Ma to hide with me, but they wouldn't. They wouldn't."

Moze's words came quickly, flowing in a choppy stream. His eyes were unfocused, as if he were seeing the horrors of that night all over again. Ellie's hands clutched the fabric of her skirt, fingers turning white under the pressure. She wanted him to stop, so much wanted his tale to be a joke, but he would have it out. She could tell. Like some poison trapped inside a boil, it'd burst if he didn't open it up and let it seep away. She leaned forward, knees almost touching his, so close she could smell the sweet air of peanuts on his hot breath.

"I saw them. Da showed them the papers, and then the Hawker just laughed at him, used his stun-kill gun, smashed him right in the face. When Da fell, his face was gushing blood so red. I'd never seen that kind of red before. And the Grave Hawker," he gasped raggedly, angry tears flowing from his eyes, "smashed him again and again with the butt of the stun-kill. Ma saw, and when she saw, she ran at him. She threw up her hands and blocked the blows, though I know Da was gone. She begged them to stop. To leave us. I couldn't hear, but I know whatever the Grave Hawkers said to her made her scream. They picked her up, and Da, and threw them into the tram, and off they went. That night, they hit Liberty Lawrence. They stole over two hundred free poppets and almost a hundred citizens and burned our church."

Ellie sat, mouth gaping open, unsure how to react. She reached out and put her hand on his clutched hands. Their gesture so like prayer but leaned forward, holding up his head like it weighed so much, was so full of his sadness. She tasted the horror of his lost folks in his words. Lost right in front of him. How could it be true? The Grave Hawkers weren't evil. They protected the plantations. "I'm so sorry. I just...I don't even know what to say. How horrible."

Moze's tightly folded hands opened to her tender touch, enfolding her hand. They trembled and twitched as he saw the shadows of that day inside his head. What he said went against everything she had ever been taught about life in the wilds and the Grave Hawkers. Grave Hawkers help people. Yes, they gather the dead for poppets, but only the dead. And they hunt stolen poppets. The way he described them, they were some kind of lawless evil destroying everything. How could it be like he said? Maybe he was just mistaken.

She asked softly, afraid the wrong word would hurt him anew. "How do you know they were Grave Hawkers?"

"That's what they do, isn't it? Steal poppets." Moze pulled his back straight, rigid as a bar.

"No. They recover bodies after burial; that's all. They are the paid retrieval crew that goes and picks up the bodies DesLoge Com reanimates. I don't know who those people were, but they couldn't be Grave Hawkers."

"Why not?" Moze's voice was even and disturbingly calm.

"Because they work for us, you know. We would never accept living people and bodies without the proper forms and death notices. DesLoge Com standards clearly state—"

"The trams..." Moze's voice thundered, cutting through her words and silencing her. He grabbed her hands, hard. She gasped, and he loosened his grip, releasing her with deliberate gentleness.

She weighed his expression. He believed what he was telling her.

He pulled a deep breath and wiped his hands on his pants. "The trams were marked."

"What do you mean?"

"They were marked clear as day. I saw it myself, Ellie. They said DesLoge Com on the sides."

Ellie's heart dropped into the pit of her stomach. It couldn't be. "We have to tell Cordelia. She needs to know this."

Moze shook his head, stood, and turned from her. He

folded his hands across his chest, and all she could see were the white wrinkles brightly standing out in his tightly fisted hands. He turned and glanced at her for a moment, then the heat seemed to go out of his posture. He sagged a bit and let his hands dangle until they found his pants pockets. "I need you to keep this secret for now, Ellie. Please?" He walked to the window and leaned one arm against it. "I want to trust you. I need you not to tell her, please."

Ellie nodded. If only she could get him to trust Cordelia, too, maybe this wrong could be set right. Well, she couldn't bring anyone back, so it couldn't be completely made right. But this DesLoge Com involvement had to be a mistake. "But Cordelia could—"

"Promise?"

She nodded, but he didn't look convinced. "Yes, Moze. I promise. I won't tell Cordelia until you say I can."

Moze nodded. He picked up the star chart and spun it slowly. There was something he wanted to say but couldn't. She could tell by the way his gaze found her, then shifted. He was working up courage while he fiddled with the wheel. Finally, he put it down and returned to her side. Taking long breaths with pursed lips, his gaze searched the ceiling as if some monumental truth could be read in the swirling texture. Then he turned to her. With one deep breath, he said words that blew her whole world apart, "I'm not just some kid from the wilds, Ellie. I'm not just the Douglas heir or a kid who lost parents. I'm..." He took another breath to sustain him. "I'm a Resurrectionist."

She drew back from him as if he would infect her. Her lip curled before she realized it. Resurrectionist? Here? In the

DesLoge Mansion and the very shadow of Harold DesLoge's great works?

Moze watched her reaction, eyes wide and hopeful at first, but flashing with suspicion as her shock and sudden revulsion played through her features.

"It's not a crime, you know. At least not yet. People may hate us and treat us like criminals, but we aren't. It's still a republic, and even Resurrectionists have rights." Moze's chin rose, something akin to pride or determination setting his features in a hard, haughty stare. It was as if he dared her to dispute his right to be an idiot. Even with the tragedy in his past, why would he choose to have such a blatantly wrong belief system? Sure, it was legal, but people got strung up sometimes for being Resurrectionist, especially when their religion led them to steal poppets from good, God-fearing folk.

"They are dead, Moze. Their souls left their bodies when they died. Just because we reanimated their tissues—"

"God created those tissues."

She rolled her eyes at his fervor. "God created the radishes I ate tonight, but he didn't give them a soul."

"Really, Ellie? I know you're smarter than that. When you look at Thom, do you see a radish? Seriously?" He crossed his arms defiantly, but his eyes widened hopefully, waiting for her to respond.

Ellie glanced over at Thom. The poppet stood there against the wall, perpetual grin softening his dead face. But what made his face dead? The biology books never satisfied her about this. There was blood in his veins, maybe not his, and maybe it was refillable, but it was blood. His heart beat and his muscles still lifted and bent. And he took care of her, though Cordelia would say that was good programming on the chip embedded in his brain. Thom's brown eyes looked off into the distance respectfully, as a good poppet's eyes should. But sometimes, usually at night when she babbled at him about her lessons and her day, she thought she'd seen his pupils dilate and focus on her. Perhaps a twitch of a real smile.

"I can't believe you're a Resurrectionist," she said. She drew her hand across her arm nervously.

"Don't tell anyone. I don't want everyone to hate me. I just... I wanted to be honest with you."

Ellie looked at him, his secret given to protect or reject. The secret in her hands. She wasn't used to such power over another. Aunt Cordelia would have acted immediately. There would have been some kind of consequences or bargaining or some power play that would end up with Moze in her debt but not her friend. As she gazed into his eyes, full of the promise of truth and friendship, his open hands, his body leaning into this discussion in a way that Natan's guarded haughtiness would never allow. She looked at him and knew this secret was worth keeping. That she could forgive him this. That it even made him more real to her.

"I won't tell." Elle's stomach flopped, and her heart raced. She knew that tradition and family should be first in her consideration and fought the bitter taste of guilt. She pressed her lips together and glanced back at Thom.

Moze pulled her out of her seat, smiling huge and spinning her around her sitting room floor. He laughed but then grew sober. "I hope we can still be friends. Can we?"

She nodded.

"You owe me a dance, you know." Moze held out his hand to her. "My lady, shall we go back to the ball?"

"Yes, let's." Ellie warmed to the idea of returning to the swirl and distraction of the party. She allowed herself to be led away, though she couldn't tamp down the feeling that this secret might hurt later.

DOCUMENT 6: FROM THE POST VID GAZETTE, SANTELOUISA'S MAIN OUTLET FOR NEWS

A constable was called to Manson Willow Heights, where Lizsett Gorman, widow of DesLoge Financial COO Jonathan Gorman, is alleged to have caused a disturbance during the dinner hour. She was seen walking her poppet, formerly her husband Jonathan, on a chain about the exclusive neighborhood. Witnesses report that she was seen to beat her poppet viciously with a cane. They report that she screamed obscenities, which is why the police were called.

Witnesses report that she said the following:

"Not good enough, Jon? Who's not good enough? Not beautiful? Who is not beautiful now, Jon?"

Each word was punctuated by a savage thrash to the poppet's legs, arms, or back.

Witnesses suggest that, in life, Jonathan had been known to raise his hand to his wife on many occasions.

Authorities requested that Mrs. Gorman continue her

activities in the privacy of her home, to which she is reported to have replied, "I shall do with my property as I will. I have broken no law."

Gorman was issued a citation for disturbing the peace, which carries a $10 penalty.

The poppet was returned to DesLoge Com for bone reconstruction. The poppet Jonathan will be returned to Mrs. Gorman within the next few dome-days.

This reporter finds Mrs. Gorman's purchasing of her own husband's remains unseemly, but according to the Constitution of the US NOAM Amendment 46: Poppets are property and without souls subject to whatever treatment and use prescribed by their legal ownership. Gorman is within her rights.

CHAPTER 6

Moze led Ellie back into the swirling party at the foot of the long, curved stair. He donned his stovepipe hat and long dark suit jacket, though he'd lost track of the Lincoln mole during their walk. His hand was hard, not at all like Natan's soft gentleman's grip when he kissed her hand gallantly. But the roughness didn't bother her.

He swept her to an open spot. As they turned, she caught sight of the people in her life watching with differing expressions. Some seemed to admire them, smiling and nodding at the pairing of a DesLoge and a Douglas. Some just leered and whispered. Ellie imagined that, behind their cupped hands, secret poisons sprinkled into hostile ears. So many eyes on them. It made Ellie want to crawl under a table.

The Widow Douglas watched with an obvious joy, her warm eyes and wide smile showing teeth. Hard to fake that. She must be happy to see sober Moze fitting into polite society. Sasha's gaze burned her. At first, Ellie wondered if her friend was jealous or worried about her taking Moze away, but it didn't look like that kind of girlish anger. Nope. In that second before Sasha's face shifted back to a pleasant, non-committal smile, Ellie thought she saw fury. Where would that come from? Natan didn't seem to mind her dancing with Moze. He had Joceylin clutched to him as if they were made of the same skin. His gaze barely left Joceylin's to register that she stood with Moze. He dismissed her from his view as quickly as he'd found her. It was a time-honored tradition of gentility that men had their wives and that they had their dalliances. He was expected to dally with other women, especially now, before their official courtship. Later, after their childbearing years, both of them could pursue other "interests." Juni did so with abandon. Ellie had worried that, after his display all week long, Natan would press his claim on her, as young men did sometimes when their blood got hot and they felt threatened. She wasn't ready for the responsibility of a true courtship.

Ellie bowed to Moze, aware that everyone now watched her dancing with the boy from the wilds. Guest of honor or not, it was something to talk about. As his hand touched the small of her back and she curled her hand into his, she picked out her mother, eyes unfocused, probably with drink, but watching her with an expression so near regret or sadness that Ellie almost wanted to stop. But then Juni looked away to a gentleman tugging at her arm, and she threw her head back in a laugh that relieved the butterflies swirling in Ellie's throat.

Finally, the music started. A foxtrot. Though most of her

classmates had hated to learn the old dancing, she'd relished the precision of the steps. Moze naturally picked his way around the floor, spinning her to the beat and smiling comfortably.

"You're pretty good at this," she said. "Better watch it, or the comportment teacher will recruit you."

"Ma taught me this." His voice cracked as he said it. Poor Moze. So much pomp and gaiety forced on him. Was it all too much? Did he think them heartless? She imagined how she'd feel if she'd just lived through an attack on her home and her family. Would she be as genteel as he was? She didn't think she could be.

The people framing the floor seemed to melt into a soft, pastel swirl.

"How long has it been?" She hoped her words weren't going to cause him more pain but thought she should ask. "Since the attack, I mean."

"Six months. Usually feels like less, but when I'm here with you... It's like escaping from a deep cave. You make me lighter. I'm glad we're friends, Ellie. I'm glad you aren't what I thought you'd be."

For a second, her ire rose. What he thought she'd be? A snob? A monster? When she glanced at him, her anger dissipated. She knew he'd meant it in a good way. She could see that from his face. He admired who she was. Maybe he was the only one in all Santelouisa who liked her and not who she would be someday.

She allowed him to direct her across the dance floor, watching those around them rather than stare into his sad eyes. Cordelia sat, her chin in her hand, looking bored by it all, but Ellie knew better. She could see her aunt watching everything, sharp needles piercing the smoke and laser lighting. Cordelia's gaze caught on something. Her eyes widened, and she stood up. Ellie strained to see what her aunt had seen.

Natan stalked toward them, Joceylin in tow, her icy white hair streaming behind her as he dragged her forward. Still hand in hand with Joceylin, Natan shoved Moze back with his free hand. He stumbled, dropping his dance embrace.

"Yes? How can I help you, Natan?" Moze's words, so gently spoken, didn't reflect how he'd moved into a boxing stance.

"You should not be dancing so close with my future fiancée."

Face placid, almost pleasant, Moze glanced down at Joceylin's hand in Natan's and said, "You seem to have another lady about you. Perhaps you are unclear about how to treat a fiancée?"

The dance floor cleared, and a circle opened, large enough for a fight.

Ellie spoke up, hoping to stop it. "Here now. You weren't even interested in dancing with me until now, Natan. Of course, I will dance with you. Perhaps you should allow Moze to dance with Joceylin." She pushed their hard chests, separating them. Joceylin's eyes darted back and forth, color rose in her cheeks, and finally she turned with a huff, pulling her hand out of Natan's with a jerk. She retreated through the gathered crowd, leaving him alone with his scene. His features clouded as he watched her go, but he turned back to Ellie and his beau claim.

Ellie stretched her hand out to him impatiently. Courtesy demanded that she dance with her guest of honor. What had made him so jealous? He'd never seemed the jealous type before Moze. "Shall we dance now, Natan?"

"As you wish." With a curt jerk, he swept her away. His hands found their marks, and with a nod to the DJ, the music resumed. She didn't look at Moze, but he would forgive her for this social nicety. Natan's cold hands held her, but his eyes didn't. He looked off in the distance, not toward Joceylin, but at his sister, Sasha, seated at the head table. Did she have something to do with this? Ellie wondered what her bestie had hoped to accomplish by pushing them together this way. Like an angry bee, her frustration buzzed just behind her eyes and in the skin and tendons of her neck. The dance seemed to go on forever. With each spin, her stomach turned, and she stared down at her feet, hoping to avoid his, though he kept stomping on them anyway.

The song finally ended, and they bowed stiffly to each other.

Ellie gathered her courage and grabbed Natan's hand, pulling him to her. She whispered, but she set her face in a gaze she hoped looked just like the face Cordelia reserved for stern reprimands and poppets. She was not pleased with him or his sister and didn't care who would see it. "I do not bother you about your...fascination with Joceylin Eregel. It is honestly beneath me and you to engage in these games. Just know that Moze is my friend." Natan started to say something, but Ellie leaned in closer, saying, "I am above your pettiness. I am a DesLoge, and you will treat me that way.

You are not my husband. If you wish to be, you will not treat me this way ever again."

Natan stared at her, shocked. At least he was paying attention.

"He is just my friend. Okay?"

He nodded, bowed again, this time with his more natural, languid grace.

"Fine," he said. "Enjoy your friend."

He walked away with a dismissive air. His measured steps were meant to convince everyone watching—and everyone *was* watching—that he was perfectly relaxed and happy. Everyone would be sure that the two lovebirds had mended their spat. What they couldn't see, and what Ellie was beginning to understand, was that Natan didn't really care about her at all. He made a beeline across the floor to Joceylin, who sat perched at a high table, white-blond hair and shockingly blue eyes fixed on him. This fixation with Joceylin had always been only a minor concern for her. It was what the moneyed people of US NOAM understood—that marriage wasn't for love, but for position. Joceylin's family's standing guaranteed that the two of them would not be matched. Ellie's family and position could not be beaten by anyone in US NOAM, let alone by Joceylin's father, Simon, who owed his position and money to being the leader for the Grave Hawkers.

Ellie saw Joceylin try to ignore Natan as he returned to her, broadcasting her anger. He stroked her hand and leaned in. Whatever he said did the trick. Joceylin laced her fingers with his and smiled. He had done his family proud by staking his claim on Ellie, but clearly he wanted more to be with Joceylin. Poor Natan suffered as much from his family destiny as Ellie did from hers.

The dancers gathered back around her, shrieking their pleasure at the next Antedevolution song the DJ spun—*The Cupid Shuffle*. They lined up to perform the dance, just like the old-timers used to do when they were children. Ellie started the forward steps, but Moze pulled her out of the crowd.

"Ellie, I just saw something I want to show you."

He took her into the dining room. Ellie was sure that she and Natan had just ruined the act they'd performed on the dance floor by immediately returning to their original partners, but Moze insisted. Why not? She wasn't Natan's yet.

Thom followed them and stood a few feet away, waiting to serve.

The dining room had been set aside for the older Santelouisans. They gossiped and sipped tea around a long rectangular table that dominated the room. Moze hurried her past them, his gaze intent on the wall of photos that rotated the family's candid shots. He stopped, staring at the nearest frame, watching intently as the images shuffled past. Juni at graduation. Harold and Cordelia's wedding. Juni holding Ellie. Ellie with Thom at the lake. Cordelia holding Ellie in her lap, stiff and formal like a Madonna and Child statue in the old churches. The images of their lives flashed bright, then faded after a few seconds.

"Where is it?" Moze asked, the frustration causing his normally musical voice to creak. "Where...? Look! There, look!"

"Freeze image," Ellie said. The frame obeyed.

It was the same picture she'd found before—Juni and her friend with their men, boys hardly looking more than nineteen or twenty, though with Plastiques it was so hard to tell.

"That's my mom and dad," Moze said.

Ellie nodded, not surprised. "Cordelia said our moms were besties."

"I don't have any pictures of them. Can you send me this one?"

"Of course." Ellie looked more closely, but the image wasn't high res enough to be more than a shade of a moment of happiness. She wondered if Moze looked more like his mother or his father, then shook her head sadly. She'd never find out. They were dead. She reached her hand out to him and clasped his—just a gesture of care. Why he'd decided to like her, to share so much with her, the heir of DesLoge Com, seemed some kind of cosmic joke, but still she felt for him and all of the loss he'd borne. This image, so full of the promise of young love and a future, had to her been a clue of a past she'd never known. But for him, it might be an image of love he'd lost, something he'd never know again. She gave his hand a gentle squeeze as he gazed with wide, blinking eyes at his loving parents.

"Isn't this sweet?" A shrill voice said from behind them.

A claw-like hand clamped down on Ellie's shoulder.

The force of the hand spun her until she stood face to chin with Sasha. Her face was set in the same hateful grimace she'd seen earlier. "Moze, you need to excuse us. I need to talk to my bestie."

He nodded and walked a few feet down the wall to watch more pictures as they flickered in the frames.

"You're embarrassing yourself, Ellie DesLoge. Throwing yourself at Moze like this. What of my brother's feelings? Do you care so little for him? For me?" Sasha's voice was conversational, but the jagged edge of her words cut just as deep when spoken quietly. Ellie felt her face flush as she leaned closer to Sasha.

"What are you talking about? Moze is my friend. We danced once."

Sasha's muscles stood taut in the neckline of her beautiful white halter dress, making her look years and years older, harder, and desperate. It was like her eyes were going to boil right out of their sockets, they gaped so wide. For a moment, she was near unrecognizable—someone Ellie didn't know at all.

"No, it's not acceptable," Sasha said.

Ellie took a step back, shocked. "What do you mean, not acceptable? I didn't—"

"You disappeared with him. I saw it. You can't treat Natan—"

Ellie shook her head. This was ridiculous. "Stop now, Sasha. You know me. Besides, what about Joceylin and—"

"Shut your mouth, Ellie. You know his dalliance with that trash doesn't matter to our plans. He's a dumb boy, but he's my brother. You can't just cast him off like this."

"I'm not. My God, have you lost your mind?"

Sasha leaned in and whispered, so rapid fire that drizzling spittle spattered Ellie's face. "All this for that...that boy. His family isn't better than mine. Yes, his aunt is a Senator, but we're the Parkers, for God's sake. That's got to mean something to you. Besides, I just heard he's a Resurrectionist.

A dirty, coward, traitor Resurrectionist. What will Cordelia say when she finds out?"

Ellie shook her head. True or not, Sasha's outburst soured the whole evening for Moze. Where was her sense of propriety? "I don't care right now, Sasha. I don't care, and you are being awful."

Moze's head had jerked at the word Resurrectionist. Next to him stood Thom and Jule, attending their owners, both placid as lambs. Sasha's clenched her teeth. "Jule!"

The beautiful poppet stepped forward. Jule's beauty mattered because the Parkers must always have beauty around them. But beauty doesn't always protect you from violence. Sasha's anger had grown to a point Ellie had never seen. She watched her friend turn and shove Jule to the ground and begin kicking her with vicious precision in the ribs and stomach where the damage wouldn't show.

The oldies at the table stopped talking, watching the attack on the poppet. Ellie's own hand crept to her mouth, covering her winces. What could she do? Jule wasn't hers. Moze started to step forward, but she shook her head at him. If he stepped in, it would give him away. No one would violate a property owner's rights. It was the law.

The two of them stood there, impotent and dumb, as Sasha kicked poor Jule.

Thom stepped forward, his leg tangling with the carpet, or maybe Jule's arm. She didn't see, but he stumbled, falling across Jule's prone body. Sasha couldn't stop the last savage kick, which connected with Thom's shoulder joint. An audible crunch ended Sasha's rampage.

Time seemed to freeze as Ellie shuffled forward and fell

to her knees beside Thom and Jule. Neither poppet's face showed the effects of the beating—not winces, gritted teeth, nothing. Thank God, their pain centers didn't regenerate with the chemicals of the DesLoge poppet resurrection. But the damage was clear. Thom's tar black fluids leaked with a slow, thick intensity out of the hole his broken bone ripped through his skin.

"Oh, my Thom. My poor Thom." Ellie pressed her hand against the wound, blocking the flow of poppet blood from his body. She cried quietly, but everyone could see her outburst over a poppet. The oldies grumbled and whispered to each other as the poppet doctors came forward to claim Thom and Jule for treatment. The doc's hoverdiscs carried both broken poppets away.

Sasha hissed at Ellie. "See what you made me do!"

She stalked away toward her family, now gathered in a corner of the ballroom, faces shadowed by the half-light.

Moze lifted Ellie up and whispered, "He'll be okay. I've seen worse on the living. Good old Thom will make it. I promise."

Leaning into his warm chest, Ellie felt that someone finally understood her tender feelings for her beloved Thom. She nodded and pulled away because it was proper. But she smiled at his gesture. Again, she felt like he was her friend because she was worth something all on her own. Because of actual care and not some social posturing or position seeking. Moze smiled at her, a bit too warmly, while Ellie felt the weight of hundreds of sets of eyes, watching them, judging their interaction. She wasn't sure how to recover from the scene, but Moze turned to the frames on the wall. He seemed to understand her discomfort and created a polite distance and an acceptable topic by asking her about the pictures. Ellie heard the hive-like buzz of gossip begin to die back into a background hum.

"Can I ask you something?" Moze pointed again to the frozen picture. "Maybe this isn't the right time, but how do you know Ridley Brown?"

Ridley Brown? Her mind felt like it was being stung by bees. Thom falling and getting hurt and Sasha's rage were quite upsetting enough. Now Moze knew the name from the box—Ridley Brown. How did he know him?

Could Moze help her unravel this mystery? "How do you—"

"Come, Moze, time to go now." The Widow Douglas turned the corner, her shawl wrapped around her narrow shoulders. She smiled gently at Ellie. "Sorry to steal him, Ellie, but your aunt sometimes invites people best left off of any list. People I don't want my grandson—or you, for that matter—to be around. But she always says it's part of the business. Watch out for him, Ellie."

Moze's gaze turned from his Gran back to Ellie, watching the exchange with worry.

"Who, Mrs. Douglas?"

"Simon Eregel, over there." The widow jerked her head toward Aunt Cordelia at the main table. Next to her sat a smarmy, leathery man with straight black hair and pocked-up leathery skin. Clearly a man who had been outside the dome. "Old Red Boots himself."

Widow Douglas grasped Moze by the elbow and took him away. Ellie bit her lip and waved as he looked back and shrugged. Red Boots? She glanced back at Simon Eregel as he inserted himself at the head table, a swine among pearls. Juni leaned away, ignoring his intrusion, but Cordelia listened to him intently. Eregel...Joceylin's father? Uncle? She'd never met him, but from his haughty expression and pushiness, she believed he had to be Joceylin's father. He laughed with his mouth wide open, then ordered a poppet to give him a beer. He leaned back and propped his feet on the table, dragging his filthy heels across the white linen. Red boots. The red boots she'd seen in the vid at the factory when Cordelia had called her to tell her she'd be out late. What had he said? Something about Ridley Brown.

Ellie couldn't get everything to line up in her head. It was all too much drama. Between the pressure of hosting a high-society party, her bestie's nasty behavior, the Natan and Joceylin connection, and mystery men popping up, her head spun like a top.

All she could really focus on, the only thing her mind could see, was the kick that had broken her Thom's shoulder. She knew her aunt would have something nasty to say about her embarrassing sentimentality, her very public tears shed over a poppet. But Thom had always been there for her. Sasha's vicious kick hurt him.

Juni, a little stumbly, dismissed her escort back into the corner they'd been drinking in and came over to Ellie. She put her arm around her shoulder and let her body go slack against Ellie's side.

"Go upstairs, now," Juni whispered, her warm hand gentle on Ellie's arm. "Go before you do any more damage." Juni's eyes, usually so distracted, seeking the next beautiful person or colorful bauble, fastened on Ellie's, sharp, with a rare focus. She twitched her head, a shooing gesture, toward the stairs.

Ellie nodded and headed for the steps. With her head spinning and her poppet gone, it would be a difficult night for her indeed.

DOCUMENT 7: US NOAM HIGH COURT RULING ON POPPET RIGHTS
HIGH COURT RULE: DINSH V. BRAZEA ESTATE

Dinsh v. Brazea Estate was a case decided by the High Court US NOAM, which denied the legality of manumission executed by Elis Brazea, a citizen, to free a poppet woman and poppet child he had called his wife and son. Dinsh, the head judge, ruled that Brazea was trying to evade US NOAM law against manumissions by calling them his wife and child. Both the female poppet and child poppet were declared legal property, prohibited from inheriting or leaving.

Upon Brazea's death, the female and child poppet were sold, and Brazea's estate went to the US NOAM since he had no legal heirs.

After Brazea died, the legislature passed HB 801 US NOAM into law, establishing the precedent that any persons pretending/faking/suggesting that poppets are family members, spouses, or progeny are considered legally mentally incompetent. Even if, as was true in this case, the poppets in question had in life been wife and son to the living, once a poppet, they can no longer be considered human.

CHAPTER 7

Ellie tossed her covers back and leaped out of her bed the next morning. She pulled a robe around her, tying it at the waist, then pushed her sloppy hair back into place. Only one thing really mattered. She said, "Call poppet maintenance."

The vid screen flickered and lit up. An older man with a gray DesLoge Com lab coat stood in the frame, his eyes wide. "Miss DesLoge? How may I help you?"

His hands washed each other in the air as he stared into her face. She'd had a few contacts with the lab workers. Cordelia had toured her around, introducing her to the heads of departments and loudly proclaiming her the heir to the throne each year on Devolution Day. Ellie didn't recognize this man, but from his shaking hands and overly wide eyes, she imagined he'd met her or at least knew of her. It occurred to her that since he was used to Cordelia's stiff and proper manners, any kindness she showed him might seem like a trick coming from her heir, so she decided to be all business.

"Your name?" She crossed her arms in a mimic of Cordelia's "all-business" pose.

"I'm Jackson, Miss DesLoge. We met once... Never mind. I expect you are calling about your poppet." He reached out of her view to grab his compad. He flicked the screen several times and bit his lip, staring hard at the reports. Clearly, he felt pressure. Ellie hoped that didn't mean bad things for Thom. Jackson gathered a large breath and turned the compad screen so it faced her. Though she couldn't read the report, an image of Thom strapped to a table with bags of fluids and brightly lit cords laced in and out of his arms met her gaze. Ellie felt her tongue grow thick with the nausea in her guts. "Um, we aren't ready to send him back to you. It'll be a few days. We have to repair this shoulder and humerus bone."

Ellie nodded once, matter-of-factly. "I'd like him returned as soon as possible."

"I understand you are quite attached to him." Jackson smiled an overly familiar, smarmy smile like pretty wrapping round a rotted fruit basket. It settled her stomach instantly, distaste elbowed aside by frustration. Why did it always come back to this? To her weakness?

Pushing her hair back, Ellie hoped that the flush on her cheek didn't show on the holovid. For all of her bluster, he clearly wasn't buying her tough act. He knew. Of course, he knew. She'd crawled on the floor last night in front of everyone, crying about a broken poppet. She could hear the whispers and sneers moving at the speed of sound across every level of society in Santelouisa. Her weakness and sentimentality had to be the topic of every wagging tongue. Cordelia must be so disappointed with her.

"Yes, well, please complete the repairs quickly. Vid off." The screen flickered to black, though Jackson's mouth hung open with unsaid words. Ellie didn't want to be rude, but she couldn't stand the thought that some technician judged her for her stupid tears. A technician at her own lab! She stomped across the room to her closet, dialing up an outfit for school. The closet hummed as it sorted through the elements she'd chosen for the day. Practical, muted colors. It spit out her uniform with the addition of a soft gray sweater, round-toe shoes, and no jewelry. Ellie slipped on the clothes the closet chose. Blending into the background would please her greatly today. She shivered, thinking about dealing with school and all of the nasty whispers that were sure to happen in the hallway, but DesLoges didn't hide from their problems. They faced them head-on. She grabbed her compad and bag and checked that she had her Joltlace on, and headed out of her room, though each step was like walking through wet concrete. A deep breath, and she rushed down the stairs, past other poppets. Ellie felt Thom's absence in each tread. She peeked into the dining room, but Cordelia wasn't there. She wondered if her aunt was still in bed. It had been a late night. She hoped she could avoid her dear aunt for a day or two until this all died down. Maybe then she'd be able to meet her stern gaze and explain away her weepiness over Thom.

She stepped out the front door into the silvered morning light but halted on the wide entry stairs. The driveway circle, neat and tidy, stood empty. Thom usually called for the autocar. As she looked out at that empty drive, her eyes filled with salty tears. Blinking hard, she was just able to hold them back. She felt his absence beyond just a missing ride to school. There was a Thom-shaped hole in her life that everyone expected her not to care about. Why was it so hard to be what they wanted? How could they not care about the poppets who cared for them? It had never made less sense to her than now with her Thom broken and strapped to a table at the factory.

Late to Antedevolution Literature class, Ellie rushed in, muttering an apology to Mrs. Loar as she went to her seat. All the gazes of her classmates weighed on her like bricks. They watched her every day. That was normal. But today, their eyebrows arched and their mouths smirked. Judging. Always judging. Ellie, trying to project an air of confidence, focused on the image that Mrs. Loar showed the class. The holograph rotating above their heads depicted a dark-skinned man, dressed only in ragged short pants, sitting on a stool. The black-and-white vid with frayed edges and a grainy texture made the image more immediate to the eye, so much more real than if the color were true to life. The poor man's back looked craggy, an alien landscape encrusted with fibrous scars and angry ridges. His head turned away from the light that shone on his back, so Ellie couldn't see his eyes. She thought perhaps the photographer didn't want to show his eyes. That, perhaps, in those eyes you'd see pain you couldn't stand. His muscles hung loose, as if he wasn't in danger anymore, but they were like thin cables, clearly defined by the work he'd done all his life.

"The Antedevolution period is rife with tales of slaves

doing the work to free the owning, producing class to be able to think, create, and imagine. This poor man's body bears the stripes of a life of slavery."

Ellie glanced over at Natan to her right. His head sat heavy in the cradle of his hands, as if he'd fall asleep at any moment. Joceylin, next to him, raised her hand.

"Mrs. Loar, that's why we have poppets. I mean, we had a working class, and it rose against us. Once we won the war, we realized that no human wants to be low class or do that kind of work. So, we have poppets to do those jobs."

"That's right, Joceylin."

Natan, awake now and nodding along with the teacher, whispered something to Joceylin. She giggled prettily and turned so she faced him with the totality of her beauty. They weren't even trying to hide their connection. Ellie turned away. She didn't need this kind of public humiliation right now. Ellie knew her brown hair and eyes and her shorter, thicker body was nowhere near as pretty as Joceylin's, with her icy hair, blindingly-blue eyes, and petite frame. Joceylin commanded a room with her purring voice. So what?

Ellie tried to focus back on the discussion, hoping she looked aloof and carefree. She was sure she actually looked awkward and uncomfortable, but she'd at least pretend that it didn't matter. From this angle, she could see Moze. He didn't notice her. He leaned forward, completely immersed in the discussion of slavery.

"Let's do a project, shall we?" Mrs. Loar rubbed her hands together in glee as all her students groaned. The image melted away into a bulleted list of requirements, which every student dragged down to their compads. "I am sending project pairings to your compads now. Make time for the next few days to do research about historical slavery together."

Everyone's heads dipped to check their personal compads. The screens flashed, and depending on the pairing, scattered groans and squeals tore through the room. Ellie didn't know who to hope for after last night's fiasco. Mrs. Loar always paired people in uncomfortable ways. How many times had she been paired with Joceylin or Natan? Mrs. Loar's blundering attempts to break down social barriers between her students led to the most awkward conversations Ellie had ever had to suffer through. She stared at the screen as it switched to Mrs. Loar's control, lighting up with the name Moze Grayson.

Mrs. Loar strikes again.

She and Moze as a pair would cause all of the tongues to wag, but at least she could talk with him without having a fight. Besides, how could Natan or Sasha blame her if the teacher put them together? She looked around nervously and saw Sasha's gaze dart away from hers. Ellie hoped maybe Sasha's hateful display last night was now causing her some regret. Though Ellie couldn't remember Sasha ever regretting anything in all the years she'd known her.

"The subject is slavery and its effects in the Antedevolution period. I want you to use the literature of the period but find extensions of what you read and know. How the literature reflects truth about the condition of slavery and workers, and how we've overcome those issues. Meet now with your partner, and plan for the research you'll have to do." Mrs. Loar lowered into her cushioned chair and propped her arms up on her long oak desk. She waved her hands like an orchestra conductor with a new aria and said, "Go on now."

The chairs and desks scraped as students moved toward their partners, mumbling discontent. Only Mrs. Loar would assign such a thing. Why couldn't she just assign a paper? She seemed to pick at the buttoned-down ideas of the past with some purpose only known to her. Sometimes her lessons made Ellie feel like they lived a privileged life, but more often they made her question exactly why they were living in a dome with their lives planned and pre-programmed for them.

"Hi, Ellie," Moze said, scooting into the desk next to hers. She looked up and smiled at him, then gazed around to see who was watching. Some students glanced their way. Sasha so studiously avoided looking at them, it was almost like she *was* staring. But not Natan. He'd been partnered with Joceylin, and his eyes never turned from her.

Ellie shrugged and turned back to Moze. She flicked the screen of her compad, scanning the images and information Mrs. Loar had loaded. "Quite a project. She wants some original research. I guess we'll be going to the archives."

Moze nodded, leaned forward in the seat, looking at her with his warm eyes. "How's Thom? Have you heard anything?"

What a question. How strange it sounded to her—how wonderful. In that moment, Ellie thought she could see the wilds and what they must be like through him and this kindness. She looked around once more to see if anyone was listening, then whispered, "He's still being worked on. Should be back to me soon. Thanks for asking."

Though the others might think less of her for her worry, he wouldn't. He really believed that Thom was more than an empty-headed poppet.

"Want to go downtown to the research center?" Ellie asked.

Moze bit his lip, thinking. "I've got...services in the morning. They're downtown. Maybe we can meet after?"

"Services?" She whispered right back. Here? In the city? "Maybe you shouldn't be talking about that, I mean—"

"Ellie." Sasha hissed from her table and slid her hand across her compad, sending a note into Ellie's, encoded only to her so Mrs. Loar wouldn't be able to open it. Sasha nodded pointedly and turned back to her partner.

"Sorry," Ellie said, pulling the note up on her screen and turning it so Moze couldn't see. She read the note quickly, not wanting to be rude.

Meet me at my locker after. Natan wants to talk. I'm sorry about Thom, but Moze is a problem. See me after, Bestie? Please?

Ellie bit her lip as she considered her friend's gesture. Sasha wanted to make peace not even a day after her nasty display at the party. Her stomach churned as she thought about the scene last night, the violence. Her bestie had always been high-strung, but the brutality of last night— the meaty kicks and cracking of bones. Sometimes, she wondered if she really knew anything about Sasha at all. Still, she was her bestie. Besties for life, negotiated and sealed by their families. She owed her at least this. She caught Sasha's gaze and nodded.

Moze leaned toward her, pretending to be studying the comvid instructions.

"I'm sorry if being your friend has caused you problems. I can tell I'm really cutting into your normal life, but..." Moze glanced around nervously. "Look, I'm not like you. My farm, my parents, and my life never had so many rules before. I just...I want to make things right. Can I maybe come tonight and bring a dessert to Cordelia as a thank you? Maybe I can take some of the heat for what happened last night, you know, with Thom and the argument? You are worried about that, right?"

"Yeah," Ellie said. Not something she'd normally admit, but with Moze, anything less than the whole truth might crush the fragile flower of their friendship. Everyone else tolerated her at worst, groomed her for a future profitable relationship at best. But with Moze, there weren't the formal expectations she normally had to weave her way through. "But I'm sure you don't have to do that. I'll talk to her. I'll deal with it. Maybe she won't even be mad about it. She was kind of busy..."

"With that Simon Eregel."

"Did the widow—your Gran—say anything about that? She seemed pretty upset."

Moze nodded and leaned in but stopped before he came to close, glancing at Natan.

Natan glowered at him from across the room. Ellie felt her jaw tense up as she stared right back, trying to telegraph just how annoying his jealousy was to her. The Parkers needed to settle down.

Class crawled by so slowly. From that point on, Ellie had tried to just stay on task, researching the literature of the Antedevolution period. Huck Finn and Harriet Beecher

Stowe and proclamations and addresses so full of life, horror, violence, and passion. Sometimes the ancients and their abuses stunned her, but sometimes, like now, when she worried about her poppet Thom, she wondered just how much different things really were.

Moze promised to see her Saturday, dropping the idea of a dinner visit. Probably because she'd been horrified. Cordelia might misunderstand, ban him from the house or from her life. And, right now, he seemed to fit in the place that Sasha had never quite filled.

Sasha was a real problem. The scene she'd made at the party and her dislike of Moze. Even Natan seemed to be having problems with her. She had to deal with Sasha, bestie or no.

Once the class released, Ellie walked down the hallway, trying to keep her head high and her face proud to mask the embarrassment she felt as the others whispered about her and Moze, her and Thom, always something about her. Her face burned, but she hooded her gaze so that she looked like she couldn't be bothered. It was a look she'd worked on for years, though she wasn't certain it was successful. It made her feel like she had some armor on.

She turned into Sasha's cubby locker, the metal door gaping open in welcome. Inside, Sasha, and Natan waited for her, looking sheepish. Sasha patted the cushion next to her on the little couch, so Ellie sat, perched on the edge. A moment of uncomfortable silence stretched between them. Natan picked at his finger, doing his best not to meet her gaze. Sasha reached over and shoved him lightly. He glanced up and, for a second, his gaze met hers. In that second, she could see the inner Natan—a boy, sweet and frightened. But then the moment passed, and his gaze seemed to harden, a devil-may-care grin bloomed on his face. With a quick glance at his sister, whose smirking happiness was barely hidden behind a curled hand lightly grazing her lips, Natan clicked his heels and bowed. A formal salute.

"Ellie," he said, "I've been thinking we need to begin our formal courtship." Again, his gaze caught hers, and his mask slipped. For a moment, it seemed like he might give her his real feelings, but just as quickly as he revealed eyes ringed in fear, his jovial, rakish boy mask descended. What she'd thought was earnest care for her before she now could see was fiction. The Parkers were playing a high stakes chess match, and Natan was their reluctant knight.

Fakes, Cordelia had often told her, were the daily hazard that the great must suffer. Never tolerate a fake. Of course, she'd also say that the Parker family mattered in Santelouisa, and that they were important enough to forgive some minor fakery. Ellie sighed and leaned forward, offering him her hand. It was the courteous thing to do. As he grabbed it in his own hands, she didn't feel the electric excitement she used to. Instead, she felt how clammy and soft his hands were— soft like her own. Velvety, but not in a good way. "Can we have you to dinner tonight? We can discuss this further."

Discuss this? Ellie looked back and forth between brother and sister—Natan's rictus smile and Sasha's tilted head, eyes half shut in a side glance. What was this? Ellie could sense a hidden communication between them. Juni had often spoken to her about the pressures of being a

DesLoge when Aunt Cordelia wasn't around. She'd told

her that there were always subtexts in every interaction. *There are secrets embedded in lies wrapped in polite subterfuge that you will be handed each day. You will need to see through the fog of polite jockeying and find the truth as DesLoge heir,* Juni told her. *Always be aware of their motives.* The Parkers could move up only one way—through a union between her and Natan. It had always been clear to her that this was the best match for her, but she'd never really thought about how that upward movement mattered so much to them. A refusal might be interpreted as an insult. What could she do?

"Fine, that would be great. What time?"

"I'll come for you at half-evening."

She smiled tightly as Natan bowed at the waist, then turned on his heel and left.

Before she could bolt away, Sasha grabbed her wrist, though not hard. She pulled Ellie into an awkward, onearmed hug, whispering, "I'm so sorry. Really. I wish I hadn't gotten so mad. It's just...we're going to be sisters. Just like we always said, you know. Forgive me?"

Sasha put her hands on Ellie's shoulders. Such a friendly gesture. So uncomfortable, but Ellie owed it to her bestie to accept her intensity. Sasha's words flowed out, unwound in a vivid ribbon. "Natan's an idiot, but you aren't, and when I saw you with Moze and you disappeared, I just felt like you were leaving me. Moze is an outsider and doesn't know our ways —that you are spoken for. All he can do is drive a wedge between our families, and I won't let that happen. Besties are forever, you know?"

Sasha sniffled.

Crying? Really?

Ellie bit her lip and shrugged. Sasha never cried about anything. Sasha brought her other arm into the hug and crushed Ellie to her. The gesture broke through the pressure of the fight and the awkwardness she felt. Their families linked them in childhood, ceremonially at an Ascensionist service for the whole community to see, then emotionally by bringing them up as near sisters. They'd had all their young elite classes together. They'd served as each other's planner for each birthday celebration, as formal besties do. In all of the social entanglements of Santelouisa society, the bestie bond was one that only a formal and very public divorce could sever. Besties sometimes lived together after their childbearing years. The bond could save a failing family or restore a tarnished business reputation. Sasha and Ellie had grown into that bond. Her bestie, the girl she'd laughed with and trusted with all of her secrets, the only one she believed to be true to her.

Ellie watched Sasha use her silk sleeve to swipe the tears off her splotchy red cheeks. Sasha had made a mistake, just a stupid mistake. Yes, Thom had been hurt, but the lab was fixing him. She couldn't hold it against her forever.

"Forgive me?" Sasha asked.

Ellie said, "Sure. Besties, right?"

"Besties."

They leaned their foreheads against each other for a sweet moment, then Sasha pulled away. "I look a mess, don't I?"

She didn't. Other than her round red cheeks, Sasha always looked amazing. But there was no telling her that.

Ellie reached out her hand and shoved Sasha's shoulder lightly, smiling.

"I've got to go. Big date tonight," Ellie said, hoping her voice's forced musicality would mimic the sweetness and excitement she didn't really feel.

"I'll order up your outfit." Sasha was already spinning combinations of fashionable flair on her compad, ordering Ellie's closet to work overtime. "You better hurry on home. Won't Cordelia want to see you before?"

"Right," Ellie said. She rose and excused herself, calling for an autocar on her compad. She walked with too many things swirling in her head. Natan wanted to declare—or at least that's what his family had decided. Like leaves trapped in a tornado, the two of them swirled around each other. Not really wanting to but being made to be together. She'd always thought that they would discover that they loved each other or somehow some strange adult magic would take hold, and he would be more to her than just the handsome brother of her bestie. She'd always had this fantasy that one day their gazes would meet across a room and music would play and they'd sweep into each other's arms, but clearly that wasn't in the cards.

Just a couple of chess pieces being moved around a board, Ellie thought and pulled her sweater closer as she walked. She pushed the heavy oak door open and stepped out into the silvery dome-noon, so bright that for a moment she couldn't see. Then, with a lurch, her body recognized the waiting serpent that froze her on the marble steps like some broken little bird.

"Share a ride?" Joceylin blocked the door of the autocar that had arrived to get Ellie, leaning like she belonged.

This day never seemed to get any better. Why not? "After you," Ellie said.

And true to her word, she climbed into the autocar with the daughter of "Red Boots" himself. Widow Douglas's warnings about the Eregels came raging back into her mind. As the car pulled away, Joceylin pulled out a nail file and began sawing. Without even looking up, she said, "If you think your life is hard now, just wait until you really cross me. And if what I heard today is right, you are just about to make me your worst enemy."

DOCUMENT 8: VID-AD IN ALL MAJOR DOME CITY NEWS STREAMS.

Additionally, this is the transcript for many of the vid-show sponsor commercials that ran throughout the Devolution period of US NOAM.

From DesLoge Labs... Reanimix for your poppets.

As brilliant as Harold DesLoge was, he couldn't defeat biology. Even dead and reanimated tissue requires energy to work, lift, and do all the things that poppets do. But who wants to waste good food on them?

Or if you feed them your trash, do they seem to slow down midday? Do they run out of energy?

Feed them inexpensive, enriched Reanimix Formula Tabs. Reanimix Formula Tabs are an easy-to-administer tablet that provides slow release, dense calories that allow poppets to work almost around the clock without needing special preparations or specialized application times like breakfast, lunch, and dinner.

Heavy-duty labor? Try Reanimix Triple Strength with triple calories to keep the poppet strong and active through even the toughest job. All this at a low DesLoge Labs price.

Keep 'em working. Use Reanimix!

CHAPTER 8

Joceylin's kicky satin skirt and pixie-cut blouse did not reflect the viciousness of mood radiating from her as the autocar coasted from the Academy toward DesLoge Mansion. Ellie tried to stay calm, but her heart hammered in her chest. Joceylin represented everything she didn't like about people at Academy de Bellum. Usually, her constant seeking of attention and her fake attempts at gaining Ellie's friendship were nasty reminders of the facts of Santelouisa's social strata. But at the same time, this Joceylin, hard diamond eyes set in an expression of stone that marred her doll-like features, was for once real and demanded her attention.

This Joceylin ordered the car to drive in circles, going nowhere as she stared at Ellie. She muttered and clenched and unclenched her fists.

"Um, autocar, take me to DesLoge Mansion," Ellie said.

"No," Joceylin said. "Continue the ten-block circle until I release you."

"You can't keep me in here. I don't know what you think I did, but—"

"You haven't done anything to me. Not really." Joceylin crossed her arms and huffed loudly. "You've never taken me seriously, never tried to be nice to me, never allowed me to be nice to you. That's all fine and good. Daddy says there will come a day when you will deal with me, and I'll be useful to you. Then maybe you'll think I'm worth your time."

Ellie sucked in a quick breath. "I've never been cruel to you—"

"Sure, you have, but I can take it." Joceylin waved her hand in dismissal, then tucked her smooth, white hair behind her ear. "I have to be tough. Then, when I take over from my father, I'll be your partner, like it or not. I can wait for that."

She flicked her hand toward the shops and beautiful homes they were circling, places that neither of them would ever go to because they were for the middles. Middles were the people who worked for them in the factory and at the shops.

"What would these people do without us, without what our families provide for them? Between you and me and the Parkers, we fulfill everyone's needs. It starts with your poppets, which my family helps to provide."

"What do you mean, provide?" Ellie asked.

Joceylin laughed at her, sneering. "Ellie, so precious, so sweet. Where do you think the bodies come from? You know about the Grave Hawkers, right? You know about them, but do you think they are just some guys out in the wild who pick up bodies here and there? That they are like some quiet little grave robbers getting product for the DesLoges?" She turned to the window, breathing in ragged breaths, as if she'd been crying hard.

Ellie shifted across the autocar and sat next to Joceylin. Truth—it's what she'd always craved. From her mother, from her friend, and from her aunt, but it was a rarity in her life. This moment with Joceylin tasted real to her in a way that most of her life tasted like cotton candy.

"You're in line for—" Ellie started to ask.

"I'm the Grand Wizard's daughter. I'll be the next Wizard of the Grave Hawkers, and you'll be my silent partner. I'll provide you with raw materials, and you'll create the product that makes life in the dome-cities possible." Joceylin turned toward her, face set in ice, legs crossed tight and hands folded, white at the knuckles. "You and me, we're the same. Lives set in stone. I'll be kissing your ass my whole life and, behind closed doors, you'll be kissing mine."

The foul language razored through Ellie's reserve. Her mouth dropped open at the suggestion that their lives were linked this way. But, as she thought about it, the hints of this relationship between DesLoge Com and the Hawkers had always been there.

"Here's the thing, Ellie. I'll put up with your arrogance, your ignoring me and treating me like I'm beneath you, because like Daddy says you'll need me someday and then, by God, then you'll treat me right. It'll be a love fest every day when I'm bringing you the bodies you need for poppet production. We're the reason your family can dominate the industry and provide everything folks need. All your family does is live off the discoveries of Harold DesLoge. You're like a bunch of fat leeches. But my family...we're the ones who really make everything work. When your aunt wanted her pretty blue eyes, I picked them out. Me! I found the body and delivered it to Dr. Parker."

Ellie leaned back in the seat as the weariness of her family connections settled on her like chains.

"What do you want from me, Joceylin? What is this all about? You're telling me how we'll be friends. How you'll be the answer to my prayers. Great. I still don't understand why you're driving me around in circles." Ellie tried to match Joceylin's tone, the edge of her words, but she was pretty sure that she still sounded like a frightened little girl.

"I want you to give up Natan."

"What?" Several swift seconds ticked by in silence as Joceylin's demand clattered around in her mind. "Natan is my beau. Surely you can't expect—"

"That he could be mine? Why not?" Joceylin's voice rose and grew to a screech. Her hands, claw-shaped, raked across her thighs, leaving red tracks. "Why not? He is only your beau because of tradition. Because your family is higher up in the social strata than mine is. You don't like it any more than Natan or I do. We are all slaves, Ellie. Slaves to tradition and expectations. We might as well be poppets."

"I know you and Natan like each other, but—"

"It's not like. We love each other. I know that's a foreign concept to you DesLoges. I know how all that matters to you and Natan's family is what tradition dictates, but I will not bow to tradition. All this time that your families have been playing this game of planning a bright, perfect future for you and Natan, we've been in love. He's been what he had to be with you for his family, but with me... Ellie, with me he is his best self. He's happy with me." She gazed out the window at the homes and the neat lawns that streamed past the window.

Ellie could see the thunder that sat on her perfect, smooth brow.

Joceylin turned, slow, like it was through a thick fog. Finally, they sat, nearly nose to nose. It felt to Ellie like they were the two most powerful girls in the world.

"I want him, and he wants me. Have you ever really wanted something, Ellie? Ever? From where I sit, it looks like you've never done anything for yourself."

Ellie stared at her for a moment. She was the grandniece and heir of Cordelia DesLoge, and no one talked this way to her. This conversation went against everything that they'd been taught, told, and brought up to be. For a moment, she thought about demanding that Joceylin stop the autocar, get out, and walk. She thought about tearing into Joceylin and her ridiculous demands. Imagine telling her, Ellie DesLoge, that she couldn't have or didn't deserve her promised future. She'd be within her rights. Joceylin was, according to Santelouisa tradition, beneath her. Beneath her. The idea suddenly seemed so brutal. Tradition. Sure, Joceylin wasn't a DesLoge or a Parker, but she, too, had been taught that tradition mattered above all else. What gave her this courage?

"Stop the car," Ellie said. "Just stop right here."

She shoved past Joceylin, out onto the sidewalk. Truth. She'd never had a chance to really practice it, but Joceylin and her awful father got to speak it with abandon. She leaned against the autocar as Joceylin got out and stood next to her. They watched the middles walking through the park that the ancients had built in the middle of Santelouisa. Inside were the largest collection of trees and the only animals that most of them would ever experience inside the dome. Middles who would enjoy lives of tradition and prosperity built on the strength of the empire that DesLoge and the Grave Hawkers maintained laughed and loved and remained unconcerned by the two teens squaring off like titans in front of them. Ellie looked at Joceylin—really looked at her. The bright white hair, smooth skin, ice-blue eyes, and angry smile. She seemed bigger, less empty now standing with her arms crossed and a heat-filled gaze locked on Ellie.

"Does Natan know what you are doing? I mean, does he agree?" Beautiful Natan, her beau, her future—at least that's what she'd always thought.

Joceylin shook her head no.

"I'm sorry, Joceylin. I wish I could agree to this. I can't, though. It's like you said, tradition is the master of our lives. I'm not sure how to overcome it. Even if Natan and I both wanted to, we'd be destroying our families."

"I promise you now, Ellie. If you allow Natan to go against his heart, for tradition's sake or whatever, I will never forgive you. If you take him from me, we will be enemies."

The force of her words hit Ellie like a fist. Had she ever felt a love like that? Maybe for Aunt Cordelia, but...no, that was tempered. Maybe for Thom. Ellie and Joceylin's names might be the thing that held them fast to their futures, but did it have to step in the way of love or beauty or truth? Ellie knew somewhere in her heart that this decision—this request for a future—had to matter to her and to them all, beyond the anger or disappointment of their families.

"What do you want me to do? If I deny him, it will be an insult to his family."

Joceylin stalked off. She turned and kicked her foot at the front end of the autocar. "Damn it! I don't know what to do. I just know that if you take him from me, if you take him and you don't even love him, I will never forgive you." Ellie stared at Joceylin, seeing her pain and her beauty, but most importantly, she was seeing her reality. No matter what she did at school, how she excelled, she'd still only be a Grave Hawker. How could the Parkers forgive her for that? How? They would, since money was almost enough to forgive her lower status. Joceylin would be their next choice, but only if Ellie refused Natan. The devastation of the insult she imagined would topple her aunt's trust of her, throw her mother into a panic, and who could guess what Sasha would say about it. If last night had been a taste of her anger, Ellie actually felt a glimmer of true worry that such violence might turn on her if Sasha's dreams of a Parker–DesLoge alliance fell apart.

"Let me think about this, Joceylin," Ellie said, suddenly so tired of this day. Even with the dread she felt creeping across her skin like a cold breath, she had to admire the guts of Joceylin's request. From here on, Ellie thought, I need to treat Joceylin with more respect. This—what would you call it? A kidnapping? A threat? Whatever you call it—took courage.

"One more thing." Joceylin shifted her weight from foot to foot. She looked up, locking gazes with Ellie's.

Whatever she prepared to say next looked to be a painful admission. Her body seemed to hunch around the words as they formed, as if they were a dagger wrenching up through her guts.

"If you do this for us," Joceylin said, her words slow and breathy, "I will forgive you for every little thing. You will be someone I owe, no matter what happens between Natan and me. My debts become my family's debts, and our debts become the Grave Hawker's debts, you understand? This is my promise. Forever."

Ellie nodded. She'd never valued Joceylin before, but now, standing eye-to-eye, she realized that this girl was to be her flip side, her silent partner. If she wanted to be effective, having the Grave Hawkers in debt to her would be a good thing. She was sure that Cordelia would have relished a deal like this, even if the Parkers suffered for it. Besides, Ellie couldn't deny the passion in Joceylin's voice. Who was she to trample on love?

"I'll talk to Natan, then let's see what I can do," Ellie said.

Joceylin smiled, white teeth bright in the dome-noon-silvered light. Another autocar pulled up, and the door popped open. As Joceylin entered it, Ellie noticed the red boots propped on the rear-facing seats. Simon Eregel's leathery face leaned out and smiled. He gave a tip of his hat, pulled the door shut, and off the car sped, leaving Ellie feeling like a pawn in a monumental game of chess. Why was it that she was the only one who didn't get the rules of this game?

Ellie put on the outfit Sasha had dialed up for her that afternoon. Tight skirt riding too high on her legs, shaping her too-large hips into something they weren't and never would be. The shirt, low and bagging across her small chest, no matter which way she plucked or tucked it, highlighted her lack. Why would Sasha try to put her in such an outfit? Is this the kind of thing it took to get the attention of her beau?

She pulled the items off in a huff. Black pants, an emerald wispy shell top Cordelia had given her over a white tubewrap. Sensible but pretty. Nothing that Sasha or Joceylin would choose, but she wasn't them. She walked over to the closet of her treasures and picked through the hidden box she'd found. On a whim, she took the leather-thonged necklace out and put it around her neck. It didn't go with her beautiful Joltlace, so she tucked it into the tubewrap.

Her vidscreen popped on. Cordelia paused a moment, looked her over, then said, "Plans?"

"Hello, Aunt Cordelia. Yes, I wanted to talk to you about that."

"Where are you going?"

"On a date."

"Natan Parker? He's coming to court you? You're too young for that."

Ellie nodded. She turned to face her aunt. "Are you here at home? Can I come to see you?"

Cordelia swept back. The birth tubes of the reproduction lab, backlit and sparkling, lined the walls behind her. Few people got to see the birthing center, where poppets were chemically imbued with the secret recipe so they could rise. "Much too busy to come home today, my love. Supply problems. So, the Parkers are making a play for you, eh?" Her aunt's eyes swept down her outfit, weighing what she wore. But at least that judgment was tempered with the love she could see in her aunt's eyes.

"A play? I don't know about a play. It's just that they misunderstood when I danced with Moze."

"Yes, a lot of people had concerns about last night—about your little problem with Sasha. Listen, my girl, I don't really care to have the Parkers take over this company."

"But he's my beau. I thought that you wanted—"

"That doesn't mean anything to me, silly girl. Beau! There are many boys to choose from besides Natan Parker. You can have any appropriate boy you want. He's just the most convenient." Cordelia swept her arm as if she could gather all of the DesLoge Com lab up in her grasp. "This is yours. If you don't claim it, others will."

"But the tradition—"

"To hell with traditions, girl. If you want him, fine. If you don't, fine. But you must find a way to claim all of this and make it yours. To be the mother of all the world. If marrying the Parker boy will give you the strength, then you do that. If not marrying him is better, I will be with you on that, too. Your mother, poor Juni, might protest. She dreams of a white wedding. Her own wedding was... well, let's just say it wasn't ideal. But you, my Ellie Bird, you may be able to choose differently—choose better."

Ellie drew back, shocked but delighted. Cordelia sometimes surprised her with these moments of lovely acceptance, so different from what she'd worried about all day. Ellie ran her hand up and down her arm, feeling the skin there drawn up in bumps. Aunt Cordelia had a way of reaching right into her heart when she wanted to.

"Now, I think that you do need to work on your public face. That display you put on with your poppet. Crying in public. Good thing Sasha was acting a complete fool, or we'd be dealing with a real public relations fiasco. For now, it's just some tongues a waggin' about your too-soft heart. But you'd better never put on another display like that again."

"Yes, ma'am."

Cordelia smiled, appraising her. "You are much more than you think you are, Ellie Bird. You've got the heart of a lion—just like me. We're fighters, we are, and I'm glad I'm not a Parker tonight."

Ellie grinned and grabbed her sweater. "I love you, Aunt Cordelia."

Cordelia smiled and waved her hand. "Go on, child. I'll see you soon. We will talk of your future then. Just don't let the Parkers or anyone else dictate your life. Be strong for me."

She nodded as the screen went dark. Cordelia told her so few things, but in this, at least in her love, she was complete and clear. Ellie hurried through the door and down the stairs, two at a time. The new maid poppets lined the hallway, programming clearly incomplete. One had opened the door, letting Natan in, but swung it closed with a rude slam as soon as he crossed the threshold. Another of the maid poppets stripped his jacket off but didn't seem to know what to do with it. Natan pulled at it, swearing softly, but she wouldn't let go. The poor maid poppet groaned and huffed as he tried to get the jacket out of her fisted hands.

"Release, Lydia," Ellie said, reaching out to take the jacket from her. She smiled and shook the jacket out straight, handing it back to him. He returned the smile, but his was tinged with nervousness. "Sorry. Thom usually..." Thom. She'd gotten through the day trying not to think about him, but it came rushing back now. Maybe her first date ever would be enough to get her mind off of how much she missed him.

Natan bowed to her, but the gesture seemed suddenly oldfashioned. Stupid. It might have been sweet if she didn't know about him and Joceylin, or if she hadn't come to dislike this whole process. She returned the greeting with a shallow, but appropriate dip of her own—all of society's niceties were like dances in a grand ballroom. Each orchestrated step led to another, as if there really was no choice, just measured movements.

In Devolution Society, because of the limits on births and the strict stance on dome city intermarriages, all families created upwardly mobile alliances striving to collect more power, more prestige, and more poppets. Not that all of the "leaders" of society, the politicians, for example, came from the families of the highest poppet ownership. Widow Douglas, for example, didn't own poppets. She'd utilize poppets at the senate, and while she was out, but never in her home, to Cordelia's dismay. Mrs. Douglas's name's currency, its very value, came from its connection to the government for hundreds of years back. When she married, she married another family of great politicians, thus increasing her social capital. Names and their preservation held more value than anything.

The Parkers and the DesLoges were the same. Because they were the most important industrialists, highest earners, and owned the most poppets in all the dome cities of US NOAM, the joining of their families through marriage had seemed a foregone conclusion.

As she watched Natan rise from the deep traditional bow, foregone conclusions were beginning to get on her nerves. What the Parkers wanted. What her mother wanted. What about what she wanted? Or what Natan wanted?

She reached her hand out. He started to kiss it, but she pulled his hand down, and clutched it gently with hers. "Come on Natan, let's just get out of here, okay? Where will we go?"

Natan paused, seemed to collect his thoughts, nodded, and pulled her toward the door. Lydia opened it for them, and they stepped out into the dome-twilight.

"I thought we would go to dinner at my house. My parents would love to see you. Then, we could go to the theater. We have a box. I'm not sure what's playing."

Natan's words clicked and clacked across the rims of her tolerance. His voice, his cadence, and his clammy hands all combined in such a way that she knew the night would pass slow like molasses on a cold plate. In the car, he prattled on about his teams and the sports she never cared to watch. She smiled, nodded, and tried to be interested, but her mind fed her images of Thom and Moze and Cordelia and Joceylin. Especially Joceylin.

At dinner, his mother and father and Sasha all discussed the latest rulings from the Senate, the particular quality of the silks coming from CharLanta this year, and the latest uses of their new version of Plastique. All of it rattled around in her head until she knew--was absolutely convinced--that there was no future for her with any of them. They were putting on a show for her, talking in polite circles without ever really engaging her or Natan. She and Natan were pawns in the colossal game. The only thing joining with the Parkers would bring was her own despair. She wanted to blurt it out right then, to throw her napkin on the ground, and stand up and scream that they wouldn't be her future.

Only Sasha's friendship motivated her to keep the peace.

She ate the creamy coconut dessert whips and complimented their choice of poppets, as any well-mannered girl would. Then, she said, "Natan, will you take me home, please?"

They walked to the door together, a family—father, mother, Sasha, Natan—all the loveliest people. Their beautiful poppets lined the hall behind them, all but Jule. Jule was, of course, laid out next to Thom on a slab knitting new bones. Jule and Thom broken beneath the boot of Sasha, who laughed and hugged and promised to get together tomorrow. Ellie couldn't add it all up.

She said her goodbyes, and she and Natan walked down the magnolia-lined path. The river sang in the distance—a rushing, rhythmic noise. The silver dome-light muted the velvety green of the path, and the silence between them blossomed until both struggled to fill the void.

"I wanted—"

"You were—"

They both stopped.

"You first," Ellie said.

He shoved his hands into his pockets, rounding his back around this moment. His head hung as he looked off toward the river. Ellie watched him as he seemed to search for his words—words Joceylin had already given her in the car. His normal bluster and bravado had gone. This was the real Natan. A boy, like many others, nervous and unsure. But unlike others, he had a family destiny to mind. Other boys in their class probably had similar worries, but none quite as binding as the destiny with which Natan's family saddled him. She could see it now. Why hadn't she seen it before?

"I hate this, Ellie. You're more like a sister to me, you know?"

A sister? Wow. She hadn't expected the pain she felt.

Rejection hurts in its many forms.

"You don't like me either, right?" he asked.

"I don't *not* like you. I mean, I've always thought you handsome. But no, I've never really fancied you. I've always thought we'd figure it out when the time came. But here we are."

Natan grabbed her arm and pulled her around to face him. He stared deeply into her eyes, searching them. Finally, he shrugged. "I love Joceylin. I didn't mean to, you know, fall for her. But I did. I've been seeing her for a long time now. I know you don't really like her. Neither does Sasha. But that's just because you guys don't know her. She's smart and funny. She laughs with me. No one else makes me feel like I'm valuable. Me—not my name. Doesn't matter to them, though." He bumped her with his shoulder, not in a mean way—like he would a friend. They walked. "Sasha and Dad—they think I can be more than I am. They think... Well, I just don't think I can be a DesLoge, Ellie."

They moved along together, the silence more comfortable than before. He reached out and took her hand, gently this time. She let him hold her hand as they walked. Why not just be truthful instead of polite?

"I don't want you, Natan. I don't want anyone right now. If I step out of the way, will they let you have Joceylin? Her family is powerful."

"Powerful, yes. But not acceptable. Grave Hawkers aren't the kind of people that we Parkers marry. We marry industrialists. I spoke to Mother about it. She's the only one who cares what I want. She tried to talk to them for me. To tell them that we didn't have to always follow tradition. I mean, we control Plastiques. We have so much power already. But all they think of is how much more powerful we will be with the DesLoge name attached to us. It doesn't matter what Mother or I say. Dad and Sasha never listen to either of us."

He kicked a rock down the path.

"I wanted to hate you, Ellie. I wanted to. But you've always been nice to me."

Ellie nodded, wishing she was anywhere else. How weird it was to be talking about rejecting every plan, every expectation they'd ever shared. It had been a security blanket. When other kids at the Academy jockeyed for power, position, and standing with their relationships, she'd been always guaranteed the best beau by virtue of birth. There had been a certain simplicity in accepting what you are given. Only one real law ruled their lives—birth is destiny.

They rounded the path and pushed open the heavy

iron gate. It wheezed and sang a rusted song in complaint. From here, she could see the blazing windows of the DesLoge mansion with the massive oak branches hugging it from cellar to roof. Here on the grounds, she pulled him over to a gazebo covered in clematis flowers—one of the flowers that thrived in muted dome-light. They sat together for a few minutes, thinking, enjoying being on the same side.

"If I deny you, they could just go looking for someone else if they think Joceylin isn't respectable enough."

"I'll make her respectable, damn it!" Natan growled. "They don't know her. No one does."

"I think I met the real Joceylin today for the first time." Ellie smoothed her hands across her hair, pushing it back from her face.

"Do you care for Moze? Is that why you are so glad to free me?" The words weren't said with bitterness. His face was open and full of questions, his eyes twinkling.

Ellie shook her head. "No, it's not that. Really, it isn't. This isn't about me."

Natan nodded. "I hear Sasha and Dad sometimes. They really think they have this all in a bag. That if you marry me, you and I would be easy to deal with. They figure that eventually Cordelia will pass it down, then the sky is the limit."

She shivered to imagine the conversation between Sasha and Mr. Parker. It probably looked the same way conversations between Juni and Cordelia looked when they discussed her future, as if she wasn't even in the room—third person, never asking what she thought. It infuriated her. It made her feel powerless. All these people deciding things, making plans, never asking what was right or wrong, or even what either of them wanted.

"I hate this, Natan. Just go and be with Joceylin. If it is what you want, really what you want, then what can they do if I am the one who calls it off? I will deny you tomorrow, if you're sure."

He whooped and jumped up, pulled her into a spinning embrace, and danced her around the gazebo like a floppy rag doll. "Thank you, Ellie. Oh God, thank you."

"Put me down, Natan. It's fine. You're free." Just saying it made her feel lighter, the way he must be feeling too.

He bowed and kissed her hand, the formal response a Belle of a Beau could expect. Then he hugged her again, so close she thought she'd be bruised—the response of a friend. She returned his hug, circling him with her arms, honestly so glad that they'd broken it off. He leaned his forehead against hers and, eye to eye, he whispered one last "thank you." Then he took off at a trot, not toward home but toward a waiting autocar she could see at the end of DesLoge drive. Ellie squinted at the car. A flash of white hair confirmed that Joceylin waited for him.

Ellie turned toward the mansion. She needed to figure out how to deny Natan without destroying her relationship with Sasha. Could they still be friends? Would Sasha see this as a personal betrayal even though her brother could now be happy? Happiness. That was what she needed to focus on.

She opened the front door and stepped in. "Quite a show out there."

"Oh Juni, you scared me!" Ellie shrieked.

Juni came forward and grabbed Ellie's hand, dragging

her to the sitting room. She nearly tossed Ellie into the armchair. Juni sat, her thin body perched on the front edge of the chair, legs crossed at the ankle and beautiful black hair, smooth and rippled with light, hanging down her back. She looked like, at any moment, she could be swept up into a cloud with the angels. Not like the picture that she and Moze had found. That Juni hadn't been Plastiqued up to perfection. She'd been younger then, her face rounder and more real in the image Ellie had been studying each night. Back then, with her too-big nose and thinner lips, her mother had looked so happy.

Now, she looked livid.

"What's this I hear?" Juni's hands folded and unfolded, fluttering like birds in her lap. Nerves? Juni never seemed to be affected by anything. Her usual calm facade cracked and crumpled as she spoke. "I can't believe just how ridiculous you are. It's some kind of payback for how I was. I just know it."

"What?" Ellie leaned away from her mother. She wasn't used to this kind of clarity coming from her.

"You're going to ruin everything!" Juni leaped up and paced. She trailed her fingers across the lampshade, the tabletop, the marble mantelpiece, then back again. Drumming. Drumming her fingers all the time.

Ellie stood, feeling like she needed to be ready to defend herself or maybe even run. Juni had never hurt her before but, then again, she'd never really taken an interest in what Ellie did, let alone get angry at her for something. That was too much effort. Juni turned, seemed to harden, drawing up until her shoulders squared and her neck muscles corded up.

She marched over and grabbed Ellie by the shoulders, shaking her.

"You aren't really going to let the Parker boy get away, are you? Is your head full of bubbles? If you marry him, you will cement your claim to DesLoge Com. Don't be a little fool!"

Ellie pulled out of her grip. "What are you talking about? Aunt Cordelia said—"

"I know what she said. She said it to me, too. But look at me! What she says and what she does can be two different things. Think about it!"

The dome breeze ruffled the velvet curtains, so cool and refreshing usually, now made her shiver. Think about what? Cordelia had been nothing but wonderful to Ellie. Raised her when Juni wasn't around for her. Loved her. Took care of her.

"You are walking on a thin line made up of traditions, expectations, and a stony heart that will toss you away if you become inconvenient. You are not so precious that she can't get another one of you. Do you understand? I know she makes you feel like you are so special, but if you do the wrong thing..." Juni crossed her arms across her thin chest, nails digging into her shoulders. "What you've got with Sasha as a bestie and Natan as your beau, that makes you valuable to the company, don't you see?"

"I am valuable to the company, no matter what. Cordelia told me so today." The heat in her cheeks, the anger, didn't mask the deep well in her gut. This unexpected wash of cool fingers and fear sweeping over her felt like truth.

"That's what she says, what she believes...but Ellie, my little Ellie...." Tears from nowhere, tears like a stream overflowed Juni's eyes. Eyes that never cried or cared or seemed to see her. Eyes that were only hers now. "Ellie, she'll shove you aside. She will. She's done it before." Ellie looked closely at her mother. "She did it to me."

Ellie started to reach out but jerked back her hand. She didn't want to be rejected. Juni turned toward the tall French doors overlooking the river and the beautiful yard of trees grown at great expense, a testament to DesLoge power.

"I didn't marry right."

Ellie joined her mother at the door. "What do you mean?"

"I mean, I didn't marry my beau. I denied him and married your father."

The hairs on Ellie's neck stood as if her skin had come to attention. The dome-light was muted in the night phase, but even so, the shimmers off the river seemed bright. Or maybe it was just that she stared too hard, keeping her eyes wide. She hoped that her mother would keep talking.

"Who is my father?" Ellie's heart hammered, chest thumping like the inside of a great bell. "Who?"

Juni gasped in two lungful of air and sobbed it right back out. Painful. This conversation, the most talking they'd ever really done, clearly hurt Juni. It cut her deep enough to make her real. To make her react. Juni shook her head, raised her fist to her mouth, and sobbed lightly into it. She shifted away from Ellie, away from her probing. Perched on one foot, the other toe tapped, rolling on her pump's rounded toe. Ellie put her hand on Juni's arm, just a feathery touch to let her know she cared.

"Go ahead. I won't ask anymore."

"I can't tell you, Ellie. I can't because if I do, Cordelia will find out, and she will deny me. Me. Her own flesh and blood. I'll be put out and sent to the wilds with nothing. I...I made my life long ago." Juni planted her foot and pulled Ellie into a one-armed embrace. "Listen, I chose to marry my love. At first, it was okay. She accepted us, but later she found out who he was. She couldn't forgive me. Even when you...even when we produced an heir, she couldn't forgive me. She made me... I had to give you up, you see? I had to... go away."

Ellie felt like she'd been hit. Her body tensed around the horror of it all. Cordelia had stolen her?

"Why would she say that I don't have to marry him then?"

Juni shrugged. "A test? Maybe she hopes someone more appropriate will come along. Maybe the Parkers will be inspired to offer some kind of compensation or some innovation to keep the match alive. But here's the truth—you are replaceable."

The awkward embrace became a full-blown hug—the only one her mother had ever given her. After a long moment, Juni pushed her back to arm's length, looking closely at her face. Her gaze slid down to her neck, to the leather thong necklace hanging there. Her eyes widened. One long, elegant finger dipped, hooked the leather string, and pulled the small bag out of her shirt, where it had been hidden all night.

"Ellie, where did you get this?" she whispered. "You can't let Cordelia see it."

Ellie re-tucked the necklace. "You've seen it before?"

Her mother nodded again on the verge of tears, though

this time Ellie wasn't sure if the tears were angry or fearful. "That's a Resurrectionist key. The man who owned that... well, he isn't welcome here. He's dead, though. Long dead."

"Ridley Brown?" Ellie asked.

"Don't say his name! Don't ever say his name, honey. It's trouble. He's a Resurrectionist who hurt Aunt Cordelia. He's off limits. Put that necklace back where you found it, and never mention him again."

Juni walked away, sniffling, to the door. She paused, purse draped elegantly on her wrist. "Marry Natan, stay in her graces and then someday...maybe we can both find a path to goodness. I'm sorry, Ellie. I'm so sorry."

Then, with a whirl of her silky skirt and sable hair, Juni escaped the gravity of DesLoge Mansion and Ellie's problems.

Ellie made her way up the stairs, bodily exhausted and nearly dragging herself along. But her mind whirled with worry. Who should she believe? Cordelia, who said she wanted her to be independent of the Parkers? Or Juni, who said she had been tossed to the side? Ellie fell into her bed, clutching the pillow to her body. What should she do?

DOCUMENT 9: VID-AD ANNOUNCING ARRIVAL OF NEW STOCK AT DESLOGE COM

To be sold,

Next Harold-day—

A shipment of 94 prime, strong poppets consisting of 39 males, 15 young males, 24 females, 16 young females.

Just arrived from the wilds. Available at DesLoge Com Market.

CHAPTER 9

The closet spit out a skirt of soft flowing gauze that skimmed the top of her knees, one of her favorites. Its mint color made her feel jolly, and its flowing shape at the knee made her hips less noticeable. The cami shell top, pink with little roses all along the edges, and simple gray shrug weren't showy, but they were cute. Cordelia would approve. Fashionable enough, but still practical. She pulled the clothes on, tying and settling the skirt, and brushing the cami into place.

The call clicked and beeped as the maintenance manager answered with a snappy, "DesLoge Poppet maintenance, how may I help? Is this an emergency?"

Ellie slid her feet into flat silver shoes. "No emergency," she said, leaning forward and strapping the wraps. "This is Ellie DesLoge."

"Miss DesLoge." Surprise in the efficient voice. "Calling about the poppet called Thom?"

"Yes, how long before he will be returned?" Ellie flicked on the vidscreen. The flash of light blinded her for a moment, then she could see the tiny woman, who'd sounded so efficient, with her feet up on the desk, reading *Belle*, the magazine of beauty and culture. Perhaps she hadn't noticed the vidscreen pop on.

Ellie cleared her throat. The woman glanced up, wheeled back, and fell out of the chair with a clunk.

"Crap." She popped back up and brushed her hands through her hair. "Sorry. Let me check on him."

She started to move off screen, but Ellie stopped her.

"Wait. I'd like to see him, please."

"Uh, that's not standard operating procedure, Miss DesLoge."

"What?"

The woman seemed to draw herself up, puffing up like some selfimportant bird. "Yes, I can make a report, but..."

Ellie had seen Cordelia handle things like this a thousand times. The trick, according to Cordelia, was to puff up bigger than your adversary. She squared her shoulders and pulled the comvid close to her so that her face filled the screen. She gathered up her voice and her anger, like she'd seen her aunt do so many times in the past.

"You will do as I ask. You will show me my property and give me a complete report. You will do this, or I will have your job. Now!"

The woman's face paled. "Yes, Ma'am."

She hustled away, the vidcamera panning after her toward a wall of flesh—poppets—every type and size hanging from rings that encircled their hands, legs, and necks, holding them in place. The technician hopped on a hover disc and whizzed upward a couple of stories, then jetted some thirty feet to the left. Thom's swollen face came into the frame as the woman's hover disc stopped in front of him. He looked pretty bad to Ellie, but then again she was unnaturally attached to her poppet. She shoved the thought down before it overwhelmed her courage.

"Well?" Ellie raised her voice even louder. "What's his status?"

"His arm's near mended. His face needs a bit more restructuring. Nose broken. You can have him back tomorrow. We will have it fixed by then."

"What of the other one? Jule?"

The woman faced her, was about to speak, but then thought better of whatever complaint she might have made. Ellie smiled at that. Cordelia used her gruff nature to cut through the self-important resistance of her underlings. On Ellie, it felt like being a toddler dragged around in Mommy's nice heels. She liked the look but hated the fit. Not for the first time, she wondered what kind of CEO she'd be when it was her turn to take the helm of DesLoge Com.

If Cordelia let her. If.

Juni's warning sat heavy on her.

She shook her head to clear the thought. "So? Jule?"

The hover disc carried her back to the ground, where she stepped off in one swift motion. She walked into the next area where poppets lay, scattered in pieces, enveloped in liquid. Some of the poppets writhed on metal tables while doctors sewed them together and dosed them with the base chemicals used to make Plastique, correcting rips, stabs, breaks, and tears.

Jule lay on one of the tables. The signs of massive blunt force trauma were clear in the ribs that sat in jagged forms trying to heal. Her face's delicate bones couldn't hold the swollen eyes and blackened cheeks with their usual grace. She looked as if this face would swell with the fluids of healing right off her skull. Maybe seeing this... maybe it was a bad idea.

"Thank you." She switched off the vidscreen, though Jule and Thom still seemed to hang there in her mind.

She stalked out of the room and downstairs into the kitchen, not even bothering with the dining room. The house poppets milled about doing what they were programmed to do. A thorn sat in her mind, twisting each time she looked at them. The world of Santelouisa, her world, sometimes seemed a beautiful song that purred and lilted and lifted everyone to amazing heights—civilization, innovation, art, and society, all enriched, all incredibly fulfilling. Other times, times like this one, it was like the song soured and false notes crept in, destroying the harmony. Here in the kitchen, with all of them, the poppets, swirling about making her life work, Ellie felt empty.

Em, the chef poppet, whipped eggs and milk together into a froth and added fresh basil, all grown in the wilds on farms like Moze's. When the chef poppet poured the egg concoction into a sizzling iron pan, Ellie watched his face for any of the signs of what the Academy had proclaimed sentient beings, live citizens, possessed. Joy. Anger. Sadness. Actions taken without direction, reflex or training. Devotion.

Love. Pain. The ability to speak. Thought. That was the one that Ellie always struggled with inside. Thought. How could they see what went on inside a poppet's head? How could anyone be sure they didn't think? At the Academy, the official answer had been that thinking creatures would find a way to give indications that they thought. Poppets didn't. Did they?

Ellie shook her head and took the plate that Em passed to her. Soft yellow eggs fluffed and grilled, veggies layered in and steaming. How could something without a soul make magic like this? The bite she took confirmed it. Between muffled chews, she said to Em, "Oh...mmmmm, Em. So...delicious."

Though he didn't react or stop his ceaseless chopping, folding, and kneading, she thought she saw a slight dip of the head. A few more bites, and she allowed herself to be shuffled out the door. Poppet maids she didn't even know pushed her bag and compad into her hands. She stepped into the waiting autocar. Time to meet Moze.

She went downtown early on purpose. She wasn't where Moze wanted her to meet in just thirty minutes. Instead, she was on her tiptoes, peeking through the window of an old factory in the GasBright district. Set aside for the young and unmarried Santelouisans, this part of town seemed unfinished, always becoming something. Bare brick walls and iron gates, brightly lit neon shops, where pleasures of all kinds could be had. Here, the black sheep children of good families could rebel against tradition without exposing themselves to the horrors that old-time runaways suffered.

Sasha had dared her to do this, but until now Ellie had not felt up to visiting this part of town.

Last night, when the elder Parkers had gone to see about dessert and Natan sat sulking at the table, Sasha had pulled her aside and handed her a paper with this address on it.

"Just go see. He's a Resurrectionist. I know it."

"No. The widow goes to church with your family, Sasha. Why would you think such a thing?" Ellie had lied to her bestie. Of course, she knew he had been a Resurrectionist in the wilds. He'd told her. Ellie felt awful. What kind of friend lied like that to a bestie? Even remembering it made her head hurt.

"Go, before you go to the library with him. You should see how crazy they are."

Ellie had agreed, mostly because she didn't want to talk about it anymore, but here she was, balancing on a neatly painted little crate that sat outside of a mostly curtained window. She pressed her face against the glass, silently cursing the whole bestie thing. If she didn't do it, she'd have her own conscience to deal with. Such is sentience. Sometimes she wished she could be as empty-headed as a poppet.

Ellie shivered thinking about Jule and her beautiful bruised face. That wish of a moment ago, she surely didn't mean it.

Movement beyond the curtains pulled her attention back, and she pressed her face hard against the glass. She worried that the people walking behind her were getting an eyeful of her unders, but if they were GasBrighters, a little flash of a girl's panties probably wouldn't shock them. Not that Ellie really knew what went on behind the brightly curtained glass of the closed shops. She only knew that girls of good families didn't go inside those shops if they valued their reputations.

Movement again but unidentifiable. She jumped down from the crate and made her way back behind the building. She pushed the wooden door and stepped through into a sweet-smelling hallway. Walking down the hall, she passed door after door, all closed but, behind them, she heard occasional muffled murmurs and thumps. Her heart raced as she moved through the last threshold into the wide-open space of the warehouse. Scattered large machines still bolted to the floor sat like hulking sentinels. In the center of the space were chairs—white wooden chairs set in a squared pattern, open at the corners for people to walk through. Each side of the square held five rows filled with people, eyes closed and silent. No sound. No echoes. No speakers chanting out a benediction.

Ellie moved behind one of the machines, sure they'd all snap out of their meditation and rush at her with an angry rebuke.

No movement. Not a word. Watching them in their silence quickly became, well...boring. The church Ellie went to, Soul Ascensionist, wove sound and color and movement into every church day. No one left without the shouted singsong of the preacher ringing in their heads. The music, full orchestration backed up by the talented star singers of Santelouisa, stayed with her for days after every service. This silence was strange.

She scanned the people sitting in rows so quietly. Men and women sat together, each caught up in their own thoughts. Some faced upward, eyes squeezed shut in concentration. Some with heads bowed seemed to stare at their hands clasped in their laps. Others...wait. Poppets? Poppets sat among the parishioners. Why were they there? They stared ahead, toward the middle of the square, which sat empty. Like a poppet mind.

"I am moved," a woman said and stood. She walked to the center of the square.

"Praise be," the congregation answered.

She raised her hand toward the ceiling. All the parishioners—not the poppets—did the same. Like sprouting blades of grass, arms sprung into the air. After a moment, she dropped her hands, as did the rest. Ellie couldn't see why they did—wait! A poppet stood next to the speaker. Who had sent it?

"This is Brad." The woman put her hand on the poppet's shoulder.

"Brad," they all answered, voices mixed in a swirl of sound.

Silence again, but this time it buzzed with potential. The parishioners leaned forward in their seats. The poppet's hands climbed slowly and surely toward the ceiling. When its hands reached the highest point, Ellie noticed the hands of the other poppets raising in answer. What was going on?

Finally, she picked out Moze's face among the crowd, his eyes open wide and full of bright intensity. The woman in the center seemed near to swooning with the power of her happiness, and she raised her hands again to join the poppets. They all began to sway, as if some unspoken command had been issued. Ellie crept forward to hear better because the woman's whispers didn't reach her ears.

"...Holding on..."

"...Life eternal..."

The group stood in one shuffling exhalation. Like a blossoming, their movement filled the air and the space of the factory. Ellie's fascination led her forward another few steps. Her fear of them evaporated. What were they doing? The whole congregation stretched their right arms toward the poppet and the woman in the center of the square. They put their left hands on the shoulder of the person to their left, creating concentric squares that together seemed to electrify the air around her. The hairs on Ellie's neck rose as the spiritual currents of the room spun.

Suddenly, the woman's voice rose to just above a whisper but still boomed out across the room, gathering its power in the echoes and hums of their perfect attention.

"Brad...He was Bradlin Forrest."

The woman's eyes squeezed shut, and she leaned closer to the poppet next to her. Her hand remained on his shoulder, but the rest of her body moved closer to the poppet's quiet form.

"Husband, father."

Ellie moved out from behind the machine. It was too far. She couldn't see enough. Another machine was closer, so she hurried across the cement floor, which had to have been swept clean many times to be as dustless as it was. From here, she could see better, but she wasn't well hidden.

"Bradlin's children and wife died in front of him before the Hawkers stole his life away."

How could she know that? Was this some kind of trick?

"I see his wife. He calls her...Sherl. Blond hair, almost white. Blue eyes. Small frame, maybe 110 pounds."

The poppet turned, his hand lowering until it lay on her shoulder. They formed a closed circuit, looking into each other's faces.

"Two children. A boy, Jacen, was only three years old. Redhead like a carrot. Freckled and sweet. Little Cecal, a girl with her mother's hair. Six years old."

One of the men near Moze spoke up. "My neighbor has the boy. I've seen him. Jace, they call him. He's their daughter's poppet doll. I will shepherd him."

The congregation replied, "Praise be."

The poppet in the middle had turned toward the man who spoke about Jace.

Who had programmed him to do such a thing? At her church, the pastor talked about how the Resurrectionist church zealots deceived their members using "brain washing"—some kind of technique that made poppets do things that they hadn't been programmed to do. She watched Moze's face, so fascinated by what happened in the center of the chair square. He believed. For a moment, she thought about running. Running back home, away from this strange display, away from this boy, but in the end, what was she going to run to? A crazy mother who thought her worthless? An aunt who might disown her?

A defunct beau and a violent bestie? Ellie watched the pop pet shaking, shuddering like he was cold, with the woman's hands on him and her voice slicing through the air like a blade. The strangeness of their connection held her against her will, though on the inside good little Ellie screamed out that she should run.

Silence stretched out in the hall.

"Will no one volunteer to find his poor little Cecal?"

None spoke. Ellie's eyes found Moze. He was looking right at her. She leaped back behind the machine, pressing her body to it as if she could fade into it somehow and escape being caught.

"I will search for her, Bradlin Poppet," said Moze.

"Praise be," the flock said in answer.

Ellie hurried back to the hallway and the exit that led out into GasBright Square. She reached the door and pushed it open with care, hoping the muffled creak wouldn't make it back down the hall of doors. Maybe Moze hadn't really seen her when he spoke up about Cecal Poppet. He could have been looking at someone in line where she stood.

She wandered down the street to a coffee house she'd seen on the way in. On the corner stood a streetlamp, the most famous in all Santelouisa. Iron and black, with globes of actual fire as big as her head. Flames, honest burning flames, were only allowed here in GasBright Square and at the homes of the richest families. Only those places contained the safety devices that the law dictated for protection. An unchecked fire in an enclosed dome would be disastrous with smoke and a lack of escapes. Ellie shivered when she thought about it.

This lamp, a holdover from the Antedevolution city, enclosed with non-combusting plastiglass, the same material as the city dome, served as a landmark for all who lived here or visited Santelouisa. It harkened back to the time before, when Santelouisa had been open to the air and to the people of old, no matter what class. The lamp represented the passions and failure of that time. By itself, the ever-burning lamp consumed more power and more fossil fuel than the entire dome consumed now. The inky smoke leeching off the flame gathered at the base of the monument in a vile cloud, sucked out through a low pipe and into the underground of the ancient layers of the city. A monument to waste, to the way things used to be, burning as a brilliant reminder of the city's sad past. That's where Moze wanted to meet.

Ellie grabbed a sweet coffee and a seat next to the window where she could see the lamp and Moze when he came. She wasn't sure what she would say to him if he had seen her at the Resurrectionist meeting. The service seemed crazy, near treasonous now that she had escaped it. Pretending to somehow read a poppet's past like some psychic from the old movies that Antedevolution people used to watch. Things like that were ridiculous.

The coffee smelled of cloying cinnamon and hazelnut. When she sipped it, the bitterness made her mouth pucker. Clearly, the poppets here lacked Em's talent as chefs. Ellie looked at the poppet behind the counter. The female seemed halting in all her movements, disjointed like a broken doll. Her skin, creamy as buttermilk, shone under the soft globe lights selected for their warmth and beauty, like most things in Santelouisa.

Ellie knew that beauty mattered in the dome. The work her aunt and the Parkers and everyone else did was to make life lovely. To make every minute safe and sweet. She sipped at the drink, savoring it even if it didn't rise to the DesLoge standard, feeling close to all the dome dwellers.

The dark of dome started falling, a thickening and warming of the air that happened every day. The silvering of the dome itself softened the light. Roads began to light up, and soft white footlights lined the raised surfaces of every curb, every step, every building corner until GasBright Square blazed and twinkled from every surface she could see, living up to its name and reputation.

"Have you ever been here before?" Moze was right next to her.

"Oh, you scared me!" Ellie was surprised that he'd snuck up on her. "No. Never."

Moze pulled a chair out and straddled it, propping his crossed arms on the top of the back. He looked at her without talking for a long moment, seeming to evaluate her. Ellie squirmed under the scrutiny.

"Do you want anything?" She waved toward the lovely poppet behind the counter.

He shook his head, not even looking. "I know you wanted to go to the archives, but I think I need to show you some things. Things that Aunt Cordelia will never show you."

"What about our project? We need to get to work."

"Don't worry. Everything we see tonight will apply to a project about slavery."

She gazed into his eyes—eyes like chocolate—framed by his jagged golden halo of hair. "You'll be able to keep us safe here, right?"

She wasn't usually frightened in Santelouisa. Crime was a product of the former era when there were people who

didn't have much. The elimination of the poor had elimi-
nated violence and theft. But still, her classmates' whispers
about GasBright Square sometimes shocked her. He nodded.
They stood and turned to leave, but as they did, Moze caught
sight of the pretty poppet working the cappuccino machine
with clumsy jerks and shudders. He studied her for a
moment, taking in her platinum locks, upturned nose, and
tiny hands. Ellie watched for a moment, trying to figure out
what he was looking at, but he pulled her gently forward, out
into the open square.

The humid air pressing down on her body filled her
lungs with a wringing heat. Though it took some getting
used to, it made her skin shine with a fine layer of sweat.

"Why is it so hot here?" She fanned herself as they
walked together toward the red lights of the lower square.

"It's what the clientele here likes, I'm told." He walked
like he owned the place, confident in his steps and his shoes.
A casual observer wouldn't see a boy from the wilds if they
looked at him. Sure, he dressed more simply than most in his
denims and his white cotton shirt, but he moved like he
belonged. He always moved that way. Like he danced. She
quickly looked down to her own feet, embarrassed by her
fascination with Moze.

"How do you know so much about GasBright Square? I
mean, you are new here."

He smiled. "My church is here." He looked at her in a way
that told her he knew she already knew that.

"Um, Moze," she said, words stuttery as they came out. "I
saw... I mean, I kind of—"

"Look, here we are." He squeezed her hand and said, "I

just need you to trust me. Help me tonight. I'm all yours for the project and for research. I'll even dust your Ellie Museum, if you want. But tonight, let's see if we both don't learn something new."

They stood in front of a huge glass-fronted building that seemed to shine from all sides with neon signs, bright chrome, and lit-up pedestals that held poppet after poppet. *Buy or Rent Here*, one sign said. Another, all in bright green, said *Special Orders Accepted*. Above it all, on a sign shaped like an arrow pointing down toward the main entrance, a brilliantly flashing yellow and orange set of letters proclaimed *DesLoge Com Poppets*.

"What is this?" She asked even though she'd already guessed.

"It's funny how little they've shown you. I guess you aren't in on the day-to-day of the company's business, huh?"

"No, I mean she—Aunt Cordelia—tells me some stuff, but not... What is this place, Moze?" She didn't wait for him to answer. Really, why should she? This place had her name on it. She ought to know what it did. So, she walked in.

"Wait. Just wait, Ellie." He tried to pull her back. She shrugged him off, weaving through the dozens of pedestals that held poppets of every type, each wearing the plain uniform of black short pants and a red shift top embroidered with the teal insignia of the company across the front. The poppets, not yet activated, stood stock still in a stasis beam that held them up in various friendly poses.

This male poppet, maybe fifteen years old at death, had his hand extended in a mock handshake. This female, an older lady with a hefty price tag on the base of her pedestal due to her skill as a seamstress, had the tools of her trade—a needle threaded and scissors at the ready. So many poppets.

Moze touched her shoulder. "Don't you ever wonder where they come from?"

Ellie continued walking through the display toward the middle of the showroom. "They come from funeral homes, of course. Where else would they come from?"

Moze shrugged. He paused in front of the special orders department and hooked a thumb at a sign outside the high marble threshold into a showroom dominated by a large vidscreen. The sign said, *Special orders require 3–6 weeks of fulfillment time. We will make your poppet dreams come true.*

The room stood empty, but for the large screen and a compad table near it. They stepped up to the table, and an instructional holovid began to play. Aunt Cordelia, the beloved face of DesLoge Com, spoke to them glowingly, her face softened by the plasti-makeups applied by the greatest of artists available. Only Ellie would recognize that this wasn't Cordelia's real face, with its so expertly prepared smile and lilting gaze. Only Ellie could see the fiction. Cordelia's visage seemed to appraise them, then it spoke. "I congratulate you on your excellent taste. Who wants a poppet designed with someone else in mind? The most discerning citizens design their own poppets. Please select the characteristics you would like to purchase."

Ellie started to step up to the table, but Moze beat her there. He dialed in features. Long brown hair, brown eyes, heart-shaped face, medium build, and small hands. Who was it he was describing?

He looked at Ellie for a moment, then went back to selecting. "My mom," he said.

"Why are you doing that? You said she died in the wilds. You saw her. I mean, did she—"

"The Hawkers got her," he hissed. "I saw them loading the hover trams with them. That's what they do."

"Shhhhh..." Ellie saw the salesman watching them from the corner, leaning against the doorframe in that way that adults do, filling a space puffed up like some kind of goofy mating bird. A quick jerk made Moze see the salesman watching them so closely.

Moze leaned toward the compad, as if he needed to adjust his order and let his fingers swipe across the screen, though he didn't change the parameters. He lowered his voice. "It's what they do, Ellie. They steal people. They stole my mom and everyone we had on the farm. What do you think they do with them?"

"I don't know. I—"

"Can I help you all?" The salesman ambled toward them, his steps heavy. His gait reminded her of an old-day cartoon show with the bulldog cop, whose cheeks flapped and fluttered while he walked his beat. The salesman's cheeks were nowhere near as impressive. Ellie put her hand up and covered her mouth so her nervous giggle wouldn't show.

He crossed the distance and finally stood next to them, reading over Moze's order. His haughty pose made him look like he understood things in the world that she and Moze wouldn't get for many, many years. "Nice choices here, son, but you don't need a special order for that. We've got merchandise in stock that fits your parameters. You are authorized to purchase poppets for your household, right, kiddies?"

Ellie started to tell her employee that she was a bigwig, but Moze grabbed her hand, silencing her. "I am, sir," he said. "I'm the Widow Douglas's ward. I'm looking for a housekeeper with the ability to farm. We have a little garden that needs some constant weeding. So, I'm hoping for...an outsider."

The man rubbed his pointy, white-bearded chin as he considered this. "The Widow, eh? Don't get many orders for her house."

Moze leaned on his bent knee in a way that reminded her of Natan when he tried to impress his boys. Moze pursed his lips, nodded, and said, "That's the past. Now that I'm here, I'm building up the staff. I'm looking for a certain type, and we're willing to pay more."

The salesman's eyes lit up, dollar signs or a hope of a bright, happy future seemed to play across his features. "Yes, sir. I'll gather some of the specs on what has come in and what we're expecting soon. I'll have the artist come in and give us an image based on your needs. We'll see what we can find. Follow me."

The salesman led them into a private showing room where a vidscreen reeled through hundreds of options that Moze used as a template to identify his mother's features. The process was slow. He pointed Ellie to a compad that sat on a desk made of sleek red wood with a padded chair behind it. She picked up the compad and sat down next to him, cradling the dark screen on her lap.

"Ellie, are you wondering why we are here?"

She shook her head angrily. Did he think she was stupid? "Because you are a Resurrectionist? I mean, I get it. You are trying to find your mom, right? I don't think it's healthy, but I won't stop you. You aren't going to be satisfied until you've searched."

Her words sounded colder than she'd meant them to sound. He drew back from her, brows hardened and mouth thin.

He stared at her for a minute, like there was something else he wanted to say, but then he turned back to the vid. "Just put your palm on that compad."

"Okay." She did as he said. The compad lit up, asking for a password. She turned toward him to ask what to do next, but the screen flickered, then showed the outline of her palm. The compad copied and highlighted her fingerprints. Circles and checks appeared on spots and whorls. The pad dinged, and a stream of information flowed past her eyes, rolling names and addresses, image files, and training briefs.

Moze nudged her with his elbow. "Send it to your compad, Ellie."

"That's not right. It's stealing."

"It's not stealing if you're the heir. Come on, Ellie. It's your company. I think you have a right to know what's going on in your company."

"It's Cordelia's company. Moze, I'm willing to help you, but I don't want to do anything that's going to make anyone else mad. Really, I've got Sasha yelling at me about Natan. My mother is not making any sense. I don't know how to make everyone happy. And then there's you."

She pulled her hand off the compad, stood, and began to

pace. She wasn't exactly angry, but she felt her heart racing anyway. If he was going to be a part of her life, and she did want him to be, she needed him to understand what was at stake for her.

"Look, I'm here," she said. "You told me you are a Resurrectionist, and I'm not even sure what that means anymore. They say you all are traitors to what we stand for. They say that the law hasn't caught up to what we know is true, that you all are thieves and terrorists. But you...you're here, and I like you. I feel bad for you about your folks. I'm making everyone I thought I could count on mad, and I'm throwing my future into the toilet, but other than that, I'd love to commit a death-felony with you. That's what the ancients called sarcasm, in case you don't recognize it." She lilted her voice as if scorn would finally make him see sense. Yet, he stood, watching her without comprehension, without any regret for his demands.

She tried again to get him to see his prying as unreasonable or at least to understand why she didn't want to be a part of it. "This looking in company files like a spy and violating the trust of the dead given to be poppets. Only the lowest would step between a man and his last wishes—only cowards and Resurrectionists."

Moze took her hand again—this time to try to calm her. "Can we at least look at the information, just to see what it says? He'll be back soon."

Ellie looked into his eyes. Though she could tell he'd live by whatever she'd decided, his face filled with desperation. He wanted this badly. In this moment, his intensity made her realize that this was what she really craved in her own life.

She wanted desperation and excitement. She craved it, and now she had it. Here in GasBright Square, where all the nasty things happened. Here she could help him find his mother if somehow his mother was being held by the Grave Hawkers, maybe for some mistaken crime.

She laid her palm on the compad, reactivating it. "What are we looking for?"

"My mother's name. Josine."

"You really think they would use her real name?"

Moze shrugged, but his shoulders seemed to sag lower as he did. So much terror hid behind his eyes. She didn't want to believe him, but how could she deny what sat in his bunched muscles and drooping, wan cheeks? He mourned. What would it hurt to eliminate this conspiracy theory of his? Perhaps then he would move on, would become part of the culture here, and give up his crazy connections to the Resurrectionists and the wilds.

Ellie scanned the information as it flowed by. Names. So many names. Who were all of these people reported in the DesLoge Com files? Too many names to be just this store. Too many to be all the poppets in Santelouisa. She looked him in the eyes again, then he turned toward the door. The handle jiggled, and the door opened an inch.

"He's coming, Ellie."

She flicked her hand across the information, selecting it all. "Copy to Ellie DesLoge's personal compad."

"Voice command accepted," the compad said.

Ellie tapped the screen as the door swung open, closing the files.

"Okay, young man, I've downloaded some future choices into this vid file. Would you like to review it?"

Moze shot her a glance and stood, dusting off his jacket's shoulders. She stood with him and sighed loudly, dramatically. The salesmen turned to her for the first time, staring at her not-so-remarkable features for a second, then the light of recognition flickered in his eyes. Shock bloomed on his face, mouth drooping, nose flaring, eyelashes reaching for the ceiling as his eyes widened.

"Holy crap, little lady. I didn't know it was you." He deflated, and his jowly haughtiness became something so much smaller.

"I'd prefer you call me Miss DesLoge. Your name is?"

"Vishon Burr, Miss."

"Thank you for putting that information together for us, Mr. Burr. Please send the file to the Widow Douglas's home vid for us." She flicked her fingers in rapid succession, a dismissal she'd seen Aunt Cordelia use often when her patience had run out. "I'm in the mood for an inspection. What do you say, Mr. Grayson?"

Moze nodded and stood next to her, tall and elegant. He crooked his arm for her hand and cracked a private grin as the man stumbled all over himself to show them around. Whatever he wanted her to see, she'd make sure they had the chance to see it.

"I'll go with you on this, but in the end, you need to explain yourself, Moze," she whispered through her fake, haughty grin.

They walked behind the large, swaying butt of Mr. Burr as he led them back through the showroom.

"And," Ellie whispered, leaning close, "you need to tell me about Ridley Brown."

They moved toward the back of the massive showroom. Ellie pulled the leather-thong necklace from her top and wiggled the pouch in front of him. He must have seen something like the bag before because his eyes lit up like they recognized the treasure she wore.

"Put that away. If the wrong person saw that... I promise."

"Good," she said.

Mr. Burr pushed open the double door into the next room. A much smaller, less sumptuous room. Here, there were counters, straps on the wall with deactivated poppets plugged into machines that pumped their fluids for them, naked poppets in pens, standing crowded away from the gates that would let them out.

"What is this room?" she asked. It smelled of bleach and body odor, but that smell wasn't the most unpleasant thing in the room. More unpleasant were the dead poppets stacked in the corner. Husks.

"Well, Miss DesLoge, Mr. Grayson, this is the trades room. You'll notice that these poppets aren't up to snuff. They're used, but we'll repurpose them. Waste not, want not."

Ellie pushed her hair back over her ear as she thought about this. She'd never considered what happened to poppets when people upgraded or got rid of old ones. Why hadn't that ever been a question she'd asked? She walked over with Moze to the pen, where poppets of all ages crowded into a back corner, their naked bodies covered in ashen skin. Were they cold?

"Why aren't they clothed?" Moze asked, his hand rubbing the arch of his eyebrow.

"Easier to see defects, to fix problems as they come in. Besides, they don't care, do they?"

Moze's eyes seemed to harden, not happy about the naked poppets. Ellie stared at them. What did he see that she didn't? To her, these looked like background. They were, as her aunt had said, machinery. But something about them, about their condition, was hurting Moze. She wanted to see things as he did, if only to understand why he would become a Resurrectionist and stand against all the advances of the domed cities.

Thom.

She looked into the faces of the naked, crowded poppets and tried to imagine what she would feel if her Thom crouched there, naked and alone. Something inside her bent at that thought. She shifted her hand until it caught Moze's and clasped it tightly, trying to drive away his anger and her own confusion.

"When will they be..."

"Returned to service? Well, some we will send back to DesLoge Com for complete reprogramming. Some of them have picked up corruptions, and until those tics are removed, they aren't fit for service."

"Tics?" Ellie asked.

"You know, they have ruts. Ruts? You've never heard? So, when a poppet has been with a family for a long time, they develop habits."

"Attachments," Moze said.

"No, son, that's not possible. They don't have human

potential like that. Their brains are dead. You learned this in your biology classes, right?"

Moze nodded, jerky—not really agreeing. Angry. He was like her Rosetta Stone, decoding things she'd never really considered before. Why would she have? She'd been brought up to believe, to cleave to these ideas. Poppets didn't feel, think, or have attachments. No way, because the DesLoge chemical compound was patented and guaranteed to revive the muscles and motor centers without accessing the higher thinking centers. Without a soul, thinking was ridiculous. Thom's sweet smile, his patient walk, and so many instances of lingering doubt about his lack of a soul surfaced in Ellie's thoughts.

"Not attachments? Habits then? Patterns? Routines?" Moze said and looked at Ellie, his gaze holding more meaning than even his pointed words. What did he want her to see?

"You are suggesting intelligence, son. I promise, without programming, there is none."

Ellie thought back to the Resurrectionist church. The poppet worried about his family, at least as the church women portrayed it. They'd pulled the names of the children from him. The poppets had moved together, supporting each other. She thought of Thom falling across Jule's body, taking the blows meant for her. Hadn't the past few days been empty at home without Thom and his strange, silent love? Of course, Aunt Cordelia would say she was anthropomor-phizing him, like when you draw a dog with big, human-looking eyes.

Ellie pushed past the salesman, past Moze, and went into the pen, examining the poppets.

"These are blanks?" she asked, using the word Cordelia did so often, so effortlessly in conversation. Ellie never really thought about the cold vein of disconnection that the word really suggested. She fought the urge to shiver.

"Yes, Miss."

She walked into the center of the poppets, their bodies so drawn and gray, and examined each. They weren't worn out, as her aunt had told her. She looked in their faces, pretending to check their teeth and the quality of their eyes the way a horse trader in the wilds might examine a new pony. Some had lovely hairstyles and supple skin, even though they were naked. These had been the poppets of households of care and repute. Clean nails, inset gems in their skin, whitened teeth. Cared for. Poppets you'd be proud to have in your mansion, your house, or business. The poppets all stared past her, disengaged as poppets should be until commanded to be otherwise.

Moze came up next to her, silent, but watching all of her movements. He stood stiff, like a right gentleman of Santelouisa, but from his eyes and his smile, she knew he approved of her observations.

"How much will a lot like this sell for once it's been reconditioned?" Moze asked.

"Hmmm, do you want an estimate, or do you want a true price for purchase, sir?"

"I want an exact price. A pre-auction price, but please be fair."

"Yes, I won't abide you overcharging my friend, Mr. Burr," Ellie said.

Burr dipped his head, turned his rounded body quickly back toward the main showroom, and hurried away, saying, "I'll be back, but it may take some doing to get the best price."

As the man moved past and out of the room, Moze pointed at her leather necklace.

"What?" Ellie whispered, her hands trailing up, fingers touching the lump under her sweater. "My necklace?"

She pulled the leather thong, bringing the bag out of her blouse—leather pouch tied off tight. With the poppets crowded all around, she tugged at the pouch, opening it. She reached in and pulled the wooden carved figure of the tiny woman out into the light. In her hand, it seemed so small and fragile, a bit of delicate beauty. She offered it to Moze, thinking he wanted it, but Moze shook his head. He pushed her hand away, she thought, but then realized he pushed it outward, toward the poppets crowded in the corner of the pen.

As her hand raised before them, the poppets seemed to focus, like their programming suddenly kicked in. Their eyes were fixed upon the wooden figure solemnly standing in her dress with her scarred forehead. Ellie gasped as they moved toward her, toward the figurine.

Moze put his hand over the hand of the nearest poppet reaching toward her with softened longing. Their faces hung slack, pleasantly as they always did, but their movements and their grasping said something different.

He closed her hand around the figure and guided her to

place it back in the bag. As she did, the poppets lost their focus, faded back into the default they'd been given. Blankness. They settled back into their fearful waiting for the chemical wipe that would come. But what had they been doing, reaching for the wooden woman? What did she mean to them?

Moze pulled her away, his eyes shifting to the doorway. As they left the pen, he said, "She is a symbol, not unlike the triangle flame of your Soul Ascensionism. She is the Moses. I am named after her."

He led her toward the back of the room, toward the desiccated pile they'd seen earlier. She crept forward, not really wanting to see what lay there.

"They moved toward the necklace, Moze. They responded. I know that wasn't in their programming. Do you know what that means?" Ellie's breath came in quick bursts.

He stood and faced her, waiting for her to come to whatever conclusion she would make.

"I knew this, Moze. I knew there was more to them, to Thom. They said there was no higher thought, but for them to react to a symbol like that... To react to something that they haven't been programmed for. I can't believe it. We have to tell Cordelia."

Moze shook his head and pulled on her arm, moving her back again toward the pile. "Not yet, Ellie. You need to know the whole thing. I need to show you the rest of the poppet story before you go off half-cocked. Be patient and trust me. I have to show you more about poppets—things that nice girls and regular folk don't really ever know. We Resurrectionists know because we have been fighting against poppet use for so long."

The idea made Ellie nervous. This went against everything she'd ever been taught. He called it poppet use. He thought they were sentient. What had the bio teacher said to justify poppetry? He'd said that sentience requires certain attributes like higher thought, free will, a culture and religion, a sense of self preservation, a conscience, and the potential to reproduce. She remembered because the explanation had, at the time, seemed so interesting to her.

The philosophical ideas behind poppetry, the idea that they really were just machinery had never sat right with her, but the explanations had made it easier to accept their service.

She'd never seen a dead body before, but because they were poppets, she'd dismissed them when they'd walked by earlier. Moze squatted down next to the pile, which was hip-high. He pulled the arm of the nearest poppet away from his face. As the arm fell away, the poppet's eye sockets yawned empty in his face, gaping and grim.

"Ughh," Moze said. "Transplants."

Ellie knew about this. Her aunt's eyes were transplants. Sasha's family made its living doing transplants along with chemical preservation on the aging of Santelouisa each day. Still, she'd never looked into the face of a poppet used for transplants. She'd imagined jars somehow, little glasses in farms where they grew eyes and teeth. But deep down, Ellie had always suspected reality might be like this.

She moved closer, needing to see. Needing to face just what her family's company was involved in.

On top of the pile was a smaller poppet, maybe five or six, white hair—a beautiful child. Ellie looked her over, top to toe, trying to figure out what had been used from her. Finally, she pulled the child's hands from under her. Three fingers had been removed from her hand, right at the palm. Just three fingers. Ellie pulled those hands into hers and flipped them over so she could see her palms. Something was there, written in blue, smeared ink. Ellie wiped her fingers across the cold, dead skin.

"Is it a tattoo?" Moze asked.

"Maybe," Ellie said. "If it is, I can't read it."

"Let me see." Moze took the hand, gently turned it into the light, and squinted. "Oh, no. Damn!"

Ellie had never heard him use bad language before. "What?"

She couldn't imagine what would make him so angry, but as she looked at the face of the little poppet—the sweet little angel face now dead and destroyed for fingers—just fingers, not even something vital. She felt her own anger bubbling.

"Her name." Moze shuddered, stifling a deep, wracking sob. "Cecal. This is little Cecal."

Cecal. From the service. He'd said he would find her, and he had. He picked up her tiny body from the pile, cradling it to him. He whispered words she couldn't hear but she could feel the comfort, the plea for forgiveness that wouldn't come. All this for a poppet. She shouldn't care about it, but her emotions were roiling, shifting from anger to bitter sadness.

"Moze." She touched his shoulder. No response. Just him holding the body close. "Moze, come on now. She was..."

"Just a poppet? Yeah, just a poppet. But this was a girl just a few months ago. Just a few months."

"How do you know that?"

He laid the body back on the pile and pulled her hands together across her tiny chest. "Because I saw her alive in the spring."

"You knew her?" Ellie pulled back. She'd never seen someone she'd known turned to poppet. Aunt Cordelia had it in her will that her body would be cremated. No one would stop her, even if it were against the "body and soul" law. It could happen, though.

"Her family lived in Liberty Lawrence, KS. We went to church together." He lifted his sleeve and showed her a faded blue set of marks on his left arm—his name tattooed on his arm. She reached out and traced the letters. *Moze Grayson of Liberty Lawrence.* "Our parents had us all tattooed. There were so many Hawker raids. So many attacks. They wanted to be able to find the turned, so they marked us. She got her tattoo the same day I got mine last year."

"So, you could be returned home? Like a ransom?" Ellie asked.

Moze shook his head. "So, we could be identified. They didn't tell the little ones that. It was bad enough that it stung. Lots of kids cried and squealed, but not Cecal. She was just a little kid, but she was so brave."

Ellie pulled Moze to his feet. "Let's go tell your church about her."

Mose glanced at her, a question in his eyes.

"I saw. I'm sorry. It's just...Sasha thought...Sasha thought... She sent me." She wondered how much she should tell him about what Sasha thought and what Sasha wanted her to find. Sasha's assumptions that she would be horrified by the Resurrectionists and run screaming back into the safety of her planned-out life, safe from such peculiar truths as these —well, it hadn't worked that way.

And what about Moze? What must he think of her? A spying sneak. He'd made an offer of friendship, offered her a chance to learn about people and things that had been purposefully hidden from her, and had made her feel better about her attachment to her poppet. How had she repaid him? Followed him. Invaded his privacy. Judged him for being different. What must he think? "I didn't mean..."

He shook his head and stared at the pile of poppets.

"I bet Sasha thought that my crazy church would scare you off, right? She doesn't like me because she doesn't understand. To her, to most of the people here, I'm a threat or I'm insane because I don't agree with... this." He touched Cecal's little grayed hand before leading Ellie back to the door. "I'm glad you were there. I thought I saw you, but when I looked again, I couldn't be sure. We aren't crazy, Ellie. You saw the poppets with your own eyes. They still respond and feel. They even think."

"I don't know exactly what I saw at your church, Moze." Moze started to answer her, but Salesman Burr reappeared, moving in quick, thumping steps, sweating as he reached them. "Sorry! First, I want to say how honored we are here to be serving you and your friend, Miss DesLoge. We have come up with several prices...the retail so you can compare, a discount, and what I think is the best of the offers, the employee discount. Since you are here Miss, you can of course take whichever of these you'd like. They are your poppets. We would just write them off to the Accounting Department."

All Ellie could think of was how Aunt Cordelia read everything related to the business every morning. Her throat constricted as she imagined having to explain the purchase of used poppets that she didn't want or need.

"No, no. He will be paying for them. The discount will be enough."

As he led them away to pay, she looked back and saw the poppets crowded together again and staring into the distance. Soon, these poppets would be at the Resurrectionist church, saved from reprogramming and parting out. Saved from being a Cecal.

DOCUMENT 10: FROM ACADEMY DE BELLUM-PUBLISHED ENCYCLOPEDIA

Eregel v. New Kansas: A High Court case held that the Federal Fugitive Poppet Act superseded a New Kansas law called the Kansas Freedom Act, which prohibited poppets from being taken out of New Kansas and into servitude, no matter their previous state of servitude in the domed cities.

Case Background

A poppet woman named Margaret was taken illegally by Resurrectionists to New Kansas from Santelouisa, where she had once been property to a man named John Ashore. In New Kansas, the Resurrectionists claimed that she lived in freedom and independence. Ashore's heirs decided to reassert their claim on her as property and hired Grave Hawker Simon Eregel to recover her.

Eregel led an assault and abduction on Margaret in Liberty Lawrence City, Kansas territory. They took

Margaret to Santelouisa, where she was destroyed by Ashore's heirs. The four men involved in the recovery were later captured by Resurrectionists and tried under the Kansas Freedom Act, which appoints penalties for Grave Hawker recoveries and the ultimate fate of the poppets returned. Eregel and his companions pled not guilty to kidnapping and manslaughter and argued that they had been duly appointed by John Ashore's heirs to arrest and return Margaret to Santelouisa.

Eregel and his companions appealed their sentence to the High Court on the grounds that the New Kansas law was not able to supersede federal law. The Fugitive Poppet Act states that property rights are to be protected in all lands and territories of US NOAM, regardless of local laws.

CHAPTER 10

Back in GasBright Square, dome-dark's silvered evening accented the beautiful bright neon signs of each shop, each bright bar, and every destination that the young, the risqué, and the experimenting citizens visited. Their panting excitements, their temporary flouting of societal restrictions, and the heat of their frenzies blanketed the square in a thick humidity that made Ellie's clothes sticky. Her skin drew up as an artificial breeze blew across the sheen of sweat on her skin. Moze's silence wound around her like a spring, tightening inside her chest. He looked defeated. This is what poppetry did to him.

She wanted to say, "None of this will matter when I take over DesLoge Com," or "I can free any that you want me to free," or even "We can change it all, together."

Together. That's how she wanted him to think of them. She'd never felt that way about her and Natan. Or her and

Sasha. Maybe she did feel that way about Aunt Cordelia sometimes, but this was different. How he felt—how he saw the world—opened her eyes to a new way of being. For the first time, she considered these traditions and antique beliefs to be something that might be wrong.

"Moze, I'm sorry I let Sasha talk me into following you. It seems so stupid now, but I just wanted her to feel like she still matters to me, you know? I wanted to do what she asked to keep the peace. I didn't want to hurt you."

Moze laughed. "You aren't what they told me you'd be, Ellie."

Ellie smiled back, wondering exactly what they had told him.

They turned off of the main road, walking with a smaller, less bright-looking crowd. Here, fake firefly lamps flickered weakly at street level, illuminating only the feet of the passersby. Numbers were lit neon red against the dark of the covered alley snickleway. As they walked, Ellie's mind turned over the idea that someone had discussed her with him. The idea frightened her a little.

"What did they tell you about me?" Ellie matched his steps but worried about the darkness of the street and the type of people they followed. Not that there were any unsavory, dangerous people in Santelouisa, right? After the War of Devolution, all the undesirables died or were pushed out. There weren't any poor people, thieves, or violent people left. Were there? How many times had Aunt Cordelia promised her that the dome cities were all safe from such things? Still, she moved a bit closer to Moze as they walked in the dark.

"They...my church people. When we found out that Gran

wanted me to meet you, to be a part of society, they told me that you'd be a...snob. Cold-hearted. I mean, you indirectly own thousands—hundreds of thousands–poppets."

For a minute, she wanted to protest. She'd never thought of it that way. She did own Thom. She shrugged.

"But I don't."

"Just because you don't directly control them or move them around doesn't mean that they aren't yours. Anyway, I decided when I met you that I'd try to help you to understand what the rest of the world believes. You've been here in the dome for so long that you think this is all good and moral. They told me that you'd never see it any other way, but then I saw you with Thom, and I knew you weren't what they said you were. There's nothing cold about your heart."

The sweetness of his words made her blush, but it was too dark in the alley for him to see it. She focused on following him. They arrived at a door lit by flaming letters that spelled out *Inferno* above its frame. He pulled her to the side, leaning in close, his breath on her face. "Pretend that you are into me. Like we are having a real private kind of conversation, but watch the people going in. What do you see?"

His hand rested next to her face, providing cover for her gaze. His face, so close to hers, turned toward the door. Her heart raced at his closeness. Though he didn't touch her, she'd never been this close to a boy before without dancing and chaperones being involved. She could hear his breath, and it made her want to hold hers so that she didn't pant in his ear like some out-of-control animal. Why did he affect her this way?

She tried to focus on the people who went into the entrance marked *Inferno*. Though the dark made it hard, she could see that the people going in wore spectacular outfits—the latest in gold-threaded iridescent fabrics cut in angled strips around the knees of each lady. Lights sparkled along the hemlines, twinkling like sunlight on the rippled surface of a lake.

"They're Juni's type," she whispered. "Upper-class socials."

Moze moved even closer, whispering in her ear. His hand moved down onto her hips, as if their intimacy felt natural to him. Heart thundering in her chest, she pushed lightly against his chest in half-hearted protest. He caught her hand in one of his. "Listen, Ellie. They're something you don't know about, because good girls like you, decent people, don't do what I'm about to show you. But I can't let them see you here. I need to put a mask on your face, okay? To protect you."

She looked into his eyes. He held her gaze, steady, somber—brown eyes. From his pocket, he pulled out a beautiful black mask made of satin and florescent feathers. He lifted it to her face and gently held it there. Ellie reached back and tied it, understanding that he intended to protect her from whatever happened past that glowing doorway.

"This isn't some school project," she said. This made them real partners, and she knew the shift mattered to them both.

"Nope. This is a life project, Ellie my belle."

She giggled. "My belle?"

"Someone called you that once, someone you don't

know. I knew the moment I met you that I wanted to call you that." Moze leaned in, a kiss on his mind—she could tell. Her first kiss? Here on an adventure, fear in her galloping heart.

He kissed her on her temple, holding her hand to his heart. "You are my friend, right, Ellie?"

She nodded, heart slowing. Her disappointment overwhelmed the fear. Where did she get the idea that he wanted anything more than friendship? Focus, Ellie!

He looked like some cad making time with a fast girl. If she didn't have the mask, there would be talk. But now she was safe.

"I hate to do this, but you must see everything. This may be the night you learn to hate me. This may be the end of our friendship, but I know things that make me who I am. I know about what happens here when good people like you aren't looking. Please just...just forgive me for this."

Before she could respond, he pulled her into the line leading into the brick-fronted building, neonless and awningless, marked only by the flaming numbers and the yawning darkness of the open door. A small vidscreen lit by brightly colored dancing static asked to see money, and a drawer popped out to accept the bill. Moze dropped in a five thou—a huge amount. And who operated with cash in the dome city anymore?

"Wha..."

"Shhh." He squeezed her hand to silence her and pulled her close so she could hear over the crowd of people behind her.

She noticed that many of them wore masks and dramatic

clothes that swept across shoulders and stood starched up around heads like headdresses.

The vidscreen's colors vibrated, and a voice asked, "What do you require today?"

"Complete access," Moze said, his voice lower than normal, play-acting at adulthood.

"Code?"

Moze held up his hand in front of the screen and flashed hand signs faster than she could follow. His fingers flew like some invisible keyed instrument sat under them. The screen flashed with each movement, lighting their faces with a disconcerting glow. Ellie wondered how Moze, new to the city, knew what to do to get them in.

The people behind them grumbled about how long they were taking, but finally the screen said, "Present your palm."

He lifted their clasped hands to the screen and looked into her eyes, then pulled his hand from hers and placed it on the screen. She followed his lead. The screen went dark for a moment as the center of her palm began to itch, but only for a second. Moze held his hand back out to her, took hers, and turned toward the door.

"I'm sorry for this, but it's necessary." They stopped at the door until the doorframe flashed red and a silvery film that looked a bit like the dome, melted away.

"Containment field," he said, pulling her into a dark hallway. Once past the door, the sound of an electronica orchestra clashed another series of rhythms that seemed to grow up around their feet, as if the floor itself vibrated with a hammering heartbeat.

Ellie's palm glowed with golden phosphorescence. The

mark itself swirled and doubled back, a winding serpent eating its own tail. Such a lovely mark, but she rubbed at it. Aunt Cordelia didn't approve of body mods that weren't poppet-based. This kind of art tattooing was, in her view, common and base, something mid-management teens did before they realized that they should resist such banal pursuits. The Parkers made a pretty penny on skin transplants when body mod freaks hit the age of accountability where they either had to clean up or get out. Most chose the shiny pink transplant skin grown from the most pampered poppets at DesLoge Com. The skin transmuted into the natural skin color of the transplantee through melanin treatments, though Sasha told her those hurt like crazy.

"It's a temp. Don't worry," Moze shouted over the din. He led her into a large open space where the electronica music bloomed. Bodies wrapped in translucent light shields and brightly colored dressings flew and dipped in the layers of floors that stacked up the side of the tall room. Winding iron stairs lit with a flash of bright white light every time anybody stepped on them. From the ceiling hung cages, platforms, and neon ropes that held dancing, spinning poppets dressed in old showgirl feathers or tuxedos. Such beautiful poppets, top-of-the-line models with intricate dance programming. They must've cost a fortune. Moze slipped a mask over his face that matched hers. They were sorely underdressed for this compared to the others, but Moze pulled her out onto the dance floor anyway. He kept her close to him, much closer than he had at the ball she'd hosted. Her body fell into rhythm with his, even though she felt shame about his hands and his thigh pressing against her.

"Listen, Ellie, we're going to make our way through here slowly...see everything."

The music shifted, and the crowd moved tighter to them. He cradled her close to keep her from being stepped on and steered them toward the stairs.

"No matter what we see, don't react. Don't let them know who you are. You need to act like you've seen it all before and like it's no big deal, okay?"

She nodded. "Moze, I'm scared."

He looked her for a moment, his brown eyes held a guarantee that at the end, they would be okay.

"Me, too, but we'll get through this."

They swung toward the stairs with the swirling, beautiful mass of people. Finally, he pulled her by her hand onto the first stair, letting the song go on without them. She stepped up, moving forward with his hand on her elbow, guiding her. His hand, shaky and damp on her skin, held her softly as they ascended. The first landing, twenty feet above the main floor, glowed green, with neon plants and ten-foot-tall leaves. Ivy with red and purple fibers bursting into vibrating flowers as big as her hand twisted in the music's beat, casting their glow across the faces of the men and women entwined in couches and hammocks beneath them. Moze led her forward, stepping around the legs and feet of the people making out, to the far end of the balcony. The next winding staircase hid behind massive elephant ear plants.

They mounted the next stairs, climbing up to a level, where brightly burning white and blue light edged each and every table, chair, and wall. People here sat and drank, faces close in conversations that had to be yelled above the booming music.

The brightness of the tables reflected off the faces, making them glow like angels. She turned toward Moze, who shook his head. This wasn't it.

He pulled her toward another set of stairs, one without lights, that wound into the darkness at the top of the room. At the foot of these stairs, they stepped into a silky silver shield like the one that had guarded the front door. The electric shiver of the barrier passed across her skin, holding her in place. Moze pressed her hand on a vidscreen that glowed weakly on the side of the staircase.

The silvery veil parted, and they stepped up onto the stairs. Along the curved wall, a dim yellow light marked their path, but with each step, Moze's hand got tighter on hers, and her heart's hammering deepened to match.

Without words, Ellie could feel the weight of their passage here. This was the members-only area he'd paid so much for. This was what he really wanted her to see. The air was thick with heat, and the smell of bodies sat in her mouth like foul food you didn't want to chew. Ellie fought to keep her face neutral as they mounted the last step and moved toward an old-fashioned oak door. Moze put his hand on the door and tilted his head, an invitation for her to do the same.

Ellie took a deep breath. She looked back across the nightclub and the excitement happening behind her. The Inferno, from this perspective, looked like a tilt-a-whirl ride. On each level, the people enjoyed each other, not worried about the conventions of Santelouisan society and tradition.

"Don't let them fool you." Moze shook his head. "They're parasites. We all are. You have to see it."

Ellie pressed her hand to the vid screen. No sense in keeping the blinders over her eyes. She needed to let him lead her through all of this.

An air-filled hiss escaped around the door. Behind, a darkened hallway, white and sterile, yawned. Her heels clunked on the white tile underfoot. At the split at the end of the hall, they paused.

"Here we go," Ellie said. No reason to wait any longer for whatever awful thing was ahead. They turned left and marched down the hallway. With each step, she gathered her strength or at least faked it well. No matter what, she had Moze with her. No matter what awful thing he'd been trying to work up to showing her, she could handle it, right?

At the end of the hallway, Ellie put her hand on a brushed silver doorknob that seemed to throb with angry heat. She jerked away and looked back at Moze, just a step behind her. He nodded, his face so somber that she knew he was afraid of what she would learn here.

"We'll be friends after this. I trust you."

He smiled. "I hope we can be. Truth is painful sometimes, Ellie."

His hand covered hers on the knob and turned, swinging the door open to a room that looked like a cake from a Valentine's day wedding. Red flounces, heart-shaped chairs, velvety wall hangings, a carpet of bright red and white fibers deep enough to shift under foot—rich in a way that the actual wealthy wouldn't be caught dead employing in their own homes. Rich in a way that suggested no end to wealth.

Tables loaded with the most precious food goods that money could buy. Chairs around the room were occupied by people snacking and whispering.

There was a sense of expectation, a unified hush held them in near silence. What were they waiting for? Moze pulled her back behind the others, against the wall. He didn't look at her, but kept his gaze aimed at the dominating art on the wall—an image of a beautiful woman, nude, posed as if she'd just woken from sleep. Definitely, a picture of a woman of the night, or as the wise men of Journey called them, streetlight person. A hooker.

Ellie turned to Moze to ask him about it, but his gaze sharpened as the light of the room took on a new rose tint. The image of the woman grew brighter, then disappeared. From behind it, a line of poppets walked into the room, strung together with gold braid rope.

They shambled across the room in lacy things that barely covered them. In some cases, they had no lace. The male poppets had gauzy wraps around their middles hiding their private parts, but the wraps drew the eye. No dignity. At least in her house, the poppets had some dignity.

An older man in a tuxedo leaned closer to her. "First time here, my dear?"

She nodded.

"No names. Just pick the one or ones you want. Oh, the two of you are sharing, huh?" He gazed at Moze with a greed in his eyes that made her stomach turn.

"Better watch out, sir," Moze said, voice carefully carefree. "If you spend your attention on us, you might not get your choice."

"Yes, yes. Quite right. Mustn't let you distract me, pretties."

Ellie knew the man. Even with the half mask over his face, she would know him from his jowls and his smarmy voice. This man had shaken her hand, sat at her dinner table, and kissed her aunt's cheek. Ellie shivered.

"The mayor," she said to Moze under her breath.

Moze's gaze flickered to hers for a moment, then returned to their appraising of the poppets. Ellie was sure his play acting would pass with anyone who didn't know him, but the streaks of high, angry red on his cheeks gave away his internal turmoil.

A scarlet-haired woman dressed in a bustled, high-necked dress that would have been appropriate for a Victorian belle, sashayed in after the long line of poppets on the golden string. Her white painted face, red lips, and eyes framed with diamonds looked like a mask. A spotlight fell on her glittering face.

"My loves," she said, her voice deep like a man's. "My darlings, I give you love. The chance to love that which is forbidden."

The people in the room seemed to lean forward as she spoke. Mouths open, eyes wide, and hands clenched.

"Remember the rules, dears."

The guests laughed, and the mayor answered, "There are no rules, Madame Voyle."

Moze squeezed her hand as the others stood, leaving a trail of dirty dishes and cups behind them. They crowded forward, grabbing for the poppets. All of them had been incredible looking in life. Plucked in their prime. Dead at the age of their greatest beauty. Ellie had a terrible feeling about this. How did they get these poppets?

Moze pulled her toward the poppets as Ellie watched the mayor grab a tiny brunette with dark skin and a long neck, so young that, even dead, she looked like she was just out of her childhood—thirteen or fourteen. He wrenched her around to him, covered her mouth with his, and his hand found her breast. Ellie suppressed a heaving scream.

The mayor's mouth broke away, but his hand didn't as he dragged the small poppet down the hall and out of sight. Others followed him, dragging their own pretty poppets into rooms along the sides of the hall. Some took one; some took three. Poppets on golden ropes were dragged into rooms. Ellie's heart ached as she imagined what was happening in those rooms.

"Don't be left out, my dears. What about this one?" Madame presented a blonde, petite girl. "This is little Georgia. Only seventeen when she died. Pretty as she can be. Like her, my boy?"

Moze shook his head. "The mayor invited us in with him."

Madame waved her hand at the hallway. "Don't be late then, my dear."

He started toward the hallway. Ellie didn't want to go; she didn't want to see any more. As they walked toward the room, her skin crawled, imagining the mayor's hands on that little poppet's body. But no laws prevented it. Poppets were just property—even if they only looked thirteen. Nothing to protect them from this outrage. Nothing to keep them safe from the pedophiles who couldn't abuse live children. Her stomach jerked as she thought about him with that little poppet, perhaps proud that he'd found a legal outlet for his sick sexual tendencies.

Moze pulled her past the doors. Some were closed with noises of stringent sex—angry, violent actions—vibrating through the door. Some were open. Though she tried not to see, people and poppets formed geometrical shapes—gray skin and pink skin and brown skin all smashed together. Poppets' blank faces and rigid bodies being abused.

Ellie couldn't help the tear that rolled down her cheek as she fought the urge to scream, to lash out against these beasts. She wiped at her cheek with her shoulder as Moze pulled her into one of the rooms, one with a woman already there. She had two poppets sitting on the bed before her, and Ellie squeezed her eyes shut, not wanting to see whatever she was doing to them.

"Shut the door, dear."

Ellie opened her eyes, shocked. The widow! Moze's venerable grandma stood in front of the poppets, her mask cast aside on the bed.

"Hello, Ellie, dear. Sorry to spring all of this on you, but time is short. Things are speeding up now. We had to bring you in without much preparation. Step up now. You can help me. Come on, both of you."

Widow Douglas wore a flashy neo-French revolution shelf dress that swung out wide from her hips. Many partiers from Juni's social groups wore such dresses to their themed parties. But the widow wore it as well as any woman half her age, and she wore it for a reason. She pulled her wide skirt open and exposed another layer of clothes—a light-colored skirt full of pockets with flaps closed by plain brown buttons. The widow opened the pockets and pulled out instruments and concoctions.

"Moze, can you give them a spray vaccine, please. They both suffer from poppet consumption."

Moze took the spray and leaned over the girl poppet. "Please open your mouth."

The poppet complied, not looking at him, though, for a second, Ellie thought she saw her eye twitch, almost a wince.

"Don't worry, my girl. He won't hurt you. We're Resurrectionists." The widow patted the poppet's hand and turned it, checking for the telltale tattoo. "She's named Iris."

Ellie's face flushed as she realized that the Resurrectionists weren't as distant or weak as everyone in Santelouisa had assumed. Widow Douglas, one of Aunt Cordelia's closest friends and a Senator—a Resurrectionist. She would have to tell Cordelia about this. She couldn't keep such a secret from her. That would be traitorous. Even so, her stomach churned at the thought of revealing the widow's secret. Why should she care about this?

"I haven't heard of any Iris missing," Moze said. He motioned to Ellie. "Want to vaccinate the man?"

Ellie nodded, moving to the male poppet. "Open your mouth," she said. As he turned toward her, she realized that he'd been sorely abused. He had no nipples on his chest. Instead, two matching scars like little zippers decorated his well-defined pectorals. Ellie reached her hand out to touch the scars, but Widow Douglas stopped her.

"Don't you think that they are handled without kindness enough, Ellie? We ask before we touch them. We give them some dignity." It sounded like a reprimand, but when Ellie looked in the widow's eyes, all she saw was a request—an invitation to rise above what she thought she knew the world to be.

Ellie nodded. "May I touch your scars?" she asked the poppet. The words tasted like some foreign concoction. Every experience, every training had taught her that such kindnesses were wasted on poppets. The poppet didn't respond. Of course, it didn't. It was dead, for goodness' sake. Ellie looked back at the widow in confusion. "What should I do now?"

"You can touch them. We just want to be decent, is all."

Ellie ran her fingers across the scars on the poppet's chest, wondering what happened to him. Wondering if someone like the mayor had done this to him.

The poppet tilted his face toward her and, for the first time, Ellie realized his mouth had been slit with a knife and reinforced with stitches. The effect made him look like he smiled a clown-sized smile but, in truth, it had widened his mouth, made it bigger.

"What is this for? Why..."

The female poppet's head turned, showing that she, too, had been altered. "I don't want to describe why their mouths are this way. Just understand, everything done to them here is at the sexual whim of those willing to pay."

Widow Douglas took out a salve, dabbed a cotton stick in it, and wiped an oily substance across sores in the poppet's privates.

As she worked, she explained, "We try to help them. Madame wears them out. She lets them be used in any way the clients want. We've seen just about everything you can imagine and some things you can't. The thing is, once the poppets get to this level of degradation, Madame sends them to the other hallway."

"The other hallway?"

Widow Douglas filled a syringe with each of the poppet's fluids and stuck the full vials back into her pockets. "Moze will show it to you in a few minutes. Look, Ellie, I hope you will keep my secret. I will never harm your aunt, even if I oppose the business and the keeping of poppets. I believe in the peaceful resolution of our peculiar institution."

"Will you keep Gram's secret, Ellie?" Moze turned the full force of his kind brown eyes on her, pleading. The secrets seemed heavy, but she nodded. At least for now, she could do it.

"I will, as long as it doesn't hurt us. But if I have to, I'll tell her." Ellie kept her eyes level, chin high, never breaking eye contact.

"Fair enough." Widow Douglas smiled and turned back to the poppets. "Take her to the other hallway, Moze. Show her what else the company is involved in."

"The company? What do you mean?" Ellie asked.

Moze took her hand again and led her back to the hall. "Just come with me."

The dark hall was thick in cloying perfumes that covered a whiff of corruption. She wished she could refuse him—just turn back into her life with its absolute goods and simple truths. Her mind raced, and her feet seemed to resist, moving sluggishly toward what Moze had to show her. Whatever it was, it made him grip tight enough to whiten the skin beneath his fingers. Whatever it was he had to show her couldn't be good. Ellie wondered if she could handle all of this. The air felt thick, like cotton packed around her body. Her mind raced, and her pulse thumped beneath her skin, but she walked on with him. On into the dark.

DOCUMENT 11: RESURRECTIONIST REPORTS FROM THE GRAVE HAWKER-CONTROLLED WILDS

Printed weekly in The Marching Truth, a Resurrectionist vidcircular that made its way from the territories into the dome-city news nets. Suppressed—available only to level 5 government officials and first degree DesLoge Com employees.

Poppet Sale in the Wilds:

The buyers were generally of a rough breed—slangy, profane, and bearish—being for the most part from outside-dome plantations, where polite life is not practiced or taught. Decency and culture are sadly neglected by the petty tyrants of the rice fields and cotton farms that border the great Mizzourah River. Their knowledge of the luxuries of society consists of revolvers and poppet mistresses.

I made myself a prominent figure wherever Grave

Hawker business took root. At the poppet round-up sales, I might have been seen a busy individual, armed with a vidscreen catalogue, doing my utmost to keep up all the appearances of a knowing buyer, conducting myself like a rich planter from the wilds.

It is true that whole families of poppets are sold at once. The man and wife might be sold to the dome city of CharLanta, their sons and daughters be scattered through the cotton fields and the rice swamps of Mizzourah, while the grandparents might be left in the service of the Hawkers to wear out their weary lives in heavy grief. Let not the words of the Soul Ascensionists fool you! Poppets feel and weep and mourn. They have their souls! I have seen their tears.

The buyers handle Poppets as if they had been brutes indeed; they pull their mouths open to see teeth, pinch muscles, make them stoop and bend. Then they ask the Hawker keeper scores of questions about the poppet's qualifications and accomplishments. Meanwhile, the Hawker's whip continually lashes at the thighs and calves of the poppet to keep them spry. "Salting" they call it, though from the amount of poppet fluids on the floor, it should be called soaking.

The facial expressions of those headed to the block were always the same. It told of more anguish than words express: blighted homes, crushed hopes, and broken hearts. But at the block, it was different. Poppets regarded their sale with studied indifference, never making a motion, save to turn when told to. Then, when the sale ended, they stepped down from the block without a look at the buyer, who now held all their happiness in his hands.

CHAPTER 11

Ellie and Moze walked back past the rooms where poppets performed acts of cruel prostitution, their orifices being sold for use until they broke or wore out. The brutality of it shocked her, but not in the way she thought it would. She knew about poppet prostitution. She'd known about it because it was promoted at the Academy as an enlightened step forward. Her textbooks marveled at the beauty of the dead fulfilling a role that had once been forced on the poor, the lowest workers, and addicts—all things that didn't exist anymore in the dome-cities. The teachers, their parents, and the authorities reminded them that in the time before, in the time of illegal prostitution in the Antedevolution cities, children like her could be snatched and forced to act as sexual servants by twisted opportunistic villains and thieves of the old cities. The use of poppet bodies prevented girls and boys from being stolen, abused, and destroyed.

She'd thought at the time that it was a gentle, socially

responsible way to allow people to do immoral things. And why should it matter? Poppets couldn't feel or react. Right? Ellie hoped so deeply in her heart that they couldn't, after what she'd seen.

They walked toward the next bright layer of hell in this inferno, and all Ellie could think was that she was being ripped in half from the inside. Part of her so wanted the poppets to be what they'd always taught her—dead, unaware, uncaring things, because if they weren't, then she had to do something for them. If they weren't what she'd been taught...her mind rejected the logical consequences of that possibility.

But what about Thom Poppet? What about little Ellie, convinced always that Thom lived, thought, and loved her. Grown Ellie could deny, but little Ellie—the Ellie who seemed to control her heart—knew that he was so much more than a meat puppet with intricate programming.

"This is bad, Ellie. Just as bad—worse—than the other rooms. I'm so sorry you have to see this." Moze shook his head and slouched as he led her. His face, usually so handsome and open, seemed to darken as they walked toward the other end of the hall.

They stepped into a room quite like a Plastique doctor's office. Clear plastic suits hung along the wall.

"I think we need to get into them." Moze grabbed a suit, stabbing his legs in clumsily. Ellie watched him and followed his lead. He had seemed to know what to expect, but the horror on his face, his shaking hands, suggested that he wasn't doing as well as she'd thought. She thought maybe this was the first time he was seeing this, too. He handed her a suit to put on, the sad acceptance dragging at the handsome features of his face, pulling them down and aging them. As much as he liked her, the job of showing her this place hurt him. It had to be like staring the devil right in the eye.

"I'm sorry, too." Her words, a spot of kindness in this bleak place, seemed to calm him.

"This isn't the way we should have met. We should have met in a time of peace. We should have been able to court and laugh. Instead, I have to take you to a horror show." His features became stony, bitter.

She hurried into the suit, wondering what it was for, and followed him over to a reception window, tapping with a knuckle on the frosted glass to get the attention of the attendant. The window opened to reveal a man with a child's pale ivory face, blue veins crisscrossing the bridge of his nose. He looked to be eight years old, so small and smooth. The only hint that he might be older were the bulbous veins on his hands.

"Have you put on your splatsuit? Yes, okay. May I get you something? What is your taste?"

Moze stepped in front of her. "We want to watch. That's all."

The man ran his gaze across both of them, weighing them. Ellie felt like she was being evaluated for use—whatever use lay behind the steel door. The thought turned her stomach.

"Step this way, my young watchers." The man continued to stare at her so hard that Ellie's hand went to her mask to make sure it still protected her.

The silver steel door opened with a hiss, allowing the seeping atmosphere to assault their noses. Sweat, body odor, roses, smoke—the mixture of scents heavy and thick in the air as they walked into a large space, concrete floor and dark wooden paneled walls. Scattered seats around the room resembled antique dental chairs, and metal tables held devices that reminded her of things she'd read about in the Medieval era. Pillories, cages, racks, and embalmer beds—all the stuff of nightmares about the room.

"Exhibitionists will put on a show for you in here. We call this the Hippodrome." The attendant drew out the words, arching his eyebrows and affecting a flirtation that bordered on creepy. No, scratch the *bordered on*. He was creepy. Ellie's skin crawled with every word and lilt. "The private rooms are just that... private. What goes on in there is only available to consenting, paying participants. Now, if you'd like to book a room, become more active participants...well, then, just come and get me."

Moze and Ellie shook their heads at the same time, drawing together and away from the childlike attendant. Like babes in the woods, they both expected to be found out or exposed by this strange, vile creature.

The attendant stood with them for a long moment, looking around at the earthly "delights" he peddled. As her gaze followed his, Ellie's eyes didn't want to see the poppets strapped to the devices. She wanted to see plastic mannequins or cut-out paper dolls. She wanted to see a museum that didn't have drip trays filled with fluid or nasty chunks of skin, gray and mottled, peppering the floor.

The attendant shuffled back to his post, leaving the two

of them frozen, feeling like panicked herbivores in a tiger's lamp-like gaze. Finally, it was Ellie who edged forward toward a table with two people working—Ellie didn't know what else to call it—on a poppet boy of maybe twelve or thirteen. The poppet wasn't beautiful, but he might have been once. Ellie couldn't tell since the poor thing's eye holes were filled with metal plugs that leaked silvery tears down the poppet's cheeks. The poppet's nose had been cut jaggedly away and flapped to one side of his face. The marks on his chest—nipples gone, cut away, and sewed up with clumsy stitched seams—made her shiver.

The two men, encased in the splatsuits and covered in poppet internal fluid, laughed as they pulled skin from the poppet's back in long strips. Ellie watched, her teeth clenched at the brutality they were practicing on this poor poppet boy. How was this better? That's what they promised.

"What..." Ellie's voice was too soft to be heard over the music and laughter and clanging of metal against concrete. She stepped closer. She needed to make them stop. The poor poppet sagged against the table. Was he even functional anymore?

Moze squeezed her arm. "Stop, Ellie. We can't fix this. It's too big."

"But I can," she whispered passionately. "I have money and..." She pulled him toward her. "We can—"

"Shhh... Not here. You can't stop this here, Ellie. They'll sell you these poppets and replace them. When they replace them, they steal more people."

Ellie shook her head, angry. "This isn't right."

She backed away from the cackling men destroying the

young poppet with no eyes. She backed away into a woman who wielded a long, sharp knife against the skin of an older poppet, cut after long, deep cut. The fluid welled up and spilled onto the floor.

"Why do these people do this?" Ellie felt like she'd crawl out of her skin if they didn't get out. She turned as the woman began sawing the poppet's fingers off. "I have to get out of here. If this is nothing compared to the private rooms..."

"This is hell." Moze put his arm around her. They moved toward the door, past a janitor poppet with a bin full of body parts, sawed, hacked, and pulled apart. The janitor fed the pieces into a chute of steel. Ellie imagined it went to an incinerator that would consume what was left of the poppets when they were used up. As Moze pulled open the door, Ellie looked back at the older poppet who seemed to be reaching out, his hands clutching at a salvation only he could see. But that was impossible, right? He was a poppet.

"I want to go get Thom. Right now," Ellie said, running toward the door. She'd been without her friend long enough, and just now she found she didn't trust anyone with his life. Not even the techs of DesLoge Com. Together, they fled the brutal hippodrome.

DOCUMENT 12: HIGH COURT RULING ON FRED POPPET/SHAWN SCOTT V. STANDFORD

In a case brought by Shawn Scott, Resurrectionist pastor, in the name of his mother's poppet, Fred. The case asked that since Fred had been a citizen in life and had been reborn in US NOAM, he should be considered a citizen with all the rights and privileges due a full citizen. If his citizenship were recognized, Scott asked that Fred be granted his freedom. The High Court made two main rulings. The first ruling was that poppets weren't alive and had no souls; therefore, they were not citizens and had no standing to sue in federal court. The second ruling was that the federal government had no power to regulate poppets in any territory acquired after the creation of the United States of North America (US NOAM). The only regulation of poppet production, sale, or treatments related to poppet products originates from DesLoge Com exclusively (see Maxplosive and Joltlace creation as internal regulation at DesLoge Com).

CHAPTER 12

Ellie's head swam with the most painful images her eyes had every beheld—worse than the old-time horror movies, worse than pictures in history. Worse because it was legal. Worse because people accepted it. Worse, because there was no way to dismiss it from her mind.

Her thinking felt ripped in two. Part of her reasoned in Aunt Cordelia's voice that, though unpleasant, all of this was the cost of civilized life. That if poppets didn't fill these roles, there would be a child or woman strapped to those tables. The other part of her, the voice of little Ellie who only knew love and what should be, screamed in horror. The din in her mind pounded and ached and made her stagger. In the end, the thought of Thom settled her mind. She had to get Thom.

She and Moze picked their way across the upper level of Inferno's club toward the spiral stairs. She couldn't wait to taste the outside, to shake off the shadows that clung to her.

Knowing made her responsible. For a moment, she looked at Moze and hated him. But she squashed that. It was an infant's reaction. It was what he'd worried she would do. Blame the messenger instead of the message. No, she had to see this. She had to know what happened to the poppets after they left DesLoge Com.

As they moved down the stairs, her hands ran across the cold metal of the banister, and her feet felt the reverb of the thumping tribal music playing for the masked dancers. Among the dancers—on pedestals, in cages, hung in slings on walls and from the ceilings—were poppets that flailed in gossamer gowns that trailed and lifted in the circulating air, the colors of flame. Some poppets hung upside down by their heels. What had they been before? She could imagine them, parts of families with futures. What if Moze were right, and the Grave Hawkers were hunting live people—for this?

"Moze." She jerked him to a stop on the stair. "I think I know what I can do about this place. I'll get Cordelia to stop selling to them. If I explain what is going on here, then I think she will be just as horrified as I am. Maybe I can get her to block them from getting more poppets."

Moze pulled her close, talking into her ear. "Cordelia knows."

Her feet wouldn't move, though he tried to propel her forward. The words echoed around in her mind. Cordelia knows? She started to ask him more, but he shook his head, moving toward the stairs, herding her toward them.

She pulled out of his grasp. "What do you mean, she knows?"

He stared at her for a moment, his brown eyes full of fear,

then glanced down at the bottom of the stairs. She crossed her arms and turned away, hoping he'd realize she wasn't going anywhere. Not until he explained what he'd said.

His eyes rolled as they looked from above them on the stairs to below them and the floor. He desperately wanted to be away from here, but she wasn't going until he spilled.

"I'll tell you, but then we really have to go, okay?"

She nodded.

"You own this. The Inferno is part of DesLoge Com. She fills the orders because they are her orders. She built this with Harold in the very beginning so that the bad urges that people had could be funneled toward what she called "more appropriate targets." This place is the most famous pleasure dome in the whole of US NOAM. It's one of Cordelia's favorite projects. Gran told me that she designed this place right down to the light-up tiles, the gossamer flame suits, and the torture tables. We really need to get out of here. If we stay, they are going to figure out who you are and, if they do, word will get back to your aunt. Come on."

He grabbed her, and she let him pull her along, down the stairs. Her mind reeled from the accusations against Cordelia, her family, and her name. But what she'd seen, the horror of it, killed any fight she might have had left.

Level by level, they descended through the hot mist and thick rhythm of the club and, as they moved downward, her knotted-up throat loosened. The revelers turned toward them as they rushed down the stairs in a headlong gallop. They stared, laughed, and pointed.

"Careful, Moze. We don't want to be noticed," Ellie said. "Please."

Moze slowed, measuring his steps, though she could tell he wanted to bolt out of there as much as she did. Ellie glanced back and saw a flash of white-blond hair. Though she was masked, Ellie knew it was Joceylin leaning over the first balcony. As they moved down the stairs, Ellie saw the others—the handsome boy she'd once thought she'd love and her bestie, the Parkers, laughing and drinking with Joceylin. Seeing them together in this horrible place convinced her. No matter how she decided to handle this nightmare, Ellie knew she couldn't go back to what was expected of her. That life with Natan and being a quiet little DesLoge lady was no longer possible. Not knowing the things she knew. Her mother and Cordelia would have to understand. They'd just have to.

When they finally made their way through the exit, onto the pavement of GasBright Square, Moze maneuvered them into a snickleway between buildings—a service walkway that poppets used to deliver things during the day. He stopped and leaned against a brick wall, panting. He looked haunted with eyes so wide they nearly glowed. She wondered if she looked the same as she fought for her breath, hand cradling her side, locked in a stitch from running so much.

"I'll never get used to that," said Moze. "Never. My mother used to tell me about it. She used to say it was our duty to fight the DesLoge Empire. But she was the bestie to Juni DesLoge, and they couldn't change anything. It's all so big—so much. Maybe it won't ever change."

Ellie took his hand. "Moze, you just did. You changed everything. I don't know how or what I can do, but I do know I can't let that go on. I couldn't live with myself."

He pulled her into him, hugging tightly, as if the hug would protect them both from what they'd seen. His face leaned into the curve of her neck, his breath hot and tickly. "Ellie, I wish you could see Liberty Lawrence, what we are trying to build out there. There's none of this...ugliness in Liberty Lawrence. None of it. Just a bunch of Resurrectionists trying to figure out how to live. Come there with me, Ellie. Escape from this rot with me."

He pulled back until his face was just inches away. So close she could feel his breath on her lips. His brown eyes were so full of promises and comfort. She'd never tried to kiss anyone before. She and Natan had come close once or twice, but it felt too awkward. But this time, she did. She kissed him, soft lipped, wrapped in his arms, breathing his breath, his eyelashes soft against her cheek.

Moze slid his hand into her thick hair. So many thoughts, so many breaths. She thought for a moment about how she and Natan had been forced together for so long, and how she'd never felt this kind of breathless need for him. She wondered as Moze's lips held hers how, for so long, love had been a dead thing to her, a tradition to be bartered between families?

They broke from each other, breathless. She grinned at him, a silly grin, and touched his face, running her fingers across the dimple there. "I'm glad you found me, Moze Grayson."

He trembled, took a deep breath, and said, "It had to be, Ellie DesLoge."

The full realization of all they'd done struck her. She'd known him for just a few weeks, and now she had kissed him. She'd turned her back on tradition and expectations—for a Resurrectionist no less. She pulled back, stroking her hair back into place nervously. Moze must've felt the temperature drop between them. His happy face sagged. They were moving fast. Too fast for her. For a moment, with her back against the bricks, she thought about running from it all—Moze, Joceylin, Sasha, and Cordelia. But if she ran, who would care for Thom?

"Let's go get my Thom, please. I don't want to let him out of my sight anymore."

Moze nodded and led her back into GasBright Square through the poppet snickleway. Once they entered the crowded square, where so many bodies pressed together into a shadowed herd, they tossed the masks into a recycler. Ellie felt her racing pulse begin to settle as they made their way to the corner where the autocars shuttled past under the lantern, now burning in the dome-night. They passed the coffee shop she'd sat in earlier, thinking that they'd be learning about slavery in the olden days—not the horrors of slavery that existed right in front of her face—slavery that she'd not even recognized.

Now, every poppet they passed seemed to look sad to her. Their perpetual pleasantness a thin veneer over the truth that was their life, full of dread and endlessness. Her mind swam with the horror of their servitude. How much could they feel and know? She remembered so many little gestures and moments when Thom seemed to be ahead of her thinking, doing things without her asking. Did it reveal something in him that wasn't brain dead? With each action beyond his programming, had he shown her he was more than a poppet? Before she'd suspected it, had she tried to get him to show it? Now, she didn't care whether she could get him to reveal it—she believed. She knew that what happened to the poppets wasn't moral and that she couldn't let it happen. Not anymore. She had to get to Cordelia and Juni. She had to change their minds about the poppets. "You are being awfully quiet," Moze whispered as they stood in the pool of fiery light waiting for an autocar. "You look scared, Ellie, and that's no good. You need to put a smile on your face, or at least hide your fear. You are too well known, and people will remember."

Ellie took a deep breath and tried to smile. It felt like she pulled at her face with puppet strings. Maybe if they were in a conversation, then her expression wouldn't matter as much. She turned to Moze and said, "You promised to tell me about Ridley Brown, remember? How about now?"

The crowd pressed in, shoving them to the edge of the sidewalk. GasBright Square, known for being a place where anything and everything could happen, seemed a perfect place to talk without fear. But even here, Moze put a finger to her lips, silencing her. "Don't say his name under the dome. He's a criminal here."

"Really?" She blushed under the familiarity of the touch of his finger and stepped back, suddenly shy. A criminal? Ellie thought back to the picture of her mother being held so tenderly by Brown. "I didn't even know about him before I found a box of his stuff—the necklace I showed you and a bunch of coded papers that someone had tried to destroy."

"He was a revolutionary Resurrectionist with a price on

his head. They say he died in the wilds." Moze stuffed his hands into his pockets as they waited.

For a second, she wished that he'd grabbed her hand instead, but here in the open—that was a bad idea. An autocar pulled up, and the door yawned open. They got in together, sitting across from each other. Ellie twirled her hand in her skirt nervously, staring out the window. So many thoughts swirled through her head. How much did Juni know? Could she change Cordelia's mind about poppets?

"Ellie, I..." He stared at his feet and picked at the edge of his thumbnail.

She wasn't the only nervous one. She let her eyes run over him since he was busy looking elsewhere. For the last few weeks, she'd been denying it, but now she felt comfortable admiring him—his strong, rugged face, his well-muscled, triangular-shaped chest. She looked up at his face again and met his gaze. He grinned at her, then turned away as if he didn't want to rub it in. He'd caught her openly admiring his looks.

Her face burned furiously, and she stammered, "I wish the car would hurry up. I just want to go get Thom."

Moze nodded, then switched sides, settling in next to her. He took her hand, folded it into his own with an awkward, clumsy fist, but it made the flush creep back into her skin and a smile bloom on her face.

"Ellie, I didn't know I'd like you. Honestly, I didn't know it would be this way."

"What? Of course, you didn't. I didn't know I'd like you either, but..."

"No, you don't understand. They sent me to you to show you all this. I'm a volunteer."

The buildings melted together with the manicured magnolia trees and hibiscus bushes splashing their colors against the windows of the autocar as they flew toward the DesLoge factory. Ellie found her stomach sinking, not with the movement but with the weight of his words. "They? They who? What are you saying?"

"That I'm not here because of Gran...that's what I'm supposed to tell you. I mean, now you know about Gran and all, I want you to know the truth. The whole truth. Because you deserve to hear it from someone who cares. They sent me... I'm here to tell you, to show you about the company."

"Yeah, so. You have."

"No, I mean. Damn, I feel like such a traitor." He jerked back from her, thumping his other elbow against the window. Ellie pulled back angrily. Who in this mess would tell her the truth without any kind of strings attached? She'd thought Moze. He was all she had at the moment. All she could trust.

"I don't think I can take this, Moze. I don't think I want to know—"

"Let me tell you, please? I don't want to keep things from you now." He cupped her cheek and laced his other hand into the hair hanging on her neck. He pulled her, met her in the middle, and kissed her again. This time, the kiss wasn't so quiet, so sweet. Angry and hot, a brand against her lips. Fevered. She felt like the world spun around them at a hundred miles an hour. They broke apart after a flashed eternity that left her feeling soft, warm, and silly. Her anger had been kissed away. They broke apart slowly. Lips hovered near each other, as if magnetized. He spoke, and his breath flirted with the wet he'd left on her mouth.

"You are so lovely, Ellie girl. I don't think you know that. In every way. No matter what happens to us, please never let anyone convince you that you aren't brave and strong and beautiful. I think that's what they want to do...keep you weak. At least, that's what he thought. Now that I've met you, I..."

Her thoughts were smeared like a watercolor in the rain. "Who he? Moze, I'm so confused."

They were almost to the factory. He needed to hurry. His gaze shifted from hers to the window, like whatever he had to tell her was so shameful, so painful that he couldn't meet her gaze. Whatever it was, it wouldn't matter to her. Whatever brought them together, they were together now, right? They would overcome it, she felt sure. She reached out and folded his hand in hers this time, gave his cheek a kiss, and said, "Just tell me, Moze. I'm not afraid anymore."

"Slow down," Moze ordered the autocar. "If we get separated or if I disappear and you want me, then you pack up all of Ridley's stuff, that necklace of yours, and leave the dome."

Ellie's gasp couldn't be suppressed. Out of the dome? Impossible.

"Why would we be separated? Are you planning to leave?"

"No, but... Just listen." The harsh tone in his voice shut her up. He softened. "Ellie, use the star map. I left it for you. Follow Polaris upriver and out of the dome. Use Ridley's necklace when you need poppets to pay attention."

"Why would—"

"Ellie, we're almost there. I have to hurry. Ridley sent me. He's still alive—last I saw outside Liberty Lawrence. He used to talk to me all the time about you when he visited our farm and at church. He'd say how you were being raised by Cordelia and how she only ever hurts people. He said how he'd give anything for you to know about the rest of the world. How he wanted to save you. I don't know why he cares so much, but he wants you to know the truth, and that you always have a place with us in Liberty Lawrence."

"I can't just leave, Moze. I belong here, don't I?" How did this Ridley person know her anyway? It didn't matter who Ridley was to her really, just that she was a DesLoge right? Maybe she could make a difference as long as she dug in, worked on Cordelia with all of her love and convincing. Maybe she could make them see how torturing poppets in the dome debased everyone. She felt super-charged and electric in her anger. "I can't leave. What if I can change it? What if we can fix it all?"

Moze wrapped his arms around her as they pulled into the factory's alleyway. "I hope so, Ellie. I hope I can be here to help you because..."

His words trailed off. They didn't kiss. Instead, he pulled her against his neck and rubbed his cheek against her softly, mumbling into her hair—not words but sadness and fears. She wrapped her arms around him. Even as the car pulled up to the entrance and the door opened with a breathy hiss, she clung to him until the fears dissipated like a foggy morning's mist.

The entrance of the factory, dark this late in the domenight, had a vidscreen that accepted Ellie's palm and voice print, opening the entrance and lighting her path as they walked through the outer offices and reception areas. She'd been through here before on holidays when Cordelia felt generous toward the managers. She'd have a family open day and trot Ellie and Juni out as examples of how DesLoge was a family-friendly place to work. Those had been fun visits for her, where Cordelia had showed her around, declaring her the heir, with Juni following behind like a puppy, getting progressively drunker with each martini she drank in the back of the hovercart they used. Ellie had felt loved, important, and close to Cordelia.

This time, the offices closed in around her like dark tombs, and the emergency lights cast a reddish glow in puddles on the shiny marble floor. They walked quickly, hugging the walls and selecting their steps to be quiet, but even so the marble floor thudded and tapped their progress, echoing hollowly in the thin, after-hours air.

They passed halls that opened into labs or storage dormitories. She'd seen them before, sparkling white and sterile during the long tours every year, but she wondered if they would be different now. She wondered if, like at the Inferno, Moze knew more here than she did.

Through the final double metal doors, the factory floor opened with paths of steel. Vats of tangy-smelling chemicals bubbled within. On the walls and from the ceiling hung poppets on wires and hooks in various stages of revival. She'd seen this before, so many times that when Moze sucked in a shocked breath, she looked back, worried that something had happened to him—a trip or some kind of injury. He had stopped stock still, looking up at the hundreds of poppet bodies.

Ellie had seen this before. Many times. All of these things she'd grown to accept. But mirrored back in his eyes, she saw a shock that must equal the shock she'd felt at the Inferno Club. He'd known things, but to see it here, to be able to touch them... What must he think of her that she'd put up with this for so long—that she'd not seen this as horrific? The numbers of poppets hanging suddenly seemed clear to her for the first time—they had always been there, background noise in the music of her life.

She jogged, trying not to see the bodies hanging, trying not to see the station where the poppets would be rebrained —a chair that cut and popped a disc of bone from the tops of their skulls and shoved a chip into their frontal lobes. Moze kept pace as she stumbled and slid across the floor, angry for falling, upset for finally seeing—understanding what happened here in her family's factory.

"Ellie, are you okay?" Moze asked, kneeling next to her as she drew up her knees, bloodied and sore, and wrapped her arms around them. She lowered her face onto them and let hot tears finally run out, burning little rivers on her angry cheeks. She felt betrayed by her own ignorance. There are none so blind as those who won't see, the saying goes.

"No, I'm not okay. I'm not." She shuddered, trying not to sob and hitch like some hysteric child. It took a moment to pull enough breath, but that gave her time to put words together in a string that would make sense. "I'm grateful to you, Moze. I just don't know how to...thank you. I hate this place. Everything I always thought was okay. I just accepted it all. Everything they told us, everything they said—were all of the things they said lies? Everything I thought I knew? It's all so...horrible."

"This is a deep well, Ellie, full of sickness and lies. A deep well. No matter how many times you pull up a bucket of truth, they have so many still hidden in the deep. You aren't to blame."

She growled at the pain as she pulled herself up and moved again toward the far factory floor. "Not yet, but I will be if I don't do the right thing."

He reached out for her hand again, but this time, Ellie dodged. Not that she didn't want to grab his hand or lean into his strong shoulder. It would have been so comforting to just let the sobs and the sad waves of terror wash across her, reducing her to a messy little girl. But she shouldn't. She couldn't. Not anymore. She had to be what Cordelia was. Strong. Independent. Able to stand on her own.

Ellie pretended she didn't see the flash of bright pain in his gaze. She squared her shoulders and continued. "I think he'll be in the back. That's where they do all of the VIP work."

He nodded and followed her sure steps back toward the next double steel doors. Pushing them open, they found themselves staring down a hallway lined with white doors, framed by red shielding.

"I don't think we should trigger these doors, Ellie. Cordelia is going to know."

Silver cut lettering on a plate by the first door announced *Organ Harvesting.* Ellie stared at it for a moment. Thom wouldn't be in there, but at this point, didn't she deserve to see everything that she was inheriting?

She took a deep breath, then pressed her clammy palm against the lettering, which glowed with an internal white light. "Let her find out. I want her to know that I'm not a fool."

"Ellie DesLoge, accepted."

The door hissed open, and together they walked through.

DOCUMENT 13: PUBLISHED LAWS DEAL ING WITH THE DAY-TODAY DOME-CITY INTERACTIONS BETWEEN HUMANS AND POPPETS

Poppet Codes

Nurses

No person or corporation shall require any nurse to provide care in wards or rooms in hospitals, either public or private, in which poppets are placed.

Hover Transports

All passenger stations in this dome city operated by any motor transportation company shall have separate waiting rooms or spaces for non-servant poppets.

Restaurants

It shall be unlawful to conduct a restaurant or other place for the serving of food in the city at which live people and poppets are served in the same room.

Toilet Facilities

Every employer of poppets shall provide reasonably accessible and separate toilet facilities for the living and the dead.

Intermarriage

The marriage of a person who was formerly alive shall be null and void after the remains are reanimated.

Barbers

No poppet-serving barber shall serve live persons.

Teaching

Any instructor who shall teach in any school, college, or institution where live children learn shall teach the accepted DesLoge Com texts about history, law, and comportment. Any teacher who refuses shall be deemed guilty of a misdemeanor, and upon conviction thereof, shall be fined a sum not less than fifty cred for the first offense. A second instance will result in expulsion from the dome into the wilds.

Militia

The live militia shall be disbanded as of the Devolution and shall never be compelled to serve again. The dead militia shall be made up of poppet soldiers without chem-neuter. No militia poppets will be allowed within the dome cities and shall be under the command of live peace officers. At the disbandment, the militia poppets shall be either stored in concrete sheds, made escape proof for the safety of live humans, or destroyed in compliance with the Constitution of US NOAM.

CHAPTER 7

Walls of jars, not poppets, met their questing gazes. Glass vials filled to the rim with clear suspension gel held the plunder of the medical arm of DesLoge Com. Ellie had seen this all before but never really thought to ask where or how these treasures came to them. As she considered her own lack of curiosity, even her own naïveté, her brow hardened. She struggled with a deepening anger—at her own lack of knowledge. She'd seen this all before, but she'd been so wrapped up in her role as heir, preening under Cordelia's attentive gaze. She'd been a fool. Ellie shook her head to clear out the shame.

"Our most important exports to the other dome-cities are organs. We have almost any organ or tissue type. Since the US NOAM outlawed clone parts, we've cornered the market on, well...everything."

Submersed in the gel were beautiful eye sets, kidneys,

and hearts. Large jars held lungs and bones and even big swaths of skin patch in every color. She saw dashes of freckles and tiny scattered hairs frozen in the stasis gel, fed, and preserved for the person who would someday need them. She'd always been so proud of this part of their business. So happy that they were in the business of saving lives, not just beautifying like Sasha's family, but honestly making things better. But now, as she considered all that Moze had told her, she stared at the small hand jarred and lit before her. She wondered where it came from. Did it come, as Moze suggested, from the wilds? From some stolen child? She was afraid to turn the jar and look at the palm in case some blue-inked name would give more evidence to

Moze's claim against the DesLoge family.

Together they walked back past the displays into a lab. "I've never been in here before," she said. They crossed the floor to a vidport where Ellie's palm opened the compad files for them. "Search Thom Poppet of DesLoge."

"Searching," the vid said. It played a blooming holographic flower for their entertainment as the info sped past, its red petals morphing and growing into different hot-dome fauna to entertain them. The image melted into glowing red letters. "Thom Poppet is in Bay 18356 of the storage level."

Moze stepped up and said, "Search Josine Grayson."

"Searching."

Ellie turned to look at Moze, but he'd turned away from her and the vid, staring off toward the back of the room. He was caught up in his own thoughts, eyes large and woeful as a deer's. His poor mother. He hadn't given up on her, though he'd seen her stolen. She reached out and pressed her hand against his back, rubbing lightly.

"No Josine listed. There are unclassifieds being processed in the intake lab, level sub-three." The comvid's voice print knifed cold down her back. Unclassifieds. She had to find out what those were.

"Use floor lighting to direct us to Thom Poppet, then to the unclassifieds," Ellie said.

"As ordered, Miss DesLoge."

"And don't report this to Cordelia DesLoge," Moze said.

The comvid didn't recognize Moze's voice as a voice of authority, so Ellie repeated what he'd said.

"Sorry, Miss. She's already been informed of your presence, all of these inquiries, and of your presence at other company facilities tonight. She has made no recommendation for action but continues to monitor your progress. I also reported your request that she not be informed."

"Thanks a lot," Ellie said, throwing up her hands. "Activate lights. Let's get going. I'll have a lot to explain tonight."

"Yes, Miss. Have a nice night."

The base of the walls flashed with crystalline blue trails that arrowed off toward a single stainless-steel door with no window and no doorknob.

"Open," Ellie said. A muffled thump and click signaled the door's opening. On the other side, wires hung like jungle vines from metal walkways. Poppets hung from peg walls, wires, and tubes piercing and entangling them. Stainless steel trays held instruments of every type—scalpels, thickly curving needles, and kidney shaped pans. Discreet grading in the tile tilted toward small metal grates that dotted the floor. The poppets, though motionless, were hooked to machines measuring their heart muscles, their lung capacity, the chemical bath in their brain, and the activity of the chip implants. These wounded poppets represented the daily pain that a personal poppet might suffer.

The types of injuries each poppet had were displayed on a containment pad wrapped around their bodies, holding them in place. A shorthand holographic report was projected on the air in front of each poppet as they walked past. This one, a ginger haired-female, run over by a truck—legs broken, one nearly torn off. The damage seemed extensive, but the large stitching across the thigh held it together as it healed. The scar would be incredible, but poppets don't care about scars.

Even as she thought it, Ellie rejected the pat answer from her well-trained DesLoge company line about poppet's cares. Now, every time her training told her that poppets were thoughtless and devoid of feelings, the new Ellie, a wiser Ellie, felt her stomach turn. So much false information.

Moze studied another poppet; this one's face was a mess. Swelling rendered the features a puffy ruin. The blond hair was caked with brown, thick chunks that hung in clumps around the poppet's mottled head. The poppet's name was projected in red letters in front of her ruined face. *Jule.*

"What?" Ellie rushed over and squinted her eyes, trying to see the familiar poppet in the mess in front of her. "I thought she'd be much better than this. My God. Look at her."

Moze read the chart as Ellie brushed the hair out of Jule's face. The poppet woke, though her eyes stared off into a distant place only she could see. Her mouth opened and closed, her lips working around the splits and lumps from the beating she'd gotten at Moze's party. Ellie had never suspected that her bestie could be that vicious.

"Poor Jule," Ellie said, running her hand down the poppet's cheek. She could feel the rough scars that they'd sprayed with the Parkers' Plastiques to make her face plumper and smoother.

"She's not stable enough to move, according to the doctor's record." Moze thumbed across the vidscreen. "They are rebuilding her organs. Without the machines, she'd be gone. Damn. Ellie, your bestie—"

"Yeah, I had no idea," she said. "You think you know someone. You grow up together and play pretend future together, but I guess when things go wrong, the cracks in a person really come out. She's good in lots of ways. Just pushy, you know? When she doesn't get her way..."

Moze didn't respond. He looked Jule in the eye and said, "We'll be back for you, Jule. Stay safe here."

No response, of course. What did he expect? They followed the flickering blue floor lights through the maze of wired-up poppets. They walked in silence, scanning the figures, looking for Thom's kind face.

"Moze, what did you mean back there? With Jule?"

"I mean that I'll steal her if I can. I'd steal them all."

"You can't do that. No matter how you feel about poppets, they don't belong to you. Stealing is wrong."

Moze laughed, a biting sound that reminded her of bitter lemons. He waved his arms around him. "Do you call this right? You have a factory that neuters humans and creates docile little slaves. Stealing is nothing compared to that, Ellie. Nothing."

Ellie felt the heat of anger rise up in her cheeks again. "We may be wrong and cruel to some poppets. Maybe we need to change things, but without my uncle's intervention, all of them would be dead in a grave. We are saving them. Some people are just...assholes."

"Ellie. Such language. That's not ladylike." Moze turned to her and smiled, the first genuine boyish grin she'd seen all night.

The smile caught. She couldn't help but smile back. "Well, it's true."

He nodded, turning past a staircase and walking into a room of poppets stacked tightly in rows. Tubes laced into the poppets' nostrils and pumped fluids and nutrition into their stomachs as they stood, lashed to stands that held their weight in the smallest amount of space. Ellie's eyes strained to count the number of poppets there.

"The record says these are fixed. They'll be going home in the next few days. I bet he's in here."

"Thom? Thom!" Ellie shouted. All the poppets' heads jerked up, acknowledging her words and waiting for orders. Near the back, a pair of hands raised above all the heads—hands she'd recognize anywhere. "Thom, keep your hands up."

Ellie shoved her way through the thin aisle, weaving toward Thom's waiting hands. She rushed forward and grabbed him, hugging him so tightly that her own ribs hurt. She sobbed into his shoulder. "Thank goodness, Thom, you're okay." Thom's hands fluttered against her shoulders and back. She caught Moze staring at her, his eyes wide. She realized how she must look, hugging a poppet. How ridiculous. She dropped her arms and pulled back from Thom, though she took his hand.

The old poppet let her hold his hand as Moze pulled the dripping tubes out of his nose, leaving a trail of creamy yellow paste dribbled across Thom's shoulder and on the floor.

"Ughnnn," Thom verbalized.

Moze paused and looked at Thom's face. "Does he always make noises like that?"

Ellie shook her head. "Usually, he just does that around me, when I'm talking to him a lot. I think it's just a program they gave him to make him more...human. Not, like, human like you and me, but..."

"God, Ellie. He *is* human like you. Can't you see that? Haven't you been paying attention?" Though his voice was hard, angry even, his hands were gentle as they freed Thom.

"I don't know about them being human. I think I've seen things that are cruel and ridiculous and need to change, but I haven't seen any humanity in them. They are not what they were. No matter what you want to think, Thom isn't the man he was when he was alive. The thing he used to be, his soul or whatever, left when he died."

She pulled Thom out of the stands to the open floor. He leaned on her, stumbling a bit, but she propped him up as they moved away from the lashed-up poppets.

"Unnghh," Thom said again, pulling himself upright. He adjusted his filthy shirt, tucking it into his pants, and then took his place, the place he'd had all her life, at her side. Ellie couldn't help the smile that bloomed on her face as the warm satisfaction of having Thom back radiated through her.

With Thom rescued, they sought the unclassifieds in the intake lab. Any fear Ellie might have felt seemed shot now with confidence. Confidence inspired by Moze and Thom—the two most dependable men she'd ever known.

Flashing blue lights led them deeper into the complex. Together, they walked down the stairs and through room after room of materials, clean drain tables out of horror stories like those of the Antedevolutionary age, when corpse were pumped full of fluids and poisons, then dropped into graves to slowly rot away. Ellie shook her head, wondering what were they doing here.

Moze stopped, signaled that he saw something, and pushed them back. He peeked around a door frame lit by the blue lights. A comvid flashed on, and the voice warned they'd arrived.

"There are white coats in there." Moze grabbed her hand. Ellie laced her other hand into Thom's, just in case. "Get ready...okay, now!"

They burst through the door as the room swelled with sound. A whoosh and sudden temperature drop unsettled the air, biting Ellie's cheeks with frigid little kisses. The white coats—DesLoge scientists—had their backs turned toward them. A winch arm lifted a cluster of clear tubes, smoking and ice-covered, out of a freezer car. The unclassifieds had been flash frozen like the meat that was served in Santelouisa. Like the meat, the unclassifieds came from far away, outside of the dome, so they had to be preserved until they could be processed. Cordelia had told her about this—

freshness of specimen, quality of product, words that seemed at the time so proud. She remembered being at Cordelia's side, feeling like the work that DesLoge did was incredibly important. She remembered standing so tall, beaming at her aunt, who beamed right back. That day, they'd been so close. But now, what would she say to Cordelia?

The winch lowered the tubes onto the floor, where the white-coated workers moved in with cables and hoses, beginning the process of defrosting them. The hoses pumped water that raised the temperature on the edges of the container slowly so that the internal tube of ice floated freely in the sleeve of glass.

"The dead inside the ice will be brought back to freshness. It only takes a few minutes," Ellie told Moze. Thom followed behind them, waiting for Ellie to direct him. She noticed that Moze turned and looked at him a few times, making the same quiet signals to be still or to move forward that he made to her, expecting Thom to understand.

They moved forward until they squatted behind a metal staircase, closer to the scientists and their work. A vacuum lowered into each tube, and with a breathy slurp attached to the iced specimen, lifting it into the air and dropping it into biotin bath. It was a soup of healing, warm photocide cells that used the water encasing the specimen, breaking out the oxygen and hydrogen to fuel their revival of the compromised organs of the dead. The process made DesLoge the only poppet manufacturer in US NOAM. In the world. She'd never seen it in action before, so she leaned in, hoping that she'd see the effects of the microscopic revival as they happened.

Moze turned to them, his eyes wild. "If something goes wrong here, just run. Understand?"

Ellie nodded, but worried. What did he imagine would happen here, other than the creation of a poppet?

"They're just doing their job, Moze. Nothing's going to happen here other than us making more poppets. Really, these dead will be revived and chipped. That's all."

Moze turned to her, his eyes rounded, the whites glistening bright. Fear.

What did he think? Her heart raced as he leaned in. For a few seconds, he gazed into her eyes, then he said, "This isn't what you think it is, Ellie. It's not."

He surged forward, grabbed her shoulders, and kissed her. It was quick. Desperate. His lips smashed hers at first, painfully, but then softened. He pulled back, then said to Thom, "I think things may go bad here. If they do, get her out. You are a good one, Thom. Follow Grandma Poppet to the promised land. You understand me, don't you?"

"Urgh," Thom grunted, shifting next to Ellie and balancing on the balls of his feet. She'd never seen him do that before. The ice slips melted, and biotin-produced oxysteam blasted in the air, creating a fog that crept around their legs. The scientists spoke into their comvids and read the dials that glowed along the tubes that pumped the biotin and suctioned away wastes. The dead emerged slowly from their blocks of ice. Their forms shadowed against the bright light that shone behind them, obscuring their features. What Ellie could see was that the bodies of the dead were not at rest the way she imagined they would be. Instead, their hands were raised above their heads, legs splayed out, kicking, or curled.

Heads craned forward or thrown back. Why would they all be that way?

Their skin wasn't the gray or blue that the texts said it would be.

It was pink. Ruddy and perfect. What was going on? Moze coiled beside her, tense in every muscle, face grimacing in pain. Pain? "What..."

He shook his head and motioned toward the scientists and the new dead. The nearest one was a male with dark skin and jaggedly cut hair. His body, still rigid from being frozen, was held up by cradling wires that wrapped around his crooked arms, swinging him back and forth. Another of the dead seemed further along. Its body softened from the treatment, dangling and limp. Twitching? Did the biotin restore the lifelike movement poppets had—what the company called afterlife? Ellie scanned back in her memory. No, it didn't. It just repaired organs and skin and prepared the corpse for the chemical bath that would come and restore it. Why was this creature twitching, then?

The nearest scientist picked up an instrument—a long cylinder with a clear tube attached. He hit a button, and the familiar orange chemical—Harold's greatest invention—climbed up the tube. He moved behind the more supple of the defrosting dead and placed the instrument at the base of its skull while his fingers flew across the screen of his comvid.

Moze pointed. "Did you see that?"

"What?"

"He moved."

"Who..."

The scientist twisted the instrument, a rasping noise, metal on metal, and a spike was driven into the bottom of the specimen's skull. The creature's arms jerked up as the chip connected with its brain stem, converting the electric signals of the chip into the new programs that would drive the poppet's flesh.

"He didn't move," Ellie said. "They told me that any jerking or movement is just an adjustment to the injection of the chip and the chemical bath."

"Ellie, he moved. He moved before they changed him." She turned toward the other specimens in time to see the next of the poppets changed with the snick of the instruments. Another corpse, a female, nearly free of all the ice, dangled ready to be changed.

"No, Moze you're just seeing things. It's all a reflex, like—"

The female screamed. As the scientist approached her, she screamed with all her voice, slicing through Ellie's ideas.

Ellie moved around the stairs, following Moze out into the open. They inched forward, trying to see. The scientist leaned toward the female petting her long shining brunette hair that curtained her face but didn't mute her sobs. He murmured to her, words beyond their hearing over the whir of machines and the dribbling, melting biotin liquids.

"That's some kind of mistake. He'll get her down," Ellie said to Moze.

He didn't hear. His eyes were fixed on the naked female curled up and swinging in the wrap of tubes that held her. She struggled and moaned, trying to get away from the hands of the men who tried to steady her, grabbing for her shoulders.

They discussed the Santelouisa's ball team as they worked on the woman, pulling at and organizing her tubes. Though her hands slapped at them, they dodged and worked around her struggling.

Words emerged from the woman's moans and her wails of "Why?"

Surely, they would stop. They had to recognize—

"Hey, hold her will you, Dave," one said to his partner. He grabbed her hair and jerked her head forward. Dave, the other white-coated technician, grabbed her flailing arms and pulled her head to the floor.

Ellie stumbled forward, throat closing around the horror and the words that wanted to pour out. What were they doing? The woman was alive, and they knew it.

Moze stumbled out of their hiding and raced across the divide of the factory floor.

"Moze," the woman screamed. "My baby! Jeffers! You killed my Jeffers, you son of a bitch!"

The man ignored her, placing the instrument on the back of her head.

"No!" Moze screamed as he ran. "Stop!"

"Moze—" The woman's head jerked to the side, then collapsed on her neck like a broken spring as the technician twisted the instrument that ended her screams.

"No!" Moze's wail turned into a growl as he jerked the instrument from the man's hand and turned it on him, jabbing the point into the technician's neck. The man collapsed, hands clawing at the metal jutting out of his throat, pulling it free. Blood pooled in a fast slick around the dying doctor.

"Ma!" Moze screamed, finally reaching the woman. He cradled her head in his hands, lifting her face. "Ma." Dave scrambled away, hitting alarms as he went.

"Help me get her down." Moze's voice splintered as he stroked his mother's hair back from her face.

Too late. They were too late.

Ellie grabbed the comvid screen and ordered all the specimens to be dropped, the biotin expelled, and their restraints pulled back.

She turned back to see Moze on the floor rocking his mother, whose eyes had lost their sharpness. The chip. She'd been turned by the procedure, and now she was nothing but an empty vessel waiting to be filled. The others, those whom the men hadn't changed yet, were like Moze's mom had been before the procedure, wailing and angry. They emerged from the biotin blind. They muttered and shuffled along the floor until their sight cleared, and they seemed to get control of their hands and legs. The factory floor lit up with yellow splashing pools of flashing alarms lights warning of the massive escape.

"Moze." Ellie kneeled, put her arms around him and pulled, but he wouldn't let go of his mother. "You have to get up."

Thom walked back and forth in front of them, grunting and groaning. He began to gather up the naked, stumbling unclassifieds, dragging them toward the lockers, where uniwraps hung in bunches. He dragged out handfuls and gave them to the shaking, recovering unclassifieds.

Ellie didn't know where they came from or how this had happened, but she'd be damned if it would happen ever again. And what should she do about the dead technician? Moze had been defending his mother, but would the law recognize that his mother was alive before the attack and that he'd been defending her? Ellie didn't know what to think.

"We have to get them out of here, Moze. We have to get you out of here. What will they do to you?"

Thom helped lift poor Josine up and got a uniwrap on her. Then he pulled them, Moze and Josine, toward the door. Ellie helped herd the others along behind them, answering questions and stressing the need to hurry quietly. The unclassifieds did as they were told, especially since they recognized Moze from Liberty Lawrence. While they hurried down the hallway, Ellie tried to access the comvid, but she was suddenly locked out. The screen stayed dark. Was it Cordelia's doing?

They ran down the hall and out the back of the factory, across the lot and into the alley behind. Just as Ellie ducked into the poppet snickleway, peacekeeper lights washed across the front of the factory.

"We have to keep moving," Ellie said.

Thom led them farther into the tight alley and then into a dip between the walls. Several poppets sat in the space, faces turned toward them as they stumbled into the nook. The resting poppets stood and began to move forward, programming urging them to help, but Thom met their gaze, standing at the front of the group of escapees. The three resident poppets nodded and wandered back to their walls, slumped down to the ground, but continued to watch.

The live group of unclassified—Ellie wondered if it would be better to call them kidnapped—muttered to each

other, watched Moze, and stared with unrestrained confusion at Ellie. Was she so well-known that these wilders would
recognize her? Did they blame her?

Thom came back and squatted down next to her.

Moze, red-faced with rage that could find no outlet, clung
to his mother, withdrawn from Ellie and the others. He
needed her now, even if he didn't know it. She had to save
him from this fresh hell, if she could. A common comvid
screen on the wall, lit red, had registered their presence. It
would report them if she didn't do something about it.

"Damn." Ellie placed her hand on the screen and said,
"Juni DesLoge! Give me Juni DesLoge. Emergency."

The comvid flickered, and Juni's face floated as a holo
beside her. Her mother looked startled.

"What, Ellie? I was sleeping." Her childish voice a
singsong whine. Juni's eyes cleared, the sleep fog lifted, and
she cast around, taking in what was happening. "Oh God,
Ellie. What's going on? Are those poppets?"

"No, they are people who were being made into poppets.
Juni. They were alive, and they tried to change them."

Juni shook her head, unbelieving. "No, you must be
mistaken. At DesLoge Com?"

"Yes, I saw it myself. Juni...they have to get out of here. I
have to get them to the Widow. She can get them out. Right,
Moze?"

Juni looked toward Moze and at the people they'd saved,
then she glanced away. Ellie could hear another vid in the
background. She saw Juni's eyes widen, fearful and bright. "Is
it true? Did you two murder one of our lab men?"

Ellie bit her lip, looking to where Moze dragged his

mother along. "It's true. But he was killing people. Juni...that man killed Josine. They made her a poppet, even though she was alive."

"Josine? Oh no." Juni shook her head, shock and sadness playing across her face. After a moment of looking lost and delicate, Juni's features hardened. "No, don't go to the Widow with Josine. They'll expect that. They already know it's you and Moze. Go to the mansion, but don't go in. Go down to the river and wait at the boathouse. I'll be there in a bit."

The holovid collapsed on itself. Ellie turned to Moze, who watched her from the corner of his eye. His anger had no focus and sat right on the edge of his face. She had to be delicate with him. His rage could undo the whole group if they weren't quiet.

"Moze, we need to go. You heard her. She'll help us. She'll meet us." Ellie tried to project a confidence she'd never actually felt with her mother. Moze turned to her and weighed her with his eyes. Ellie moved close, running her hand down his arm and then across Josine's forehead. She was non-responsive. A poppet with no programming. Just a zombie without the appetite, like in the old days.

"I couldn't...I couldn't save her, Ellie. She's one of them now, and I can't fix it. I can't bring her back."

Ellie's beliefs from the world she'd always understood tried to come out of her mouth. That Josine's real soul was gone and that all that was left was the meat that had carried her. As she looked into Moze's eyes, she knew that none of those words would bring him comfort. That he, a Resurrectionist, didn't accept that the soul was gone. In his mind, she was still in there, trapped in the empty shell that DesLoge Com had made her.

How could she believe anything she'd ever learned after what she'd seen?

"Moze, we have to go. We have to get you and the others out of here. Please."

He continued to stare at his mother, tears hanging on his lids.

Thom walked over to Moze and Josine and offered them both a hand. Moze just stared at it, but Josine put her hand into his and allowed herself to be led forward. Moze snorted back his tears and stumbled to his feet, his mouth gaping and eyes wide.

"Did you see? Did you?"

Ellie nodded and fell into line behind Thom. "I see it. I don't understand it, either. But we don't have time for this. We have to go. Now."

She caught his hand in hers, turned to the others, and found them already lining up behind her. One of the women stepped up next to them, studying their linked hands and her face. When Ellie couldn't stand it anymore, she stopped and turned toward the woman.

"I'm Ellie. You?"

"Sorry, Ellie, I'm Rose Vule. This is Conward, my brother, and Lisl, our mother."

The others nodded hello and began moving again through the alleyways, slowly making their way toward the heights and DesLoge Mansion.

"I didn't mean to be rude," Rose said. "It's just that I've

heard so much about you, about this place, and here I am. I'm just a bit stunned, you know?"

Moze ignored them, lost in his own world, but he allowed himself to be led through the back streets. Thom was doing a great job keeping them off the main streets as much as possible. Their group, the Vules, Josine, and the male who'd died first, were dressed in uniwraps.

They'd be easy to identify if the group moved into the open.

Thom stopped in front of a doorway where a comscreen had been shattered. Strange. Things like that were usually repaired quickly in Santelouisa. Thom raised his fist and banged on the door. The pattern, two louds and three softs and another loud, didn't match any kind of training or programming that she'd ordered. Ellie wondered if Moze had snuck some new programming in when she hadn't been looking, before this horrible thing happened to his mother.

The door swung open, and a familiar face glanced out at them. Gertrude. Ellie sighed with relief. Gertrude didn't just run the antique shop she and Sasha had always gone to. She had always been like a friend to her, though the kindness that was usually in Gertrude's face evaporated when she saw Ellie standing there.

"What is this? Is this a trick? Are you all trying to get me in trouble?" Gertrude crossed her arms over her chest and blocked the entrance. Ellie moved toward her, intending to talk her way in, but Moze shook his head.

"Show her the necklace," he said.

She knew better than to argue. Ellie reached inside her

shirt and drew out the wooden woman amulet, dangling it in front of Gertrude's hardened features.

Gertrude's gaze traveled from the amulet, across the group of them, then lingered on Ellie. She sucked the corner of her lip in between her teeth and bit down.

Ellie reached for Gertrude's hand. The older woman allowed her to step closer.

"Can you help us?" Rose asked. She and her family all seemed ready to bolt, but Moze put a hand on Gertrude's shoulder.

"Please. We're in trouble." Ellie squeezed the woman's hand. "Please help."

Gertrude nodded, looking past them and down the street toward the lights of the peacekeepers weaving and bobbing over the tops of the buildings.

"Come in. All of you."

They all made their way into her store, huddling together as Gertrude gathered up clothing from her stock to replace the factory uniforms. The Vules were already talking to her about their escape.

"Ellie," Gertrude said, holding up her hand to silence the Vules, "what are you doing out with these folks, and where did you get the Moses figurine? What are you doing with this lot?"

Moze sighed and pulled his hand off of his mother. "Thom, will you watch her?"

Thom sat next to the static Josine as Moze pulled himself up. "Gert, Ellie's okay. Ridley's taken a special interest in her, so I showed her the Inferno. She knows."

"I saw it all, Gertrude. Every horrible thing." Ellie felt her anger and all of her disappointments crystallize, condense into hot tears. Gertrude, a familiar face, now a stop on some kind of secret Resurrectionist pipeline. What was next? Ellie's mind was spinning with all of the new constructs, the new information and horrors fresh on her memory like a painful, weeping sore. "I'm so scared of all of this. What kinds of monsters are there when a place like the Inferno can exist? What do I do with what I've seen?"

As Ellie's tears came like a flood, Gertrude wrapped an arm around her, squeezed, and whispered, "I'm sorry for you to find out this way, but I've always hoped you would figure out the bad that DesLoge Com does. I look at your Thom, always the same smile I knew when he was alive, and I wonder who is going to stop this flesh trade we all participate in."

Ellie nodded, drying the tears with the balls of her hands and turning to look at those she'd taken from the DesLoge Com. The family that had been captured, that she'd liberated, didn't make up for the horror of Moze's mother dying in front of him. How could she ever make up for such a thing?

"We won't stay long. I don't want this to come down on you. I don't want them to hurt you. I mean, Moze... One of the technicians is dead. I have to get these people out."

Gertrude looked over each of them, her gaze pausing at Josine Poppet. It was as if she saw her for the first time. "Oh... oh, Moze. Oh, poor Josine."

She hurried to Josine and stroked her hair. Ellie followed, her hand clenching and unclenching as Gertrude kneeled before Moze and his mother, mourning with him, comforting him. What would the Widow think when she found out her daughter was dead and her grandson a wanted, murdering runner? In one night, the Widow's world would be completely destroyed.

"My mother says she can get them out. She said she can help all of them," said Ellie. Her empty-headed mother had good intentions, but she didn't know anything about what was really going on in Santelouisa. What could a party girl socialite do for fleeing Resurrectionists? She'd never left the bright neons of the beautiful streets and high-end shops. Still, a spark of respect lit in Ellie's heart. Her mother had stepped up. "I don't know what she can do for us. I mean, she's kind of useless."

Gertrude shook her head, stood, and angrily stomped across the room to a bookshelf, jerking a book from behind a pile. "Useless? You think Juni is useless? Ellie, you're in for a shock."

She walked over to the window, scanning the street. "Look, you need to get it through your head that you don't really know much of anything. You've been fed this long line of lies at the Academy and by Cordelia DesLoge. You, my girl, are one of my favorite people. So sweet and attentive to an old woman peddling secondhand stuff. But look here, little one. You are deluded about everything you think you know. You see now that I am a stop on the underground railroad, but so is your mother."

Ellie looked at Moze, who'd returned to his mother's side. He nodded grimly, then continued to try to get his mother to respond to him, checking her wound, murmuring to her. The Vules fell silent and listened in.

"She's got her own story to tell, and we don't have time to

really talk about this, but you do need to think about just how little you know." Gertrude wandered around, pulling together a pile of goods, stuffing them into carpetbag packs, and handing them to the Vules and to Moze. "You aren't going with them, are you?"

Ellie shook her head. "Someone has to make sure that no one is following them. I think I can manage that much, at least."

"Just like your mother."

Normally, Ellie would have bristled at such a comparison. But after Gertrude's reprimand, what did she know? Here she stood with Resurrectionists and a murderer— none of this was covered in Dr. Venkma's history class. Just like Juni, Gertrude had said. "I hope that I'll understand this someday."

"Until then, it's best that you keep your mouth shut and get these folks on the road to Liberty Lawrence. Past Mizzourah, the Grave Hawkers thin out, I've heard. Does she want you to meet at the river?"

Ellie nodded. "Behind the mansion."

Thom grunted and took his place next to Ellie, pulling her away from the window and vocalizing quite a bit.

"Stop it, Thom. We're talking," Ellie said, pushing the old poppet away.

Moze jumped up and looked out the window. "Look, Ellie, you need to rethink how you treat Thom. Look at him."

Thom was pacing, weaving back and forth and muttering in his way.

"What? What is it, Thom?"

The old poppet reached out a hand to her and pulled her

farther back into the shop.

"Come away," Gertrude said to Moze. "All of you, follow Thom. Now."

Moze pulled his mother to her feet, and the Vules joined up behind Thom. The poppet's hand found Ellie's elbow and guided her gently away. They all made their way back into a stock room, where piles of clothing and old furniture offered easy places to hide.

Just as Ellie turned to ask Moze why he was so sure that they should follow Thom, she heard a banging on Gertrude's door. Insistent, massive booms rattled the metal door in its frame.

Ellie gasped and turned toward Thom, his face only five inches away from hers as she squatted next to him. His eyes, grayed out, seemingly unfocused, found hers. He covered his mouth with his fingers. Was he asking for silence? They could hear Gertrude open the door, rattling lock after lock, and yelling with a nasal lilt, "Coming, coming. I'm just a little old lady. You'd better just be patient."

The door yawned open, and Thom pulled her down farther, so she could only see the tops of the heads of the people at the door and their tricornered hats—hats that only peacekeepers wore. Peacekeepers here? Already?

Moze leaned forward, listening to the exchange. Mumbled questions, which Gertrude answered in a voice that suggested that she was old and hard of hearing.

She hunched her shoulders and seemed to shrink an inch or two. "What was that? A girl? A buncha kids with a poppet? How many poppets? Are they criminals? No, I haven't seen them. Am I in danger? What'd they do?"

More murmuring. Ellie could see them shifting back and forth, ready to move along and look somewhere else.

"Well, if you're sure I'm all right. I promise I'll report if I see them. Thank you, peacekeepers."

She closed the door and locked it with rattling surety, engaging each of the six locks with more noise than she actually needed—a show for the peacekeepers who hadn't lifted out of her alleyway yet.

"I've put you in danger, haven't I?" Ellie asked, reaching out to Gertrude.

"Nonsense. This is what I do all the time. I'm a conductor on the underground railroad. You just happen to be the most well-known passenger I've ever had, but the job is still the same. Follow me, each of you. Single file now."

Ellie let Thom lead the way, the Vules behind. Lisl reached out and squeezed Ellie's hand as they walked past. Then came Moze and his mother. Watching them together, knowing that he'd just become a murderer because of the horror that was DesLoge Com's tactics, knowing that she couldn't change poor Josine back, Ellie felt like her world had crashed in upon itself.

Moze passed her, sparing her no glance, only staring at his feet, his hands cradling his poppet mother's shoulders, steering her.

Ellie pushed back the tears stinging in her eyes and squared her shoulders. She fell in line and followed Gertrude as she pulled them into a closet and pushed back a thick bar of hanging clothes. Behind was a solid brick wall that Gertrude pressed her fingers against, one brick near the ceiling, two in the middle, one other off to the right—each lit up under her touch, sang out a soft tweeting note. With a rattle, a bricked-over door swung free of the wall, revealing a set of silver metal stairs that twisted downward into a deep, black vault.

"Follow Thom to the bottom. There you will find survival kits. Only take one if you expect to run," Gertrude said, looking at Ellie as she explained. "Be sure to hydrate now and to take cleaner pills for the river water. You will not see the river until you get past the DesLoge mansion. Look for the next station there with Juni. She's the next conductor."

Ellie grabbed Gertrude as the others filed past. She hugged her with all the strength she had, wishing that she could do something to keep the peacekeepers from coming back or to keep her safe. "Thanks," was all she could think up.

"Be safe, Ellie. This lot has a long, dangerous road. But you...you have choices that could change life for us all. Be wise, my girl. And be brave. Your aunt and your mother have been engaged in a long Cold War for you, but also for us all. You've been a child—an innocent with no will of your own. But now, you've got to be a grown-up. Now, you've got life in one hand and death in another. Sometimes, death isn't all there is. Sometimes there's a life to be found beyond this one."

Her eyes, blue and sharp, gazed into Ellie's like she wanted something to pass in between, something best left without words.

"Now go. Get out of here, and be safe."

Ellie stepped onto the metal landing, then took the first steps that would lead her away from the life she knew.

DOCUMENT 14: ACADEMY DE BELLUM BIOLOGY TEXT

Evolution Of Man

Improvement of Man—If the stock of domesticated animals can be improved, it is not unfair to ask if the health and vigor of the future generations of men and women on the earth might be improved by applying to them the laws of selection. This improvement in the future race has a number of factors in which individuals may play a part. These factors include personal hygiene, selection of healthy mates, and the betterment of the environment. As has happened many times in history, the stronger, the wiser, the more able have been rewarded in the marketplace. Wealth comes to those who have risen among the various levels of man. Thus, the wealthier members of society, like the strongest deer in the herd, naturally rose to leadership positions in modern society. Weaker, poorer members of the human race, beset by their own inborn genetic propensity for laziness, violence and stupidity, naturally took positions in society that required less of their limited intellect—workers, soldiers, cogs in the machine created by the wealth for the benefit of all.

Eugenics—When people marry, there are certain things that the individual as well as humanity should demand. The most important of these is freedom from germ diseases which might be handed down to

the offspring. Tuberculosis, syphilis, epilepsy, and feeble-mindedness are handicaps that have been elimi-nated through selective breeding and birth. It would not only be unfair to allow weaknesses to pass genetically through generations—it is criminal. The science of being well born is called eugenics.

Genetic Criminality—Historic studies have been made on a number of different families in this country, in which mental and moral defects were present in the parents. The "Jarls" family is a perfect example. The Jarls family's genetic mother is known as "Molly, the mother of criminal chromosomes." In three generations, the progeny of the original generation cost the old city of New York millions of their dollars. Their biological weaknesses led to their being given over to the care of prisons and asylums, and over a hundred feeble-minded, alcoholic, immoral, or criminal persons. Another case recently studied is the "Chrayer" family. This family has been traced back to the War of the States when a young soldier named Mart

Chrayer seduced a feeble-minded laborer girl. Their 480 descendants suffer from startling deficiencies. Clinical records show that 33 were sexually immoral, 24 confirmed drunkards, 3 epileptics, and 143 of their descendants were feeble-minded. The weakness of the underclass of old seems clear in these examples.

Parasitism's Cost—Hundreds of families such as those described above exist today, spreading disease, immorality, and crime in the wilds of US NOAM. Just as certain animals or plants become parasitic on other plants or animals, these families became parasites of society. Before the Worker War, they not only did harm to others by corrupting, stealing, and spreading disease, but they were actually protected and cared for by the old United States out of public money. Poorhouses and asylums existed to house such poor genetic stock. They took from society, and they gave nothing in return. They were truer parasites than any mosquito or kudzu vine.

The Remedy—When they rebelled during the Worker War, such people were deemed to be lower animals. We separated ourselves from them and their stock using the science of the domes and walls to stop the spread of their contamination. Every dome citizen who wants a baby must submit to a genetic work-up to confirm that they do not possess the undesirable mutations of the worker class. Weak embryos undergo a purge when detected. All of these prevent the reemergence of undesirables and low people inside our domed cities. If we were less kind, we would probably have killed them off to prevent them from spreading, instead of allowing them to continue to exist out in the wilds. Our humanity will not allow this, but we do have the remedy of preventing intermarriage and the possibilities of perpetuating such a low and degenerate race—the dome and separation of civilization from the wilds. Through our efforts, humanity will continue to thrive and strengthen, while the weak outsiders will devolve into non-viability as a species.

CHAPTER 14

Silence, except for their shuffling muffled footfalls on the wet concrete. The service tunnel, lit by glowing pod lights, sported the messages of a thousand escapes on its curved walls. Other escapees had etched and painted wisdom for those who followed, describing the path west from the dome city, telling of how to avoid the Grave Hawker traps that they claimed stretched out for every mile of the Mizzourah River.

Her legs were aching with the efforts of the night, so much walking, running, and worrying. Moze hadn't given her a kind word since his mother had died. And why would he? Why would he worry about some momentary attraction he felt for the heiress of the company that destroyed his life? That moment of hesitation, when Josine's life ended and Moze's changed forever, replayed over and over in her head. She glanced at him, walking ahead, his eyes never leaving his feet as they picked the path that he led his mother along.

Thom, leading the way, set a strangely fast pace that made
the Vules stumble and curse. They'd only just gotten their
feet back after being frozen. Imagining that trip, kidnapped
and frozen by the Grave Hawkers, infuriated Ellie. Her body
trembled with unspent adrenaline.

"What will you do?" Lisl Vule asked, slowing until she
matched Ellie's pace. "You know, when we leave? You might
get in trouble for what he did."

Ellie shrugged, falling into step. Ahead, she could just see
the silver of the dome-night winking like a distant eye.
"Maybe...I hope not. I'll just keep trying to fix things. I never
knew about what happened in the wilds. What we were
doing out there."

"Right." Lisl's voice sounded bitter, sarcastic. The word
hung between them like an icicle.

"What?"

"I just have a hard time believing that you didn't know
about any of this. Yeah, maybe you didn't know we were still
alive, but you know about poppets and how many there are.
You had to know that there weren't enough dead to supply all
the cities. Seriously. There are so many," Lisl said. "I've been
to Santelouisa before this, just to visit. They're everywhere.
Do you even notice them anymore?"

Ellie stared ahead, not wanting to take this but finally
seeing that it was true. On an average day, she was served by
hundreds of poppets. At the mansion alone, nearly one
hundred poppets served Cordelia and her every day. They
brewed coffee, cooked lunch, swept floors, and weeded the
gardens—all the work, all the necessities of the DesLoge
lifestyle.

"Are they just fauna to you? You only seem to notice them when you need them. I've never understood you Santelouisans. They are here, everywhere, doing everything for you. Everything. Then you act like you are doing them a favor making them slaves. You treat them like they are lower than dogs, but they are your dead." Lisl stopped and grabbed Ellie's shoulders. "They are everything to you here. I mean, in Liberty Lawrence, we have poppets, but they wander and do only what they want to do. Mostly, they flock on the edges of town. We do for ourselves."

Wandering poppets with no programming? Ellie fought the fear that roared in her mind as she considered a life so different. Ahead, Thom—her Thom—led the group, never asking for anything, always taking care of her. She'd always thought of him as special, as aware, though she'd never voiced it. But the others? If she were honest, the others were just like wallpaper in her world. Nothing but meat machines to deliver what she wanted. That's how she was raised.

Probably sensing Ellie's retreat into her own shame, Lisl pulled away from her, speeding up to rejoin her family. Ellie moved ahead too, catching up with Moze, though he didn't really acknowledge her. She didn't expect him to. He'd been deep in his own thoughts ever since the factory. She wanted to reach out and touch him, pull him into a hug that would warm both of their souls, but the tunnel mouth grew bright, and they spilled out onto the southern lawn of the DesLoge mansion. They walked along the tree line in the silvered night. Nodding daffodils and elephant ears lined the edge of the lawn, holding back the carefully cultivated wildness of the DesLoge woods.

Ellie looked up at the mansion, at the bright windows of Aunt Cordelia's rooms. Did she know what had happened at the factory—the murder, the theft, the living beings used as dead? Ellie dreaded it, but she would have to talk to her. She'd have to try to change it, to change her aunt.

The manicured lawn turned and narrowed into a stone-lined path that wound through a grove of magnolias that, according to Aunt Cordelia, had been genetically changed to bloom all year with the filtered sun of the silvered dome's light. The pink petals of the blooms littered the pathway, softening the footfalls of their steps. As they moved deeper into the shade of the trees, she pulled closer to Moze, hoping to get him to acknowledge her. Hoping for...anything. They walked in silence, listening to the gurgling of the Mizzourah and the twittering recordings of the canaries, parakeets and songbirds that were part of the mansion's grounds.

"Moze," she said out loud. She hadn't meant to. She'd thought it, loudly, hoping that somehow he'd hear her thinking his name, thinking about how she felt about him. Then it had come out, unbidden, like some errant wind.

He looked at her, turning slowly, like he was underwater. His eyes, hooded and full of sadness, finally met hers, and her breath crushed right out of her lungs. What did she think she could say to him? What would make it right?

"Moze, I don't know what I'll do when you're gone." There. She'd said something. Something to shatter the ugly silence. Something to warm his heart. Something.

He stared at her for a moment, then took a breath, deep and rattling. His gaze left hers, found his feet, one in front of the other, and her heart started to fold up on itself.

She tried again.

"How will I ever find you again? Once you go..."

"Once I go, you can go back to being Ellie, the princess of DesLoge kingdom. You can have your cotillions and your beaus, and you can go back to being part of this madness." She grabbed his elbow and pulled, slowing him down.

"I don't want to be a part of this madness. I didn't know. Really."

"You didn't know. I get that. But now you do. How can you stay here? How can you go back into that house of lies and live with her? She's a murderer."

Ellie stumbled as he shook off her hand.

"But...Moze, I have to try to talk to her, to stop her from using the Grave Hawkers or to stop them from hunting the living. I can't just leave without trying."

He turned away from her toward his unresponsive mother, not only physically with his steps, but also emotionally. He wouldn't look at her, no matter how many times she said his name. He'd retreated deep behind his own eyes. Here in the dark of the DesLoge wood, it was as if he'd already left, though he was an arm's length from her.

A white shape emerged from behind a drooping elephant ear before she had the chance to try again.

"You made it," her mother whispered from the near darkness of the thick grove. "You led them."

Juni's hand reached out and caressed Thom's face as she stepped out of the shadow and onto the path. They all gathered around her in the half-light. Juni's features were serious, set with a passion that Ellie didn't recognize.

There in her eyes sat clarity and purpose. "I can set you

on your path to Liberty Lawrence. Moze, you've been there. Can you find your way?"

He shook his head. "Rode in a closed train, under the river. No aboveground transports for the Widow Douglas's grandson."

Moze's mother, Josine, stepped forward. Her features, lit by the silvery light, almost looked alive, almost human.

Juni gasped. She shuddered and stumbled forward, her arms wrapping around Josine's slight body. She cradled Josine's shoulders while her fingers tangled in Josine's honey-colored hair.

"Oh, Josi," Juni moaned into her old bestie's cold, dead neck. "Oh, honey, I wish I could have saved you. Sweet Josi."

Juni then reached out to Moze, pulling him into the gentlest, loving hug she'd seen her mother deliver.

"I'm so sorry, Moze. I'm so sorry we couldn't get to her first."

"You let this happen. You and your stupid underground. How did you not see this coming? Gran says you track all the Grave Hawkers. When they came for us, it was like they had a plan to destroy the whole Liberty Lawrence resistance. They knew where to come, and they went after us all. And now, my ma is like this." Moze jerked out of her grasp.

Juni nodded.

Ellie's mouth hung open as the gravity of his accusations washed over her. Her mother was a linchpin in the underground—an underground she'd never known existed. Never in her life had she felt more ridiculously stupid. Sure, at the Inferno she'd been surprised, but how could she have known such things went on in Santelouisa? She'd been a sheltered debutante. But now, how could she excuse not knowing about her own mother?

For a moment, her mind went back, looking for clues that Juni was more than a vapid pleasure seeker. Her hand twisted in the hem of her shirt as she struggled with her own prideful past. She should have seen her mother for who she really was. Shame reddened her face.

Moze shook with anger at Juni's attempts to calm him. She said, "We will get you back to Liberty Lawrence, you and Josi. And maybe there Ridley can protect you."

"Too late. It's all too late. Ridley can't bring her back. Ridley can't cure her or save my Da. It's over, Juni." Moze's shoulders slumped, and he seemed to deflate as his anger bent inward. He turned to Ellie, reached out, and gently took her hands. He pulled her forward until his lips hovered just inches from hers, and his eyes seemed to light on her with heat. "It will be a war in the wilds, Ellie, like no one has ever seen. Brother against brother, city against town. When they find out about the living being turned..."

Ellie pulled his hand to her heart, clutched it there, thinking about war. There hadn't been one since the Devolutionary War. Would they militarize the poppets again to attack the wilders and the Resurrectionists? Would DesLoge Com and Cordelia pile on more sins?

"Moze, you need to come away now. I have a flat boat waiting at the dome edge," Juni said. She linked hands with her bestie, though Josine's hand flopped loose.

"Come away, Ellie. Come be with me in the wilds. If you would come, we could hide together and let this thing get past us. I'd sit it out for you to keep you safe." Moze took a sharp breath, then pressed his lips into hers, smashing his mouth against hers until it hurt.

Ellie wriggled in his grasp, pulled back, and softened her hands against his hard cheeks, gentling him until the kiss was the kind of kiss they'd both remember. She broke away slowly, touching his lips again and again with hers, savoring him.

"I can't. You can't, either," she said, just with a bit of her breath. Just a whisper for him.

Moze stared at her, his brown velvet eyes wide and warm and shocked. Then he nodded, his gaze hardened, and his fingers gripped her shoulders. "Then keep you safe, Ellie Belle, 'til we meet again in this life or the next."

He bowed to her—a formal gesture—took her hand, and pressed his lips to her palm. Natan had done such things before, and they'd always struck her as silly, childish gestures. Now, the warmth of Moze's lips and the promise he gave her made her heart ache. She had to send him with something that he and she could keep in their hearts.

"You are my true beau, Moze Grayson. I will have only you. Someday, I will find you again when I can make things better. This, I promise you."

Everyone in the group had turned, watching their promises. Juni, the Vules—even Thom and Josine—their silent witnesses.

"You are my belle, Ellie DesLoge. Only you hold my heart. I will fight, but always I will think of you. I will find you again when this ends."

She glanced down at his feet for a moment, gathering her strength. Then she raised her eyes, met his, turned her chin up, and gave him a small, bright smile. "We will fix these things, Moze. Then, we will be together. I will find you when I can."

"I have to get you out of here, Moze. Now. The peace-keepers are coming, and they will execute you. The death of our scientist is on vid. The rest has been excised, but that part is playing on vids all over. We must go."

Moze nodded and released Ellie's hand.

Together, the group walked to the river. Juni shooed Thom and Ellie away with frantic, fluttering hands.

"Let Thom take you to the mansion. You must be away from all that happens next. Please, Ellie, do what I ask," Juni said. "Go to your room, cry, and hysterically refuse to talk about what you saw at the factory. Lie about what you saw, and I will come to you soon."

Her mother turned from her and walked to the river, showing the others the way.

Only Lisl's soft goodbye sounded back across the fern-muffled path. Only their footfalls and then the absence of anything reached Ellie's ears. Thom stepped to her side, took her elbow, and turned her back toward the house. They walked together, back across the grounds,

Ellie's mind begging to scream. They entered the mansion through the mint-colored parlor and made their way to the stairs. Ellie heard Cordelia's muffled voice yelling at someone, probably a factory doc on vid. She hurried past and slid her shoes off, slipping up the stairs in silence. Once in her room, she threw off her dress and pulled on her night-clothes as her vidwall flashed with an incoming call.

She took a deep breath, then began to pretend—she

cradled her head on her arms and let the pent-up fear, anger, and loss all come to the surface. She let the tears loose and, as the vidscreen lit with Cordelia's face, Ellie's eyes swam with the rushing flood of the night's tears, right on time.

"Ellie, you're home. How long have you been here?"

"Not long. I came in quiet. I didn't want to be seen."

Ellie stood, paced, and wrung her hands. "I'm scared, Aunt Cordelia. I think Moze...he may have killed a man tonight at DesLoge Com. He didn't mean it, but... the man is dead. What will happen to him? To me?" Ellie hoped her aunt would buy her loud protests.

Cordelia seemed to study her, watching the tears and the twist of Ellie's mouth. Quickly, her emotional show began to feel wooden, so she let her tears dry up and her sobbing breath calm. "I'm sorry, Aunt Cordelia. I'm just frightened is all."

"You should be. I'll be right there."

The vid screen clicked off, leaving Ellie scrambling, setting the objects she had scattered—Ridley's papers and Moze's notes—in a box to hide. As she moved, Thom's clipped gait carried him in circles behind her, as if he were chasing her around a track.

"What is it, Thom? What?" The thick frustration of her need to be ready for her aunt made her voice hard.

He grunted and reached for her neck. Not in a threatening way. He'd never do that. But Ellie's hand followed the trajectory of his, feeling along her collarbone where he'd pointed. The necklace. The little carved woman. What if Cordelia knew what it was? Ellie's fist closed around the wooden figure, drawing it up and over her head. Just as it cleared the crown of her head, her door opened, and Cordelia swept in. Thom stood behind Ellie. She dropped the leather and wood into his cupped hand, then walked across the room to meet her aunt. She pecked her on the cheek and, since her aunt didn't complain, she hugged her, letting Aunt Cordelia feel her fears and her worries in a long, rare squeeze.

"Poor Ellie Bird. My poor baby girl." Her aunt stroked her hair and pulled her down into the seat next to her. "What were you doing there, hon? In the factory, I mean."

Ellie felt the tears well up again in her eyes, though this time they were fresh and hot with fear. She felt like the wrong answer might change everything. What had Juni told her? "Ellie, she'll shove you aside. She will! She's done it before."

Ellie cast around her gaze, trying not to look her aunt in the eyes, until she captured her chin between her thumb and her finger and pulled Ellie's face toward hers. There was no escaping her aunt's predatory stare.

"Why were you there?"

"To get Thom," Ellie blurted. Truth is always the best way to lie. Truth covers the jittery voice and shifting eyes of a created story. The thing is, the closer you are to truth, the less likely it is you will be caught.

"To get Thom? You mean, you went in there, and a man lost his life, so you could get your poppet?" Aunt Cordelia's voice was awash with scorn. "Well, I hope you're happy. You've given yourself quite a little reputation, breaking into the factory and being a party to a man's death. This sort of thing could ruin you—make you a morally unfit heir, like your mother. You wouldn't want that, now would you, my Ellie?"

Misery at being a disappointment to Cordelia tightened thick on her skin like a two-sizes-too-small winter coat, suffocating her in its heat. "I'm so sorry, Aunt Cordelia." And she was. "I didn't mean to cause so much trouble, really." And she didn't. "I didn't know what was happening until it was too late." Truth is so much easier to use to pad the things you want to hide.

Cordelia seemed to measure Ellie's words, her features cast in ice, so hard and cold. Her fingertips dug into Ellie's upper arms, hooks that held her as the evaluation went on. Then suddenly, she thawed, smiled gently at Ellie, and pulled her into a hug.

"You poor, dear Ellie. You couldn't help what Moze did, could you? You were just there to get your Thom, and why would you think you couldn't? After all, it is your company too."

Ellie nodded, snuffling miserably. As bad as things had gotten, as angry as she was, deep down she wanted this love, this comfort from her aunt. She hoped this love would remain if all her actions tonight came to light.

"You couldn't know that you'd see his mother." Cordelia's voice was warm honey on her ears, but still her hook fingers caught Ellie and jerked her into a face-to-face, eye-to-eye stand-off. "Some things are so ugly but necessary. This peculiar institution of ours makes us do things that seem vile, but they are necessary to sustain us—necessary to our way of life. Do you understand?"

Ellie didn't respond. She waited. Waited for Cordelia to

explain, to make things right like she always did. But this discussion of their way of life would from here on sound hollow to her ears. After all she'd seen tonight, the usual comforts and lies tasted like copper and heat, turning her stomach.

"Yes, Aunt Cordelia." The first lie.

"If I'd known we had Josine, I would have...well, let's just say this whole ugliness wouldn't have happened. I'll have to try to keep up with things better."

The old woman released her, stood, walked over to Ellie's desk, and began flipping through the pages, books, and pieces of flotsam she'd left sitting there. Ellie wondered what her aunt would do when she found out about the snooping she'd been doing. Would it be like Juni had said? Thinking about Cordelia being angry with her, maybe even throwing her out, made Ellie's heart ache.

Cordelia held one of the coded papers that Ellie had taken from the Ridley box. Its teeth glittering in the light, but Cordelia didn't look at it closely. She waved it then pointed it at Ellie. "Did you know that Moze was a Resurrectionist?"

Ellie kept her hands folded in front of her, calm and demure, though she ached to stretch them out and snatch the papers away from Cordelia. To do such a thing would be to admit the wrongs she'd done. Wrongs that now seemed the only right things she'd ever done. A Resurrectionist, she'd asked. Ellie shook her head but wondered if she would become a Resurrectionist now just to be able to sleep at night. "No, Aunt Cordelia. He never said."

Lie number two. How could she have lived this way, beholden to murderers and floating atop such destructions without a care? How could Aunt Cordelia be a part of such things? Cold settled in her gut as she watched Cordelia rage around the room. Moze was out there somewhere in the woods, stumbling in the dark with a dead mother because of them. He was leaving her, probably glad to be rid of the empty-headed pawn of Harold and the DesLoge Com legacy, this foul way of life.

Her aunt's gaze was hard-set and full of questions. "Well, he was. You were taken in by one of them, Ellie Bird."

"Yes, but—"

Cordelia, her stately aunt with the beautiful blue eyes and genteel manner, screamed. A high-pitched, throaty scream that shattered Ellie, crumbled the words in her mouth that would defend Moze, explain his actions and how much he meant. Instead, Thom whimpered and gnashed his displeasure in the corner. The screech, filled with fury and spite, knocked against her like a blow as it resolved from some guttural, meaningless note into her name, "Ellie!" Cordelia leaned on the table, head drooping as if in sheer exhaustion.

"You let him into the factory and now he's escaped— escaped with product and knowledge and proofs." Her voice dropped low and quiet. Dangerously calm. She swept everything off of the desk, scattering the papers, the compad, and the stolen Ridley Brown artifacts. Her aunt's hands, only now beginning to show their age, hovered over the toothed papers like she was afraid they would poison her. Then, with razored ferocity, she lunged, snatched the papers up, and stared at them. Her face was alive with pain and, just as quickly, anger.

"What is this?" Her bright eyes had latched finally on the name, Ridley, and on the knowledge that Ellie had stolen from her. "Are you a Resurrectionist?"

"No, Aunt Cordelia." She was fighting back tears now, though the sobs were wracking her chest. "Really, I just wanted Thom. I didn't know—"

"I don't know what to think of all of this. I am so disappointed. We will have to discuss this tomorrow. Right now, I need to call in some trackers to stop Moze before he gets too far. You are to stay in your room until I call for you. Thom will bring you what you need." Cordelia marched to the door with the papers clutched to her chest. "You will need to explain these...traitorous acts of yours."

"What will you do to him?"

Aunt Cordelia turned and gave her one last look filled with a fury Ellie had never seen. "I will do what must be done to save us all. I will preserve our way of life and our name, like I always do."

She stepped out and pulled the door closed behind her. Ellie heard the bolt slip into place, locking her into her room. She was stuck here and Cordelia was sending trackers after Moze, Josine, and Juni. She went to her window and looked out toward the Mizzourah. The surface seemed calm as glass. She could only hope and pray that they would be safe.

DOCUMENT 15: HIGH COURT RULING EBLAMAN V BUTHE

The High Court of US NOAM ruled that city courts cannot issue decisions contradicting the Constitution of US NOAM and laws passed by the US NOAM Congress. In this case, Resurrectionist and newspaper editor Shem Buthe was arrested for violating the Fugitive Poppet Act when he helped incite a mob, through his writing and speeches, to rescue poppet Glover from Grave Hawker recovery agent Stephen Eblaman. Buthe was released from custody by a low court judge in Jersey-Yorktown City who ruled that the Fugitive Poppet Act was unconstitutional. Grave Hawker Eblaman appealed to the High Court based on the loss of property and his good name stemming from his inability to return the poppet to its owner.

The High Court, in a unanimous opinion written by Chief Justice Tawne, stated that in adopting the US NOAM Constitution, people granted power to the government and DesLoge Com to protect property and carry out the law: "Many of the rights of sovereignty should be ceded to the US NOAM Government, and that it should be supreme, and strong enough to execute its own laws without interruption from a Dome City or territory."

The court noted that the supremacy of US NOAM law could be effective only if the US NOAM government were given power to enforce law. The High Court, therefore, found that the power of Jersey-Yorktown's low court "is limited and restricted by the Constitution of US NOAM." Jersey-Yorktown did not have the power to nullify the judgment of the High Court or to find the Fugitive Poppet Act unconstitutional. Buthe's original conviction therefore was upheld, and he will remain imprisoned for twenty years. The whereabouts of poppet Glover are unknown, but he is assumed to have been smuggled to the wilds by Resurrectionist radicals.

CHAPTER 15

Sleep never came. In the dark of her room, Thom's calm, raspy breaths were a singsong clock ticking off the hours and the deafening loudness of the empty silence surrounding her. Her mind wouldn't stop thrumming with its fears about Moze and Juni. Replaying the accusations of Cordelia, her anger, and her lack of explanations left Ellie's heart breaking. Cordelia had called her a Resurrectionist and a traitor.

She threw her covers back and stepped out of her white-lace canopied bed. Her aunt had bought it, saying it was the bed of a princess. She'd always been just that—everyone's little princess. Everyone's plaything. Never again. Not anymore.

The boy she felt something for, maybe something deep enough to be love someday, walked away from her and her reality. Even as much as he wanted her, he didn't want to be a part of this place, so full of death and dependency and poppets. So full of people without their wills—alive, dead—had she ever really thought about what they were? Was she any better than a poppet, wandering through life without ever seeing the truth of what life was like around her?

She shivered as the memories of the club rose in her mind, the fluids dripping into the grates under the torture chairs.

She picked through her clothes, choosing soft cotton pants and a white top. Nothing fancy. Nothing that a princess would wear. She pulled on her most comfortable shoes and grabbed a jacket, since the chill she felt seemed so deep in her skin she was sure she'd be shivering all day long.

"Thom, what will I do?" Ellie watched vehicles filing into the drive. Not hovercars. These were private floaters—cars that could leave the dome. Trackers. She could see the roughly dressed men and women with hardened arms and worn leather boots making their way up the stone entry stairs. So many of them.

If only she could get the word to Moze or her mother. She put her hand on the doorknob, but it buzzed a rejection, not allowing her to open the door. She was a prisoner.

"Contact Juni," Ellie said to her compad at her desk.

"There is no answer, Miss Ellie," the compad replied in its genteel feminine voice. "Shall I check for her location?"

"You can track her?"

The screen of the comvid lit with an angling, bright map that she recognized as the whole domed city of Santelouisa. It swooped in upon itself, growing more detailed as it sought Juni on the map.

"How are you doing this?"

"Juni is chipped for ease of tracking."

The map showed DesLoge Mansion, focusing closer and closer.

"Chipped?" Ellie felt the heat rising in her cheeks. Could Cordelia have been tracking Moze and the group the whole time? "Where is this chip located?"

The map settled in on the first floor of the mansion with a circled tag resting on a chair at the dining table.

"It's located in her molar." An x-ray rose from the dim corner of the map image—a file within the file.

Ellie stared at the screen showing her mother's location. "Am I chipped?"

"Not that I track."

"Why would Juni be chipped?"

"According to the DesLoge files, Juni was chipped after an attempt to escape into the wilds sixteen years ago." Sixteen years ago? Ellie had only been a baby then.

"What happened?"

A vid flipped on, reeling out across the ceiling, showing Juni being dragged toward the camera and away from a small, single-story house that sat beneath a bright blue sky. Blue. She'd been outside in the wilds. No sound came from the vid, but Juni's mouth moved in a constant angry-looking dance. Her fragile body twisted in the hands of rough men, who dragged her away and into a hover tram truck. They shackled her and slammed shut a barred door. Juni pressed her body and face against the bars, leaning out, grasping for her captors in such fierce and desperate grabs. Only then did Ellie realize that her mother seemed to be fighting to reach a man who held a bundle in his arms tenderly, like the bundle was precious and breakable.

"Freeze," she said, halting the vid's progression in a grainy, flickering shot of past life. A little leg hung out, uncovered and tender, beneath the villain's arm. Her mother was reaching for her, hands curled like claws and mouth gaping.

As she focused on that little foot, Thom wandered over, stood behind Ellie, groaning softly. Just a foot. Had to be her foot, right? He reached into the image, pawing at Juni's face and neck. He grunted, looked back at Ellie, then pawed again.

Ellie cupped the portion of the image that Thom had touched. "Expand," she told the compad. Her mother's face expanded, her neck—around it was the wooden lady Ellie had worn all night.

Thom looked at her with his grayed eyes and slack grin. His hand rose, shaking and slow, until it pointed at the necklace where it sat now, around her neck and tucked into her shirt. She'd put it back on the night before because it made her feel better. Thom gazed deeply into her eyes, as if his stare would plant some thought or idea into her mind. He pointed, then his hand turned and touched his own neck.

"Do you want the necklace, Thom?" she asked, curling it in her hand.

He pointed again, finger touching his chest. He held his hand out, flat and steady, his eyes latched to hers in their quiet intensity. Ellie did as he seemed to want her to, though her mind rebelled against the very thought that he would bid her to do anything. She unlaced the necklace and placed it in his hand.

He nodded once, a tiny movement, but loud as a scream in Ellie's mind. Had he always done such things? She'd been looking all this time for some signal of this...independent thinking. This sentience. She'd thrown herself out of trees and downstairs and to the floor, hoping to evoke a reaction, but hadn't ever seen it. Yet here it was—an outstretched hand and a tiny nod.

He took the little wooden lady on its leather string and tied it around his own neck, tucking it into his shirt, hiding it away.

"Oh my God, Thom. My Thom." Ellie threw her arms around him, hugging him tight. She'd done it before, many, many times, but this time, this wonderful time, he hugged her back—just a light pressure on her back and sides, but it was a miracle.

How many times had they told her that such a thing wasn't possible? That the poppets were machinery with no soul, no feelings, and no primacy. Every textbook, every rule, everything ever told to her said that this act was impossible. That he was empty and blank, just like an animal. But she'd known all along that was not the truth.

"Thom..." She didn't know what to say to make up for the years of suffering—the tortures, the multitude of idiotic orders and actions, when all along he felt enough to hug her. "The time at the lake? You did save me, didn't you?"

One nod. Thom stepped back into a more appropriate, stately position.

"You've always been protecting me. You've always been here for me. And I've just assumed that you would take care of me, be here and fix things. I wonder how hard that is for you. To care for the grandniece, the heir of the one who created this strange life of servitude for you, for all who are like you. Thom, I'm so sorry."

He turned away, picking up papers to neaten the room. But in that moment, Ellie saw the single tear track down his nose and drop to the floor.

A bright miracle, prismed and slow, the tear found her heart.

The door popped open with a loud click, suddenly free of the comlock that Aunt Cordelia had ordered in the night. The vid screen flickered on, and her aunt's lovely, stern face filled it.

"Ellie, I'd like you to join us for breakfast. I want to discuss your recent...activities. Bring your Thom and the materials you took from me. We'll make a fresh start, shall we?" She smiled, though her teeth were clearly clenched, and strain showing in the corners of her eyes.

"I'll be right down." Ellie grabbed the box of Ridley's things—those that hadn't been taken by Cordelia the night before. Ellie moved frantically, so she slowed, panting a little, gathering her strength. "Let's go, Thom."

Thom didn't respond, didn't agree, but he seemed ready, so Ellie started down the stairs. She stuck out her hand to Thom. "Let's go together."

As they descended the winding stair and made their way across the marble floor, Ellie wondered where Moze was. Had he made it out of the dome safely? She hoped so. Her stomach turned as she thought of the trackers that Aunt Cordelia had sent to find him.

Voices floated out the formal dining room where Aunt Cordelia usually held court. So many voices. Suddenly, Ellie froze outside the door, listening, trying to grasp what was happening before walking into the room.

"What were you doing out there, Juni?"

"What do you care, Cordelia? I was drunk, and I had a gentleman suitor. He wasn't gallant, so I walked away. The mansion seemed closer, so I walked here."

Silence. Ellie peeked around the corner.

Juni sat at the end of the long oblong table, her hands folded demurely in her lap, and her head hung, chin to chest.

"Why did you walk? Any hovercar would have stopped for you. You are a DesLoge, after all."

"I didn't want to ride. I wanted to walk."

The silence between them seemed to stretch like a thread pulling from a sweater, longer and longer, until it seemed they would fray under the stress, the high drama of their polite silence.

Ellie took a deep breath, tucking the box of Ridley's things under her arm. She tried to seem casual, but she was sure she only achieved awkward. "Let's go, Thom. We can do this, right?"

She stepped into the dining room, stopping in the door so that her aunt, the matriarch of the family, could politely invite her in. All eyes swiveled to her, noted her, and then swiveled away back to Cordelia. Ellie fought the urge to suck in a gasp of air as she noted the assembled people around the oval table. Juni, as she'd seen her, sat at the nearest end of the table. Her tangerine dress hung carelessly from her thin shoulders, and she wore a floppy hat and sunglasses, even though she was inside. Ellie recognized this now as her costume, the way that Juni managed to stay off of Cordelia's radar.

To Juni's right, farther around the table sat Joceylin, her white-haired rival, looking angry and sour, arms crossed over her small frame and every body angle set in high tension. Joceylin's eyes shifted, caught hers, and held her pinioned. Whatever had transpired played across Joceylin's face in the tension of her lips, which thinned with anger. With just a glance, Ellie understood that all they'd agreed to, the cessation of her and Natan's formal relationship, had been discarded.

Across from Joceylin, looking as miserable as she'd ever seen him, sat Natan. His eyes were cast down, and his posture, near perfectly straight back and squared shoulders, radiated misery.

Aunt Cordelia's voice was inauthentically bright. "Ah, Ellie. Welcome back, my little prodigal child. Tired from your long night of wandering?"

Ellie shook her head and walked right past Juni. Though it hurt not to acknowledge the new understanding she had of her mother, Ellie figured she should focus on pleasing her aunt as soon as possible.

"No, Aunt Cordelia. I slept well, but thank you."

Juni didn't acknowledge her, either. She just sat lump-like and infuriating. Why didn't she stand up for herself? For Ellie? After seeing her mother last night, in charge of an escape and so vital, this visage of a grown woman slumped at the table like a child with her feet tapping nervously seemed like a sour note in a symphony. It no longer made sense to her. Why was she so passive now, especially when Ellie could use a kind word or even a glance? Ellie repaid her in kind, ignoring her completely.

Sasha sat between Natan and Cordelia, laughing in her muted and proper way, clearly putting on a show of perfection. Cordelia sat half-turned and smiling at Sasha, who seemed to be in the middle of some amusing story. Both women, one so old and queenly, the other so young and eager, were above everyone around them. Both were so in charge.

That's how she'd like me to be, Ellie couldn't help but think, falling into her old patterns of self-doubt. If only I was what she wanted me to be. Ellie found her seat next to Cordelia.

"We are waiting for one more before we can really discuss what has happened among you young folks." Cordelia's gaze moved across each of them, her bitterly blue eyes like pins holding them in their place. Ellie could see them, each in their turn, squirm under the gaze of the most powerful woman in their world.

"Who are we waiting for, Auntie?" Ellie asked, hoping that the pet name would soften her aunt.

"Young Joceylin's father, Simon. He's been on an all-night hunt, and I'm hoping he'll be bringing back our mutual problems."

Ellie nodded, sucking her lip in to chew nervously. She waited, her gaze shifting between the thinly-veiled longing that settled between Joceylin and Natan like a fog and her mother, still shrunken in upon herself. Would Cordelia do as she'd said and honor any choice that she made? Allow her to deny Natan? Maybe. Or, after her escapades with Moze, would her heart be hardened? If only Cordelia would rise and hug her, pull her closer and tell her she'd be okay. Or was she, as Juni had told her, replaceable—just another defective little fool too stupid to do the right things? Was she just like Juni to Cordelia?

The front door slammed, and a draft, too chilly to be normal dome wind, tickled her spine. Thom, silent while he stood at attention, stretched his hand up to his throat and stroked the lump where the wooden necklace sat. Would the others notice his movements and understand that Thom was different? Ellie tried to catch his eye. Though he didn't look at her, he did drop his hand back to his side. Joceylin leaned forward as the heavy footsteps approached. Was she excited? No, when her hand swept back her white blond hair from her pixie face, Ellie could see the tension in her lips, pursed with worry. Sasha and Cordelia continued to laugh and talk while Joceylin seemed to be peeling apart by layers.

"Joceylin," Ellie said. She stretched her hand across the table and thumped it to get her attention. For a moment, Joceylin's green-eyed gaze swept away from the doorway to meet Ellie's eyes. Between them, it seemed questions of bravery and promises flew back and forth. Could she honor her promise to let Joceylin have Natan? Would it be wise to just go ahead and announce her intentions to Cordelia? Joceylin's gaze skittered away toward Sasha, then back—trying to telegraph some message that Ellie couldn't catch.

"Well, here you are, my friend. Come join us, please." Cordelia signaled between her and Ellie. "You don't mind, do you, Ellie?"

She shook her head and scooted to the side. The slight

felt cold and sharp, like being cut with ice. Never before had Cordelia shifted her away. Usually, she drew her closer, making sure she was involved in whatever problem lay before them. Ellie could only hope that this was some temporary punishment. Or would she wind up like her mother, a sad remnant at the end of the table, tolerated and ignored?

"Excuse me, Sasha." Cordelia turned her full attention to Simon Eregel.

Ellie watched Sasha's face, so animated and bright a moment before, fall into shadow as the spotlight of importance passed from her to the rough man now leaning back in the formal mahogany chair, propping a foot up on the table.

"Yep, quite a mess you've got here, Miz. DesLoge. A mess of epic proportions." He smiled, and his bezel-bacco-stained teeth seemed to glow blue from his worn, wrinkle webbed face. "Uh yup, that girl of yours sure made a fool of us all."

Cordelia's face grew red as he talked. "Be careful what you say. Remember, you are talking about my niece and heir."

Simon nodded, unimpressed by Cordelia's anger, and continued with an amused tone of voice. "Yes, Ma'am, I know. It'll cost quite a bit to relocate Doc's family to another dome-city. Without them here, the scandal of her being part of a murder would disappear. So, that's in the works."

"I'm beholden to you for that, old friend." She said it kindly, but as she did, her eyes found Ellie's, telegraphing bitterness over this unwanted debt. Ellie's face burned with embarrassment, but she didn't look away. She didn't want to look weak and ridiculous.

"Now, as for this other matter—our runaways. I have a crew looking for them. I just need to know how far you want to go to find them. Shall I call out the Grave Hawkers? Shall we hunt them to Liberty Lawrence? Or do we let them go the way we let go of Ridley?"

Ellie saw Juni shudder at the name. Her thin arms wrapped around her body, hugging away some imagined chill.

"No. This one can't just get away. I think we owe something to young Mr. Grayson, don't you?" Cordelia tipped her head to the side coquettishly.

This talk made her stomach churn. Grave Hawkers chasing Moze and the Vules. Would they be safe?

Juni stood, yawned, and wandered toward the window. There, she leaned against the frame sitting on the padded seat beneath it. "I'm bored, Cordelia. Can I go get a drink?"

"No, Juni. You can't drink at 10:00 a.m. It's just not done."

"Then let me go get a nap, would you? I'm tired of this."

Juni pulled her legs up and hugged them, caring little about the flare of her skirt showing the roundness of the backs of her legs. Ellie could see Simon lean in to get a better view.

What a pig. He leered, only looking away when Cordelia cleared her throat.

"Go lay down, Juni, if you must. I thought you'd care about this, since it has to do with Ellie." Cordelia let the words hang like low clouds.

Ellie thought Juni might say something. There for a second, a flash of the competence she'd seen in the forest met her gaze and made her catch her breath. In just that second, Ellie understood that Juni wasn't trying to get away from her. It was that she wanted to get away to send a message into the wilds. That she'd get the warning out to Moze and his group.

"She's always done fine without me. Besides, I'm too tired." Juni's words drew out in a long whine.

Cordelia didn't acknowledge her. Instead, she twiddled her fingers in Juni's general direction, dismissing her. Juni stood and flitted away toward the kitchen and the back of the mansion. Ellie hoped she would get the message to them, to keep them safe from Simon and his crew.

"Let's dispense with the formalities, shall we? Clearly, my niece has no sense of decorum, anyway."

Sasha tittered, as if what Cordelia had said were more witty than anything she'd heard before.

"Simon, your daughter and my niece's beau seem to have struck up a friendship that goes beyond what is proper. This is nothing against your daughter, but I think perhaps she might be overstepping herself some," Cordelia said.

Joceylin's face became red. She glanced at Natan, her gaze sharpening, demanding some action from him.

He stared miserably at his hands, unable, or unwilling, to take a stand.

Sasha sat forward on her chair, smiling with a buttery satisfaction that spread across her features.

Simon, appraising his daughter with a critical but admiring eye, said, "I wouldn't doubt it. She's smarter than most. Real quick. Why shouldn't she shoot high?"

Sasha's smile melted into a grimace. "They don't belong together. My family is to be joined with the DesLoges. I've been besties with Ellie, and my brother is her beau—has been her beau—for years and years."

"Yes, well, that remains to be seen," Cordelia said.

Sasha didn't gasp, but the lightning-quick turn of her head suggested she hadn't expected those words like a slap in her face from Cordelia.

Simon sucked his teeth. "What's the boy think?"

Natan sat, miserable and mopey, unable to meet any of the gazes. "I love Joceylin. Ellie knows. I told her."

His voice might have been unimpressive, but Ellie thought his words were pretty brave.

"I don't want him, Aunt Cordelia. I want to deny him."

"What are you saying, Ellie? We're the only family good enough for the DesLoge name! Why would you do such a thing?" Sasha stood and spoke too loudly for polite conversation. Her words were edged with an anger Ellie had seen only when something didn't go according to Sasha's best laid plans. She'd seen it in Antedevolution lit class when a paper she'd put a lot of work into had come back without a good grade. She'd seen the grimace on her friend's face before but never aimed at her.

"I'm sorry, Sasha, really. I'm not willing to take someone whose heart won't be mine."

"Don't do this, Ellie. He will marry you if you will have him." Sasha moved around the table, wringing her hands.

"Just sit down, dear. You're making a scene."

Cordelia's voice seemed to hit Sasha like a cold shower, freezing her in place. She lowered herself back down slowly. Poor Sasha's face sagged, her cheeks doing the thing she hated so.

What would it take for her to make this right with her bestie? Could she save their friendship and live up to what she'd promised Natan and Joceylin? Probably not. "I'm sorry, Sasha. I don't want him now."

Ellie turned to look at her aunt, whose cool gaze and placid, marbled features seemed to turn in orbit to fully gaze upon her. There was no approval or anger, just a curious sort of interest.

Unable to bear the weight of that gaze, Ellie stood, turned toward Joceylin, and grabbed her hand. Not a natural gesture. Surely, Sasha would see through it. But Aunt Cordelia might see the pairing as important.

"Joceylin, if I do this—if I step aside and find another to marry—will you always be loyal to me? Your strength and your connections will be important as I come into my position with DesLoge Com."

Ellie didn't dare look at her aunt to gauge her reaction. She just hoped this gambit was worth the risk.

Joceylin looked at Natan, then at her father. She turned back to Ellie. "I will be."

She reached her hand out and caught Ellie's in hers, gave her a quick squeeze, then dropped her hand.

"Aunt Cordelia, don't you think that is more useful to us than me being married to someone who doesn't want me? There will be someone. Maybe someone more like Uncle Harold."

Her aunt stared at her for a moment, then laughed loudly. "Ellie, you're usually such a quiet girl. Not a peep from you for sixteen years, and now? So much trouble in just a couple of days. Fine, Ellie, if you want to deny the Parker boy, I won't stand in your way. I must say, if it weren't for that attack on our scientist, I'd think that Moze boy was actually a good influence on you."

Her aunt waved a hand at the others. "You're all free to go. Simon, you and Joceylin will track up Widow Douglas's little murdering nephew. I'll put in a word for you with the Parkers."

Joceylin squealed with happiness, clapping her hands together and lunging up out of her chair. A word from Cordelia DesLoge is a bond. It's a promise as good as a brick of gold. Natan shyly met her joy with his own half-smile—the first he'd hazarded since the meeting had begun.

Sasha sobbed, just once, but it was enough to make Natan put his arm around her and whisper something in conciliatory tones. Sasha jerked out of the circle of his arms. She stiffened and stood. "Miz Cordelia..."

"Sasha, dear?"

"Cordelia, I'm afraid I need to protest—"

"Now listen, Sasha," Cordelia started, standing up with a quick shove against the table. She moved with the grace of a cat. "Your family will always be as important to us, to Ellie, and the company, whether or not we are actual family."

Sasha traced her finger across the tabletop pattern's swirls and scrolled inlay.

"You always told me you and I would be masters of the universe together," Ellie said. "How is that going to change, Sasha? You'll have your Plastique empire, and someday I'll be head of DesLoge. We'll be just like sisters, and we'll always work together, right?"

Simon let his chair hit the ground with a thunk. "Isn't this nice. Little misses all in a row, getting their dreams come true. Least my girl will. Maybe not you, Miss Sasha, but gals like you got futures that are written by the world." He stood up, stretched, and put his hands in his pockets.

Shifting his weight forward and back on his boots, rocking and grinning, he whispered to Ellie, "See, I know what's going on here. I know it. You've got some sympathies 'cause that boy tickled your fancy real nice. I see you got that old box I took offa your Dad when I shot him out in the wilds. Maybe you're a Resurrectionist like him?"

Ellie gasped. "How dare you. You can't speak to me that way."

He grabbed her arm and twisted her soft skin between his bony fingers. "Listen, girlie, you may be the next DesLoge queen, but you ain't yet. Not yet. Promises you make, words you say, they don't mean squat to me and mine." He gritted his teeth, blue and angled deep into his red gums, a nasty and brutal smile. "I'm gonna run your boy down 'til he ain't got feet. I'll gun him down and make him my own poppet." His sour breath was hot on her face. "Won't that be nice? Then you can come look at him, maybe talk to him. You DesLoges can do whatcha want in my book."

"Sir, you should release me. Right now." Ellie made her words hard and icy, hoping he'd take the hint.

"Daddy, let her go," Joceylin said.

Cordelia watched but did nothing. She seemed to be waiting to see how Ellie would handle it.

"Unhand me. Now."

Simon looked her up and down, raked his gaze across her almost hungrily. He released her and laughed, a chuffing, dismissive sound. Shoved her lightly as he passed. "Joceylin, let's go, girl."

Joceylin looked at her and mouthed, "I'm sorry," then hurried out of the room, tiptoeing in the wake of her father's heavily clumping boots.

"How can you allow us to be entangled with that?" Sasha said, though Ellie wasn't sure who she said it to.

Natan ran his fingers across the top of the table, tracing the wood grain in circling lines.

"How can any of you think this is okay? You are degrading us, Natan." Sasha grabbed her brother's shoulder.

He looked at her hand for a moment, perhaps with a bit of regret, then shrugged it off and walked toward the door.

"Why would you do this to us?" Her voice rose until it was a shriek.

Ellie rushed to her bestie. Cordelia didn't stop her. She watched. Ellie imagined that she weighed her reaction against what she herself would do. But Ellie couldn't worry about that. She'd try to be there for her bestie, even if she never could be again. Even if they'd always be on opposite sides from here on out.

She opened her arms, wrapped Sasha up in them, and said, "I'm sorry. I really am."

For a moment, it seemed like Sasha would let the pain and tension melt away. For a moment, she seemed to lean into Ellie's hug, but then she stiffened. She grew, hardened into something statuesque, cold and slick. She slid from Ellie's grasp.

"You and I may be besties, but right now I don't like you

even a little. I'm hurt to my deepest core by you and by your treatment of Natan's and my name."

"He doesn't want me, Sasha. Why should I—"

"Do you think anyone married for the strength of their family or the good of their nation is in love? You let a silly boy believe he could throw off his family. We were to be sisters. To work together for the good of us all. Now, after all of this, what can we be?"

Ellie looked toward Thom. Things had been so much easier before, but now the gulf between them was too big to cross. Unless...

"Sasha, I've seen things...bad things. Things you wouldn't believe if I told you. We can work together, use our names and our power to make things better. Maybe Aunt Cordelia would work with us and teach us how—"

"What things? Things that traitor Moze showed you? Ellie, you poor thing," Sasha said. Her voice dripped with a honeyed kind of pity, long vowels, and sarcasm that cut like a razor. "Nothing you can tell me will change me. You have been misled. Misinformed. He used you, you silly girl. He used you and abandoned you. Then you, like a little empty-headed fool, let my brother go. You gave us away, Ellie. You gave me away."

Sasha turned on her heel and clicked away toward the door. Ellie wanted to run after her. Slap her. Yell at her until she shut her mouth and listened. But, instead, she froze. Her friend's bitter words paralyzed her.

Sasha leaned against the jamb of the door, glancing over her shoulder at her old friend. Their eyes met, and Ellie felt tears well up to sting her.

"Sasha..."

The name hung between them, asking all the questions that neither of them would. Would they be able to get past this? Would they be besties? Would they ever speak again? Sasha's eyes shifted away, and her head shook quickly, as if the answer to every question for them would always be negative.

"Thank you for having us, Miz Cordelia. The Parkers will always be in your debt."

"Thank you, child," Cordelia said. "The DesLoges take care of their own, no matter what."

The two women locked steely gazes, appraising and reassuring. Ellie felt like an interloper in her own home watching these two iron maidens saluting each other. After long moments of dignified stares and unspoken promises, their stalemate broke. Sasha bowed her head.

Then Sasha turned, her long jacket dress dusting the floor as she walked away. Like a breeze, she flowed out the door and perhaps out of Ellie's life. For a moment, Ellie couldn't breathe. Her bestie, one of the few people who'd ever tried to understand her or tried to make her life better, was gone. She took a deep, hitching breath, trying to fill up her lungs with air because that would staunch the tears waiting at the gates of her eyes.

"Come sit next to me, dear," Cordelia said.

Her aunt returned to her seat at the head of the table, a throne for a queen who'd presided over so many scenes of drama and horror. Ellie moved for the seat next to her, stomach churning and knees weak. This was the moment of her greatest fear. Would she have the courage to say the things her conscience demanded, or would she cave and retreat back into her world of quiet acceptance? Could she be strong here? With Cordelia's weighty gaze upon her?

"Thom, get us some tea." Cordelia shifted in her seat, adjusting her skirt across her legs. The old poppet shuffled away, leaving them in the silence that sat thick as a cloud. Cordelia pulled her compad out and ran her fingers across the surface, playing images Ellie couldn't see. She tried to look unconcerned, but her heart drummed in her chest. She twisted her hands in her skirts under the table, unable to stop fidgeting. She hoped her aunt couldn't see.

Her aunt's pursed lips switched to the left side of her face —a quizzical look. Then her features softened and, with a sliding swipe across the face of the compad screen, she threw the flickering vid up for Ellie to see.

A map popped up with live action, triangles moving about followed by lines of text. The map showed an overhead view of GasBright Square the day before, with each shop and attraction identified by little symbols and descriptions. Every single person was identified and tracked. Ellie could see identification numbers, names, and scrolling descriptions, including her own. Cordelia's power seemed boundless. Only Moze's triangle had no identifiers. He must not be chipped. She breathed a sigh of relief.

But the relief crumbled as Ellie thought about the simple implications of her being tracked all night. If Cordelia looked very closely, Juni would be outed. If she looked very closely, she'd know about the underground railroad. Ellie stiffened under the realization that she couldn't allow that to happen under any circumstances.

"Let's see here. So, you and Moze were to be studying last night. I have you at a coffee shop at dusk, but you left pretty quickly to go to a factory shop?" Cordelia looked up, seeming to measure the look on Ellie's face.

Her mind was racing. "And maybe I wanted to show off a little bit. I knew that Natan didn't like me. I've known that for a while now. But Moze liked me. He liked me, and I wanted to impress him with the importance of what we do."

Her eyes felt full of tears she didn't want to drop, but maybe, just maybe those would help her cause, maybe take some suspicion off of her for the time being. Maybe Aunt Cordelia would want to ease her pain.

"Please, Aunt Cordelia, I just wanted to make Moze like me and to get Thom back. I don't want to relive last night's... misadventure. I certainly don't want anything more to do with Moze now." The lie was like a snake in her mouth, thick and full of teeth. Would it bite her in the end to say such a thing?

Thom returned, hot tea on a silver tray. He set the tray gracefully on the corner of the long table. As he poured the steaming brew into two delicate china cups, the vid continued playing, showing the movements of Ellie's triangle and the unmarked triangle that was Moze.

"Two sugars, Thom," Aunt Cordelia said, distracted from the vid by her need to tell Thom something he'd done for the last twenty years, at least twice a day.

The triangles made their way to the flat square that represented Club Inferno. Ellie took her teacup and lifted it smoothly to her lips, sipping as the triangles seemed to rest at the club. Ellie hoped her aunt wouldn't do a detailed scan, flipping the schematic vertical for a look at what Moze and Ellie had done there. As she set her cup and saucer gently back down, she tried to formulate words that would end this analysis of their night before all was exposed.

"We didn't study, Aunt Cordelia. We went dancing. I'd heard of this club that my friends all go to—the Inferno."

"We own that, too."

Cordelia stared at her, face blank but eyes sharp. Ellie tried to keep the nerves from hardening her own eyes. She just let her honest misery show through. That at least was the truth and couldn't be picked apart by Cordelia's expertly razored questioning.

"Yes, I found that out when the hand scanner confirmed me."

"We have records of hand scans. Shall I check them to see what all you did in Club Inferno?" Aunt Cordelia leaned forward. With a soft, deliberate grasp, she raised her teacup to her face. For a moment, the steam wreathed her features in a gauzy veil that reminded Ellie of the myths of Antedevolutionary England, where dangerous fairy women stole the youth and lives of those they ensnared. Cordelia's youthful but weathered gaze held that kind of dangerous wisdom and angry beauty. Ellie shivered, but did her best to hide it as Cordelia took her sip and lowered the cup again.

Ellie took a gasping breath and tried to tell a story that would save them all somehow. "I went upstairs, Aunt Cordelia. I wanted to see it all because you always say I should know more about the company. Once I was up in the more... exclusive areas, I saw things that a young woman shouldn't see. But Moze, he made me understand that the company is "—she dredged up a pretty lie as fast as her mind could work —"...serving humanity by providing the services that used to be forced upon human victims or sex workers. He explained that it was essential to a polite society that the poppets absorb *all* the indelicate pastimes that used to plague mankind. I'd read about these things at the Academy. To see them in action was distressing but enlightening at the same time."

Cordelia's mouth turned up. A small smile. Ellie seemed to be on the right track, since her aunt was no longer programming the vid. The image still flickered in the air above them, tracking the path of their movements, but now Cordelia didn't seem to be too worried about following along. Ellie dropped her hand to her lap and twisted her fingers into her blouse's hem, trying to control the tremors of nerves that her hand might give away.

"I just wanted to be with him and feel beautiful and show off for him. Then I got to thinking about how I wanted Thom back..." Ellie took a jagged breath, trying very hard to control her gushing words, to make them into an explanation that would distract her aunt from the map. "That's when we went to the factory. We found Thom. Then, we found Josine. Moze went crazy when he saw his mom as a poppet. I guess I kind of understand that. If I saw you dead, or Juni, I don't know what I'd do."

Cordelia leaned forward and reached for Ellie's hand. Ellie untangled and reached out toward her aunt, hoping her hand would be cool and dry and tremor-free. For a moment, Cordelia clutched her hand, stroked it, and looked into Ellie's eyes. Her gaze had softened, back into the loving and kind benefactor that Ellie loved so well.

The triangle vid people that represented her and Moze emerged from the flat square that was the club and spilled out. Ellie saw them pause in the alley to the west of the club. Their first kiss. She felt the heat rise in her cheeks. She tried to focus on Cordelia without letting her nerves show. How long before the triangles got to the woods? How long before Juni was exposed?

"Tell me, Ellie, because I can't see in the factory footage, what you saw before the murder?"

The image of Josine's body hanging from the post flashed through her mind, with Moze leaping to her aid, and the others, alive. How could she explain that?

"I'm not sure what I saw, Aunt Cordelia. I know we found Thom and Josine. Moze attacked the doctor and in that moment..." Could she make her aunt believe that what they'd seen wasn't a threat? "It's a blur. We found Thom and Josine, then they fought, and there were people, but I'm not sure how they got there. Moze didn't really talk any after finding Josine. But we just left because the man was dead. I didn't know what to do, other than try to get home." The triangles clustered around Gertrude's shop. So many of them. Too many to be coincidental. So many of them without the numbers and the information that marked a resident citizen, chipped and tracked, of DesLoge-controlled Santelouisa. Only her triangle was traceable.

Cordelia released her hand and slid back in her chair. She waved her hand at Thom for him to come serve her again. "What I don't understand, Ellie Bird, is that you seem to be following them into their escape. Can you explain that?"

Thom picked up the silver teapot and tilted it toward Cordelia's cup. Ellie searched for words, for explanations, but she knew that in just a few seconds, she'd be trapped. That, in those seconds, the whole underground rail road would be exposed and, maybe, whatever Juni knew about how to escape would be open to the Grave Hawkers because of her.

Thom shifted as he started to pour; his usually rock-steady hands jittered. He jerked, slid forward, and dumped the steaming hot tea across the screen of the comvid, which crackled and popped as the liquid found its way into the crevices of the device. The screen with triangles and squares slid and flickered and faded, just as the triangles left the shop.

"Thom! You clumsy oaf!" Aunt Cordelia slid the chair back and shoved him, knocking him off his feet. His arms cartwheeled as his body fell backward. He hit the ground with a meaty thump. Cordelia mopped at the screen with a napkin.

"He didn't mean it, Aunt Cordelia. It was just an accident." Ellie mopped with her own napkin, hoping that the vid couldn't be fixed. Who was she kidding? This was just a temporary reprieve. All it would take to be right back in the hot seat was a new comvid.

"Honestly, Ellie. You and your Thom Poppet. All of this, the whole situation, could have been avoided. Moze was a perfectly suitable match for you. I could have backed your little fascination. What a grand joining of two old families. You had to go get Thom. It's always been that way for you."

Aunt Cordelia stood and began to pace. Thom pushed himself up to all fours. "Stay, Thom. Stay down."

Thom froze, staring down at the floor.

"Aunt Cordelia, he didn't mean it. He just…"

"You know he's just a poppet, right? Do you, Ellie? None of this mess would have happened but for your obsession with him. You've always been obsessed with him." Cordelia's hand traced the top of her frilled white blouse. "Juni defended your strange fascination with him. Said it was just like a girl with a pony or a kitten—something to care for and to love. Something of your own. I think I've been very patient with you about this, but last night, well… things changed."

Ellie gasped as her aunt's hand dipped into the top of her blouse and pulled out the Joltlace that she wore every day of her life. As she cradled it in her hand, her smile evaporated. Something deadly moved in the crystal blue depths of Cordelia's eyes.

Ellie rushed over to Thom and pulled him up to his feet. He clutched the wooden pendant of the Grandma Moses figure with reverence. His face, neutral like usual, seemed to have shades of grim acceptance in the way the line of his mouth compressed and the sidelong glance he gave her.

"No, don't, Aunt Cordelia. Let's talk about this."

Cordelia's hand clutched the Joltlace, pulling the button closer. "I need to end this dependence you have on him. You say that you understand that poppets aren't alive, but honey, I see it in your eyes. You love this old slab of meat. That's all he is, you know. It's like loving a gear or a wrench. You can't keep up this defiance against the truth—this wrong-headed thinking will destroy us. Don't you understand?" Her aunt's hand stayed on the Joltlace, clutching it with her long fingers. Her fierce blue eyes cut Ellie, measuring her as she stood shoulder-to-shoulder with Thom. "I have to preserve our way of life. I am the mother of the dome-cities, and you will be too, but only if you get past this bad set of ideas you've got in your head."

Ellie shook her head, fighting back the tears. "I don't believe anything bad. I am all DesLoge for you. I believe in the institution, Aunt Cordelia. I swear I do."

She fought the urge to attack her aunt, rip the Joltlace from her hands and tear it from her scrawny neck. Inside, her churning stomach and pounding heart paled next to the near electrified state of her nerves, painfully slow in their reactions. Every bead of breath from her aunt's mouth, every word and every inflection, was like the grating of a fork against fine china plates.

"You must learn that these poppets aren't anything to us. They are property. Livestock, you hear? You are falling for a pair of dead eyes and motions that I've programmed into him. I need you to see that he's nothing."

"No, Auntie, please. Please, I'll do anything. Just don't hurt him."

Ellie moved between Thom and Cordelia, though her body would not be able to stop the Joltlace signal if her aunt pressed the bright blue button. Just one tap, and Thom would cease to be. One push and a creature she loved would be dead forever.

Somewhere down deep, Ellie realized that he was alive to her. Alive! That spark that she loved deserved to be protected, deserved its life. He wasn't a dead thing, no matter what anyone said.

"This is going to hurt, dear Ellie, but you will see how much better it is when you face the truth. Idiots like Moze and your little beau, Natan, they don't know what the world is really about. It is about a way of life and how you enrich the lives of your kith and kin. All of Santelouisa and the other dome-cities are our kin, girl. All of the cities depend on our poppets. My heir can't have some unnatural, soft-heartedness for a poppet. My heir's got to be an iron-fisted matriarch with the protection of our way of life foremost in her mind. Step away, Ellie."

Ellie shook her head. Hot, fast tears slid down her cheeks, and her breath hitched, but she still shook her head and backed toward Thom. He moaned and lightly pushed her forward, away from him. Dear Thom. He'd die trying to protect her.

She turned quickly, like a ballerina pirouetting on stage, locking her arm with his and pulling him toward her until his head lay against hers. "I can't let you hurt him, Aunt Cordelia. I just can't."

"Step away, Ellie, now. I saw everything. I saw how you led Moze into our factory, how you gave away secrets, and how quickly he could make you turn against everything we stand for. I saw it, but I can forgive you. All will be forgiven if you will just step away from that poppet. If you do that, you will prove you love me and that you are worthy of your name."

"I do love you." Ellie's words sounded like the wail of a siren in her own ears. "I do, but you can't keep destroying people. I saw live people made into poppets. That goes against everything you've ever taught me. I thought we only used the dead. Now, you want to take Thom."

Ellie put her arm around Thom's neck, keeping his head close to hers, cheeks touching. She could see the disgust in her aunt's sneering, arching gaze. Ellie began again, knowing she wouldn't win this. The disdain in Cordelia's eyes grew. "I can't let this happen, Aunt Cordelia. I'm sorry I'm not what you think I should be."

Ellie backed away from her aunt, step by backward step. The Joltlace glowed blue between Cordelia's fingers, and she worried that her aunt would risk the explosion, trust that the tiny charge wouldn't hurt Ellie even with her head right next to his. Under her breath, she prayed, though she wasn't sure who to pray to. Did the Resurrectionists believe in God? Or had they rejected him because of the defense of poppets in the *Book of Holies*? Such thoughts washed across her fevered mind as she moved backward with Thom into the hallway. Cordelia followed, eyes wide, flashing.

"Do you understand what you are doing?"

"Yes, Aunt Cordelia. I'm saving my friend."

Cordelia followed them as they backed out of the dining room and to the front door.

"You will have nowhere to go with him, Ellie. Once you leave, do you understand I won't let you back? I will get Thom one way or another. There is nowhere you can go in Santelouisa where I won't find you. Nowhere."

Cordelia's words pealed like a bell. This is what Juni had promised. This hard choice between what she knew was right and what would be easy. She kept her arm around

Thom, though he kept pulling and sagging in her grasp, as if he wanted to escape.

"Not letting you go, Thom. You have to stay with me, okay. You have always stayed with me."

They passed through the door as Cordelia put the Jolt-lace back in her shirt. Ellie steered Thom toward the side of the house, still clutching his head to hers.

Cordelia waved dismissively. "I will have him, Ellie. This is completely futile. You leave me no choice, my girl. I will have to choose another."

Cordelia's words slid like an ice pick into the meat of her heart. The rejection hurt, even if it was expected.

On the lawn, the poppets weeding and trimming and watering stopped to watch them—Ellie hand in hand with Thom, running for the edge of the woods. She hoped to find the same trail she'd stumbled home from the night before—the same one that Moze had taken.

Thom pulled against her hand once they were in the treeline, slowing her. He grunted and stumbled over a knobby root but seemed to know the way to go. The twisting trails she'd always played on as a child now seemed haunting and oppressive with their heavy smells and thick vines that tore her legs as she ran. Where could they go? Her mind spun as she thought about the limits of her options. Gertrude's? No, because they'd track her and trap Thom. Sasha's was out. The Parkers would side with Aunt Cordelia. Joceylin owed her, but how long could she hide Thom. Juni? What could Juni do to protect them?

The woods thickened around them, crowding out the gray of the dome and its simulated breeze. The recorded song of birds, crickets, frogs, and things that no longer existed in the dome-city but Harold's millions paid to pipe in for effect echoed around them. Thom stumbled and moaned but kept them moving forward toward the managed river.

Ellie didn't know what they'd do or how they'd find their way, but as she followed Thom, she realized that the only time she'd felt so right, so justified and powerful, was when she and Moze had been working together. When they had found Thom and Jule at the factory. This escape, no matter how it ended, had to be. They had to try because life without Thom wasn't an option.

Ahead, the foliage shifted, shook, and drew apart. A whizzing noise and a thump. Thom grunted, turned and pushed her, trying to get her to run. A dart sat deep in the meat of his neck, its red feathered head nodding as he fell to his knees, his eyes spinning in his sockets. Then, silently, he tumbled to the ground.

"Thom!"

Rough hands covered her mouth and jerked her back.

DOCUMENT 16: VID-AD IN ALL MAJOR DOME-CITY NEWS STREAMS.

Additionally, this is the transcript for many of the vid-show sponsor commercials that ran throughout the Devolution period of US NOAM

Poppet Dolls: The Toy Craze Sweeping Dome Cities Once upon a time, when Harold DesLoge first created the chemicals for awakening dead flesh, it was only legal to administer the chemicals to adults. The worry of the time was that child poppets would be too shocking for our citizens to handle. Perhaps then, in the first strange days of this poppet revolution, it would have caused some of our more delicate citizens or our children particular pain to see such tiny reanimates.

That worry is a thing of the past.

Fifty years ago, DesLoge Com introduced the first teen poppets, which, according to all accounting of the day, proved to be the hottest sellers. Many consumers of poppets preferred the young, strong bodies of teenaged poppets to the older adult versions. Though all poppets are checked for strength and durability, with most coming with a lifetime warranty and free maintenance, citizens of the cities went positively ga-ga for the new, sleek teen models.

Just twenty years later, the first child poppets made their way to market at first as playmates for children, but soon, the small poppets developed into a resource for mining companies, duct-work corrections, and just about any other project that required small hands and tiny bodies. The boon for our lifestyle justified the risk.

Profits soared as retailers struggled to keep child poppets in the showrooms.

Still, DesLoge Com didn't seem willing to take that final step. Infant poppets, according to company spokes-woman Villa Ghete, destabilized with common usage. Too fragile, too useless, and perhaps too strange. Since the High Court ruling against free birth, many citizens aren't allowed to have children due to the constraints of breeding laws, population pressures, and space. It was whispered that the citizens of the cities might be scandal-ized by the usage of poppet infants when they weren't approved to have their own.

However, with the loosening of the birth laws to allow all true citizens at least one birth child, the company must have felt the infant poppets' time had come.

Starting this week, infant poppets will be available at your local poppet dealer. There may be some waiting lists, due to low supplies, but DesLoge Com promises it can deliver the poppet babies within a 2–4 week period. So little Suz wants a dolly this birthday? Why not buy her a poppet doll of her own? Like a real baby, she can feed it, dress it, and change it. Like a real baby, the poppet doll can be programmed to cry, sleep, and even to pass gas. If little Suz gets tired of the poppet doll or grows too old to play with it, it can even be returned for recycling.

So, be sure to head to your local poppet retail center to pick up your own Poppet Doll. Be the first on your block!

CHAPTER 16

"Hush now," the voice whispered next to her ear as she struggled in the grasp of her attacker. Thom lay on the ground, motionless. Dead? Poppets could die. She'd seen it in the factory, and occasionally when one fell from great distances or suffered some massive damage. She'd seen them put down but never one of her poppets. Never Thom. She shuddered and sobbed into the heavy hand laid across her mouth. "He's fine, girl. It's a paradart. He's just in a paralysis. He can hear and see everything. He just can't move on his own."

She fought until the hands loosened. "Let me go! How dare you touch me. Thom!"

"Hush now. You're causin' him nothing but grief. He can't help you, but you're making his mind race. Tell him you're okay so he can be relaxed." The man released her and gave her a gentle shove toward Thom.

Ellie fell to her knees next to Thom, turning him over.

His eyes were open, still moist with the look of life, but frozen, locked in the distance. "Don't worry, Thom," she whispered. "I'm here."

The man who'd grabbed her wore a black cassock with a hood that grayed his features in shadow. He cupped his hands over his mouth and blew through his fingers, whistling like one of the piped-in birds. Ellie leaned back on her heels, hoping that she wouldn't have to protect them from this man. She'd had some classes, a few rounds with a local fitness instructor, a padded gloved, and a huge helmet-headed practice attacker. But a woman of her standing in one of the domed cities was never expected to have to defend herself against an actual attack. She raised a hand and made a fist, but realized how ridiculous she looked. Words would have to save her.

"I don't know who you are, but you'll be sorry if you hurt me or my poppet. We're from DesLoge Mansion." She stood and brushed off her skirt. "I expect they're on their way here now. You'd best leave us be."

Crime didn't exist inside the dome as far as Ellie knew, but she'd read all of the Antedevolutionary lit books with their graphic descriptions of kidnapping and rape and theft. What if he wanted to ransom her? Or what if he had been sent to kill Thom and drag her back to DesLoge Mansion, screaming and kicking?

"I'll say it again," the man said. "Hush now. I'm not your enemy. Do you recognize me?"

She studied his face—warm chestnut hair shot with gray, weather-beaten smile and kindly eyes that seemed to smile all along their edges. He reminded her of someone she'd always known, or had always dreamed of. She shook her head, then pushed her hair back out of her face. Her hair. In her palm and so close to her eyes, it seemed odd that her hair was the same color as his. His crackled, reddened face wasn't a city face. He must be someone sent by Moze.

He smiled at her and kneeled by Thom. "Just trust me for a minute, girl. I'm here to help you." He pulled out a pocketknife and leaned in next to Thom, his blade lying close to his neck.

"What are you doing?" She thrust her hands in between his knife and Thom's throat. She didn't know how to stop him if he planned to attack Thom, but she'd sure try.

"Shoo, Ellie, now. I'm going to take out his tracker. He would never let me cut him with you here. Cordelia programmed Thom to believe I was your enemy when I left. He's not going to let me touch him, and I have to get this out of him."

She withdrew her hands, hoping she could trust this man with the life of her oldest friend. The man hovered, the tip of his knife just an inch from Thom's skin.

"I promise it won't hurt him. It'll free him. Okay?"

Ellie nodded, and he flicked his blade, opening a tiny, deep cut like a little mouth. He dug inside and pulled out a tiny light, flickering and blue, on the tip of the knife's blade.

"Look here." He leaned forward so that she could see it, then crushed it against a rock. "With this little tracker, they can follow you anywhere. They'd be on him and you in seconds out in the wild. They're counting on that. They won't grab you here in the dome, but they will the second you are out there where they can do whatever they want. You hear,

Thom? I'm helping. Don't you believe that crap Cordelia put in your head so long ago."

"Do I have one, too? I mean, I asked my comvid, and it said..."

He nodded as he ripped open a pouch of surgeon-grade anti-biostery cream. Ellie had seen it before at the Parkers house. They used it to clean their forks and knives—an extravagance they could afford. Steam rose from the packet as it ate away at the gore on the blade. The man jerked the dart out of Thom's neck.

"Yep, you have one. You're precious cargo. The heir of the DesLoge fortune, right? The comvid didn't know to track you, though. Your chip hadn't been activated for general tracking; only Cordelia could access you. Don't worry about Thom. He'll be up and ready to go in a minute or two." He pulled the blade out of the packet and settled back on his knees. "I better get yours while he's still down, or he'll attack me. Can you lean forward for me?"

Ellie stared at him. Why should she trust this man? His face was familiar, but even so he could be any kind of villain. She stared at him for a moment, then decided she'd have to risk it. She'd trust him. What other option did she have? Soon, the peacekeepers or the Grave Hawkers would find them and then where would they be? She leaned forward, lying across Thom's back, and shifted her long brown hair out of the way.

"Do it quick."

The man touched the spot right behind her ear with his rough finger, gently but without lingering. Then quick as a thought, he cut her, the pain a brief flame as he dug. She hissed as he pulled out the blade and covered her wound with a skin strip, binding up the gaping skin neat and tight.

"Yep, this one is top of the line. Look at 'er." He rolled it gently between his finger and his thumb, wiping away the blood. Bigger. Bright blue lights and tendrils of clear wire small enough to sit on the tip of her pinkie. Such a tiny thing. He wrapped it in a leaf he grabbed off of the ground, then he took it gently in his hand and dug in his leather messenger bag, pulling out a digi-rabbit. She'd had one as a child. Even a DesLoge child wasn't allowed a live animal. Live animals didn't exist inside the dome-cities except in tiny zoos that held animals for petting. They were sources of disease, eaters of food, and, as Aunt Cordelia would say, "They make piles of poop." But digi-rabbits don't. They are a clean, safe alternative to the real wild version of an animal that no one alive and dome-bred had ever seen. They were scenery on the grounds of the mansions and in the parks. Just to make things seem more natural.

The man took the tracker and jammed it into the open gears of the digi-rabbit's mouth. He cranked the wild setting, a much faster and shyer version of the rabbit programming. The automaton found its feet, gathered its legs up under it, and then took off in a flash of bright white fur. They watched it run, top speed up the hill and toward the deeper woods, until its clicking, humming legs and thumping gait were lost among the sway of the tree branches, creaking and groaning in the dome-breeze.

"Come on, Thom. Ellie." The man offered a hand up to poor Thom, who'd lain prone until he was addressed. He pulled Thom up and dusted off his back. "Follow me."

They walked in silence toward the bank of the Mizzourah River. Back before the dome was built, the river had been wild, muddy, and prone to flood. But since the dome, workers had lined the riverbed with earth-colored bricks and thick mortar. The river silt, soft as wet velvet, was pumped through controlled irrigation canals. Those canals carried the silt into gardens and then shifted the runoff back into the river to be carried out, flushed south in the Missip trench, the poison runoff river that carried away all the waste of Santelouisa. So safe and controlled. Such a beautiful system. But now, as they escaped from Aunt Cordelia and the mansion, Ellie wondered whose hands formed these bricks she had stepped on so many times. Whose sweat mixed with the mortar between?

"Where are we going?" she asked, not wanting the silence to fill with thoughts of poppets and bricks and her own ignorance. He stepped off the path and moved deeper into the woods, leaves crunching beneath his boots. She looked to Thom, walking beside her and matching her pace. She grabbed his elbow and squeezed. The poppet's head turned, though his eyes didn't connect with hers. He groaned and turned his gaze toward the back of the man who led them.

"Here's the thing, Missy. I've got to get you safe. I made a promise to your mama long ago that I'd be here for you when you needed me. I ain't been able to be here for you afore now, things as they are. But I'm here now."

"Well, where are you taking me? To a safe house? Now that I'm not chipped, maybe I could go live with Gertrude. She might take us in."

The man's hand went up to his ear, and he froze in his

tracks. He threw out his arm, signaling her to stop. "Moses 3, say again." He pressed against his ear. Ellie thought he must have some two-way listener in his ear, allowing him to talk to his partners. She strained to hear against the wild sounds that piped through the forest. "You betcha. I can have her there in fifteen. Can you make it?" A silence suggested an unheard answer. "Grave Hawkers, is it? I'll get her there."

The man pulled her around to the back of a tree. He put a finger up to his lips and nodded at her. She nodded back. She could be quiet. They listened. Listened to the recorded frogs and loons and skittering. Underneath, mixed up with the voice of the wind and the creaking trees, she heard it— the crunching, slow and deliberate, of a group of boots. More than two pairs. More than three. Someone was following, but not closely.

The man whispered, "They're tracking the digi-rabbit. Won't be long. We need to get to the river fast but quiet. Right? Silent, if you can do it."

Ellie nodded. They crept forward down the gradually inclining hillside that hugged the Mizzourah. The sound of the crunching leaves faded in the distance and, as it did, they picked up their pace, moving ever steadily toward the first cataract, which had always been the boundary of her wandering. Thom didn't stumble, picking his footing with such deliberation. Some part of her still screamed that it wasn't right or even possible that he could think beyond his programming, but here it was, unknown terrain with no problem. Her heart ached for every moment she had ever doubted him or belittled him. All those poppets who'd served her in her life. Were they all just like Thom?

The man pulled her behind a large berm next to the cataract, a manmade barrier in the river. This side of the cataract held the known, tamed river where Santelouisans played and swam and wandered in the safety of the domed life they'd created. Beyond the cataract, upriver was the edge of the known. It was where the dome sat against the earth, cutting into the river and dropping it beneath the lip of the barrier.

"Ellie?" From around the berm came a soft voice—one she hadn't expected.

"Juni?"

Juni swept her up into an embrace—one she'd sampled so few times in her life, full of warmth. For a moment, they clung to each other, then Juni whispered in Ellie's ear. "I'm sorry it ends this way, my little girl. I've always tried to let you be yourself and live the best way you could. I still believe that you would make a wonderful DesLoge CEO." Ellie's head swam. There was the Juni she'd always known, the one who only cared about money, power, and fun. Then there was this other Juni, the one who had Resurrectionist friends and secrets Ellie would never know. "Run, baby. Save your Thom. Maybe losing you will be the thing that makes Cordelia finally understand."

"They're coming, Juni. You need to get out of here." The man climbed the berm and stared into the distance through magnifiers.

Juni grabbed two large packs from behind her. "These are survival kits. Strap them to you, and don't let them go."

Ellie grabbed the large pack and swung it around her shoulder as Juni helped strap the other to Thom's back.

"There's food and purifiers and all sorts of things you will need," Juni said. Then she seemed to notice that Thom held the box of Ridley's papers. She smiled and placed her hand on the box. "Look, it's the papers."

The man looked at the box, his brow creasing.

When he looked serious like that, Ellie could see a resemblance to the man in the pictures...to her father. "Are you my father Ridley?"

The man and Juni smiled, looked at each other for a long moment, and even giggled.

"Nah, girl. I'm your Uncle Tate. Is that enough? Say your goodbyes now, ladies."

Ellie turned back to Juni. "Come with me, Juni."

Her mother shook her head. "I have to stay. I'll keep one foot in the door here so you can find your way back in some day."

"I'm afraid to leave," Ellie said. "Where am I going?"

"Into the wilds, my girl. And you must be brave and quick. There are horrors out there."

The crunching of heavy feet approaching came over the gurgling of the river's shallow waters.

Juni's eyes filled, but she blinked it all back. "Love you, Ellie. Love you, and be safe. And when you find him—and you will find him no matter what they say—Just, when you see him...tell him I still love him."

"Him who? Juni..." Ellie stared into Juni's eyes.

Tate grabbed Ellie's arm, jerking her away. "Get out of here now, before you get yourself caught, Juni. Go!"

Ellie glanced back to see Juni's white skirt disappearing around the berm.

She snuffled back the tears and the sadness and turned to follow her uncle—an uncle. Her heart fluttered in her chest a bit as she thought of the word. "Come on, Thom, we have to keep up."

Tate nodded grimly and gestured upriver over the cataract and beyond. The crunching leaves continued to punctuate the song of the woods but never seemed to get much closer. Ellie took heart in that, hoping that her mother had gotten away clean and that they would, too. As they walked, her stepping carefully into Tate's steps and feeling Thom's movement's behind her, she wondered at this family she'd never known.

"Tate... I mean, Uncle Tate... Is that okay?"

"Sure, Ellie, that's a great joy to hear. You father and I, well...we don't get home much anymore and..."

"He's still alive, then?" Ellie skipped forward, catching up to her uncle's long, quiet, striding steps. "I mean... now?"

Tate nodded and smiled wide at her as they climbed over a rising hill, peppered with boulders and the twining roots of the weeping trees. "He'd like to know you, Ellie. Hardest thing he ever did was leave you and your mom. But they made that decision together."

Ellie shook her head. The idea of two people in love separating seemed ridiculous. "Why didn't she go with him if he couldn't stay?"

Thom grunted behind them, huffing as he pulled his body up the incline. She slowed her pace so he could catch up to them. Alive or no, he was older and less able to keep up this pace.

"She did go with him. The Grave Hawkers dragged her

back. After that, Juni stayed in the dome and became a conductor. Figured that if Cordelia wouldn't let her go, she'd help others get away. She was on one end, your dad on the other. You are so like him, you know. He's the one who taught me and your mom about the poppets, how to care about them and watch out for them."

They crested the hill and carefully climbed down the steep ridge toward the dome's edge, which crackled and hummed in the dome-noon light. This close to the dome, the hairs on her arms and neck seemed to have a life of their own, standing, dancing in the dome-breeze. She'd never been this close to it before. The knot in her throat bobbed and refused to be swallowed down.

"How can I get through this?" Panicked breaths made her pant as she stumbled down the last few yards of the hill. "Where will we go?"

"Listen. This is the path you've studied before. You remember that song? Baby Paw Dreams?"

Ellie shook her head.

"What? You never learned it?" Tate offered her a steadying hand as she hopped off of the last of the small cliffs to the flatter ground nearest the dome. The river bubbled up from the lip of the dome and on both sides. As wide as the river was, she could see metal gates framing the mouth of the river. Gates, with steps leading down and down. "I'll teach it to you, but we need to get into the underground first."

"The underground?"

"It's the only way to get out. Trust me, Ellie. We've got to get you two out of here."

Ellie followed him to the cold railing that led down into

the dark metal mouth of the underground. For a few moments—as long as a thought, though they felt like a lifetime—she wondered if she could stay. Let Thom go free and find his own way while she went back and made Cordelia love her again. It would be easy. But that moment passed as she looked at Thom. His eyes had found hers, stared at her with his soft, blank expression—yet still his eyes held hers. There was no way she'd abandon him. She'd be brave, like Moze. She'd lead him to safety. It was the only thing to do.

With a deep breath to steel her resolve, she stepped into the darkness. They clanked down the steep, cold steps, leaving the filtered light of the domed sky behind. Her hands slid down the wet metal, and droplets sounded off the walls in loud echoes. The closed-in, close blackness folded her up, squeezed against her, but she kept pace.

"Are you still with me, Ellie?"

"Yes." A whistling breath, but she answered. Thom wheezed behind her.

"Just a bit farther, and we can hide for a while. Just around the corner. Put your hand on the wall, about as high as your eye. To your left...feel it?"

She bumbled into the walls—rough and chalky beneath her cold hands. Her finger fluttered up the face of the wall until they found a narrow band that ran side to side. Kind of like a lip or a chair rail.

"Got it."

"Good. Keep one hand on that, and follow my voice." He was moving forward, fading farther into the darkness. Why couldn't they light a torch or something? She shuffled her feet so she wouldn't lose her footing and counted each step.

Twenty...fifty...eighty. Then the wall turned, and the lip led her off to the left.

"Keep coming... Now, I've got you. Reach back for Thom, too."

She flung her hand back toward what she hoped was Thom. His hand was there, as if he could see in this black, soupy dark. Like a train, they followed Tate into the velvety blackness, with only echoes defining the space.

"Just a bit more."

A door creaked, and dry air puffed across her face. Tate pulled them in, and the door creaked again, then closed with a deep click. A chuffing rattle and then a light. Tate held a fluorescent light tube in his hand. The brilliant neon light filled what looked like a large closet. Clothes, coats, blankets —all hung from hooks on the walls, but they looked out of place in the cinderblock closet.

"This is a way station on the underground railroad. You know your mom is..."

"I do. I just found out," Ellie said, the new pride for her mother plain in her words. "She saved my friend Moze and his mother."

Tate nodded. "After that first escape, when they dragged her back here, she had to stay. Your dad wanted her to run with him, but then who would keep track of the DesLoge Com movements? Only someone from the inside could position us to really change things."

Ellie bit her lip as she considered Juni's position in the company. Always there, always ignored. She'd been invisible at each and every event, standing in the background, watching Ellie stand next to Aunt Cordelia soaking up the limelight, pretending to cling to the men who flowed in the wake of the good ship DesLoge. She'd been mad at Juni, angry at her stand-offishness and her willingness to leave her to Cordelia. How much of that had been part of her cover? Juni seemed heroic to her. She'd always accepted Juni's indifference as part of her drunken flirtations—that her lack of control excused her lack of interest in her daughter. Now, she found that indifference was actually a smoke screen. That she had been part of her mother's cover. She shook her head, trying to drive out the ugly thoughts about her mother and her feelings of abandonment.

"Here." Her uncle extended his hand to her. "Eat this."

She took the stringy dried meat, sniffed it, and said, "No, thank you."

"Can't afford to be a snob about this, girl. You need to eat. It's turkey jerky. Here ya go, Thom."

He handed a strip to Thom, who looked to Ellie for permission.

"Thom, you need to go ahead and eat," Tate said. "You don't need permission out here. There's no Joltlace gonna hurt you."

Ellie slapped the turkey jerky away from Thom. "What are you doing? That is meat."

"Yeah?"

"What do you want to do? Make him a man-eater? He needs poppet chow. Anything else will make him..."

"A monster?" Tate laughed, picked up the jerky off of the ground, and took a bite from it. "You're gonna have to feed him, Ellie. No room in those knapsacks for poppet chow. Besides, Thom isn't some monster. He's chipped and trained, and his chemicals are all in balance. You have to understand that all those tales they told you are from the earliest days of poppet making. They keep telling 'em to scare the kids and keep people in the dome. Like, somehow the tales of scary, meat-eating poppets would keep the kids from a'wandering outside the dome."

Ellie turned to Thom, whose grayed features nearly glowed in the neon of the florescent light tube. His gaze alternated from downcast, staring at the ground to her own eyes, to Tate's hand and the jerky. He was hungry. She'd never had to worry about feeding herself before, let alone feeding someone else.

"I suppose we have to. You go ahead, Thom. Eat if you're hungry."

The old poppet let his head sag and his shoulders curl up in a shrug, a comical expression of acceptance. He chuffed, a happy sound, as he reached for the jerky.

"Did you see that?" Tate asked. "He reacted to you. A real reaction...not some programmed nod or bow. That was...that was..."

"That was really my Thom."

Tate stared wide-eyed. "I don't know how you've done it, girl, but you've managed to either retrain this old boy, or you've given him a reason to be better than his programming."

"He's always been more than Cordelia or anyone knew. I think I've always known that. It's just... I couldn't live with what that meant for me and for my life, you know? Having to give up everything. Having to leave."

"Yet here you are, for him, right? That's what Juni told me. That you left to save Thom."

Thom chewed slowly, eyes distant, but she could tell he was listening.

She nodded. "How am I going to take care of us on the outside? I've never taken care of myself, even."

"Look, we can't move until dark. The peacekeepers are looking for you both inside, but they will send Grave Hawkers out for you soon. We have another six hours of light, and it'll take about an hour to get through the underground to the outside. While we wait, maybe I can teach you about some things." Tate handed her another strip of jerky. "Let's start with directions. How will you find your way to Liberty Lawrence KS? It's two hundred and fifty miles away, you know?"

Two-hundred and fifty miles. The whole of Santelouisa is only twenty miles wide. The air seemed to thicken around her, weighing down her lungs. "How... I mean, there's no way we can do that, right? Walking? There's got to be some other way?"

Thom grunted around the jerky.

"Do you have a starwheel? That'd be helpful. If you don't, then I'll have to—"

"I do. Thom, don't we have—"

Thom was already rooting in his bag and, with a happy-sounding wheeze, his hand came out clutching the star wheel. He scooted closer to her and placed it gently in her hands.

She spun the top cardboard circle around, trying to make sense of the dots of white and the overlays.

"Find the bear's eye star there...got it? Okay, so that's gonna be the brightest star in the sky—your best friend." Tate spun the overlay until the bear's eye star sat at the top. Then, he leaned back and started tapping his feet, humming a tune that wound around her memory like a mist hanging in distant valleys. Stars. She'd see stars for the first time. Tiny points of light that traced a path across the velvety vaulted sky, spinning and turning in some endless dance. She'd seen pictures in her book, seen them in films and on the shows from the Antedevolutionary television. But, to see them for real? She wrapped her arms around herself against the tremors she felt would come. "Once you find it—"

"How will I know I'm following the right one? What if they all look the same?"

Thom grunted, began to rock and...hum? Thom's grunts formed a melody, solemn and low, halting like he didn't have the notes in their entirety. Like it was a foggy memory he'd just discovered in the corners of his mind.

"The Bear's Dance. Good idea, Thom." Tate took a piece of paper from his pocket. Paper was rare—for special occasions because it used so much energy and materials to make. Instead, they all used comvids. She must have worn her confusion on her face because Tate noticed and said, "Only paper for you now. Comvids are traceable."

He used a thing he called a pencil, laughing as she marveled at the lines it produced. He drew a rectangle with an extension, pointing to each corner, naming a star and explaining its position. In a flipped pattern, there was another, smaller but the same shape. "Two bears, a mother and a baby, circling in the sky. Forever together. You will need to start at the brightest star and follow the paw of the baby up the river. There are some places where you will be secure, and there are some things to avoid. I'll teach you the song, and it will keep you safe."

With a voice higher than his muscular frame suggested, Tate began to softly sing the words. Words he'd repeat over and over in the glowing dark, singing her to sleep and awake until she could sing the words back.

WHEN THE SUN *dawns above the dome, And the first true rooster crows, Follow the baby's paw*

The old Mizo is awaiting for to carry you home If you follow the baby paw.

FOLLOW THE BABY PAW, *Follow the baby paw,*

For the old Mizo is awaiting for to carry you home If you follow the baby paw.

THE RIVERBANK WILL MAKE *a mighty good road*

But the bends bring Hawkers until Jeffer's town. Climb up the mansion hill and breathe, traveling on Follow the baby paw.

FOLLOW THE BABY PAW, *Follow the baby paw,*

Under the river, up arrow's rock full resurrection If you follow the baby paw.

. . .

The river slides between two hills, Follow the baby paw,

The gate can crush you, Independence bound, Follow the baby paw.

Follow the baby paw, Follow the baby paw,

Mission and Blue and Breen hills gone too. Follow the baby paw.

Where the great big river meets the little river Follow the baby paw

Hawkers hold, few can cross

But the old road can carry you home

And Liberty waits beyond the old battleground Follow the baby paw.

They sang until her voice was hoarse. She watched Thom rock and hum and grunt in rhythm. It was just like Moze had promised. Thom was so much more than just a machine. Moze. She'd driven thoughts of him so far out of her mind in the escape. If they hurried, would they find Moze and his party? That thought, that possibility, was enough to settle her stomach. Her back suddenly felt straight and strong like a steel rod, and the star song swung like a dancing bear in her mind.

Thom put his hand on her shoulder, startling her. He seemed to be aware of her pain, even if she hadn't voiced it. His other hand followed hers up to the letters of her name, ran across it. She buried her face in his shirtfront and clung to him, letting her tears come. Thom petted her hair as she wept. She tried to quiet her sobs, the bitter sadness she felt about failing to reach Cordelia, failing to save anyone except herself and Thom, leaving Juni behind. In the end, she could have left with Moze, should have left with them.

"Oh Thom, we have to find him."

Her uncle rolled over and wiped his hand across his face. He looked at her through bleary, sleep-swollen eyes. "Have you slept? You need your sleep for the trip."

"I slept some. Moze came through here."

"Of course, he did." Tate rummaged through his pack. He pulled out a toothray and applied it to his teeth. Around the device, Tate's words sounded stunted and comical. "I 'rought 'im 'ere."

"You? Why didn't you say that earlier?"

He took a long drink from a water bladder, then wiped his lips against the back of his hand. "Didn't think to. Sorry about that. But he sure was a sad kid, lost his mom and his girl all at once. Guess that was you, huh?"

"You don't have to be mean about it. I helped save him. The peace officers were coming for him and I..."

"Don't bother yourself, Ellie. I heard it all from him. Listen, you can't get that upset about some words said in passing. Out in the wild, people spar with words and tease each other to pass the time of day. If you act like you are bleeding anytime someone gives you a bit of sass, you're gonna tip them off to where you're from. You do that, and they'll hurt you, take advantage for the fun of it, or they'll take you prisoner, sell you back to the city alive or dead depending on their mood. There's some good people out there, little Ellie. Good as gold. But the others, they'll kill you as soon as look at you. Use you up. They're hard out in the badlands between here and KS. They've had to be. They eat bark and jerky meat and think nothin' of it."

"Uncle Tate, how long before we leave?" Moze. She had to keep him in her mind because that made the fear of the unknown seem a distant mote in her mind.

She and Thom changed out of their fancy "city clothes" into homespun, practical clothes that would be less obvious in the wilds. As they changed, Tate went through the backpacks that Juni had given her, laying the materials out on the floor and explaining each—from how to operate the solar shield shelter to the spark gun, a signal that would attract Resurrectionists if she needed them. He had them practice operating the gear, setting up the small, camouflaged shelter, and discussing the proper way to handle first-aid emergencies. So much to remember and so little time.

After a while, Ellie found that her eyes were too heavy to keep open as Tate talked, and soon she found the dark.

DOCUMENT 17: FROM THE POST VID GAZETTE, SANTELOUISA'S MAIN OUTLET FOR NEWS

On Saturday morning, two Grave Hawker retrievers posing as customers at a Liberty Lawrence KS's coffee house seized Shadrach Poppet, who had escaped from Santelouisa. Shadrach was taken across the state line for a hearing. Resurrectionist lawyers Robert Morris, Richard Henry, Gray Lorg, and Sam Wall offered their services as Shadrach's counsel. They immediately filed a petition for a writ of Habeas Corpus with the Supreme Border Court seeking Shadrach's release from custody. Judge Lemuel, Chief Justice of the Border Court, refused to consider the defense's Habeas Corpus petition. Later, a crowd of Resurrectionists entered the courthouse, overcame armed guards, and forced their way into the courtroom.

In a chaotic struggle, Resurrectionists took Shadrach, carried him off, and temporarily hid him in an attic. From there, the Resurrectionists helped Shadrach escape into the wilds. On an order from the US NOAM Congress, nine

Resurrectionists were indicted and imprisoned in the border prison. Ultimately, each of the imprisoned Resurrectionists was broken out of the prison and fed to non-neutered poppets by border-land Mizzourans, all suspected to be Grave Hawkers. Border prison guards offered little resistance to the uprising.

CHAPTER 17

When Ellie opened her eyes again, she found herself propped up on Thom's lap, the old poppet keeping watch as she rested. Her uncle lay curled up around the chemlight stick, his throat constricting around wet, breathy snores. She pulled herself up, stood, stretched, and went to the door. On the back, in the yellow half-light, the metal had been gouged and scratched by countless blades. Initials stood in sharp relief, jagged little cartoons with foul-mouthed punch lines, declarations of love, messages to those who would come after—all people who had run before her. People who'd discovered the ugly truth or had a poppet to save or who couldn't live in the dome with all of its controls and restrictions anymore. She ran her fingers across each word, each image, trying to draw strength from those who had blazed a trail that she'd have to follow.

Near the top, carved in deep jagged strokes, she found her own name written in tall, blocky letters. "Uncle Tate!"

When he didn't wake, she huffed and grabbed the light-stick from his sleep-loosened grip. With the torch in hand, she returned to the door, up on her tiptoes, until her nose nearly touched the letters that formed her name. There was more.

"Ellie DesLoge," the message said, "I do and will always think of you as the love I cannot have. You will be my inspiration. Forever yours. Moze."

Her heart staggered in her chest. How she would have loved to hear these things from his lips. If only they'd had more time.

Ellie shivered and pulled her jacket tighter. "I'm scared, Uncle Tate."

He nodded. "That's a right healthy attitude for a girl off on her own in the wilds. Be cautious. Be brave. I'll do my best to get you there safe."

He stood and stretched. "Let's get moving, then. By now, they've found your tracker. Won't take long for them to start on the Mizzourah. We'll need to get ahead of them if we're gonna get to Liberty Lawrence KS."

"But Moze—"

"Moze will see you in Liberty Lawrence KS. Have faith."

Faith. No one had ever asked her to have faith before. Cordelia had ordered her to have a backbone, Juni wanted her to be patient, and Sasha had told her to be accepting. But faith? Such a thing was the plaything of Resurrectionists and fools; at least that's what they'd taught her at the Academy. Of course, everything they'd taught her had proven to be false—just things they wanted her to think, not things that were true. Moze had been true. For him, for what he'd become to her, she could have faith.

She nodded.

Thom grunted and gave her a little push toward their bags, wandered over, and slung his pack onto his back with a quick surety. Uncle Tate handed her a jacket and some pants...men's pants. She'd never worn them before. She pulled on the pants and rolled the jacket up, hooking it to the top of her pack. She wondered how long it would be before they caught up with Moze. If only she'd gone with him in the first place.

She pulled her skirt back down over the pants. She looked ridiculous, with her legs, knees down, clad in the rough spun cotton trousers. "Why do I need these?"

"Because it gets cold at night on the river, and because the bugs will eat you up."

"Bugs?" Ellie'd never seen a live bug. She'd seen the ones the Academy kept in stasis, but she'd never been touched by one or bitten by one. Up close, their mouth parts had been something out of a nightmare. How many nightmares waited for her just beyond this metal door?

Tate opened the door and stuck his head out, listening. Silence, a near silky silence with droplets on metal, and a whistle as the wind passed across the face of the steps they'd descended before.

"Okay, let's get with it." Tate threw the door open and walked down the metal pathway, his footsteps clanking and echoing loudly, a bright noise in the velvet dark. Ellie stepped out behind him, her own boots shuffling along the metal sidewalk as she tried to minimize her own noises. Thom's steps were the only ones that seemed to be wrapped in quiet.

"There's a few places in here where we'll need to be quiet, but here we're in the guts of the dome. This is where the machinery and the inner works are all behind these walls. Nobody comes down here unless something goes wrong and, of course, nothing ever goes wrong, right?" Tate's laughing voice bounced off the walls. They continued down the walkway, their path lit by runner lights at their feet that twinkled on as they walked toward them and flickered out once they'd passed.

"I don't know what I expected," Ellie said. "I guess when they taught us about the war and the threats outside, I never really understood why we needed the dome cities. I mean, the domes keep everything out, but so do walls. Why did they need—"

"Because in the time of the War of Devolution, the ashes and poisons drifted into the cities and hung like clouds over the parks and the homes. Walls kept the poppet armies out, but their stench—well, that was too much to bear. So they built the domes. Then, it didn't matter what kind of bomb dropped or if the fires raged outside. Life could continue, lawn parties and cotillions under the gray washed protection of the dome. And boy, did they rain down some shit on the plains and the outer towns."

Ellie's face reddened. She wasn't used to such plain talk and the taste of the bitterness in his words, the violence against their way of life that wove together his sentence, made each word sharp like a dagger, wounding her.

As Tate turned down a set of winding steps, she heard a distant hum that had been just on the edge of her consciousness before. It resolved into the babble of water. Lots of it. The Mizzourah cut through here. Just beyond the outer wall. They would need to get on the river to get to Liberty Lawrence KS. Tate cut his gaze back and forth as they walked. His pursed mouth alerted her to the depths of their danger. His mood seemed to darken as they moved farther into the tunnel.

"Maybe we lost them? I mean, they can't track us anymore."

"Don't count on it. Maybe they did give up for now, but, hon, we're like fish in a barrel here. Most dangerous trip in the world is the crossing between poppet territory and free territory. I won't be happy until we're in the woods." Tate shifted his pack on his back. "Thom, how you doin' back there? Still with us?"

Thom grunted musically.

"When we get to the bottom here, you have to be really careful. There are things hidden down here."

Ellie stumbled on the steps, then righted herself. They'd come down some ten flights, twisting until her head spun. She stepped off of the last stair and onto concrete. Here at the bottom, the air felt wet and thick. It wrapped around her like a blanket. The concrete glistened as the wide ribbon of dark Mizzourah water slipped past in the capped channel. The plexi walls revealed the churning muddy water and even the occasional channel cat, big as a hovercar, all bulging eyes and mossy scales and whiplike whiskers. "What I don't understand is how we got to that point, you know? I mean, how did we get so that we didn't think we needed the outside anymore? We made it work, but how'd that decision get made? You know, to turn our backs on so many of our own people and to shut ourselves away from them, from the world? Seems like we gave up a lot to keep our way of life. That's what the war was about, right? Our way of life?"

"That's what they say in the books, I know. That's what they teach now. But my dad was there. He says there was more to do with greed and fear than with the workers and their demands. More to do with a new kind of labor replacing the old. Like when the machines replaced people in the old days before the war, and before the computers replaced the machines. There were these people, Luddites, who liked to destroy the machines and mess up the work they did. Same thing here. Same idea, except the domes kept out the Luddites. They couldn't walk in or fly in or anything."

They'd gotten to the lowest level and, in the distance, a light burned brighter than dome-noon. It shone like a spot across the rippling surface of the deep channel of the Mizzourah. For a moment, she couldn't go any farther. Out there was the wild, full of unknowns. Full of dangers. But perhaps out there, she'd find Moze and freedoms. Safety for Thom. Like the mouth of Plato's cave, the opening to the outside world lay bright and frightening in front of her. Would she step out into the true world or would she crumble and choose to shuttle back down the steps into the belly of the cave and be reshackled to live in fear? She shook her head, drew up her back up straight, and strode forward. She would face it, no matter what it would be.

"So, do you take people all the way to Liberty Lawrence

KS?" Ellie asked her uncle, his back bobbed and dipped in front of her like a shadow puppet in the brightening light of the dome opening.

"Sometimes," Tate said.

She could see the profile of his face, scruffy cheeks and heavily lidded brown eyes now in the half-light. "Sometimes I do, when the runner doesn't know jack about the wilds I do. For you, I'm gonna run all the way to Liberty Lawrence."

Ellie giggled, feeling lighter as they moved into the light. "I don't see you running. This is more like trudging."

"Hmmmm, nope. Not trudging," Tate said, picking up her joke and tossing it back. "Slogging."

"Um, shuffling? I know Thom is shuffling."

Thom grunted his protest.

"What, Thom? Not shuffling...we're certainly not traipsing."

Tate laughed. "How about fluttering or sashaying?"

Ellie snorted. "I'm not that coordinated. Just ask my comportment teacher."

"Oh, la de dah! Comportment." Tate snorted and slowed, letting her pull up next to him as they stepped into the pool of light that marked the last twenty-five yards of the tunnel. "Sheesh. You better be glad that I'm going with you, little debutante. The wilds are no place for waltz lessons."

Just like that, Ellie's jovial mood evaporated. What did he mean? She wasn't some baby. She stiffened her back and hurried forward, stepping full into the light of the entrance and allowing the brightness to wash across her face. "You don't have any right to speak to me like..."

The direct sunlight blinded her, sharp like a hot blade.

Her hands rubbed at her eyes as she adjusted, squeezing her lids shut against the pain. Beyond her pain, there was a shuffling.

"Oh, no. Down!" Tate's voice, edged with steel, rang out to her right.

She fell into a crouch. Thom's moans and grunts grew urgent in her ears. He pressed her down and shoved her to the side until she was shuffling blind on her hands and knees, Thom herding her like a sheepdog. The metal grid platform cut into her knees as she shambled to the left, her eyes foggy as she crawled. What was going on?

Two shots, loud as thunderclaps, rang out—shattering the air. Guns weren't allowed inside the dome, so Ellie had never heard a shot before. It was just like the movies she'd watched from the Antedevolution period.

Her eyes cleared, and she could see five men ranging out beneath the raised-up metal walkway they were on. There was nowhere to go. No cover. Nothing to duck into. The men, decked out in long duster cloaks and wide brim hats, wore their shade-like masks as they stared up at Tate. Had they seen her and Thom? Thom continued to push her along the wall, shielding her with his body.

"Shoulda known it'd be you, Tate Brown." The familiar voice crawled up her spine like a spider, creepy and ticklish. Simon Eregel. "She's got to come back with me, Tate. You can't have her. Cordelia won't allow it."

"You can't fire on us here, Simon." Tate slipped his arm out of his backpack and tossed it to Thom. "You'll hit the dome." He whispered, just loud enough for Ellie and Thom to hear, "Take the pack and run when I start firing. You'll need to get as far from them as you can. Stay off the river until you can't see the dome anymore."

Ellie felt her heart leap, hammering and pealing in her chest. He was talking like he wouldn't be there. Like he wouldn't lead them.

"But you promised," she hissed at him, though it wasn't true. He'd make her no fool promises. He'd never promised her a thing. "You can't just..."

Thom grabbed up the pack and strapped it to his front. He scuttled up into a crouch and pulled her up into the same.

"Sorry, Ellie. I can't go with you. Not now. Just...be careful, little debutante," Tate said. He seemed to swell up under the stares of the Grave Hawkers. He raised his hands slowly from his sides, lifting them as if in prayer toward the sky. When they were straight up, he said, "Get ready now."

So bright, such a blue sky, beautiful and strange, but so big and open. She felt pressed like some flower in a book. Her breath came thready and quick, but she gathered up her strength and grabbed Thom's hand. Past the stairs, she could see trees—so many trees. Some tall, white, leafy, weeping. So many kinds. She'd seen some of them inside the dome. But never had they been so green.

"Tate," she said, unwilling to raise her voice above the babble of the river in case they didn't know exactly where she was. "Please, Tate. I don't know how to get there without you. I'm scared."

He smiled at her, then said, "Get to Ridley and get Thom safe. He's more important than you can know, Ellie. Get out now and don't look back."

Tate lowered his hands to his neck, crossed behind his head, and, with a jerk, he pulled out two flashing silver guns. As his hands dropped level, he crouched, though there was nothing for him to hide behind. He had the high ground. Dr. Venkma had taught her that the high ground was worth big numbers in a battle. She couldn't leave him to face the Grave Hawkers by himself. She belly-crawled over and grabbed at his feet.

"Give me a gun, too! I'll help."

Tate spared her a glance. "You are a stubborn girl, Ellie." He gritted his teeth, locked his arms, and drew a bead on the men across the knoll. "I'll shoot," he shouted. "I'll kill you bastards where you stand!"

"This is unnecessary, Tate. Just let us have her. No harm'll come to her. She's too valuable. You know, I'm not going to hurt my partner's kin." Simon's voice boomed above the river's, amplified by the bowl of the small valley they stood in, until it seemed to answer itself with a lilting echo.

"She doesn't want to go back. She's free now, Simon. I mean to see her be safe."

Simon didn't answer. Not with words, anyway. He did laugh, openmouthed, and with an edge that felt like a slap. Tate didn't seem to find it funny. His face hardened into that of a statue. He angled his pistol and fired off two shots. A yelp and one of the men fell, his chest an open gaping mouth filled with shot and gore. "You must run now, little Ellie. You must run, and don't look back."

"No, Tate," she said.

He fired again on Simon's men. They had taken better positions, hidden behind trees and rocky outcrops, with only their shadows telling their positions in the noon-day sun. Thom grabbed her, pulled her to her feet, and shoved her toward the stairs.

Tate called after her, "Thom is special, Ellie. Get him to the Resurrectionists. Keep the wind on your face." He fired again as one of the shadows advanced toward the bottom of the stair on the other side of the walkway. They'd be on them soon. "Hurry, Ellie!"

Ellie gritted her teeth and turned. "Come on, Thom."

She jogged as fast as her knocking knees would carry her. Their steps clanged on the metal grid platform. She leaped down steps two at a time. Behind her, the shots whizzed from Tate's gun, though he seemed to be shooting only at shadows, not at the men. Of course. If Tate was a true Resurrectionist, he wouldn't normally kill. Not unless someone's life was on the line. Not unless the death would save others. That's what Moze had tried to explain to her when he'd been talking to her about his philosophy. What Moze had done at the factory had broken him because it went against his beliefs. Even as she raced, she felt a pang for all Moze had lost.

They reached the bottom of the stairs and thumped onto the solid ground of the wilds, her first steps into that new world. She felt a buzzing at her ear, then next to her, the trunk of a tree exploded. A bullet? Fired at her? Her heart, already hammering, seemed to skip a beat and surge forward. Her feet couldn't move fast enough to keep up with her hurtling body, so she tumbled forward into the dirt.

"Don't run far now, Ellie. I'll be coming to gather you up in just a bit," Simon's voice called after her.

Thom pulled her up and shambled to the treeline. The woods opened up and swallowed them, branches whipping her face and legs as she ran. She risked a glance over her shoulder. A bad idea. Tate's ammo must've run out because he launched himself at his attackers. They tumbled down the metal stairs.

She saw Simon pulling himself up on a horse. He and four of his men wheeled their horses and spurred them on toward the woods, straight at her. She turned back, panting as she pushed herself, running harder than she'd ever run. But horses! They'd run her down in a minute. They'd save her, sure. But Thom. What would they do to Thom?

"We have to get off the trail, Thom. We have to hide."

Thom grunted and swerved to the left, guiding her into a deep thicket. The ground dipped away under her feet, but she stayed true and kept running. She could hear the thundering hooves of the horses back on the trail. The shouts and snorts and the frustrated whinnies of their pursuers dampened in the distance, but a breath of fear seemed to blow right across her neck.

Behind her, cursing and crashing in the branches she'd just run through, Simon's voice shouted orders at his men. She hurtled across a clearing and tumbled, tripped, and rolled in the tall weedy grasses. Thom's hands were on her. With a jerk, he pulled her to her feet, but held her still, exposed in the open meadow. There in front of her, frozen, staring, was a deer—pointy antlers, white tail—just like in the movies. For a moment, the world slowed down as they stared, almost nose to nose, at each other. Life.

A whooshing sound past her ear. A thunk, meaty and full

of weight. Thom fell forward into the deep grass, pulling her with him. In that moment, the deer leaped away and broke for the tree line. Another whizzing thunk, this time a geyser of dirt flew up next to her head.

"Thom. They're shooting at us."

He crawled, hand over hand, toward the treeline. He turned, looked back at her, extended his hand and, when she grabbed it, pulled her up to even with him. The moment exploded, stretched out in long breaths that were oddly punctuated by her pounding feet, Thom's grunts, and moments of absolute clarity—the trees' green shone so vivid, so much louder in her eyes than the ones from the dome. The evergreen needles and the grand maples' platter-sized leaves hung like bright velvet flags. Light, golden, and fresh.

And guns shattered the peace.

"Thom, what will we do?" Ellie screamed. Near the edge of the clearing, just a few more steps to freedom. The forest, all the fears and worries, seemed to be nothing compared to the possibility of losing Thom to a bullet.

Thom grunted, nearly screaming in her ear. "Rughsh-hhhhhhh."

Behind them, right behind them, a horse and rider burst through the trees. With head ducked low and hooves pounding, the horse carrying Simon advanced. His gaze locked on her, teeth gritted in hate, leaning forward in the saddle until her vision filled with teeth—the horse's and Simon's, lit and wet with slobber.

Thom jerked her sideways, out of the path of the cutting hooves. The flanks of the horse passed so close that the breeze smelled of foam and hair and hay, a smell cloying and frightening to her inexperienced nose.

They scrabbled into the trees, but the woods were open, brushless, and accessible with few places to hide. The horse would surely run them down.

Thom yanked her along, weaving. Simon wheeled his horse around for another pass. They ran up a rough scrabbled bluff overlooking an oxbow in the river. Thom pulled her forward, leaving Simon to spit curses as his horse refused to follow up the steep, rocky path. Simon jumped off the horse and watched them climb the hill.

"You're gonna be trapped up there, little bird. Trapped with your old poppet and your dignity. But I'm gonna take both of them away. You'll see." He smiled at her with his rotten teeth.

Ellie and Thom scrambled over the top of the hill and skittered to a stop on the edge of the cliff. The wide oxbow of the slowed river stretched in front of them, so far below, wind rippling its ribboned surface.

"Trapped and mine to carry back to that old biddy bitch aunt of yours. Maybe I'll break you up a bit beforehand, just so as you'll know who's boss."

He ambled, just as pleased with himself as he could be, up the side of the hill. Ellie pressed Thom behind her, shielding him with her body, though he struggled to get her behind him.

"No, Thom!" At that moment, she felt so much rage, white hot and climbing from her gut into her throat like a fist.

Behind her was Simon and a promise of death for her

Thom. Ahead of her, a sheer drop into a brackish side channel of the muddy river.

"We gotta jump, Thom." Ellie grabbed his hand and pulled him to the edge. "Jump or die, and that's it."

Thom groaned and pulled back against her hand, protesting. As he did, Simon's laugh echoed up the hill.

"Be there in just a sec, Princess. Take you back to your auntie, but like your ol' mama, I won't take you back pristine. I'll take you back how I wanna take you back, a little broken."

She tasted bile. He'd attacked Juni. He'd dragged her back, away from her husband, and had used her. Was that why Cordelia looked down on Juni?

Ellie glanced around desperately, looking for another escape—another path for them to take. Nothing. Another shot. The bullet whizzed between them, just missing Thom's head. There would be pain for her. Horror. He would abuse her and carry her back, but Thom would make it no farther than this bluff. He would be shot and discarded. Left to lay here in the needles and worm trails to be pecked on and picked on.

Ellie would not allow it. "We have to jump, Thom. He'll kill you and hurt me if we don't."

Thom shook his head.

He'd die for her. Ellie knew that. She had to save him.

Simon came into view, bucking his gun's butt into his curled palm. He was lining up for another shot. His gun's silvered barrel winked in the sparkling sun as it swung around.

"No." She pushed into Thom, moving him to the edge of the bluff.

"What are you doing, girl?" Simon asked. His eyes opened wide as he mentally measured their steps to the ragged edge of the rock they stood on.

She shuffled away from him a few steps, her toes clinging to the edges of the cliff.

"You know, you're just making this worse. Come on and stop fooling around, and I'll make sure you go back safe. I'll be so gentle." He pushed his fingers together into a ring and kissed them, a nasty little gesture. A gesture that made her feel small—stinging eyes and a twisting stomach. In that moment, she could see the cracks in his fingers, highlighted in negative by the deep black stains in his skin like little rivers.

She wouldn't allow him to touch either of them. Not her, not Thom. She wouldn't let him win.

"Thom." She said it like a song. Like a prayer. She turned to her old poppet, showing her back to Simon and his gun. Let him shoot if he would kill the DesLoge heir. She was sure that he'd never risk that. "Thom, let's go find freedom."

She wrapped her arms around him in a hug. In that hug was the only real love she'd known as a child. In that hug, she wrapped him in hope, in protection. Then she pushed.

"No!" Simon's shout fell away as she and Thom flew.

The side of the bluff rushed past as they tumbled together through the blue of the sky, a blue she'd never seen except in fabrics and paintings—a blue so bright it hurt her heart. Thom clutched her, hugged her, and curled her into him like a baby. He moaned as they fell.

Simon peeked over the edge of the receding cliff, but still

she could make out the hardness of his lips and the anger of his brow.

Then, the tumbling ended.

They smashed into the surface of the oxbow in the river, the deep channel opening up like death's own embrace.

Down deep, Ellie bounced out of Thom's clutching arms and along the muddy channel's bottom. She hadn't filled her lungs, and even if she had, the pressure of the river's pounding current would have pressed the air out in a stream of bubbles. The current caught her up and carried her back toward the dome, back toward Simon's men—only a quarter mile on, and she'd be back in their sights.

She kicked hard and swift, pulling against the current, up the stream. If she could turn toward the shore, if only she could...but her lungs were so empty and her mind so full of light and explosions. Her ears popped, and water leaked down her throat.

Something snagged her. Caught on her pack, pulling her into a fight against the sucking force of the current. It was a chance. She fought the pressure and reached her arm up to grab the branch, to maybe pull herself to safety. She clutched, eyes squeezed shut against the muddy Mizzourah, but her hands knew the softness of what she clutched, the pliability of it. It wasn't a branch that held her. What was it?

Then, it pulled.

Thom!

He dragged her to the surface as her lungs gasped inward, an implosion that would have been her end if he hadn't dragged her to the surface.

She sputtered, spitting out the coppery water. Thom

hung from a thick branch that sat low above the calm surge of the oxbow side stream, clinging to the strap of her bag.

"Nrgggghhhh," Thom grunted. "Phuh."

Her hands flopped against the surface of the river, useless. She felt the sucking pull of the water yanking her back, deeper.

"Hurrrrrrrr. Phuh Urp," Thom muttered.

Ellie felt her arm slipping, sliding out of the harness of the pack clutched in Thom's hand. Panic climbed up her throat in a choking gasp.

"Phuh Urp, Ellllllllieeeeee." What?

The urge to fight, to kick and flop and flail left her. His voice. She'd never heard his voice before. It was just like she'd dreamed it would be. Soft, creaky old man, and sweet. Like singing and cookies and a warm blanket. He'd said her name!

"Phuh Urp!" He seemed to be yelling. Demanding. His fingers were locked around her pack, but that was slipping. He was telling her to pull up. Pull up, Ellie! She grabbed his forearm and locked her wet grasping hand around his wrist.

She struggled against the current, pulling up like Thom demanded. He lifted her onto the branch, pulling her up inch by inch until she lay across the branch huffing and panting, staring down into the deceptively flat surface of the Mizzourah.

"Urp, Ellie." Thom clutched at her shoulder. Her mind spun as she followed his directions, scrambling across the log with him.

"You talked, Thom." Ellie put her feet on the bank, safe. Thom, lips pressed closed and grim, shook his head, and gestured up to the ridge they'd just leaped from. The winking silver of Simon's pistol? Just a glimmer off a glassy rock? She couldn't be sure. "Okay, let's get out of here, Thom. Are you ready?"

Thom nodded.

They crept along the brush into the deeper woods, leaping over mud pots and crawling through little gurgly streams. What had Tate said? About twenty miles as the crow flies? Only that wouldn't be safe...to find the old highway road that cut straight as an arrow through the wilds would be suicide. It would be giving up. The Grave Hawkers ruled the road, but the Resurrectionists ruled the bends and fords of the river.

He'd whispered the *Baby's Paw* song into her ears until she'd memorized it.

Now they'd have to find her way—she and Thom alone. For hours, they stumbled along, vines snagging their feet and branches whipping their arms, silence between them. Silence because Ellie couldn't straighten out her thoughts. How much had she lost? Her mother? She'd never really had her. Aunt Cordelia? Yes, that loss smarted like an open cut in saltwater. Even so, she couldn't believe her aunt had made her love—her acceptance—contingent on Thom's death. So many things would be different if she'd only...

"Elllliiieeee," Thom said. Thom said. It was such a foreign thought. She stopped turning the blame and the wonders over in her mind and stared at Thom's face, gray but pliant, gaze latched on hers. He grunted. Not all words had come back to him, but here he stood doing something that everyone in Santelouisa said was impossible. It went against everything she'd ever been taught, or told, but it didn't surprise her. Not at all.

She reached up, grabbed him around the neck, and hugged him.

"Thom, I knew you were in there. Somehow...I always knew it."

Thom's arms paused around her shoulders, an awkward hug. Then he pushed her out to arms' length and stared at her, eyes locked on her face, grayed lips pulled up slightly at the corners, just a suggestion that he might remember how to actually smile.

"Elllllliiieeee saaaaa. Saaaaaaaa." He released her arm to thump his chest.

She knew what he was trying to say. She knew, and it made her sob, her eyes flooding with tears. He was thanking her. Thanking her for saving him.

"No, Thom. You saved me lots and lots of times. I remember." She grabbed him again and hugged him tight, glad that she'd done the right thing. Glad to be with him, even if they never were safe again. "We'll keep each other safe. We'll find Moze and Ridley, and we'll be together."

Thom jerked his head once in an awkward nod.

"Let's get on the river, Thom. They can't get us on the river."

The sun's bright rays, orange and pink, flared on the horizon as they pulled the raft roll out of Thom's pack. They worked in silence, sweet and warm and full of hope. By the sunset, the silvered canopy and the tin foiled platform floated above the ground, just waiting to be launched onto the churning brown ribbon. They strapped their packs into waterproof blisters that recessed into the sides of the craft. When they launched, Tate had promised, the raft would skim across the current, carrying them against the flow and up the river toward Liberty Lawrence KS, Moze, and freedom. The raft, a chameleon that could reflect the sky and the water and the line of trees opposite would silently, skillfully protect them from the eyes of the Grave Hawker settlers between here and there.

Of course, nothing had gone the way it was supposed to. Nothing.

Ellie looked back toward the dome, so large in her life for so long. Now it seemed tiny. Tiny compared to this raft. Not that it was big. Just that it was bigger than anything she'd ever had to do or deal with before. One step, a shove off onto the river, and she'd be trusting her life to it.

Thom jumped into the raft, folding his knobby legs under him and letting his palms turn up on his knees like some ancient Eastern wise man. She smiled. If he could do it, she could.

With one knee braced on the platform, her body teetering on the edge, she used her other foot to push the raft into the current. With a few touches, the raft's propellant system swung the raft toward the west, upriver.

Someone wise once said, "You can't pray a lie."

Ellie had been praying lies all her life, but on the breezy current above the river's deep face, her lies, her ignorance, and her choices fell away like some dead fish's scales. She reached over to Thom, grabbed his hand, and told him what all her life had been the truth.

"You are my mother and my father and my best of

friends, Thom. I mean to free you. I mean for you to be just as free as me. Is that what you want?"

Thom's eyes grew bigger, more alive in their brightness, though the inside of the raft was dark.

"Yeeessssss Ellllieeee. Frrrrreeeeennnddd. Ffffrrrrreeeeee."

He was her miracle. A promised real life. She'd get him to Liberty Lawrence KS. No matter what.

ABOUT THE AUTHOR

Donna J. W. Munro has spent a big chunk of her life teaching high school social studies. Her students inspire her every day. She has an MA in writing popular fiction from Seton Hill University. Her pieces are published in *Dark Moon Digest # 34, Sirens Ezine, the Haunted Traveler, Flash Fiction Magazine, Astounding Outpost, Door=Jar, Spectators and Spooks Magazine, Nothing's Sacred Magazine* IV and V, *Corvid Queen, Monstrous Feminine* (2019), *Hazard Yet Forward* (2012), *Enter the Apocalypse* (2017), *Killing It Softly 2* (2017), *Beautiful Lies, Painful Truths II* (2018), *Terror Politico* (2019), and several Thirteen O'Clock Press anthologies. For more of her work check out www.donnajwmunro.com and follow her @DonnaJWMunro on Twitter.

POPPET CYCLE BOOK 2 RUNAWAY

Available Soon

Ellie and Thom make their way upriver, alone, through Grave Hawker territory to get to safety in the West. Along the way, she is attacked by her former "bestie" and learns more about the system of human trafficking, which feeds the need for new poppets.

At the same time, Moze has made it to Kansas City in the west and is working with Ellie's long-assumed-dead father to create a revolution. He agrees with the Resurrectionist movement, but he wonders if they aren't just as bad as the Grave Hawkers.

.

ACKNOWLEDGMENTS

Thanks Johnny Worthen, for taking a chance on a YA zombie novel. Thanks Michael Knost for being my writing fairy godfather. And HUGE thanks for Tony Acree for rescuing my poppets from oblivion.

I have the best family in the world. Without them, I'm nothing. Mom (Sheila Schaefer), Grandma Bonnie, Becky, Rio, Matthew, Brandon, Jan, John, Fred, Karen, Ethan, Erica, Nate, Cara, Ruby, Nola, Evie, Karen, Kirk, Kenny, Carla, Avery, Zeke, Cassidy, Steve, Denise, Kim, Will, Abby, Hannah, Whitney, Timmy, Sandra, Ellie, Nathan, Ethan, Steven, Linda, Cheryl, Tony, Stephanie, Doug, Wendy, Mason, Mitchel.

My writing family is an incredible resource. First, thanks to Seton Hill's Writing Popular Fiction program for help- ing me make the leap into novels. Thanks to my mentors: Nalo Hopkinson, Lawrence Connolly, and Mike Arnzen. My tribe held me up in the hard years. Deanna (Una) Sjolander, Matt (the Duv) Duvall, AG Devit, Christe (Chicken) Callabro, Natalie Duval, Tanya Twombly, Sally Bosco, and J. L. Gribble.

Thanks to Adam Hardy, first person to hear about the pop- pets and get excited with me.

The extended family of writers who helped me (and who you should now read): Judi Fleming, Diana Dru Botsford, Jennifer Brooks, Rhonda Mason, and Sally Bosco. These ladies sharpened this book immeasurably. My first readers/cheerleaders were Matt Munro, Sheila Schaefer, Teresa Spaulding, Joan Zwick, Katie Goodson, Alexis Black, Sandra Schaefer, and Linda Nelson (my friend and fan). Thank you for asking about the poppets and keeping me believing in them. If I left you off this list, just know I appreciate you!

Anton Cancre and Steven Saus—thanks for introducing me to Obsidian Flash. It's one of the best things that's ever happened to me.

Anna LaVoie is a developmental editor with an amazing eye and a real love for enriching writing. She runs Literally Yours editing and is worth every penny. I owe her so much more than this little thank you. Anna, you are a gem. Thanks for being in the trenches with me.

Jennifer Della' Zanna jumped in and line-edited the hell out of this book. She's an editing godsend, a comma wrangler, and just one of the kindest people I've met in the writing world. Thanks for jumping in when I needed SO MUCH HELP!

Thanks to Amy Baur Bartak for inspiring my heroine, Ellie DesLoge. You're one I'll always remember— awkward, big heart, and funny.

Thanks to the thousands of teens I've taught and laughed with as a social studies teacher. You are all in my books and stories in some way or another. Thanks for the inspiration. I'm humbled to be a part of your greatness.

I owe special thanks to my two dads. John Munro, my

father-in-law, a poet and philosopher who believed in writing and quiet. He's probably laughing at me right now. My own dad, Ed Wagenblast, who loved my writing, bought me all the books he could afford, wrote with me, encouraged me to think, and believed I could do anything. The stories he used to tell people embarrassed me, but that absolute belief in me, the regard he had for my talents, and the incredible love he gave molded me. I miss him every single day and always will.